NATURAL CAUSES

LASSITER/MARTINEZ CASE FILES (#3)

Inspired by Actual Events

JOSEPH BADAL

NATURAL CAUSES
LASSITER/MARTINEZ CASE FILES (#3)
by
Joseph Badal

PAPERBACK EDITION
* * * * *
PUBLISHED BY:
Suspense Publishing

Joseph Badal
Copyright 2019 Joseph Badal

PUBLISHING HISTORY:
Suspense Publishing, Paperback and Digital Copy, April 2019

Cover Design: Shannon Raab
Cover Photographer: iStockphoto.com/nambitomo
Cover Photographer: iStockphoto.com/vchal

ISBN: 978-0578445212

JOSEPH BADAL'S BOOKS & SHORT STORIES

THE DANFORTH SAGA
EVIL DEEDS (#1)
TERROR CELL (#2)
THE NOSTRADAMUS SECRET (#3)
THE LONE WOLF AGENDA (#4)
DEATH SHIP (#5)
SINS OF THE FATHERS (#6)

THE CURTIS CHRONICLES
THE MOTIVE (#1)
OBSESSED (#2)

LASSITER/MARTINEZ CASE FILES
BORDERLINE (#1)
DARK ANGEL (#2)
NATURAL CAUSES (#3)

STAND-ALONE THRILLERS
THE PYTHAGOREAN SOLUTION
SHELL GAME
ULTIMATE BETRAYAL

SHORT STORIES
FIRE & ICE (UNCOMMON ASSASSINS ANTHOLOGY)
ULTIMATE BETRAYAL (SOMEONE WICKED ANTHOLOGY)
THE ROCK (INSIDIOUS ASSASSINS ANTHOLOGY)

"Natural Causes" is dedicated to the courageous, dedicated men and women of the Bernalillo County Sheriff's Office who unselfishly put their lives on the line every day.

PRAISE FOR NATURAL CAUSES

" 'Natural Causes' by Joseph Badal is a first-rate thriller, a powerhouse of a story that will keep you turning the pages into the wee hours. The pacing is relentless, with a sense of menace that grows almost unbearable. Lassiter and Martinez are two homicide detectives for the ages. I loved it!"
—Douglas Preston, #1 Bestselling Coauthor of the Famed *Pendergast* Series

"Another outstanding entry in a terrific series. Detectives Susan Martinez and Barbara Lassiter are smart, tough, and compassionate protagonists worth rooting for. They are compelling police professionals, not super-human crime fighters. Joseph Badal's plotting is deft, his pacing is perfect, and his writing crisp. Highly recommended."
—Sheldon Siegel, *New York Times* Bestselling Author of the *Mike Daley/Rosie Fernandez* Novels

"Joseph Badal has done it again with 'Natural Causes,' the 3rd in his *Lassiter/Martinez Case Files* series. His two female detectives follow a serpentine, dangerous path that will have the reader guessing to the last page. Don't miss this one."
—Robert Dugoni, *New York Times* Bestselling Author of the *Tracy Crosswhite* Series

" 'Natural Causes' introduces one of the nastiest villains you'll love to hate, one who offers a dangerous challenge to our two heroines... compared to her, Mexican cartels are a bunch of bungling amateurs."
—Steven F. Havill, Author of the *Posadas County Mystery* Series

"What's not to like about 'Natural Causes'? Smart, tough, and witty investigators Barbara Lassiter and Susan Martinez return to unravel a series of "natural" retirement community deaths and face a clever and dangerous psychopathic killer who pushes them to their limit, and beyond. A thriller with twists and turns that will keep you on a finely-honed edge."
—D.P. Lyle M.D., Award-Winning Author of the *Jake Longly* and *Cain/Harper Thriller* Series

" 'Natural Causes' is a blistering, bracing and bold thriller that races out of the gate and finishes in an all-out sprint. Joseph Badal's third tale to feature detectives Barbara Lassiter and Susan Martinez sets them on the trail of a killer targeting residents at a retirement community that gives a whole new meaning to the phrase 'golden years.' But Badal also sprinkles in organized crime and politics into his already savory literary mind snack, resulting in a tour de force of a crime thriller that is not to be missed."
—Jon Land, *USA Today* Bestselling Author of the *Murder, She Wrote* Series

"Inspired by actual events, 'Natural Causes' manages to be chilling, complex and humane in equal doses. A terrific read for suspense fans of all stripes."
—Dennis Palumbo, Author of the *Daniel Rinaldi Mystery* Series

"What if a resident of a retirement home is murdered? What if he's not the only victim? Can Detectives Barbara Lassiter and Susan Martinez identify a psychopathic killer? Joseph Badal's latest novel, 'Natural Causes,' will have you on the edge of your seat to the very last page."
—Alan Jacobson, *USA Today* Bestselling Author of the FBI Profiler *Karen Vail* Series

"Another thrill ride by acclaimed suspense author Joseph Badal. It's relentless from start to finish. Badal just gets better and better."
—David Morrell, *New York Times* Bestselling Author of "Murder As a Fine Art"

NATURAL CAUSES

LASSITER/MARTINEZ CASE FILES (#3)

JOSEPH BADAL

Inspired by Actual Events

THURSDAY
OCTOBER 2

CHAPTER 1

"Johnny would have loved today."

"If he wasn't dead, you mean," Max Katz said, his Brooklyn accent giving no indication he'd lived in Albuquerque for forty-two years.

Alberto Martinez shrugged to make his too-large sport jacket shift on his shoulders. Then he looked at Katz, at his furrowed face, at his mahogany-brown eyes. "Jeez, Max. I'm sitting here thinking about this beautiful fall afternoon and how Johnny loved it when the leaves changed color and the air became crisp and cool, and you just gotta ruin it."

Max spread his arms. "What'd I say?"

Alberto slowly shook his head. "You remember how Johnny used to put it? 'This is the kind of day that makes a person glad to be alive.'"

Max just nodded, although Alberto could tell that his old friend had something to add. Max always had something to add.

Alberto straightened his tie, stood, and, in the wake of his shadow, moved away from the bench in the park across the street from the church where his friend, John Matthews, had been eulogized. He removed his straw Trilby fedora, ran a hand through his thick, white hair, and watched Johnny's children shake hands with mourners as they exited the church.

"You wanna do it the way Johnny did it?" Max asked as he came to stand next to Alberto, doffed his newsboy cap, and stared at the cluster of people outside the church.

"What do you mean?"

"You know, give your body to science. No casket, no burial."

Alberto considered Max's question for a long moment. He smiled as he remembered the conversation he'd had with his friend a year or so ago, when Johnny had announced he was donating his body to science. He'd told Johnny that the only thing the medical students would find in him was an abundance of gas and fossilized chili peppers. John Matthews ate Mexican food at least four times a week—the hotter the better. He'd replied, 'Boy, would I love to be there when they cut me open. Imagine those students' faces when the gases erupt.' Alberto now turned away from Max so his friend wouldn't see him wipe away tears.

"You gonna answer my question?" Max asked.

Alberto pulled a handkerchief from a pants pocket, wiped his eyes, and blew his nose. After replacing the handkerchief in his pocket, he said, "Yeah, maybe. It's a good way to avoid the cost of a casket."

Max nodded. "You want to go to the reception?"

"Nope. Johnny told me he didn't want me hanging around with a bunch of people who hardly knew him and never came to visit." Alberto took three hundred-dollar bills from a pants pocket with a flourish. "He told me if he died before I did he wanted me to take a few people from the home to a bar and drink to his health."

"What the hell," Max exclaimed. "He ain't got no health."

Alberto gave Max a diamond-hard stare, then shook his head. "Then we'll drink to his journey to Heaven and hope St. Peter opens those pearly gates for our friend."

"Sounds like a plan." Max replaced his cap on his head and pulled it down snug over his forehead. "By the way, where's your niece today? She came to the last service, the one for Vicky Caulfield. Thought she'd be here."

Alberto put his hat back on and squinted at Max. "You gotta stop obsessing about my niece. You're almost three times her age and, in your prime, you didn't look good. Hell, you're bald as Mr. Clean, your legs are too short for your body, and you got a nose the size of a cucumber."

"Hah. That's what you think. The gals thought I was hot stuff. They still do. I gotta beat them off with a stick." He mimed the gesture.

Alberto smiled. "You crack me up, Max. We live in a retirement home with two hundred residents. Six couples, one hundred and eighty widows, and eight widowers, including you and me. The ladies won't leave you alone because they don't have much to choose from."

"Hell," Max said, "it's not just looks that count, you old bastard. It's personality, and knowing how to treat a lady."

Alberto wasn't in the mood to argue. Besides, Max was a friend—and he didn't have a lot of them left.

"You mind stopping by Charlie's Bar?" Bernalillo County Sheriff's Office Detective-Sergeant Susan Martinez asked from the passenger seat.

Detective-Sergeant Barbara Lassiter, Susan's partner, shot a quick look back as she maneuvered the county's unmarked vehicle through traffic. "I already told you I was fine with it," she said in her even, always-slightly-hoarse voice. She glanced at the dashboard clock. "We're off duty in fifteen minutes, anyway. I have nothing else to do tonight, and I love your Uncle Alberto. He's a true gentleman."

"What's Henry doing?" Susan asked.

"He's at a symposium in San Diego. Be back tomorrow." Barbara chuckled. "He's so damned smart, I can't imagine him learning anything more. How about Roger?"

"We're having dinner tonight."

"You guys getting along?"

"He's the best thing that's happened to me in a long time. I can't thank you and Henry enough for introducing us."

Barbara smiled. Whenever Susan talked about Roger Smith her tone adopted the sing-song strains of Northern New Mexico. Barbara said, "Roger's head over heels for you."

Susan tapped her nails against the passenger side window.

"What are you thinking?"

"My uncle told me this will be the fourth funeral he's attended in the last few months. All fellow residents at the retirement home."

"You worried about him?"

Susan shrugged. "Sure. He's eighty years old."

"But he's in great shape for his age. He could live another ten, fifteen years."

"The funeral today was for a man younger than Uncle Alberto. John Matthews was seventy-eight and didn't have any health problems that I was aware of. You just never know."

"What did the man die from? Cancer?"

Susan shook her head. "Nope. They think a heart attack."

"Ah. The proverbial natural causes."

"My uncle told me Mr. Matthews donated his body to UNM." After a beat, Susan added, "I admire him for doing that, but I don't think I could do it."

"Why's that?"

"Think about it. Say you're eighty years old, your boobs are flat as pancakes, and you got skin hanging down like a wrinkled drapery. Do you want some twenty-five-year-old medical student looking at your naked body?"

Barbara laughed. "What would I care? I'd be dead."

Susan scoffed. "What if your spirit's floating above your corpse watching the whole thing? I mean, my spiritual morale would be shot to shit."

Barbara laughed again. "Change the scenario. What if you died today and your body was worked on by some twenty-something medical student?"

Susan snapped her fingers. "Now that's a different story." She ran her hand over her chest. "I'd want the entire class checking this out."

CHAPTER 2

Chief Medical Investigator Frederick Gaston Beringer had been a fixture at New Mexico's Office of Medical Investigation for three decades. He'd started there as a pathologist and taken over leadership of the organization twelve years ago. At sixty-five years of age, he was now as well-known in the medical community as pathologists Henry Lee, Cyril Wecht, and Michael Baden. The main difference between Beringer and men like Lee was that Beringer wanted nothing to do with television. He was no publicity hound. He'd told colleagues and students that appearing on the "boob tube" was an insult to science and medicine. Some colleagues thought his revulsion toward the media had to do with an article in *The New York Times* in which a reporter had described Beringer as resembling a six-foot, four-inch combination of Ichabod Crane and Boris Karloff on a bad hair day and had gone on to wonder 'whether students at UNM could tell the difference between Beringer and the average cadaver.' Whatever the reason for Beringer's antipathy toward the media, he was a giant in his specialty, respected by his contemporaries, and revered and liked by his colleagues and UNM Medical School students where he often lectured.

Standing erect at the front of a twenty-foot by one hundred-foot autopsy theater, he looked out at the one hundred twenty-four medical students clustered four-to-a-stainless steel "down-draft" table. He said, "Good afternoon" into a microphone as a video camera projected his image on six big screen televisions spread throughout the large room. Beringer stood behind another of the stainless steel tables, on which a cadaver draped by a sheet had been placed.

He cleared his throat, took in a deep breath, and exhaled. Since his day had begun at 6:00 a.m., he'd done two intense autopsies, attended a combative staff OMI meeting, and taught a class. Now 4:00 p.m., this was his second class of the day. He was tired and sleep-deprived and thought, for a moment, about his wife, Estelle. *She'll meet me at the door, glass of Malbec in hand, and ask me how my day went. Then we'll sit down to dinner, after which we'll watch one or another of an episode of* Masterpiece Theatre, *and then I'll fall asleep by 8:30. What a ball of fire and what good company I am!* But despite his fatigue, he was happiest when he was acting as a pathologist and training medical students.

"For almost all of you," he began, "what you know about pathology and autopsies is what you learned by watching television and movies. What do you think the biggest difference is between reality and the nonsense portrayed by the entertainment business?"

He didn't pause for a second. His question had been rhetorical. "The difference," he said, "is that here we treat our subjects with respect. A cadaver is not some meaningless hunk of tissue and bone and fluid. Rather, it's what's left of a person who had dreams, accomplishments, disappointments, and relationships. A person who made mistakes, suffered pain and loss, and, perhaps, committed crimes. If you believe in God, then you believe a cadaver had a soul, which now might reside in heaven." He paused a beat and then added, "Or hell."

There was a smattering of chuckles.

"Your textbooks will tell you that an autopsy is an examination of a dead body to determine cause of death, the effects or indications of disease or, in some cases, to identify a dead person. Forensic pathologists—physicians trained in the study of diseases and abnormalities—perform autopsies with the assistance of autopsy technicians, sometimes called *dieners*, from the German for *helper*, and autopsy photographers.

"Pathology comes from the Greek word *pathos*, meaning feeling, pain, or suffering. It's the study and diagnosis of disease through examination of organs, tissues, cells, and bodily fluids. The term encompasses both the medical specialty which uses tissue and body fluids to obtain clinically useful information, as well as the related scientific study of disease processes."

Beringer paused and scanned his audience. Then he said, "But never forget that the subject of an autopsy was a real person, just like you, and deserves respect and care.

"Before we begin the autopsy, I want to cover a few administrative points. Usually, when a body is given to the Anatomical Donation Program at the university, it's embalmed, then stored at zero degrees Fahrenheit in one of several cooler rooms. The body is kept there for about eighteen months, and is then cremated. In the case of our subject today, he was not embalmed because we decided we didn't want to have any degradation or false readings caused by the embalming solution." He nodded at his autopsy *diener*, who carefully folded back the sheet, exposing the cadaver. Beringer stepped forward and read from a card he removed from his lab coat.

"John Joseph Matthews was a seventy-eight-year-old; five-foot, nine-inch; one hundred and sixty-eight-pound male; with blue eyes and a full head of pure-white hair. He exhibited symptoms of cardiac arrest three days ago, was transported to Presbyterian Hospital, where he was officially pronounced deceased at 4:17 p.m. He had no tattoos, birth marks, or significant scars. From interviews with one of his daughters and a younger brother, and from an examination of his medical records, we learned that Mr. Matthews had been remarkably healthy his entire life, with only one hospitalization associated with a discectomy involving the L5, S1 region. His most recent chemistry panel and complete blood count performed as part of an annual physical ten months ago showed that his overall health was excellent. The test assessed his vascular, liver, kidney, and blood cell status as excellent. The CBC measured the number, variety, percentage, concentration, and quality of platelets, red and white blood cells, and concluded that he had no infections, anemias, or other hematological abnormalities. Based on the test results for total cholesterol, high-density lipo-protein, low-density lipo-protein, triglycerides, and the total cholesterol/HDL ratio, Mr.

Matthews's cardiovascular system was in unusually good condition for a man his age. The chemistry panel also measured blood glucose, which is critically important for detecting early-stage metabolic syndrome, diabetes, and coronary artery disease. Again, all results were in the normal range, as were the assessments of calcium, potassium, and iron levels."

Beringer paused again to allow the students to digest the information he'd presented. Then he looked around the room again, seemingly making eye contact with every one of them, and, in a deep, resonant, almost-dramatic voice said, "So, what killed John Joseph Matthews?"

CHAPTER 3

Susan gazed across the bar at her Uncle Alberto who appeared to be listening to his friend, Max Katz, regale a handful of septuagenarians and octogenarians who were residents of the Vista de Alameda Retirement Home with an anecdote about John Matthews. The other men and women smiled at Max, but Alberto Martinez's glum expression and slumped posture told Susan how badly Matthews's death had affected her uncle. At his age, Alberto had, more or less, become accustomed to attending funerals. But something about the loss of John Matthews seemed to deeply trouble him.

While Barbara conversed with a couple of other Vista de Alameda residents, Susan moved to the table where her Uncle Alberto and the other men and women sat. Just as she arrived there and took a seat next to her uncle, the group—other than her uncle, who merely smiled and shook his head—burst into laughter.

The group's reaction only spurred on Max. "Wait, wait. Did you ever hear about the time that Johnny went deaf?"

One of the other men said, "You gotta be kiddin'. What happened?"

Max looked at Alberto, smiled, ignored his friend's frown, and said, "Alberto here kept telling Johnny that he needed to go see an ear, nose, and throat guy about his hearing. But Johnny just said, 'Hey, I'm old. My hearing's not the only thing that's not working so well.' Six months go by. Every time someone would say something to

Johnny, he'd shout, 'What did he say?' So, after six months, Alberto and I went with Johnny to an ENT. The gal takes one of those metal thingamajigs with the light on the end and looks in Johnny's ears. She makes this clucking sound, picks up some tweezers, and pulls from each of his ears some god-awful-black-looking thing that resembles an old-time musket ball about the size of a pinto bean."

Susan couldn't help but admire Max Katz's story-telling skills. He paused for effect and waited until someone in his audience asked him how a musket ball could have gotten into someone's ear. When one of the women asked just that question, Max shook his head. "It wasn't a goddamn bullet; it was a fossilized cotton ball the doc pulled out of each ear."

Max now laughed so hard, tears streamed down his face. "Can you believe it? He stuck the damn things in his ears one day because it was cold and windy. Then he forgot about them for six months. When the doc removed them, they were hard as rocks. She asked Johnny, 'Can you hear me now?' like that TV telephone commercial."

"What did Johnny say?" one of the elderly men asked.

Max smiled at the man, waited a few seconds, then said, "Johnny yells at the top of his lungs, 'Holy shit! It's a goddamn miracle.' "

The group bellowed with laughter. One guy hit the table so hard with his fist that a couple wine glasses shuddered and threatened to tip over.

Susan saw a slight smile crease her uncle's face. But his glum look quickly returned. "We're about to leave, Uncle Alberto," she said.

Alberto straightened in his chair, stood, and hugged Susan. "Thanks for coming, *mi cara*. I really appreciate it."

Susan kissed her uncle's cheek. "I'm sorry about your friend. I know he meant a lot to you."

He nodded. "He died before his time."

Susan didn't know how to respond. She wasn't about to tell her uncle that his friends had lived long lives and that death often came as a surprise, even for people John Matthews's age. But she held off. After all, Alberto was eighty years old. The last thing he would want to hear is some inane platitude.

"You call me, okay, *Tio*? If you want to talk."

"Sure, *mija*. Thanks again for coming."

As Alberto went back to his chair, Susan returned to the table where Barbara talked with two elderly men. "Can I break up you lovebirds?" she asked. "I have to get home."

Barbara stood and told the men, "It was nice to meet you."

Then Susan felt a hand on her shoulder and turned.

"You can't leave already," Max Katz said, his expression crestfallen.

Susan took his hand in hers. "It's been a long day, Max." She looked over the old man's shoulder at her uncle and noticed his slumped posture. She whispered to Max, "Do me a favor. Keep an eye on my uncle. He seems torn up about Mr. Matthews."

Max wagged his head from side to side. "They were really close." Then he smiled. "Don't you worry, Susan, I'll take care of him." He chuckled. "He's the only friend I got at Vista de Alameda. No one else will put up with me."

"Thanks, Max."

Barbara moved toward the bar's front entrance. Susan waved to her uncle, smiled at Max, and followed Barbara out to the parking lot.

Frederick Beringer shuffled through the front door of his home, kissed his wife, Estelle, and dropped his briefcase next to the umbrella stand inside the door. He shucked his suit jacket and hung it on a clothes tree, took a glass of wine from Estelle, and moved to his recliner in the den.

"You look tired, dear," Estelle said. "More than usual."

"Function of age and a long day."

"What happened? You told me this morning you'd be home after your last class. It's 8:00. Your class ended at 6:00."

He sipped from his wine glass, then set it down on the table next to him. "Why don't you sit down?" He pointed at the couch across from him. "I need your opinion about something."

She visibly brightened as she sat.

Beringer smiled. "You know, one of the things I like most about our marriage is our ability to talk about medical matters."

"In addition to my sexy body and drop-dead good looks."

He smiled again. She was just as shapeless and plain today as she'd been the day they'd met, forty years ago in medical school. But her smile was still a beacon of light that could lighten his most morose moment, and her sense of humor could wash away any worry. Most of all, her intellect was world-class.

"That, too, sweetie. But I need your brain, not your body at the moment."

"My, my, aren't you the romantic one."

Beringer laughed as he scrunched back in his chair. "I had an interesting one today."

Estelle beamed. "Next to romance, there's nothing I like more than a cadaver story. But I think you should first change into something more comfortable and come to the dining room table. Your dinner's been ready for a couple hours. We can discuss your case over warmed-up lamb chops, *haricots vert*, and Basmati rice."

It took Beringer fifteen minutes to change. When he entered the dining room, his meal was already at his place at the table. He pulled back Estelle's chair, waited for her to sit, then took his place across from her. He opened his mouth, but she held up a hand.

"How about you eat a little food, then you can tell me what's on your mind, and you can finish your meal while I tell you how to solve your problem."

"God, you're a pushy woman."

"What did you eat today?" she asked.

"I can't remember."

"Nonsense. You never forget anything." She scowled. "I'll tell you what you ate today. You had an English muffin and cup of coffee before you left here this morning. Then I'd bet all you had the rest of the day was a gallon of coffee and whatever you could scrounge from the break room at the medical school. And probably junk food from one of the vending machines."

Beringer tried to put on a blank expression, with limited success.

"That's what I thought. Eat," she ordered.

They sat in silence for a few minutes and ate. By the time he'd consumed half his meal, he began to feel halfway rejuvenated.

"This is good, sweetie."

Estelle shot him a glowing smile as she put down her fork and sat back. "Okay, get it off your chest."

Frederick leaned forward, elbows on the table, hands folded as if in prayer. "In my last class, we had a body that had been donated to the school. Elderly gentleman who passed away earlier this week from cardiac arrest. Natural causes. Not surprising, considering he was seventy-eight. But the man was one of the healthiest specimens his age I've ever seen. No serious illnesses and excellent lab results from a recent physical. But, like I said, a cardiac incident isn't unusual in a person his age." He sat back, reached for his wine glass, took a sip, set it down.

"So, I summarized the toxicology screen for the class. There were only a couple differences between the labs from his annual physical and the labs done in association with his autopsy. First, there was evidence of his having taken sleep medication. Diphenhydramine hydrochloride was in his system."

"Maybe Unisom or something similar?" Estelle said.

"Probably. In any case, the report also showed that cotinine was present."

Estelle had been about to sip her wine, but stopped, lowered her glass, and stared at her husband. "Cotinine? That's what nicotine transforms into when it metabolizes in the body. He must have been a smoker."

"Not according to his family. But I dissected the lungs, just in case. The tissue was pink. The man probably never smoked a cigarette in his entire life." He took in a long, slow breath and then exhaled. "What do you think?"

Estelle leaned forward—fully engaged, she pushed her glass and plate away, rested her elbows on the table, and frowned. "Where was the cotinine discovered?"

"There were slight traces in his urine and in his liver."

"Did the man use e-cigarettes?"

"Not that I could determine. I had my assistant call his daughter. She claims her father thought that people who used stimulants were weak. The man didn't drink coffee, tea, or sodas, and definitely did not use tobacco of any kind."

"Huh. You know I read about a woman who had a cardiac

incident when she rolled over in bed on her e-cigarette, broke the vial, and then absorbed a dose of nicotine through her skin. Maybe the man had a girlfriend who smoked one of those things."

"He lived in a retirement home."

"So what?" Estelle said. "Those places are hotbeds of sexual activity."

"You made that up."

"Okay, so it was a slight exaggeration."

"Any other thoughts?"

"Was there anything in his medical records that would indicate clinical depression?"

"Are you suggesting that he took a sleeping pill and then swallowed a dose of liquid nicotine?"

"No, because there would have been an emetic response. He would have vomited the substance if he'd swallowed it. Was there any staining of his skin?"

"No. I thought of that and rechecked in case I'd missed it the first time. There was nothing like that."

She looked up at the ceiling for a few seconds. "I think you should research how nicotine might otherwise have been introduced."

FRIDAY
OCTOBER 3

CHAPTER 4

Lt. Rudy Salas shouted in his high-pitched, squeaky voice, "Lassiter ... Martinez, you're up."

Susan cringed. "Oh, that man's voice is like fingernails on a blackboard."

"Hope it's not a ripe one," Barbara said as she got up from behind her desk and stopped at Susan's desk.

"You break me up," Susan said and stood. "A homicide detective who can't stand the sight of dead bodies. You ever think about a different career?"

"All the time. But how would you cope without me?"

Susan said, "There's that."

Salas waved them into his office and pointed at two chairs in front of his desk. "Got an interesting one for you."

"I hope *interesting* isn't a euphemism for *gory*," Barbara said.

Salas shot Barbara a disapproving look, then said, "The sheriff just received a call from a friend of his at OMI." Salas picked up a slip of paper and read from it: "Dr. Frederick Gaston Beringer."

Susan said, "Sounds German. Of course, the *Gaston* could be French. Do I sense that this case might entail a trip to Europe?" Before Salas could continue, Susan raised a finger and added, "Wait a minute, isn't there a Beringer wine? Is this guy related to the winemaker?"

Salas scowled. "You finished, Martinez?"

"Yeah, sorry boss," she said, sounding insincere.

The lieutenant shook his head and mumbled something indecipherable. Then he said, "Only a couple years 'til I retire and will no longer have to put up with your wise-ass sense of humor."

Barbara noticed the faux hurt look on her partner's face and silently prayed that she wouldn't say anything more.

"Anyway," Salas continued, "go to OMI and talk to Dr. Beringer."

"Do we have the name of a deceased?" Barbara asked.

Salas referred again to the slip of paper. "Name's John Joseph Matthews."

"What're the odds?" Barbara asked as she drove the sheriff's department's unmarked Crown Victoria up Lomas Boulevard to the UNM Medical School. "Yesterday we went to a wake for John Matthews and now we're investigating his death."

"All I keep thinking about is my Uncle Alberto's reaction to Matthews's death. It was as though he thought there was something off about it."

"You know they were great friends. I'm sure your uncle was just distressed about losing a close friend."

"I don't know, Barb. It was like . . . he *knew* something was wrong."

"We'll see. Let's not get ahead of ourselves," she said as she pulled onto Yale Boulevard, then turned east onto Camino de Salud. She entered the parking lot and put a "BCSO-Official Business" placard on the dashboard. Then they walked to the front entrance, showed their badges to the security guard, and asked directions to Dr. Beringer's office.

Beringer's office looked like a room out of the *Hoarders* TV show. The man stood up as his assistant introduced Barbara and Susan and quickly guided them to a small conference room adjoining the office. He smiled deprecatingly. "At least we can sit in here," he said.

"We understand you called the sheriff, Dr. Beringer."

"That's correct, and please call me Fred. Sheriff Munoz and I are old buddies. We've been members of the Albuquerque Rotary Club for years."

Barbara removed a small notepad from her purse and flipped

over the top. "The sheriff told our boss that you have concerns about the death of a Mr. John Matthews."

Beringer steepled his fingers and looked first at Barbara and then at Susan. He dropped his head a bit and looked at them through Schnauzer-like eyebrows. "We found nicotine in Mr. Matthews' system, along with a sleep medication."

Susan said, "That would seem to be anything but unusual."

The doctor nodded several times. "Quite so. Except, in this instance, Mr. Matthews didn't smoke or use any stimulant and didn't take any sleep medication. And, he was in unusually good physical condition for a man his age. Of course, cardiac arrest in a seventy-eight-year-old is very common, but . . . ."

"What are you suggesting, Doctor?" Barbara said.

"I think there's a possibility that Mr. Matthews died from a lethal dose of nicotine."

"Nicotine?" Barbara said. "As in tobacco?"

"Well, sort of. Nicotine is a highly toxic chemical that can be fatal. But it's not easy to identify poisoning if no evidence exists of drug ingestion. It can be easily overlooked by physicians and considered as a case of sudden cardiac death. This is what I believe happened when Mr. Matthews was transported to the emergency room at a local hospital."

"How much nicotine are you talking about?" Susan asked.

"A lethal dose for an adult is around sixty milligrams. Nicotine kills by blocking certain chemical receptors in the brain which, in turn, disrupts control of certain nerve functions. Nicotine poisoning can cause you to lose control of involuntary muscle functions, like breathing."

Susan asked, "How much is sixty milligrams?"

"In liquid form, less than a tablespoon."

"My God," Barbara said. "How does someone buy the stuff?"

Beringer's eyes hardened and his jaw muscles twitched. "You can buy the stuff at smoke shops or on the Internet by the gallon or barrel."

"If it's poison, isn't it controlled by the FDA?" Susan asked.

"That's an excellent question," Beringer said, "but the answer is no. Go on the Internet and look up liquid nicotine. You'll find

American as well as Chinese companies, among others, offering it for sale. They sell it to the e-cigarette industry. People who smoke e-cigarettes refill their devices with the liquid. Initially, many e-cigarettes were disposable devices that looked like real cigarettes. But today the cigarettes are more often larger, reusable devices which can be refilled with liquid. The liquid is generally a combination of nicotine, flavorings, and solvents."

"So, someone could have laced Mr. Matthews's food, or iced tea, or whatever," Susan said.

"Not likely. Eating or drinking a lethal dose would cause an emetic effect in a human being."

"Meaning?" Susan said.

"If Mr. Matthews had ingested a lethal dose of nicotine, he would probably have become ill, but he would most likely have vomited the poison along with whatever else it had been mixed with."

"Even if he'd taken a sleep medication?" Barbara asked.

"Although he had some sleep medication in his system, it wasn't enough to make him comatose. He would have had to be comatose to preclude regurgitation but, if he was comatose, he couldn't have eaten or drunk anything. I suggest he was injected with the stuff after the sleep medication took effect."

"What about the possibility of suicide?" Susan asked.

"Of course, that's a possibility. But, considering all I've learned about Mr. Matthews, I find that highly improbable."

"In other words," Barbara said, "you believe Mr. Matthews was drugged so that he would fall asleep, then injected with a lethal dose of liquid nicotine."

Beringer waggled his hands in front of his chest. "My problem, Detectives, is that I didn't find any evidence of an injection site."

Susan groaned.

"Yes, I understand, Detective Martinez. I'm not making your job easy. But, in my bones, I feel that I'm right about this. I believe Mr. Matthews was murdered. I plan to re-examine the body, centimeter by centimeter. If there's an injection site, I'll find it."

It was a few minutes after 10:00 a.m. when Barbara and Susan returned to their car. "What do you want to do now?" Susan asked

"Would you mind calling your uncle? Check if he's at the retirement home. Ask if he would meet with us."

"Sure. Why?"

"I have a few questions for him."

"About what?"

Barbara shrugged. "I'm not sure yet, but I'll think about it as we drive there."

CHAPTER 5

Alberto Martinez and Max Katz stood across from one another at the pool table in the Vista de Alameda recreation room. "You wanna go double or nothing?" Max asked.

"*Eres un bandido, Max*," Alberto said. "How much have I lost to you playing pool over the past three years?"

"At last count, it was over one hundred thousand dollars." Max made a dismissive gesture. "But what difference does it make? You never pay me."

"It's not the *dinero, amigo*, it's the principle. You take advantage of me."

Max laughed. "You shoulda spent less time in the library when you were a kid and more time in pool halls, like I did. Do you want to play again, or not?"

Alberto shook his head. "Susan and Barbara are on their way here. I'll wait for them in the lobby."

"Susan's coming?"

Alberto squinted at Max. "Yeah-h-h."

"You want me to join you?"

"Go find a woman your own age, you old reprobate."

"It's not chronological age that matters." He tapped the side of his head with a finger. "It's your psychological and mental age that counts."

Alberto put his cue stick in a rack and laughed. "Okay, Max, you can join us, but only if you don't make goo-goo eyes at my niece."

Max dropped his cue stick on the table and hurried to catch up with Alberto. "Why are you meeting with them?"

"They want to ask me about Johnny." He shrugged.

"What about him?"

"I don't know. But you knew him almost as well as I did. Maybe you can help."

Dr. Beringer ordered two autopsy technicians to bring John Joseph Matthews's cadaver into the main autopsy theater. While he waited, he flipped on the theater lights, converting the dark, windowless room into a bright, glary enclosure. As the techs entered and moved the cadaver to the autopsy table, Beringer said, "We're going to examine every part of Mr. Matthews's body. We missed something. Take my word for it, this man was murdered."

One of the techs asked, "What are we looking for?"

"Let's begin by going from his skull to his toes. Bruises, abrasions, burns, skin discolorations, the like. I'll start, then, Phil, you'll follow me; Stan, you'll finish. Hopefully, one of us will find something."

Alberto Martinez left his chair in the Vista de Alameda lobby when he spotted Barbara and Susan talking to the facility's bus driver outside the building entrance. He waited until they finished their conversation, then moved toward the revolving door. When the two women entered the lobby, he hugged Susan and shook Barbara's hand. Then he turned and pointed at Max. "Okay if he joins us?"

"Sure," Barbara said. "Is there a private place where we can sit?"

"I booked a small conference room after Susan called me." Alberto turned to lead the way from the lobby, when an elderly woman of about seventy called out, "Alberto, your guests have to sign in."

Alberto apologized to Barbara with a sidelong look. "Sorry, I forgot."

After Barbara and Susan signed the visitor's log, Alberto led them all to a conference room where they sat around a small, oblong table, Barbara and Susan toward one end and Alberto and Max at the other.

"What's this about?" Alberto asked.

Susan said, "What we're about to tell you must remain between us. You can't tell a soul about any of it."

"Okay," Alberto said. Max nodded.

"You know Mr. Matthews donated his body to the medical school?"

Alberto said, "Right."

"The school used his body in an autopsy class. Part of the process includes a complete toxicology screen, which showed the presence of a sleeping medication as well as nicotine."

"No way," Alberto blurted. "Johnny didn't take any drugs. Not even an aspirin. And he sure as hell didn't smoke."

"How about e-cigarettes?"

"Not a chance," Alberto said.

"Are either of you aware of Mr. Matthews being depressed or worried about anything?"

Max said, "John Matthews was one of the happiest guys I've ever known. He always had a joke to tell and was the first person to step forward when someone needed assistance. He was positive about everything."

"That's true," Alberto said. Then his eyes went wide. He looked at Barbara, then at Susan. "Are you suggesting that Johnny killed himself?"

Barbara said, "We're not suggesting anything of the sort, but we are trying to touch all the bases."

"There is no way Johnny committed suicide," Alberto said. "No way in hell."

Max touched Alberto's arm. "Then that would mean someone murdered Johnny, wouldn't it?"

Alberto's mouth opened and his eyes widened again as he first stared at Max, then turned his gaze to Susan. "Is that what you and Barbara are doing here?"

Susan compressed her lips and nodded.

"Holy shit," Max exclaimed.

Barbara looked at Max. "Remember, we need you to keep this to yourselves. If, in fact, Mr. Matthews was murdered, then anyone he interacted with would be a suspect."

"Including the two of us," Max said. "Maybe I shouldn't be in here."

Barbara laughed. "You and Alberto have been excluded from the list of possible suspects."

"Why?" Max asked, almost looking disappointed.

"We asked the bus driver to show us his daily passenger log for the day Mr. Matthews died. You and Alberto, along with eight female residents, went on an excursion to Santa Fe. According to the pathologist at the Office of Medical Investigation, the nicotine would have to have been introduced into Mr. Matthews's body within an hour before his cardiac arrest. You were having lunch at Jambo Cafe at that time."

Barbara said, "Were you aware of him having any financial problems?"

Alberto shook his head. "Johnny never worried about money. He could have lived in a cave if that was his only option. Didn't care about material things and didn't have any debt."

Susan waved a hand around, indicating the building they were in. "It must be expensive to live here."

"It's expensive to get in, but not very expensive to stay in," Alberto said. "When a single person signs up to live here, he pays three hundred and fifty thousand dollars, which goes into an annuity account. The earnings on that account help support the facility. In addition, we pay fifteen hundred dollars per month rent, which includes two meals a day, weekly housekeeping, and utilities. Couples pay more upfront and twenty-two hundred dollars a month. It's a hell of a deal. Johnny made the upfront payment out of the proceeds from the sale of his Albuquerque house. Between Social Security, pension income, and savings, he had more than enough to cover his rent, a Medicare Supplement Insurance plan, and incidentals."

"How do you know so much about his finances?" Barbara asked.

"We were best friends. I was a banker for fifty years. He came to me for advice. I helped him prepare his tax returns."

"Do you know if he had a life insurance policy?"

Alberto squinted and seemed to consider the question. Then he said, "I think he did. But he never told me for how much or who the beneficiary was."

CHAPTER 6

Despite the cool air that flooded the autopsy suite, Beringer was drenched in perspiration. The examination of John Matthews had already gone on for three hours, but they'd found nothing that would prove the man had been intentionally poisoned.

Beringer once again inspected the corpse's feet, including between the toes, through a high-powered magnifying glass and under the intense, hot light of the overhead fixture. He stepped back and waved in one of the techs. The man finished his examination, and then the other tech did the same.

The second tech said, "Nothing, Dr. Beringer."

Beringer heard the fatigue echo in the man's voice. "Let's take a break, guys." He sighed and added, "I know we've missed something." The looks he got back from the two men told him they were skeptical

Maybe I'll go through the files again, Beringer thought.

The two techs groaned and moved out of the room. Beringer went to a table and chair and sat down. He opened the computer sitting there and slowly read Matthews's medical files. He went through them page by page, item by item, but nothing leaped out. He stared at the screen and read the tabs at the bottom: MedFiles/ Wyatt MD; MedFile/PresHospEmer. He and the techs had scoured the files. They'd now each extensively examined the man from scalp to toes three times, including inside his mouth. They'd even removed two bridges, but found nothing unusual, except for some minor irritation around a cap on a molar. There was a tiny injection site in the man's gum, where a dentist had injected Novocain. That site had been confirmed by Matthews's dental records.

After signing out on the Vista de Alameda visitors' log, Barbara and Susan left the building. Outside, Susan asked, "What are you thinking?"

Barbara covered her face with her hands. When she dropped them, she said, "Excluding the ten passengers who went to Santa Fe and the bus driver, there are another one hundred ninety residents and thirty staff members who were on site when Matthews could have been poisoned." She sniffed. "I don't even want to think about interviewing all of those people. Why don't we go after the low hanging fruit?"

"What's that?"

"That old woman behind the reception desk was pretty aggressive about our having to sign in and out. Maybe Matthews had a visitor on the day he died."

"Might as well check since we're already here."

They went back inside the complex and asked the receptionist if they could see the visitors' log for September 29th.

The gray-haired, seventy-something woman wore a nametag that read: Agnes. Her freckled face and pert nose made Barbara think of a leprechaun.

"You'd have to talk with Ms. French about that."

Susan said, "And where might we find Ms. French?"

"She's giving a talk in the community room." The woman pointed toward a hallway off the lobby. "It's down there, just past the library."

"Thank you, Agnes," Susan said, and turned toward the hallway.

Barbara walked shoulder to shoulder with Susan, leaned in toward her, and whispered, "Would you ever want to live in a place like this?"

"I asked my uncle when he told me he planned to move in here why he would want to give up the independence he had in his own home. He told me that living in his home meant making his own meals; yard work; repairs and maintenance; utility, insurance, and tax payments; and worrying about someone breaking in. In the retirement home he has none of that, gets maid service, a manageable monthly rent, and plenty of company."

"Does that mean you would like to live here when you're old and gray?"

Susan laughed. "Hell, no. Too many old people around."

"You'll be old one day."

"Never happen," Susan said.

The door to the community room was open. Inside, Barbara saw a stunning woman in her mid to late thirties standing in front of eight rows of folding chairs occupied by about fifteen elderly women and one man. The woman wore black heels, a black skirt, and a white blouse. She was of medium height; had long, bleached blonde hair, a brilliant-white smile, and an athletic figure; and exuded understated sensuality. Barbara thought she looked out of place in a retirement facility, then silently chastised herself for being narrow-minded.

A poster on an easel next to the woman read: BEQUESTS TO VISTA DE ALAMEDA. The woman said, "Thanks to all of you for coming today. If you would like to discuss a bequest to Vista de Alameda, we can arrange a meeting for you with our attorney."

There was a bit of anemic applause, then the audience stood and left the room.

"Ms. French?" Barbara asked, as the woman moved into the hallway.

"Yes, I'm Lisa French. Can I help you?"

"Ms. French, I'm Barbara Lassiter. This is my partner, Susan Martinez. We're detectives with the Bernalillo County Sheriff's Office. Do you have a minute to speak with us?"

The woman looked at her wristwatch, hesitated for a moment, then said, "I have a meeting with our owner in fifteen minutes. Why don't we go to my office?"

French's office was neither chic nor elegant. It appeared to Barbara that it was set up to make a prospective tenant feel comfortable. There was enough room for a two-seat couch and two chairs, in addition to French's desk and chair. The large, framed photographs on the walls showed healthy-looking, smiling elderly people involved in a variety of activities. They appeared to be on holiday. Barbara and Susan took two chairs in front of the desk.

"What is this about, Detectives?" French asked as she sat behind her desk.

"We're investigating the death of John Matthews and wanted—"

Her face suddenly red, French interrupted, "Why would you be investigating Mr. Matthews's death? He had a heart attack."

"Actually, that was the preliminary determination by the emergency room physician," Susan said. "There's new information, however, that has raised some questions."

"What information?" French asked.

"We can't disclose that at this time. It would be helpful if we could look at the visitors' log for the day of Mr. Matthews's death. September 29th."

French appeared flustered. Her complexion had gone from red to pale-white and her eyes ping-ponged between Barbara and Susan. Finally, she said, "Of course. Of course. Let me get the logs."

After French left her office, Susan said, "She seems a little high-strung."

"Probably shocked by our visit."

"Just imagine her shock if it turns out someone here killed Matthews."

"P.R. nightmare," Barbara said.

French returned with a three-ring book that had an inch-thick stack of six-column log pages. The columns were titled: DATE, VISITOR NAME (Please Print), VISITOR SIGNATURE, PURPOSE OF VISIT, TIME IN, TIME OUT. "Mr. Matthews passed away on September 29th." She turned pages and, when she stopped, turned the binder around and handed it to Barbara. "Mr. Matthews had only one visitor that day. His son, Scott." She smiled. "He's a good son. He visits several times a week, without fail."

Barbara ran a finger along the line where Scott Matthews's name was printed. She looked at the times the man had signed in and signed out. She passed the binder to Susan, then asked French, "Would you mind making us a photocopy of that page?"

"Not at all," she said. She took the binder and left for a minute.

After she returned, she gave Barbara a copy of the page.

Barbara and Susan stood and thanked Lisa French, who stood as well. As they turned to exit the office, Susan turned back and asked, "Are you aware of anyone else who visited Mr. Matthews's room on September 29th? Maybe a staff member?"

"No, but I can check into it. Every member of the staff is required to log in online any time they schedule a meeting with a resident. They also have to record the purpose and the results of the meeting into our system. So, for instance, if a maintenance man has to perform work for a tenant, he logs into the system, and schedules the time and the unit number on his work calendar. He does the same thing when he arrives at the unit and when he leaves. Also logs in the results of the visit and whether further work is required."

"Sounds like a pretty good system," Susan said.

French smiled. "We're very careful about staff interaction with our tenants." After a beat, she added, "It also allows us to stay on top of our employees' performance. After any visit by a staff member, our receptionist calls the resident to check on whether they are satisfied with the employee's work."

"When can we expect to get a copy of any visits Mr. Matthews had with a staff member on the 29th?" Barbara asked.

"I can do that for you now," French said. She sat back down, tapped on her computer keyboard for a minute, then stood again and said, "Sorry, but Mr. Matthews had no staff visits that day." She swiveled her computer terminal ninety degrees so that Barbara and Susan could see it. She pointed at the screen. "See, no visits."

"Thank you again, Ms. French," Barbara said.

"Happy to help."

On their way to the Crown Vic, Barbara asked, "What did you think of the security system?"

Susan waggled a hand. "Okay, I guess. There is one glaring weakness in it, though."

"Like, what if an employee decides to murder someone and intentionally doesn't log in a visit with that person? That *is* a glaring weakness."

"Great minds," Susan said.

CHAPTER 7

Lisa French's hands shook as she returned the visitors' log binder to Agnes at the front desk. "I'll be in Mr. Armstead's office," she said. "I don't want to be disturbed."

French left the lobby, turned left down the hallway, and stopped at Stuart Armstead's office door. She knocked, waited for him to say, "Come in," and opened the door. She closed it behind her and leaned back against it.

Her boss looked at her. "What's wrong, Lisa?"

"There were two detectives here a minute ago. They wanted to know who had visited John Matthews on September 29th."

"September 29th?"

"The day he died."

"Why would they want to know that?"

"They didn't say so definitively, but I got the impression they don't think Matthews died of natural causes."

Armstead squinted, as though confused. "Impossible. He had a heart attack. Of course he died of natural causes."

"His son, Scott, visited him shortly before his heart attack. He signed in at eleven thirty in the morning and signed out thirty minutes later."

"So what?" Armstead said. "Scott Matthews must visit his dad four or five times a week."

French shrugged and felt her face flush.

"Any interest from the residents about bequests to the facility?" Armstead asked, changing the subject.

French forced herself to calm down, smiled, and said, "A couple. I'll follow up with them."

French returned to her office, kicked off her heels, reclined on the couch. The detectives' visit had unnerved her. She lay there for several minutes and wondered what she should do. She thought about the time of Scott Matthews's visit with his father on that fateful day. *How lucky is that?* she thought. Then an idea that had tickled a corner of her brain suddenly germinated into a full-fledged plan. She quickly stood, moved to her desk, and lifted the receiver from her phone console. She dialed a number from memory and breathed out a relieved sigh when Frank Calderon answered.

"Frankie, it's Lisa."

"Hey, Sis, what's happenin'?" Before she could answer, he added, "You sound stressed."

"I need to see you."

"Sure, when?"

"How about now?"

"What's wrong?"

"Not on the phone."

"Okay," Frank said. "Meet me at Emilio's, down on Edith, in thirty minutes."

Frank Calderon moved away from the corner of the warehouse building on Broadway toward the pair of men who stood in front of a third man who hung by his wrists from a rope suspended from a steel girder. A large, plastic drop cloth had been placed on the floor beneath the third man, whose head lolled forward; blood dripped from his nose and mouth, and from multiple cuts on his tattooed arms and chest.

"You fucked up, Junior. I don't pay you enough that you gotta hold out on me?"

The man moaned as he struggled to right his head. Tears poured from his hooded eyes, down his face, onto the drop cloth, and mixed with the blood trails already there. He licked his split lips and moaned again. "It was . . . for my mom." His breath came in short gasps. "She needed surgery. She's too young . . . for Medicare and don't have . . . insurance. Won't happen again, Mr. Calderon. Promise."

"Oh, I guarantee it won't happen again," Calderon said. He turned to one of the other men and rasped, "Get this *pendejo* out of my sight. I don't wanna ever see him again, ya hear?"

"*Si, Jefe.*"

Calderon then pointed at the other man and ordered, "Johnny, get the car. We're goin' for a ride."

"What did you get from Dr. Beringer?" Lt. Rudy Salas asked.

Barbara was about to answer when her cell phone rang. She looked at the screen, said, "I gotta take this," and raised her eyebrows as though to ask her boss's permission.

Salas gave Barbara a "go ahead" hand gesture, then turned to Susan as Barbara walked out of the office. "You learn anything?"

"Dr. Beringer's suspicious about Mr. Matthews's death. The man was in great shape . . . for a guy his age, had no history of heart problems, and wasn't a smoker. But he had nicotine in his body."

"So, how'd that happen?"

"That's the million-dollar question. Beringer found both nicotine and a sleep medication in Matthews's body, but found no injection site where nicotine had been introduced."

"Maybe someone laced his orange juice," Salas suggested.

"According to Beringer, no one could drink that much liquid nicotine without barfing. I did some checking on the Internet. You can make someone pretty sick by introducing liquid nicotine through the skin, but there was no indication of skin irritation anywhere on Matthews's body."

"Through the skin?"

"Yeah, Lou. There was an incident where a woman rolled over on her e-cigarette, crushed the liquid nicotine vial, absorbed the liquid through her skin, and went into cardiac arrest as a result. There was a guy in California who put liquid nicotine in his wife's shampoo bottle, which made her progressively sicker."

"Did it kill her?"

"Nope. She divorced the bastard in time. Same guy drugged his second wife with Ambien, then injected liquid nicotine behind her ear. That wife croaked."

Salas shook his head and swiveled in his chair. He looked out at the sun-lit Sandia Mountains and said, "Sounds like this stuff could become a popular murder medium. If an autopsy isn't performed, killers could be walking around free as birds. Someone has a heart attack . . . big deal. Heart attacks are a dime a dozen."

Susan nodded as Barbara returned and sat down.

"Sorry about that, Lieutenant. That was John Matthews's attorney."

Salas raised his eyebrows.

Barbara looked at Susan, then back at Salas. "Matthews had a one-million-dollar life insurance policy. His four children are the beneficiaries. Other than that, he had a small investment account with a mid-five figure balance, and a checking account that never had more than five thousand dollars in it."

Susan added, "The only visitor that Matthews had on the day of his death was his son, Scott."

Salas asked, "Did the lawyer say anything about the kids?"

Barbara uncrossed her legs, then re-crossed them. "The children—two sons and two daughters—are in their fifties. Three are happily married and successful. A doctor at the "U," an engineer at Sandia Labs, and an entrepreneur who owns the largest plumbing contracting firm in the state. Only one of the children has been a problem. Can't hold a job, always in debt, sponging off the father."

"You want me to guess?" Susan asked.

"Sure," Barbara said.

"Scott."

"Damn, you got it right the first time."

Salas scowled. "When you two finish screwing around, maybe you should check on the son."

"That's a great idea, Lou," Susan said. "I wish I'd thought of it."

Salas glared at Susan, then said to Barbara, "Get your smartass partner out of my office and do some police work for a change."

Back at their desks, Susan asked, "What else did the lawyer tell you?"

"Scott Matthews has a graduate degree in chemistry. Worked as a researcher at a pharmaceutical company. He owes his credit union a bundle. They're in the process of foreclosing on his house and repossessing his pickup truck. He's been all over the lawyer trying to get him to expedite the insurance settlement so he can get the bank off his butt."

Susan said, "A good insurance investigator will discover what we've already learned. There's no way they'll pay the beneficiaries until they make certain Matthews died of natural causes . . . wasn't murdered by the kids. The fact that Scott visited his father just before he died of nicotine poisoning . . . ."

She let the thought hang in the air.

Barbara nodded. "Why don't you call Dr. Beringer? See if he's come up with anything else. I'll call Scott Matthews and arrange a time for us to meet."

"Beringer," the pathologist answered.

"Dr. Beringer, it's Detective Susan Martinez calling. Just checking in to see if you've discovered how the liquid nicotine was introduced into John Matthews's body."

Beringer expelled a groan that sounded as though he had the weight of the world on his shoulders.

"We've examined the man's body multiple times, with no results."

"The only thing we're hanging our investigation on is your theory that Mr. Matthews was murdered by an injection of nicotine. Are you telling me that you're about to change your conclusion?"

Beringer's voice rose as he said, "Hell, no, that's not what I'm saying. I'm telling you I've never been more certain of anything in my entire career. John Matthews was murdered."

"Or, he killed himself."

"He would have had to self-medicate with a sleep drug and then quickly inject liquid nicotine for that to have happened. He couldn't have swallowed the nicotine. I already told you that. He would have had to inject himself or absorb it through his skin. We found no evidence of percutaneous absorption. And we haven't yet found a damned injection site. And, what about a syringe? If he'd self-injected, wouldn't there have been a syringe by his body?"

"We're basing our investigation on your gut feeling, Doctor. If we don't get a ruling that Matthews was murdered, we'll have to drop the case."

"Before you do that, give me a little more time."

"How much time?"

"It's Friday. Give me until Monday."

CHAPTER 8

Emilio's Café was a fixture in Albuquerque's North Valley neighborhood, having served some of the best New Mexican food in the city for almost four decades. Emilio Calderon, Frank Calderon's uncle, had opened the place. It passed to Emilio's daughter, Guadalupe, eight years ago, after her father died in a car wreck.

Frank preferred to sit outside on the small patio, away from "nosey ears," as he put it. But the weather in October could be "iffy," and today was one of those "iffy" days. The sun shone bright—which it almost always did in Albuquerque—but the temperature was down around forty degrees. He hugged his cousin, Guadalupe, looked around the restaurant, and selected a corner table away from other customers. It was the middle of the afternoon, so there weren't many people there.

"¿Quieres algo de beber??" Guadalupe asked.

"*Una cerveza, por favor.* Pacifico."

As Guadalupe turned toward the bar, Lisa French entered the restaurant. Guadalupe greeted her: "*Hola prima. Mucho tiempo sin verte.*"

"Yes, it's been a long time, Guadalupe." French made a nervous gesture with her hands and added, "I'm always so busy."

Guadalupe just smiled. She knew Lisa did all she could to avoid her family and her heritage. She'd even dyed her hair blonde to look more "*gringa*," as Guadalupe frequently told other family members. She always spoke Spanish to her cousin because she knew it irritated her.

French spotted her forty-four-year-old brother and quickly moved to his table. "Thanks for meeting me, Frankie," she said. "I know you're busy."

"Never too busy for my little sister." He waved at Guadalupe and held up two fingers. After Guadalupe placed two Pacifico beers on the table and walked away, Frank said, "What's got you upset?"

French smiled at her brother. "You're looking good, Frankie. You get better looking every year. Even the gray in your hair makes you look more distinguished."

Calderon grabbed two handfuls of stomach fat. "Nothing distinguished about my gut."

French reached across the table and poked his stomach. "I think it's cute."

"Cute, my ass," he said. "Now tell me what the hell's on your mind."

"I . . . the retirement center could be in trouble."

"Could be or *is* in trouble?"

She closed her eyes for a second and shrugged.

"I see. So, what do I gotta do to get . . . the retirement center out of this trouble?"

French opened her purse on her lap and took out a manila envelope with a little bulge in its side. "I need the thing in there put in a guy's home as soon as possible. Whoever does it can't leave fingerprints."

"What's this *thing*?"

"I don't want you to even look at it. It's better you don't know what it is."

Calderon glared at her. "So, you want me to arrange a B&E into some guy's home and leave a *thing* there."

She nodded.

"How bad is this situation? Like, life or death?"

"You could say that."

Calderon exhaled sharply. Then he changed the subject. "What's going on with your former husband?"

French's face went crimson. "What do you care about Walter? We're divorced. We're never getting back together."

Calderon chuckled. "No surprise there, considering you left him with nothing."

"Why do you always bring up Walter's name?"

"Because, Lisa, he was the most decent man you ever knew. Maybe if you'd stayed with him you wouldn't be in trouble all the time."

"He's a dork."

Frank laughed. "He's a dork who was mad about you." He sniffed, then said, "Maybe you should find yourself a nice Hispanic macho man. Would that be better?"

French sneered. "So I can cook, clean, and take orders. And service him whenever he wants."

"Everything's a compromise, Lisa."

"Huh. Tell me about it." She took a long swig from her beer bottle, placed it back on the table. "You gonna take care of this thing for me?"

"Don't I always, Lisa?"

"Thanks, Frankie."

Barbara tried to reach Scott Matthews by telephone but no one answered at his home. She tried repeatedly to get through over the next three hours, without success. At 6:00 p.m., past the end of their shift, she said to Susan, "How 'bout we swing by Matthews's house on the way to meet the guys?"

"Okay by me," Susan said.

On the ride to Scott Matthews's place, Susan and Barbara discussed Susan's conversation with Dr. Beringer. "If Matthews was, in fact, murdered, we're dealing with one clever bastard," Susan concluded.

"I wonder how many people know about liquid nicotine and being able to induce a heart attack with it."

"A chemist probably would," Susan said. "Scott Matthews is a chemist."

Barbara turned south on Carlisle Boulevard and climbed the hill toward Santa Clara. "I checked out Scott Matthews. He has a sheet."

Susan snapped a look at Barbara. "What?"

"Yeah. Assault and battery."

"He serve time?"

"Nope. The charges were dropped."

"Who'd he assault?"

"His wife."

Barbara turned left on Santa Clara and then right on Parkland Circle. The neighborhood was an older, once-high-end residential area and was still popular with the "university" crowd. She found Matthews's address and pulled to the curb.

"Why don't you take the lead?" Barbara said.

Scott Matthews's house was a one-story, territorial-style structure that sat back fifty feet from the street. Six-foot high cinder block walls extended down both sides of the property, from the front edge of the house to the end of the backyard. An attached one-car garage was on the right side of the house at the end of a paved driveway. The lawn had long-since been taken over by weeds; shrubs along the front of the house were dead; and a huge cottonwood tree in the center of the front yard had given up the ghost.

"This place is a disaster," Susan said. She tried the doorbell but couldn't hear a ring tone. After a few seconds, she knocked on the door. A man answered almost immediately.

"Mr. Matthews?" Susan asked.

"Yes, I'm Scott Matthews." His voice was hoarse and trembling.

Susan flashed her badge. "I'm Detective Martinez, with the Bernalillo County Sheriff's Office." She half-turned toward Barbara. "This is my partner, Detective Lassiter. Could we come in for a minute?"

"Why?" the man asked, his voice heavy with suspicion.

"We'd like to talk with you about your father's passing."

Matthews's face scrunched up. "What about it? Since when do the police follow up on people who have heart attacks?"

"Not very often," Susan said. She raised her eyebrows. "Just a couple minutes, Mr. Matthews."

He huffed a loud exhale, hunched his shoulders, and said, "Okay, come in." He stepped back and waited for Susan and Barbara to enter, then closed the door behind them and pointed at a threadbare couch. He took a seat in what appeared to be an ancient easy chair that was partially covered with a faded throw of indeterminate vintage.

Susan looked through the adjacent room, which once might have been a dining room. There were furniture leg depressions in the well-worn carpet. She noticed similar depressions in the carpet in the living room where they were seated.

Matthews suddenly popped to his feet. "Would you care for something to drink?"

Susan waved off the offer. "Thank you; we're fine."

He dropped back into the chair, which groaned as though a spring was about to explode.

"We're sorry for your loss, Mr. Matthews," Susan said.

The man closed his eyes and dropped his head. After a couple seconds, he looked back at Susan. His brown eyes were moist, red-rimmed. "My father was a good man." He paused and then added, "I miss him terribly." Another pause. Then: "Why are you here? I mean, why would you want to talk to me about my father's heart attack?"

"As I'm sure you know, your father donated his body to the UNM Medical School."

"Of course. Dad was a rabid Lobo fan. He never missed a basketball or football game." He blurted a little laugh that seemed to catch in his throat. "It didn't surprise any of us when we learned he'd donated his body to the school."

"Were you okay with that decision?"

Matthews shot Susan a confused look, as though he wondered why she would ask such a question. "Why wouldn't I be?"

Susan ignored Matthews's question. "How was your father's health?"

Matthews chuckled. Then he coughed out another little laugh. "Dad used to joke about what his doctor always told him: 'For a man your age, you're remarkably healthy.' That's why Dad's passing was so hard on all of us. I mean, he was almost eighty, but he'd never really been sick. We all thought he'd live forever."

Susan slowly shook her head and glanced out the front window, as though she couldn't think of what to ask next. Then she turned back to Matthews. "Had he been to a doctor recently?"

"Not that I know of. He didn't always—" He suddenly stopped. "Wait a minute. Yes, he told me when I last visited him that he'd been to the dentist's office the day before. Had a root canal." After a second passed, he added, "Do you think that had something to do with his heart attack?"

"Why do you ask?"

Matthews frowned. "What do you mean?" He looked at Barbara, then back at Susan. He leaned forward, his face now red, his eyes narrow. "What's this about?"

Susan glanced at Barbara, who nodded.

"The Chief Medical Investigator who performed the autopsy on your father believes he died under . . . suspicious circumstances."

"What! What does that mean?"

"I'll answer that in a moment. First, tell us about your visit with your father. It was on the day he died."

Matthews's eyes went wide and his fingers dug into the arms of his chair. "Sonofabitch," he barked. "Sonofabitch. That's why you're here. You think I had something to do with my father's death."

"I didn't say that, Mr. Matthews. We're just trying to find out what happened."

He stood and pointed at Susan. "Bullshit. You know exactly what happened to Dad, don't you? You're trying to find out who was responsible for whatever it was."

Barbara was already on her feet when Susan slowly stood and, in a soft voice, said, "How about you sit down, Mr. Matthews? You answer our questions and we'll tell you what we know."

Matthews looked from one to the other, shook his head as though to clear it of cobwebs, and then fell back into the chair.

Susan said, "You were charged with assault and battery three years ago."

A light seemed to go on behind the man's eyes. "That makes me a murder suspect?"

"I didn't say that," Susan answered.

"No, you didn't. But you inferred it."

"Tell us about that charge."

He looked around the room and then turned his head toward the empty dining room. "You see this place. This used to be an elegant home. I busted my ass to make a good life for my wife. Gave her everything she wanted. Country club membership, trips, fancy clothes, jewelry. I made damned good money as a chemist at a pharma firm, but I had to mortgage this place to keep up with her demands. Then Sadie decided it wasn't enough. She met a guy at the club who'd been married twice before. Good-looking bastard with a lot of money. I became used goods and she sued for divorce."

"Was that when the assault charges were filed against you?" Susan asked.

Matthews smirked. "Yeah. I contested the divorce; told her I'd never agree to it. Like a fool, I believed I could win her back. Two days after I was served divorce papers, she showed up here, beat up, blood all over her face and clothes. While I went to the kitchen to get a wet towel to clean her up, she called 9-1-1. When the police arrived, they hauled my ass to jail. To make a long story short, her attorney told me she'd drop the charges if I signed the divorce papers and gave her all the money we had, including everything in my 401-K and IRA." He waved his arms around and added, with an ironical shrug, "She didn't want the house or my truck because they were mortgaged to the hilt."

"You claim you didn't hit her?"

Matthews pointed at Susan, his lips tight and bloodless, his eyes like laser beams. Then he appeared to sag a bit and sighed. "I don't *claim* I didn't hit Sadie. I swear I never touched her. I believe she had her boyfriend beat her up. It was a setup. I got fired from my job because of the charges and haven't been able to find another—other than menial ones—since then." His head bobbed back and forth. "Now it's your turn. I want to know what happened to my father."

"Mr. Matthews, OMI believes your father was murdered. That someone poisoned him."

"That's impossible. I mean, why would anyone do such a thing? The only asset he had was a life insurance policy. The only beneficiaries are his four children."

He stopped and did the head bobbing thing again. "You think

one of us murdered our father. And you came to me because I need the money and I was charged with assault three years ago."

Susan was afraid that Matthews was about to lose it. To calm the situation, she asked, "Mr. Matthews, would it be okay to use your bathroom?"

His face was red again and he looked as though he was about to leap to his feet, but he settled back in his chair and sighed. "It's down that hall."

Susan stood and moved down the hallway. She shut the bathroom door, opened the medicine cabinet, and looked at the bottles and tubes on the three glass shelves. Her eye scan suddenly stopped at a small screw cap-topped glass bottle. The label on the bottle read: Savory Scent Liquid Nicotine. There was a multi-colored logo on the label. A warning on the bottom said the contents needed to be diluted before being used in an e-cigarette vial. She waited a minute, then flushed the toilet, and ran the water in the sink.

When she returned to the living room, Matthews and Barbara were standing, neither speaking. He moved to the door, opened it, and pointed at the two of them. "I want you two to leave."

Barbara and Susan walked out, but Susan stopped, turned, and handed Matthews one of her cards, which he tossed at her as she walked away.

Back in their vehicle, Barbara started the engine, cranked up the heater, and asked, "What did you think of Mr. Charm?"

"A bit defensive, down on his luck, and . . . he had a damned good motive for murdering his father."

"That's true, but I don't think he did it," Barbara said.

"Intuition?"

"I guess."

"Would you change your mind if I told you there's a bottle of liquid nicotine in his medicine cabinet?"

Barbara jerked a look at Susan. "Yeah, probably. You making that up?"

"Nope."

"I'll be damned."

"Yep."

"Sounds like we need a search warrant."

"Ya think?"

CHAPTER 9

During the ride downtown, Susan said, "I guess there's no need to contact John Matthews's other children, other than for background information. None of them were anywhere near Vista de Alameda the day their father died."

"Until you found that bottle of liquid nicotine, I considered the possibility slim that one of them was responsible for their father's death," Barbara said. "My Spidey-sense was telling me that Scott Matthews isn't a killer."

Susan glanced at the dashboard clock. "Damn, I was hoping to call it a day."

"Great idea," Barbara said. "Let's wait until tomorrow to get a search warrant. I'm sure the bottle will still be in his medicine cabinet tomorrow."

Susan scoffed. "I think I'd better call Roger and cancel dinner. I'll ask him to call Henry for you."

Barbara said, "I was looking forward to going to that new brew pub." She paused a beat, then added, "Henry's always surprising me." She chuckled. "I don't think of him as a brew pub kind of guy."

Susan laughed. "Roger told me the reason Henry picked the place was because the first four items on the menu are different kinds of fries. Henry knows how much you like fries. That man loves you, Barbara."

Barbara blushed. "At least he's past the puppy dog phase. Roger's still there."

It was Susan's turn to blush. "You're so full of it," she said. Barbara laughed.

"What are you doing this weekend, Lisa?" Stuart Armstead asked.

She shrugged and tipped her head to the left, the way she always did when she wanted to appear self-deprecating or was looking for sympathy. "Oh, nothing much. Maybe I'll go see a movie." She wasn't about to tell Armstead that she and her yoga instructor planned to spend the night going through sexual positions: Happy baby, plow pose, reclining butterfly, downward dog . . . .

Armstead gave her a sympathetic look. "You need to get a life, Lisa. Good looking woman like you should be out kicking up her heels."

French felt her heart rate rise. She forced herself to be calm. *I'd love to kick up my heels, Stu. But you don't have a clue about my feelings for you. I'm just using my yoga teacher to take the edge off.* She said, "You have to be careful about saying stuff like that, Stu. What with the Me Too movement."

Armstead's face reddened. "I didn't mean any—"

French smiled. "I was just pulling your leg, Stu. You're too much of a gentleman to ever do anything improper."

His face still red, Armstead just nodded.

"How about you? Any plans?"

Armstead's complexion went from red to pale; his expression went from neutral to morose. "Same old, same old. Kathy's sick as a dog."

French had watched her boss go, over a two-year span, from vibrant, lean, active, and aristocratically-handsome to depressed, overweight, sedentary, and slightly dumpy. His hair had gone from thick and only partially gray to thin and completely gray. His wife's cancer had changed his life in just about every way possible. French had come to hate Kathy Armstead for what she had done to Stuart. She knew her feelings toward the woman were irrational, but that's the way she felt. In the beginning, when she'd first come to work at Vista de Alameda, she'd developed a crush on Armstead. As time passed, that crush metamorphosed into a full-blown, one-way love affair. When Kathy Armstead was diagnosed with cancer, French was imbued with a sense of hope. She'd thought, *If Kathy dies, I'll be in the perfect position to console Stuart.*

"I'm so sorry, Stu."

Armstead gave her a wan smile. Quickly switching away from the topic at hand, he asked, "When will the new tenants move in?"

"The renovations on Mrs. Solomon's unit were completed today. Mr. Vance's unit will be done by next Thursday. All we're waiting for is the carpet installer to show up."

"What about the Matthews apartment?"

"We're painting and carpeting the unit next week. Then we'll replace the appliances. They're pretty dated. Mrs. Connelly should be able to move in a week from today."

"The one bad thing about this business is that we lose too many residents. Matthews was a great person." He ran his hands through his hair. "So were the others we've lost recently."

French nodded. "The good news, not to seem crass, is that we were able to increase the buy-in from the new tenants and bump the monthly rent. Solomon, Vance, and Connelly will come on board at much larger upfront fees and higher rents. And the new rent contracts have cost of living adjusters, so we won't be stuck with rent rates that don't keep up with inflation, like with the old schedule."

Armstead grinned at her. "I didn't agree with you at first, Lisa. I always wanted to make our rents affordable. But I have to admit, now that we've changed the buy-in and rental arrangements, the property has turned cash flow positive. With the turnover of another four units, the property will generate enough profit that I may be able to take a vacation." He chuckled but French didn't think there was authentic humor in it.

"What's the matter, Stu? You don't sound very optimistic."

A sour look showed on his face. "I feel like a vulture. In order to turn a profit, some of our longest term residents have to die, so we can replace them with residents under the new contract terms."

French wanted to go around Armstead's desk and put her arms around him, to comfort him. "Look at it this way, Stu. We're giving people a wonderful place to live. They're way better off here than living by themselves. Here, they get quality meals, maid service, free transportation, and the opportunity to socialize with people their own age. And they're secure. No one's going to break in and steal their stuff or harm them. However long they live, their lives here are infinitely better than they otherwise would have been."

Armstead nodded. "You're right, Lisa. I guess it's just the nature of the game. When you serve people in their seventies and eighties, you're going to have . . . turnover."

Barbara and Susan, along with two uniformed deputies, served the warrant on Scott Matthews at 8:15 p.m. Matthews became agitated and cursed at Barbara and Susan. When Susan told him to calm down, he moved toward her, tripped on a throw rug, flew head-long into her, and knocked her to the floor.

"Sonofa—" Susan blurted as she scrambled to her feet. She pointed at one of the deputies and told him to cuff Matthews. Then she looked at Matthews. "Assault on an officer isn't gonna help you."

It took Barbara and Susan only an hour to search his place because there was so little furniture and most of the closets were empty. They confiscated the contents of his medicine cabinet, his laptop computer, his cell phone, and files and other miscellaneous papers. They also searched his vehicle, but found nothing there. The only incriminating evidence was the liquid nicotine Susan had found in the man's medicine cabinet.

Barbara approached Matthews who was seated on the couch, his hands cuffed behind his back, and held up an evidence bag with the bottle of liquid nicotine inside. She asked, "What's this?"

He squinted at the bottle label, frowned, and shouted, "Where the hell did you get that?" Then he roared, "You planted that, didn't you?" He struggled to get off the couch, but one of the deputies placed a hand on his shoulder and forced him back down.

"You bitch," he screamed. Then he muttered under his breath, "You cops are all corrupt."

The deputies transported Matthews to the Bernalillo County Metropolitan Detention Center, where he was booked on assault charges and processed. By the time he was locked in a cell, he was so wound up that Barbara suggested to Susan, "Let's give him the night to contemplate his situation. We can grill him tomorrow." After a beat, she added, "You going to pursue the assault charges?"

"Nah. He didn't knock me down intentionally. But it was the excuse I needed to lock him up for a couple days. I didn't want him to do a runner on us."

It was 11:00 p.m. when they took the elevator to the underground parking lot. On the way down, Susan's phone rang. She saw Roger's number on the screen.

"It's late, Roger. What are you doing up?"

"Henry and I are down at Steel Bender's Brewyard nursing our hurt feelings over being jilted by our girlfriends. Henry just came up with a brilliant idea. We've ordered takeout and are going to bring it over to your place."

"It's past 11:00. We're beat and—"

"Oh my God," Roger said. "I think Henry's got tears in his eyes. What's that, Henry? You don't think Barbara wants to see you? Susan, I think his heart is broken. And, as if you cared, I'm crushed, too. How can you be so callous?"

"How much have you two had to drink?"

"Too much to drive, but not so much that we didn't have the good sense to call Uber."

Susan laughed. "Okay, okay. My place in twenty-five minutes. But I'm kicking you both out at 1:00."

Despite the late hour and her exhaustion, Barbara had to admit that the ribs Roger and Henry brought to Susan's house were terrific. "Not bad," she said.

"Speaking of 'not bad,'" Henry said, "You're looking very hot this evening, Barbara."

"You're so full of bull, Henry. You've definitely had too much to drink." She leaned over and kissed his cheek. "But I love it when you say things like that."

Barbara stared at him and smiled. Henry was a full professor in the Geology Department at the University of New Mexico and came across as a little geeky; his wire-rimmed glasses only accentuated that impression. Initially, when she began seeing him, Susan had nagged her about dating a nerd and kept telling her that there were a number of good-looking men in the Bernalillo County Sheriff's Office who would love to go out with her. But Henry had followed her around like a puppy dog when she was out of shape, when some of the cops she worked with had referred to her as "Big Babs." From the first time they'd met, Henry had looked at her as though she was the most beautiful, fascinating woman on the planet. From the moment they'd met, Henry had acted like a love-sick teenager around her. And he'd turned out to be a selfless, attentive, energetic lover. There was nothing nerdy about him when he took off his clothes.

Henry caught her staring at him and asked, "What?"

She placed a hand on his. "Have I told you lately what a great guy you are?"

He lifted her hand, kissed the palm, and then held it in both of his hands. "You tell me that with your eyes every time you look at me."

"Oh, jeez, Henry," Barbara said. "You are one silver-tongued devil. Let's go to my place."

He pointed at Roger and Susan, seated across the dining room table from them, and asked, "What about them?"

"I think they would prefer that we left."

Henry looked from Roger to Susan and slurred, "Damn you guys make a handsome couple. Statuesque, Victoria's Secret-model-perfect and Hollywood-beautiful-Susan, and tall, athletic, blond, blue-eyed, handsome Roger. A dark-haired Barbie and a blond Ken."

Barbara pushed back her chair. "*Oh-h-h-kay*, Henry, I think it's time to call it a night."

Susan and Roger laughed.

As they all stood, Roger asked Susan, "By the way, how's your Uncle Alberto?"

"Still kind of down about his friend's death. But it may be more than that. I think he's been forced to face his own mortality after four people at the retirement home, including John Matthews, have passed away in the past six months or so."

"You think his friend really had a heart attack?" Roger said.

Susan said, "Oh, he had a heart attack, all right. It's just what caused it that's in question."

Roger looked momentarily shocked. "Are you suggesting suicide?"

"I guess that's a possibility, but everything we've learned about John Matthews tells us there was no reason for him to take his own life. And, if he were going to take his own life, why not swallow a bottle of sleeping pills versus going through the rigmarole of acquiring liquid nicotine and injecting himself in some spot that even a pathologist can't find? I mean, why try to hide the fact that he killed himself?" She waved her arms around as though exasperated. "And, if he did inject himself, what happened to the syringe? It couldn't have up and walked away."

Roger said, "Maybe he somehow ditched the syringe before passing out because he didn't want the stigma of suicide hanging over his family's memory of him. Maybe he wanted it to appear that he was murdered." He paused a second, then added, "That sounds kind of lame, doesn't it?"

"Yeah, it does," Susan said. "Probably because you've had too much to drink."

"Neither of you really believe this man killed himself, do you?" Roger said.

"Nope," Susan said.

"No way," Barbara added.

"This is probably boring you guys," Susan said.

"Are you kidding?" Henry said loudly, windmilling his arms. "This is a whole lot more interesting than teaching geology to a bunch of freshmen."

"That's sacrilege, Henry," Roger said with a laugh. "Don't let the head of the geology department hear you say that."

"Screw the head of the department," Henry blurted.

Barbara laughed. "I really do think I need to get this guy to bed."

As Roger and Susan walked Henry and Barbara to the front door, Roger said, "Maybe I've had too much to drink too, but I've been thinking about something Susan just said a minute ago about her uncle facing his own mortality, about four of his friends passing away in the last six months or so." He turned to look at Susan. "What killed the other three who died? Did they have heart attacks, too?"

Barbara shrugged.

Susan said. "Heart attacks aren't unusual with people in their seventies and eighties. That's why no one initially suspected anything other than natural causes in Mr. Matthews's death. If he hadn't donated his body to the med school . . . ."

Roger widened his eyes. "I know I'm probably going off the deep end here, but what if the other deaths were originally ruled to be from heart attacks, but weren't actually due to natural causes?"

"You need to stick to Latin American Studies, Professor," Henry said. He chuckled. "Maybe you should try your hand at writing fiction." Henry looked over at Barbara. "Don't you agree, Barb?"

Barbara wasn't paying attention to Henry. She met Susan's gaze and muttered, "Holy shit."

SATURDAY
OCTOBER 4

CHAPTER 10

"Damn that Roger," Barbara said. "If he'd kept his mouth shut, I'd still be in bed with Henry enjoying my day off instead of sitting with you at Panera at 7:30 in the morning."

Susan grinned. "You're just ticked off that you didn't think of it first. Besides, we have to question Scott Matthews this morning."

"How in God's name are we going to determine if the other three people at Vista de Alameda who died in the past few months actually suffered naturally-caused heart attacks?"

"I wrote down some thoughts last night before getting in bed. We need to get access to the medical records of the people who died. If they had histories of cardiac problems then, maybe, it's a non-starter."

"But, if there was no record of heart issues," Barbara said, "what then? And how will we get access to their medical records? I don't think there's a judge in the county who will issue an order for the release of those records based on what we have at present."

"We could talk with the families of the deceased," Susan said.

"And tell them what? That we suspect their loved ones were murdered?"

"That's the only thing that will get their attention."

"Damn that Roger."

"Uncle Alberto," Susan said, "how are you doing today?"

"You don't need to worry about me, *mija*."

"I know how close you and John Matthews were. I—"

"I appreciate your concern, Susan, but I'm fine."

"What are you doing today?"

"They got a van taking a bunch of us down to the zoo this morning. We heard they have a new polar bear section."

"How about having lunch with Barbara and me? We could meet you at the zoo and then give you a ride back to Vista de Alameda."

"Max's going to be jealous when he hears I'm having lunch with you."

Susan laughed. "Tell Max he's welcome to join us."

"You sure, Susan? You know he's a dirty old man?"

"I think he's kinda sweet, Uncle."

Alberto chuckled. "I thought your mother raised you better."

"How about we pick you up outside the zoo at 1:00?"

"That's good. Three hours of animal watching should be more than enough."

"Okay, Uncle Alberto, we'll see—"

"Whoa, wait a minute. How come you're so interested in having lunch with me?"

"I was just worried about you and wanted—"

Alberto chuckled. "I didn't just fall off the chili truck, *mija*. I'm old but I'm not senile. What's up?"

"I'll tell you when we pick you up."

Stuart Armstead shifted in his chair as he watched his wife, Kathy. Her eyelids fluttered and she gripped the sides of the hospital bed. Her blue-veined skin looked thin, almost translucent. When she was first diagnosed as having cancer, tears would come to his eyes every time he looked at her. But, over the last few months, the tears disappeared and he found his time with her tedious. *I miss talking to you like we used to about the problems at Vista de Alameda, about the losses, and the creditor calls, and the deferred maintenance, and the recent deaths, and . . . .* He stopped himself when he caught her looking at him, the pained expression now replaced with one of worry.

She spoke in a high-pitched, muted voice that was almost little-girl-like. "What's troubling you, Stu?"

He stood and came over to the side of the bed. "I hate seeing you like this, honey."

She showed him a weak smile. "I hate *being* like this. Cross your fingers that the treatments will work."

He kissed her forehead and then brushed back a few errant strands of her hair.

Barbara and Susan drove to the Detention Center from BCSO headquarters and met Scott Matthews's attorney, Jeff Burns, in the reception area. Burns had his client brought to an interrogation room. Barbara immediately noticed that Matthews's demeanor and attitude had dramatically changed since the last time they'd seen him. He now seemed more frightened than angry. Seated next to Burns, he bent over at the interrogation table and stared at the cuffs around his wrists, secured to a metal loop in the tabletop.

"You ready to answer our questions?" Susan asked.

Before Matthews could respond, Burns said, "Remember what I told you. Be careful about what you say. Don't volunteer any information. If I don't like a question, I'll say so."

Matthews cleared his throat. When he spoke, his voice croaked. "Go ahead," he said.

"You understand the charges against you?" Susan asked.

"Of course. I'm not stupid." He scoffed. "Assault on a police officer. What a joke! I tripped. You know it as well as I do. You trumped up that charge just so you could put pressure on me. It's my father's death that you want to talk about."

He's smarter than he looks, Susan thought.

"Why'd you kill your father?"

Matthews sneered. "I would never have harmed my dad. I loved him."

"What about the liquid nicotine we found in your medicine cabinet?"

His head came up. He stared at Susan with wide, red-rimmed eyes; his chin quivered. "I swear on my father's grave that I don't know how that bottle got into my house." He snapped a look at Barbara. "How do I know you didn't plant that bottle?"

Barbara's eyes narrowed. "We don't plant evidence, Mr. Matthews. And swearing on your father's grave doesn't mean much if you murdered him."

Burns interjected, "Was there a question there, Detective?"

Barbara ignored him. "I guess your share of your father's life insurance benefits would have solved a lot of your problems."

Burns erupted with a shout: "That's it. I'm instructing my client to not say another word to you two." He stood and banged on the door for a jailer.

Matthews's face had gone pale and his eyes leaked tears. Then he broke down and sobbed. He glanced from Barbara to Susan, who both now stood a couple feet back from the table. He appeared to want to say something, but his mouth wouldn't seem to cooperate. Finally, he wailed, "My God, what have I done to deserve this?" He swallowed hard, dried his tears on his orange prison uniform sleeve, and looked directly at Barbara. "You're so certain—"

Burns interrupted him: "Don't say anything, Scott."

Matthews ignored Burns. "You're so damned sure that I killed my father, that the liquid nicotine was mine. You're so blinded with the myth of my guilt that you're going to miss finding the actual killer."

The jailer arrived at that moment, unhooked Matthews from the ring in the table, and marched him off. As Burns turned to leave the room, he suddenly stopped, shot venomous looks at Barbara and Susan, and, in a firm, steady voice, said, "I'm going to sue you two, your department, and the county for false arrest, planting evidence, corruption, and anything else I can come up with. I hope you've got something else you can do besides pretending to be detectives." Then he walked off.

Barbara pulled the Crown Vic into the parking lot behind 5 Star Burger on Central Avenue near Old Town and followed Susan, Alberto Martinez, and Max Katz into the restaurant. After they were shown to a table, a waitress took their drink orders. When the waitress told them, "I'll be back in a minute," Max said in his Brooklyn-accented, foghorn voice, "Whoa there, sweetheart. Maybe we're ready to give you our orders. I could die before you come back."

The young girl's face went red. She took a step back as though she didn't know quite what to do or say.

Alberto came to her rescue. "That's elderly humor, miss." He looked across the table at Barbara and Susan. "Are you ready to order?"

"I am," Susan said.

"So am I," Barbara said.

"You ladies go ahead," Alberto said.

Barbara and Susan each ordered salads; Alberto and Max ordered lamb burgers.

"Would you like an order of fries?" the girl asked.

"You bet," Max said.

The waitress tapped her pencil against her order pad, picked up the menus, and half-turned to walk away when Max said, as he pointed at Susan, "Oh, by the way, sweetie, what do you think I should do to get this lady here to fall in love with me?"

The girl's face reddened again, but she quickly regained her composure, smiled sweetly, and told Max, "Develop a sense of humor."

As she walked away, Max sputtered while the others at the table broke out in laughter.

After the waitress returned with their drinks, Alberto said, "What's up, Susan?"

"Uncle Alberto, Mr. Katz, Barbara and I want to pick your brains."

Max leaned forward, an eager expression on his face. "Is this police business?"

"Yes, it is," Susan answered.

"You gonna deputize us?" Max asked.

Alberto jabbed a finger into his friend's arm and growled, "*Pendejo.*"

"Uncle Alberto, you mentioned before that Mr. Matthews was the fourth person to die at Vista de Alameda in the past few months."

Alberto compressed his lips and waggled a hand. "More like six months," he said.

"What can you tell us about those other people who died?"

Alberto squinted, then said, "Sylvia Klein died about six months ago from a fall. Karl Quintana passed away three or four months ago. Emily Watrous died about thirty days ago. Karl and Emily had heart attacks."

Barbara then asked, as her heart beat a rapid riff in her chest, "Can you tell us anything more about the circumstances of their deaths?"

Max said, "Sylvia tripped on a curb on an excursion in Santa Fe and hit her head." He snapped his fingers. "Knocked her cold. She never recovered."

Barbara felt immediate disappointment, and then disgust. *What do I want to find, a serial killer in an old-age home?* "How about the other two?"

Alberto leaned forward. "Like John Matthews," he said, "the other two died of heart attacks in their apartments shortly after lunch."

Max said, "I had lunch with Emily, Ronnie Becker, and Shirley Masterson the day she died. We talked about going to the State Fair and were—"

Alberto cut off Max with a sharp look. "What else do you want to know?" he said.

"Do you know anything about Mr. Quintana's and Ms. Watrous's health?" Susan asked. "Did they have any chronic problems?"

Max chuckled. "Everyone in the place knows about everyone else's health problems. That, and the quality of the food, are about all we talk about."

"Karl Quintana was an ox," Alberto added. "He was strong as hell for a man his age and fast-walked on the treadmill every single day. Four miles a day. Lifted weights every other day. He was the most incredible eighty-year-old man I've ever seen."

"No heart problems?" Barbara asked.

"Hell, no," Alberto said. "The only problem he had was a dairy allergy."

"How about Ms. Watrous?" Susan said.

"She'd just had her annual physical the week before she died," Max said. "Told us at lunch that day that her blood pressure and cholesterol level were normal." He paused a beat and then added, "She used to be a dancer. I've always wanted to spend some time with a dancer, but poor Emily was uglier than sin."

"Jeez, Max," Alberto said. He met Susan's gaze, then Barbara's, and shook his head as though in apology. "Sorry about my friend here. He has no filter between his brain and his mouth."

Barbara nodded. "So, as far as you know, neither Miss Watrous nor Mr. Quintana had any health problems."

"That's right," Alberto said. "As far as I know they were healthy."

"Absolutely," Max said.

"I'm almost afraid to ask," Susan said, "but have there been any other deaths at the retirement facility in, say, the last year?"

Alberto bounced his gaze back and forth between Barbara and Susan. "You've got me really worried with this line of questioning."

Susan expelled a sigh and patted her uncle's hand. "Answer my question, then I'll explain why Barbara and I are asking."

Alberto and Max stared at one another. Finally, Max said, "Let's see, there was Seth Franks who died just about a year ago. Then Liz Smith, Leni Brooks, Pete Giacomo . . . ."

"Don't forget Anne Wisniewski."

"Oh, yeah." Max raised a finger. "And that nasty old gal, Connie Sanders."

"So, over the past year, including Klein, Matthews, Watrous, and Quintana, ten Vista de Alameda residents have passed away," Barbara said as she consulted her notes.

Alberto nodded, his eyes wide with expectation. "What's up, Barbara?"

Barbara dipped her head and thought, *we'll have to find out what kind of shape the deceased residents had been in and what killed them.* She looked up at Alberto. "We're almost certain that John Matthews didn't die from natural causes. We think he was poisoned."

"*Dios mio,*" Alberto exclaimed. "You think all of the others were poisoned, too?"

"We don't know, Uncle Alberto," Susan said. "But we're going to find out."

Max showed a deer-in-the-headlights look and his hands shook. "Maybe Alberto or I are next on the killer's list."

"Whoa, calm down," Barbara said. "We don't know for sure if anyone, besides Mr. Matthews, was murdered. In fact, his death hasn't yet been ruled a murder."

Max didn't look convinced. "I got a theory," he said. "It's the food. Nearly every person died right after lunch."

"Are you kidding?" Susan asked.

Alberto said, "The problem is that most residents eat a big lunch and then take a nap. All that food just clogs up their arteries."

Max said, "Thank you, Dr. Martinez, for your professional medical diagnosis."

CHAPTER 11

During the ride to Vista de Alameda to drop off Alberto and Max, the men threw one question after another at Barbara and Susan. Each question elevated the detectives' angst. They couldn't answer most of them.

"You told us to keep our mouths shut about all of this," Max said. "*Shish*, every time I look at someone in the place I'm going to think he could be a killer."

"Or *she*," Alberto said.

Max nodded several times. "That's right. It could be a woman. They outnumber us by twenty-five to one. I'll bet it's one of those old biddies."

"Please don't do or say anything that could make people think something's wrong," Barbara said.

"Something *is* wrong," Alberto said. "What if another resident is killed while we're keeping this to ourselves?"

"What if we're murdered next?" Max shouted.

Barbara glanced over at Susan. She felt the same way that Susan looked: fearful. "Remember what we told you. We don't know for certain that anyone was killed."

"Yeah, yeah, yeah," Max exclaimed, his accent even heavier than usual.

After they left Vista de Alameda, Barbara drove east on Alameda Boulevard. They were almost to Interstate 25 before either of them spoke.

Barbara said, "Alberto's right. My God, if there's another death at that place while we're investigating Matthews's murder . . . ."

"That would be bad enough," Susan said. "But what if we learn that other residents were murdered?"

"The whole damned department would be up the creek without a paddle."

"Not to mention that another person had died."

"Sorry. I should have said that first before worrying about BCSO's reputation."

"I know what you meant," Susan said. She released a loud breath. "You recall what Lisa French told us about Scott Matthews?"

"Sure. He visited his father several days a week. What are you suggesting? That Matthews murdered all the people who've died at Vista de Alameda? Come on, girl, what would be his motive?"

"Damned if I know. But maybe we should find out the times and dates that the other residents died and then check the visitors' log for the times and dates of Scott Matthews's visits."

The detective bureau at BCSO headquarters in downtown Albuquerque was nearly deserted. Only one other detective, Sherman Baker, was on duty. Baker was a fifty-something lifer who had more than paid his dues. He had five children by three former wives. His work ethic was outstanding, which had contributed to his failed marriages.

"What are you guys doing in today?" Baker asked. "Isn't it your day off?"

"Take a good look at us, Sherm," Susan said. "This is what commitment and dedication look like. You follow our example and you, too, might make detective-sergeant one day."

Baker chuckled. "I made detective-sergeant when you two were in high school."

"Oh, yeah, I forgot."

"What are you working on?"

"Elderly guy died at a retirement center. The OMI pathologist believes he was poisoned."

"Those places are supposed to be safe for the elderly."

"I think they're generally that way," Barbara said. "But something else is operating here that we haven't been able to put a finger on. There's a possibility that other residents were poisoned."

Baker's expression changed from neutral to horrified. "What the hell's the motive?"

"We're working on it."

Baker swiveled in his chair. "I just put my mom in a retirement center in Denver. I was blown away by the statistics for people who moved into one of those places. They call some of them congregate care facilities. They provide independent living, assisted living, and nursing care, depending on what the resident needs."

"Is your mother okay?" Barbara asked.

"You bet. She's in great shape, but after my dad passed away, she was depressed. Living in their home, always being reminded of my dad, was getting to her. She had a friend who moved into a retirement place in Denver, so she paid a visit and decided that was for her."

"Hope she does well there," Susan said. She turned away to sit with Barbara to brainstorm their case, but Baker didn't take the hint.

"You know what the average life span for Americans is?" He didn't wait for a response. "Eighty-one for women and seventy-six for men. But, you know what happens when a healthy seventy-eight-year-old like my mom goes into a retirement center and lives an active lifestyle? Where they're surrounded by their own kind, where they're secure, and eat regular meals? They can have a life expectancy of fifteen more years or greater."

"That's all very interesting, Sherm," Susan said impatiently. "Maybe you should go to work for one of those places as a promotional guy."

He threw up an arm and muttered, "Screw you, Martinez."

Susan looked across her and Barbara's back-to-back desks and said, "I know I'm getting ahead of myself, but what in God's name could the motive be for murdering a bunch of elderly people?"

"There have been serial killers who preyed on the elderly. Just like the sickos who prey on children because they're weak and easy targets. Maybe we have a psycho operating in the retirement home."

Susan looked away for a long moment. "Maybe. But if we put the psycho theory aside for a minute, what would motivate someone to kill these people?"

"The four 'Ls.' Love, lust, lucre, loathing. But we don't know if there have been other murders beside John Matthews." She let loose a frustrated sigh. "Hell, we don't even know for sure about Matthews. It will be easier to determine motive if we discover that some of the other deceased residents were murdered."

"We should contact the Quintana and Watrous families."

"I'll take Watrous; you take Quintana," Barbara said as she spun her chair to the left and turned on her computer. She Googled "Emily Watrous Obituary" and discovered that the woman had been a widow for over a decade. She was survived by one daughter, one son, five grandchildren, and a sister. The sister—Judy Granquist—was the only survivor who lived in Albuquerque. The son—Paul Watrous—lived in Belen, New Mexico. Barbara looked up the sister's and son's addresses and telephone numbers online and printed off the information. She looked over at Susan and asked, "Any luck?"

"Quintana was never married. A brother in Rio Rancho and two sisters in Moriarty survive him. I got contact information on all of them."

"The obit say what Quintana died from?"

Susan stared at Barbara for a long beat. "Just like my uncle and Max told us. Cardiac arrest."

"Same for Watrous. I think we need to split up and talk to these people. It'll be a lot quicker that way."

Susan nodded. "I'll sign out a department vehicle. You take the Crown Vic."

"You going to call the family members first?"

"Nah. I think it'll be better to just drop by."

CHAPTER 12

Saturday afternoon traffic in Albuquerque was heavy but moved well. When Susan entered Tijeras Canyon, headed east, traffic became light. Once she was through the canyon, the speed limit increased to seventy-five-miles-per-hour, so she was able to open up the department's unmarked Ford Expedition. The drive from downtown Albuquerque to Moriarty took fifty minutes. She'd put the address of one of Karl Quintana's sisters—Caterina Long—into the map app on her cell phone and followed the instructions the disembodied voice gave her. On Interstate 40, buffeted by tractor trailers whizzing past her at eighty-five-miles-per-hour, she called the Torrance County Sheriff's Office in Estancia to give them a heads up that she was encroaching on their territory, and to give them the chance to dispatch a deputy to meet her at the Long residence. The deputy on duty told her that no one was available to meet her and to enjoy herself.

Caterina and Anthony Long lived in a double-wide manufactured home on several acres south of Moriarty, on the road to Estancia. With the sun low in the sky, the temperature had dropped to the low forties, but it was a clear day. Susan understood the attraction that places like Moriarty had for people who wanted to avoid the traffic and noise of a city like Albuquerque, yet could still live close enough to access jobs, shopping, entertainment, and healthcare.

As she pulled into the Long driveway, she spotted an elderly man under a huge sycamore tree. A little girl of about five was seated on a tire swing attached to a twenty-foot-long rope tied to a thick tree branch. Both the man and girl wore thick coats and gloves. The man said something to the girl and walked over to the Expedition.

"Can I help you?" he said in a West Texas accent. He wore a suspicious, tight-lipped expression, and his blue eyes zeroed in on her like laser beams.

Susan dropped down out of the SUV, met the man's gaze, showed him her cred pack, and asked, "Mr. Long?"

"That's right."

"I wonder if I could speak with Mrs. Long."

The man looked momentarily confused, then said, "What about?"

Susan reminded herself that another reason people lived in places like Moriarty was that they valued their privacy. "I'm sorry to disturb you, Mr. Long, but I'm investigating a death that occurred recently at the retirement center where your wife's brother was a resident."

Long scowled. "My missus is still hurtin' from her brother's death. What good is it gonna do her for you to come around diggin' up memories?"

Susan decided that she needed to be a little more direct with Long. "We suspect that a man who died last week at Vista de Alameda was murdered."

Long scowled again. Then his expression changed to open-mouthed shock. "Are you tellin' me that Karl might have been murdered?"

"I'm not saying anything of the sort, Mr. Long." She put a little steel into her voice. "How about you give me a chance to talk with Mrs. Long?"

The man seemed to be thinking about what Susan had just said when a tall, willowy woman—wearing an apron over a sweatshirt and black jeans—stepped out onto the small porch set into the middle of the home. "What are you doing out here, Herman?" She came down the three steps to the dirt yard, wiped her hands on her apron, and reached out to shake Susan's hand. "Please excuse my husband, Miss, but the older he gets the more . . . protective he becomes." She smiled at her husband. "Why don't I bring this young woman into the house while you keep an eye on Madeline?"

The man gave her a sheepish look, turned, and walked over to the little girl who shouted, "Push me high, Grandpa."

"Come on inside, dear," the woman said. "It's warmer there. Soon as the sun is gone, it'll get damned cold out here."

After Caterina Long invited Susan to sit at a tiny Formica-covered kitchen table, she offered her a cup of coffee, which Susan accepted. Then Long said, "That truck out there looks official."

"I'm a detective with the Bernalillo County Sheriff's Office. Susan Martinez."

Long took a seat across from Susan. "My, haven't things changed. Hispanic female detectives. 'Bout damned time." Then she narrowed her eyes and asked, "You any good?"

Susan chuckled. "Yes, ma'am."

"Well, good for you. Now, why don't you tell me what you're doing out here in the sticks on a late Saturday afternoon? 'Specially seeing as how this is *Torrance* County."

Susan told Mrs. Long about the investigation she and Barbara were conducting. Then she said, "I understand your brother, Karl, died of a cardiac arrest."

"That's what the emergency room doc said."

"Did he have a history of heart problems?"

Long stopped and looked out a window onto the yard where her husband and granddaughter were. When she turned back, she said, "You've got my mind whirling, Detective Martinez. All sorts of scenarios are scrolling through my brain. Are you insinuating that my brother might not have had a heart attack?"

"No, ma'am. I suspect your brother *did* have a heart attack. What I want to determine is what caused the heart attack. Did Mr. Quintana have a history of heart problems?"

"My brother was as healthy as a man his age could be. No heart problems, no nothing. All us Quintanas are tall and lean." She briefly smiled. "My parents and grandparents lived into their mid-nineties. The only things that kill Quintanas are accidents, falls, dementia, and murder."

"Murder?"

82

Long chuckled. "Yeah. My grandfather was shot by a neighbor who thought he was an intruder. He was well into Alzheimer's and wandering around one night looking for a dog that had died thirty years earlier. It was actually a blessing." She chuckled again and continued, "One of my uncles was bludgeoned to death by a jealous husband. Uncle Geraldo shouldn't have been messing around with a married lady." She briefly smiled, then a pained expression crossed her face. "Karl's death surprised us all. He'd had a physical in the past year and everything had been fine. During our last phone conversation, I asked him how he was doing. He told me, 'Caterina, I'm one hundred sixty pounds of twisted blue steel and sex appeal. What could be wrong?' That's the way he ended every one of our conversations."

Tears filled her eyes. She used the edge of her apron to dry them. Then her eyes went hard. "Now, Detective, I want you to tell me what the hell's going on."

"Would you want to know if your brother's heart attack was caused by something other than natural causes?"

"Of course."

"Would you agree to have his body disinterred and an autopsy performed?"

The woman visibly shuddered. "Do you believe Karl may have been murdered?"

"It's a possibility."

She spread her arms, her face full of shock and confusion. "But why would anyone want to murder Karl? I mean, he was a retired engineer. I don't think he ever had a cross word for anyone." The tears came again, but this time she let them roll down her cheeks. "He was such a sweet man."

Susan put off asking about a Disinterment Order for a moment. "Did your brother have any life insurance?"

Long's mouth dropped open. "You think he could have been killed for the insurance?"

Susan shrugged. "Mrs. Long, we have no idea what the motive would have been, assuming Mr. Quintana was murdered."

"Yes, he had an insurance policy. It was for two hundred fifty thousand dollars. The proceeds went to his nieces and nephews."

She paused again and finally said, "The only way you can prove that he was murdered is through an autopsy?"

Susan nodded.

"I'll have to talk with my brother and sister."

Susan handed Mrs. Long a card. "Please let me know your decision as soon as possible. We already think that one resident at the retirement home was murdered. If your brother was murdered, too, who knows, maybe there were others." She met Mrs. Long's gaze and added, "If there have been multiple murders, we need to act quickly to prevent any more in the future."

"And if his body is dug up and it's discovered that he died of natural causes?"

"We hope that's exactly what we do find. But the fact that it appears one person was poisoned, means we need to make certain that there weren't others."

CHAPTER 13

It was 4:45 p.m. when Barbara knocked on the door of a large, two-story home in the Tanoan East development in Albuquerque's far northeast section. A teenage boy answered the door. Barbara showed him her credentials and asked if Judy Granquist was available.

"My grandmother isn't feeling very well today," the young man said. "Can I help you?"

Barbara didn't want to go through the reason for her visit with the young man. "Perhaps I can return at a better time," she said.

"That would be good," he said.

Barbara handed him a card and was turning to head back to her vehicle when a high-pitched voice shouted, "Who's at the door, Denny?"

The kid looked back over his shoulder and yelled, "It's a policewoman, Grandma."

"Oh, goody. Show her in."

The kid shrugged and stepped aside to let Barbara enter.

Inside an elegant living room, replete with damask-covered furniture, a wall-to-wall Persian rug, and southwest landscape paintings on the walls, Barbara stopped short of an elderly woman in a wheelchair. The woman wore a blue, long-sleeved dress, a pearl necklace and earrings, and reading glasses perched on the end of her patrician-looking nose. She had a blanket covering her lap and legs. The dress highlighted her pale-blue eyes.

"Mrs. Granquist, my name is Barbara Lassiter. I'm a homicide detective with the Bernalillo County Sheriff's Office. I—"

"Homicide?" the woman asked, smiling. "Who the hell got killed?"

Barbara couldn't help but chuckle. Granquist looked so elegant, so demure. Her fragile, aristocratic appearance had led Barbara to anticipate a different sort of reaction.

"We're investigating the death of a resident at the Vista de Alameda retirement home. During our investigation, we discovered that there had been other deaths at the home during the last twelve months. We're just crossing our t's and dotting our i's."

"Sit down, young lady," Granquist said, pointing at a chair across from her. Her eyes narrowed as they bored into Barbara. "And you came here to talk with me because my sister, Emily, died in that godforsaken place."

"Why do you say that, Mrs. Granquist? Godforsaken?"

"Those places are warehouses for old people." She leaned forward and whispered, "Besides, they're sex pits. Lots of hanky-panky goes on in those places."

Barbara didn't know how to take this woman. She began to think that Mrs. Granquist was a couple eggs short of a dozen. She took a breath. "Maybe you could tell me about your sister," she said. "Was she ill? Did she have any serious medical problems?"

The old woman coughed a laugh. "Emily! My dear sister only had one medical problem, but it didn't seem to slow her down."

Barbara waited for Granquist to continue. When she didn't, Barbara said, "You were saying that your sister had a medical problem."

"Boy, she sure did."

Again the woman stopped. Then she called out, "Denny, would you mind bringing Detective Lassiter and me iced teas?"

From somewhere a couple of rooms away, the grandson yelled, "Sure, Grandma."

Mrs. Granquist leaned toward Barbara again and whispered, "I don't really want any tea, but that boy has ears like a German Shepherd. I don't want him hearing what I'm about to tell you." A pained expression came over her as she turned her head to look toward the other end of the house. When she turned back, she said, "Darn neck hurts like a sonofagun." Then she rolled her wheelchair forward until her knees touched the coffee table between her and Barbara. "My sister contracted a disease in that place. She told me she had an STD." Granquist's expression had changed. She looked as though she'd sucked on a lemon. "Damned woman told me as if she was proud of herself."

Barbara succeeded in masking her surprise. "Was it serious?"

"No. She took pills for it."

"So, she didn't have any chronic problems?"

"No way. She was an Amazon. Always was. Best athlete at her high school and college."

Barbara tried one more time: "Your sister ever have any heart problems?"

Judy Granquist broke out into a screech-like laugh that devolved into a coughing fit. When she recovered, she said, "Emily told me she was sleeping with at least three of the men at Vista de Alameda and another two from her church." She laughed again and wiped her lips with a hanky she pulled from her left cuff. "Maybe you should talk to her lovers. They'd be able to vouch for the condition of my sister's heart." She started laughing again as her grandson entered the room.

"You okay, Grandma?"

"Honey, I'm doing just fine. You can go back to your homework." She looked at Barbara as the boy left the room. "You have any more questions for me?"

"Just one. As far as you know, did your sister have any enemies?"

Granquist seemed to consider the question, then said, "Hah. Maybe it was a jealous lover." When Barbara didn't react, the old woman asked, "Is that it?"

"Yes, ma'am, that should do it."

She stood and thanked Granquist but, before turning to leave, asked, "Do you think the family would object to disinterring your sister's body for an autopsy?"

The old woman's brow furrowed. "You think someone might have murdered my sister?"

"It seems odd to me that a perfectly healthy woman died of cardiac arrest."

"She was eighty-two years old. Heart attacks among the elderly are as common as dandelions in a lawn."

Barbara nodded. "That might be how the killer or killers covered up the crime. No one suspects a crime when an elderly person succumbs to a heart attack."

"You sound worried."

"I'm scared to death, Mrs. Granquist. If there's a murderer at Vista de Alameda, there could be more deaths in the future."

She seemed to think as she stared into Barbara's eyes. Finally, she said, "Do whatever you have to do to get Emily's body dug up."

"What about her children?"

"I'll handle those greedy bastards. They'll do whatever I tell them to do. They're all lined up waiting for me to croak so they can inherit all the money my dear husband left me." She laughed again. "They're all pissed off that Emily left her estate to me." She crooked a finger at Barbara, telling her to come close. When Barbara did and leaned down, Granquist whispered, "They don't know that I'm leaving everything to Denny. He's the only one who really cares about me."

CHAPTER 14

Stuart Armstead and Lisa French sat side-by-side in the small conference room off Armstead's office. French felt the heat coming off Armstead's leg that was barely an inch from hers. It took all her self-control to not place her hand on his thigh. Despite the ten-year difference in their ages, French found her boss one of the most attractive men she'd ever known. And, though she resented the hold that Armstead's wife, Kathy, had on him, she found his dedication to the cancer-stricken bitch admirable . . . even gallant.

"Things are looking up, Lisa," Armstead said. "This is the first quarter in three years that we've been really profitable."

French nodded. "I've tried my best to cut back on expenses."

"I appreciate that. You've done a great job." He seemed to muse about something for a couple seconds, then said, "The top line revenue's improving, but many of our residents cost us more than they pay. And the low interest rates are depressing our returns off the endowment fund."

French felt sick as she looked at Armstead's defeated expression. "We brought in the last ten residents at a higher upfront fee and the rents they pay are more in line with current market rates. Plus, the new rental agreement gives us the ability to raise rents going forward."

"I hated doing that. Our original business model was based on giving the elderly a permanent place to live, without ever raising their living expenses."

"What choice did you have? When you created that model, you thought you could rely on longevity statistics, high interest rates, and low inflation."

"I didn't pay close enough attention to the statistics about how much longer people lived when they moved into our type of facility." He wagged his head for a moment. "In fact, it's a shock how many of our residents passed away in the last two years. I don't think we've ever before had such a run of deaths."

"Mostly heart attacks," she said. "It shouldn't surprise you, considering the ages of our residents."

"No, of course not. But a lot of those who died seemed healthy." He shook his head again. "I guess it's the nature of the business we're in."

"I don't mean to sound insensitive, but if those residents hadn't passed on we wouldn't have been able to replace them with residents at a higher rate."

Armstead's brow furrowed. "I understand, Lisa. But I don't want to ever hear you say something like that again. My God, what if someone heard you?"

French felt her face grow warm.

"By the way, when's the meeting with our attorney?"

"Todd will be here Monday at 11:00."

"If we can get some residents to include bequests to Vista de Alameda in their wills, we might be able to improve our cash flow situation."

"That's a long term solution, Stuart. I mean, none of those bequests would be funded until a resident passed away. That could be ten or more years from now."

"Yeah, you're right. But at least we'd mitigate the long term effect of low investment returns and ever increasing expenses."

"I'll let you know how things go at the Monday meeting."

"I guess we're done—"

Armstead's cell phone rang, interrupting him. He picked it up from the table and answered.

French shifted in her chair and watched his expression change as he listened to the caller.

"What are the chances?" he asked. He listened for a few seconds, then said, "Uh huh. You said it was experimental, so I assume insurance won't cover the cost."

Armstead listened again. After thirty seconds, he said, "That's great news, Doctor. So, her current regimen of treatments will end and she'll start on the new program?"

He listened for a few seconds, then said, "When can you begin?"

After a pause, Armstead said, "Tomorrow? On a Sunday?"

Another pause, then, "Wonderful. We'll be there tomorrow at 8:00."

French found Armstead's reactions to the call contradictory. His words and his tone were positive; his expression seemed morose at times. "What is it?" she asked.

Armstead placed a hand on her arm. "That was Kathy's oncologist. She's been accepted into a drug regimen trial that has had wonderful results with cancer patients. And the drug company will cover all the costs. The doctor believes Kathy is a perfect candidate for the treatment. There's better than a sixty percent chance of her going into remission."

She placed her free hand on Armstead's hand. "Oh, Stuart, that's wonderful. I heard you say something about 8:00 tomorrow."

"That's right. They'll start the treatment tomorrow. We'll know if the regimen is successful after eight weeks. Kathy could be cured by Christmas."

"The perfect Christmas present," she said.

"Uh huh."

French smiled at Armstead as she thought, *that bitch will ruin everything.*

SUNDAY
OCTOBER 5

CHAPTER 15

Susan scooted back against the headboard as Roger approached her side of the bed, a cup of steaming coffee in hand. When she reached for the cup, the sheet dropped to her waist.

"Now that's what I call a wonderful way to start the day," he said.

Susan yanked the sheet over her chest and giggled. "Put your tongue back in your mouth before you bite it off," she said.

Roger sat on the bed and gently pulled the sheet back down. Susan quickly covered the scar on the right side of her chest with her left hand.

"Don't," she said.

Roger ignored her, took the coffee cup from her and placed it on the bedside table, then took her hand in his, exposing the scar left by the bullet that her former husband had fired at her.

He leaned over and kissed the scar, then looked into her eyes. "I love every bit of you. Please don't try to hide any part of your body from me."

Susan wrapped her arms around his neck, kissed him on the lips, and said, "You're too much."

He chuckled, then turned serious. "You're the best thing that's ever happened to me."

She hugged him again and said, "Damn, I wish I'd met you in high school instead of my asshole husband."

"Me too, Susan. Me too."

She laughed and pushed him away. "You want to get some breakfast?"

"As long as it's not Starbucks. I need a green chili fix. How about Padilla's on Girard."

"Oh, you smooth talking man."

"Perhaps you would like to show me some kindness for my being so considerate."

Susan smiled and wiggled a finger at Roger. "Come here, big boy."

Roger shed his robe and got into bed beside her just as her cell phone rang. He groaned.

Susan looked at the phone screen, didn't recognize the number, and answered, "Martinez." She listened for fifteen seconds, thanked the caller, and hung up.

Roger moved up against her. "Please don't tell me you have to take care of business."

She nuzzled his ear and whispered, "No, sweetie. It can wait. First, you're going to scratch an itch I have, then we're going to Padilla's. I'll take care of business later."

"Who was that on the phone?"

"A lady named Caterina Long. Her family agreed to allow us to disinter her brother's body."

"If it's okay with you, let's not discuss dead bodies until after breakfast."

"What's the matter, are you getting turned off?"

Roger disappeared under the covers and kissed Susan's stomach. She giggled when he said, "*I'd* have to be dead to not be turned on by you."

It was nearly 10:00 a.m. when Susan called Barbara to brief her on her conversation with Caterina Long.

"Excellent," Barbara said. "We'll need to get the documentation signed. I've already begun the process for Emily Watrous's disinterment. Her sister agreed to sign the docs."

"I'm thinking we should wait until Dr. Beringer officially rules Matthews's death a murder before we actually have the bodies disinterred."

Barbara didn't immediately respond. Then she said, "I've thought the same thing, but what if he can't find an injection site?"

Susan groaned. "He seems so certain that Matthews was murdered."

"I know. Let's keep our fingers crossed that he finds something."

"What do you think we should do about the others who passed away?" Susan asked.

"I've thought about that, too. Why don't we wait and see what happens with these first two?"

"The problem with that is what if the coroner finds nothing in Quintana's or Watrous's remains? We'll pay hell trying to get another Disinterment Order."

"Yeah, I understand. But if the first two show no evidence of poison, we'd probably be wasting our time following up on the others. It may be that John Matthews's death was a one-off murder."

"If Beringer is right and Matthews *was* murdered."

Frank Calderon's office was at the back of an independent grocery store that catered to the Mexican émigré community. He owned the strip center that the store anchored, as well as the grocery business. It was one of a couple dozen businesses he owned that provided conduits for laundering cash from his drug operation.

His suite of offices included a lounge for his crew—members of which came and went throughout the day, seven days a week. Additionally, there were three offices, one of which Calderon occupied. Beneath the suite, in a bunker with security that rivaled that of the White House Situation Room, were two rooms and a tunnel. The rooms had walls, ceilings, and floors that were made of three-foot thick concrete. Utilities were fed through a hidden chase that ran to the roof. The tunnel extended fifty yards from the bunker, under the alley that separated the strip center from a block of eighty-year-old clapboard houses, to a similar bunker beneath one of those houses. The bunkers and tunnel were only accessible through a trap door in that house. A large sign on the lawn in front of the house read: "Rio Grande Clothing Bank." Calderon had employees working in both bunkers.

Every day was important to Calderon. Cash flowed into the

complex on a daily basis. Couriers collected cash, carried it through the grocery store into the hall between the store and Calderon's office suite, and deposited it into a chute hidden behind a false air conditioner vent. The cash dropped to workers in the bunker who counted it, reconciled the amounts against the amounts due from drug distributors who pedaled Calderon's illicit narcotics, and then pushed shopping baskets full of cash to the bunker under the house at the other end of the tunnel. There, the cash was wrapped in clothing donated by thousands of well-meaning Albuquerqueans for poor people south of the border and boxed for shipment.

But Sunday was the most important day of all. That was the day cash was transported from the bunker under the house. Calderon had picked Sundays to ship cash because he'd figured that there were fewer cops on the streets on Sundays, especially during dinnertime. A tractor trailer truck, its side walls emblazoned with the words: "Rio Grande Clothing Bank: Helping Those in Need," pulled up to the house every Sunday evening, on-loaded hundreds of boxes—some filled with used clothing and some stuffed with cash wrapped in used clothing, and then was driven to one of three different Mexican ports of entry: Antelope Wells, Columbus, and Santa Teresa. Once inside Mexico, the driver took the shipment to a safe house, where he was met by a representative of *Banco Comercial de Guadalupe*, whose crew extracted the cash from the boxes, repackaged it, and then delivered it to one of the bank's branches. Once deposited, Calderon directed the wire transfer of the money to a variety of international banks situated in tax havens.

Calderon couldn't help but marvel at how effective the cash management system was. At least once a week, he mentally thanked his sister, Lisa, for setting up the system. She'd worked for him all through college, back when he was just starting in business, back when it was just Lisa, a half-dozen distributors, his strong-armed guy, *Churro*, and himself. He'd pushed Lisa out for her own protection after she graduated from UNM, but he still paid her five grand a week in cash.

Dr. Frederick Beringer had let his assistants go home hours ago, but he couldn't shake the feeling he'd missed something. It was nearly midnight as he once again looked at the computer files listed under John Joseph Matthews's name. Detective Martinez's Monday morning deadline weighed on him. His tired eyes went to the DentFiles/SharpeDDS tab. *That's the only file we haven't closely examined.* About to again discard the idea of going through the dental records, he blew out an exasperated breath and clicked on the tab. *Oh, what the hell,* he thought.

MONDAY
OCTOBER 6

CHAPTER 16

Susan's sleep had been restless and brief. She crawled out of bed at a little after 5:50 a.m. While making coffee, she considered calling Dr. Beringer. But she quickly pushed away the idea. *If he'd discovered something,* she thought, *he would have called.*

Her hands were shaky from lack of sleep as she sipped from her cup. Her cell phone rang, causing her to spill coffee on the table and on her T-shirt. She muttered a curse, put down the cup, stood, and moved to the kitchen counter. When she looked at her phone's screen, she recognized the 272 prefix for the Office of Medical Investigator. Her heart rate leaped.

"Martinez," she answered.

"Sorry about the hour, Detective," he said. "It's Fred Beringer. I just finished my report." He paused a second. "I found the injection site."

Susan felt a shiver hit the back of her neck as she waited for Beringer to continue.

"It was about as clever as anything I've ever seen. The deceased had a root canal procedure the day before his death. The dentist had put a temporary cap in place. Whoever killed Mr. Matthews removed the cap, injected the soft tissue under the cap, then replaced it."

"Sonofa— A temporary cap can be removed and replaced that easily?"

"These days, caps are computer generated right in the dental office. Even without adhesive, they fit quite snugly. All someone had to do was pop the cap loose, inject the poison into the tissue under it, and then replace the cap." He exhaled a loud breath that whistled over the phone line. "When we initially examined his mouth, we assumed the slight swelling and discoloration around the tooth was caused by the root canal. It wasn't until we removed the cap that we discovered the injection site."

Susan said, "You told us before that the toxicology report showed the presence of a drug in Mr. Matthews's system."

"That's right. Diphenhydramine hydrochloride. More than likely an over-the-counter sleep-inducing medicine."

"In other words, Matthews was medicated so he would fall asleep. Then the killer injected him with liquid nicotine."

"More than likely. We found a large amount of the sleep drug in his system. Not enough to kill him, but more than enough to ensure he didn't wake up while the killer removed the cap and injected the nicotine. My guess is that the killer crushed the pills and mixed them in a drink of some sort."

Susan paused for a long beat, then said, "Someone knew he'd had the dental procedure."

"Logical assumption, Detective. He was probably transported to the dentist's office in the retirement home's van. I assume they log the trips by passenger name and destination."

Susan called and woke Barbara as soon as she hung up with Beringer.

"My Lord, Susan. Do you know what time it is?"

"Of course I know the time. I'm a detective. I can figure out things like reading a clock all by myself. Now, do you want to whine, or would you like to hear what Dr. Beringer just told me?"

"Just tell me it's good news."

"It's good news as far as proof of murder can be good news. He found where John Matthews had been injected. Someone removed a temporary cap on one of his teeth and injected poison into the soft tissue beneath the cap."

"I'll be damned."

"How soon can you get to the office?"

"One hour."

"Okay," Susan said. "I'll meet you there. Dr. Beringer sent me a scanned copy of his findings. I'm going to take his report to the D.A. and get an affidavit prepared for Disinterment Orders on Karl Quintana and Emily Watrous. I'll take the Quintana affidavit around to the family members for their signatures. As soon as you get the signature from Emily Watrous's kin, we'll need to get with a judge to issue an order."

Barbara said, "I don't anticipate a problem with getting a judge to rule in our favor."

Susan laughed. "I agree. Can you imagine the headlines if a judge denied the order? Judge rules in favor of murderer. Refuses Disinterment Order."

"I can't imagine how the press would ever learn about such a decision." After a second, Barbara said, "Oh, I forgot. You have a cousin who's a reporter at the *Journal*."

Susan laughed again. "I also have an aunt who's a Bernalillo County Metropolitan Court judge."

Barbara waved at Detective Sherman Baker as she walked past his desk. "You been here all night?"

"Yeah." He smiled. "But I'm off for the next two days. Gonna visit my mother up in Denver. Did I tell you about the place where she's living?"

"Oh, yeah, Sherm. That retirement center sounds great."

Before Baker could start in again about the retirement center in Denver, Barbara went to her desk. She found Susan behind her own desk, a forlorn expression on her face, her cell phone clutched in one hand.

"What's wrong?"

"I've been sitting here for the past hour waiting for someone at the D.A.'s office to answer my call."

Barbara looked at her watch. "You realize it's just a little after 7:30."

"So what?"

Barbara scoffed. "How about you and I walk over there and button-hole the first A.D.A. who shows up for work?"

Susan stuffed her cell phone in her jacket pocket, snatched her purse from a desk drawer, and picked up a file from her desk blotter.

Barbara pointed at the file. "That Dr. Beringer's report?"

"Yes, ma'am," she drawled.

As they walked from the building, Susan asked, "Have you considered what we might be dealing with here?"

"What do you mean?"

"I tossed and turned all night thinking about it. Let's say that half the people who died at Vista de Alameda in the past twelve months were murdered. That would mean we're dealing with one of the worst serial killers in New Mexico history."

Barbara groaned. "I've thought a lot about that possibility. Just to make your day even more exciting, what if these murders have been going on for more than a year?"

"Which would make it even less likely that Scott Matthews was his father's killer."

"I think we need to talk to the D.A. about releasing Matthews on bail."

A woman with a coffee container in one hand and a briefcase in the other entered the D.A.'s offices at 7:45. She shot a sideways look at Barbara and Susan, who stood in the waiting area, then walked past them.

"Are you on staff here?" Susan demanded.

"Yes. Who are you?" the woman asked as she stopped and turned around.

Susan displayed her badge. "Detective-Sergeant Susan Martinez, B-C-S-O. This is my partner, Detective-Sergeant Barbara Lassiter. If you're an A.D.A., we need a minute of your time."

The woman gave them a squint-eyed look. "I've got a very full day, Detectives. Why don't you call and make an appointment? I'm sure I can fit you in later this—"

Susan interrupted her. "How about you give us your name?"

The squint-eyed look appeared again. The woman looked as though she was considering whether to answer. Finally, she said, "Elinore Freed."

"Okay, Ms. Freed. Here's the deal. We have a pathologist's

report that proves a senior citizen resident of a retirement center who had earlier been declared dead from natural causes actually died of nicotine poisoning. We have strong indications that at least two other elderly people who lived at the same center—a man and a woman who had heart attacks and died—were also murdered."

Freed's sour expression had changed to one of slight interest. "What do you want from me?"

Susan said, "We want you to draft something we can take to a judge to get a Disinterment Order issued for two bodies."

"You don't need a judge. All you have to do is get a letter from a relative of the deceased addressed to the State Registrar at the Bureau of Vital Statistics requesting disinterment. Include a check for twenty-five dollars. You should also include a letter from a funeral director requesting disinterment."

"And how long will that take?" Barbara asked.

Freed shrugged.

Barbara said, "We already knew all that. The reason we're here is that we need to expedite the process. We figured the D.A.'s office could do that."

Freed frowned. "What the hell's the hurry? The people you think were poisoned are already dead."

Susan raised a finger. In an irritated voice that caused the lawyer's eyes to widen, she said, "We hadn't quite finished explaining the situation. In addition to the three deaths we just mentioned, there might be at least another half-dozen. All murders. And, if that doesn't elevate your level of interest, what if another resident is murdered while we're waiting for the State Registrar to process a request?"

The ADA's jaw dropped. She wheeled around, dumped her coffee container in a wastebasket next to the reception desk, and said, "I think I can rearrange my schedule."

Two hours later, Barbara and Susan left Judge Isabelle Baca's chambers, Disinterment Orders in hand. On their way back to BCSO headquarters, Barbara suggested, "Let's go see the lieutenant. We ought to brief him."

Susan smiled. "You know, instead of briefing him, we could just wait until the media gets hold of this. Salas will go nuts. I love to watch him when he loses control."

"That's just mean, Suze. Just plain mean."

"Okay, okay. We'll go see Salas."

CHAPTER 17

"What the hell is this?" Lt. Rudy Salas asked as he scanned the Disinterment Order in his hands.

Barbara cut a look at Susan and saw a smile creep onto her face. She reached out and gripped her partner's arm and slightly shook her head. Then she looked at Salas. "Lieutenant, we thought we'd better bring you up to date. This could be front-page news."

"Really?" Salas said sarcastically. "You think? I can see the headline: Body Snatchers at Sheriff's Office Dig Up Remains."

"Huh," Susan blurted. "You can tell the sheriff that he'll look like a bloody genius when we discover that the two people mentioned in that Order were poisoned."

Salas seemed to think about that for a moment, leaned back in his chair, and swiveled from side to side. "You made your case regarding the Matthews murder. But this could be a stretch. We dig up two other bodies and find nothing, we're going to look like idiots. Especially the sheriff. Who do you think he's going to crap on if that happens?"

"You trust us, Lieutenant?"

A sour expression appeared on Salas's face. "Don't pull that on me. You two are good but you're not infallible."

"We know something's off at that retirement place," Susan said. She quickly went through what they'd learned about Emily Watrous and Karl Quintana, their health conditions, their sudden heart attacks.

Salas blew out a loud sigh. "Okay, you two, put this thing in process. What's your plan if there's evidence that Watrous and Quintana were poisoned?"

Barbara shook her head as a pain shot through her stomach. She knew what she was about to say would rile her boss. "To summarize, there have been ten cardiac-involved deaths at Vista de Alameda in the past year. I have no idea how many more occurred in the previous year or two. At a minimum, we'll need to get Disinterment Orders on the bodies of the other seven residents who died from cardiac arrest over the last twelve months." She let that sink in as she watched Salas go pale. "Then we'll have to put a security blanket over that retirement home, checking into every resident, staff member, visitor, and anyone else who could have poisoned those people." She took a breath, then added, "We'll need every detective in the department working this case. Maybe even the Feds."

Salas looked even paler. He gasped, "Oh my God. This'll be a P.R. nightmare and a media shit storm."

Barbara nodded. "That's one of the reasons we're here now, Lieutenant. We thought you'd want to inform the sheriff."

Salas nodded. Then he wagged a finger. "You know, a lot of these retirement centers are church-affiliated and have bigwigs from the community on their boards." He groaned. "This could get dicey. I don't suppose you've checked to see who's on the Vista de Alameda board."

"Nope," Susan said. "And who gives a shit? We're detectives, not politicians. I'm sure glad we have you to provide cover for us." She smirked and added, "That's why they pay you the big bucks, Lieutenant."

Barbara gave Salas a sympathetic look. Her boss now looked queasy as well as pale. He muttered something that sounded like, "I'm too old for this shit," then asked, "What does all this mean regarding the Matthews's case?"

Susan said, "We should call the D.A. and suggest he let Scott Matthews out on bail."

"Which means we got nothing on him that'll stick."

"That's about right, boss. Besides, Barbara and I don't think he's guilty."

"Then why'd you arrest him?"

"Seemed like the thing to do at the time," Susan said.

Salas groaned and waved them out of his office.

Alberto Martinez felt exhausted from lack of sleep and emotional overload as he took the elevator down to the Vista de Alameda community room. The death of his best friend, John Matthews, and what his niece and her partner had told him and Max about nicotine poisoning, had disturbed not only his sleep but his waking hours as well. He would have stayed in bed, despite the late hour, but the staff had posted a notice on every resident's door announcing an 11:00 a.m. meeting. Since he missed the prior meeting, he felt obligated to attend. *Probably couldn't sleep, anyway,* he thought.

The meeting had already begun when he entered the community room. He caught a look from Lisa French who was in the process of introducing an attorney named Todd Paisley as he found a chair in the middle of the room. After the introduction, Paisley stood, thanked French, and moved to the center of the riser at the front.

"Thank you all for attending. The reason for this follow-up to an earlier meeting conducted by Ms. French is to inform you that your board of directors asked me to prepare documents creating an endowment program that will help subsidize our operating expenses, instead of having to dramatically increase rent rates in the future. In the furtherance of Vista de Alameda's mission of providing quality residential care, the board wants to keep rents at a level affordable for residents. We don't want to convert our facility to a place where only the wealthy can afford to reside.

"The entry fees you were all charged when you moved into Vista de Alameda have been invested in funds that throw off income intended to cover operating expenses. But, with the historically low interest rates of the past decade and the continually rising costs of operating the facility, the income from investments has not been sufficient to subsidize those costs.

"So, for those residents who can afford to do so, we are asking you to consider including Vista de Alameda as a beneficiary of your estate. You could make the facility the beneficiary of part or all of any life insurance policy you might have, or you could bequeath assets to the endowment. You would be able to provide a long term benefit to the elderly community in Albuquerque by helping to sustain the financial health of an elderly residence committed to providing a safe and healthy lifestyle."

The lawyer paused, looked around the room, and asked, "Are there any questions?"

Alberto saw Max Katz's hand shoot up. Max had taken a seat in the first row, just a few feet away from where the attorney stood.

"Yes, sir," Paisley said.

"If I understand you correctly," Max said, "you mentioned that this plan is a long term solution to correct operating deficits."

Paisley smiled. "That's correct, sir."

"I understand that new residents who moved in here this year are paying more up front as well as higher monthly rents. Also, their rents can be increased as time goes on."

Paisley looked over at French, who nodded, joined the attorney on the riser, and said, "That's correct, Mr. Katz."

"So, if you're already raising fees and rents, and can keep raising rents, why should we consider leaving money to this place?"

The cold look on Lisa French's face reminded Alberto of a rattler about to strike. She opened her mouth to speak, but Max cut her off. "Besides, I heard Vista de Alameda is now operating at a profit."

"How—?" French blurted. But then she stopped and closed her eyes for a second. When she opened her eyes again, she said, "One quarter of positive income doesn't make a trend, Mr. Katz. And this bequest program is not intended to replace raising fees and rents; it's to mitigate how high fees and rents would have to go otherwise."

"Mitigate?" Max said.

Several of the residents in the room snickered.

French shot Max a supercilious smile. "Reduce, Mr. Katz. Mitigate means to reduce."

There was another burst of snickers, then French asked, "Are there any other questions?"

A lady behind Alberto shouted a high-pitched, "Changing our wills would be expensive."

French smiled. "Vista de Alameda will pay Mr. Paisley's fees to amend the wills of any residents who decide to participate." She smiled at Paisley and added, "And Mr. Paisley has agreed to charge half his usual rate."

A low murmur of voices rolled through the room.

"Remember, you'll be helping people just like yourselves," French said. "Mr. Paisley will meet with any of you who would like to discuss this program." She pointed at a secretary seated at a table by the door. "Shirley can set up appointments for you with him."

As the meeting ended, small groups of residents congregated in several spots in the room and in the hall outside. Alberto watched them and guessed from their expressions which way they intended to go: support the program or ignore it. It surprised him that many of the men and women seemed to be favorably inclined to bequeath money to the facility.

He ran into Max out in the hall. "What did you think?"

"It's bullshit." Max chuckled. "And putting legal perfume on it won't mitigate the smell."

Alberto laughed. "Mitigate, huh?"

Max grinned. "That Lisa French thinks I'm stupid. But she's a looker. I'd like to *mitigate* her between the sheets some time. Maybe she'd be less of a tight ass."

"It's time for lunch. You wanna eat here or go someplace else?"

"Here's okay. It's lasagna day. It's the one meal they serve that I really enjoy."

Alberto moved off as Max fell in beside him. After they'd separated themselves from the other residents who'd been in the meeting, Alberto said, "You know, if you put Vista de Alameda in your will, they'd have a good reason to knock you off."

Max grabbed Alberto's arm and stopped him. "What do you mean? Are you insinuating that someone on the staff murdered John Matthews?"

Alberto turned to face Max. "I'm not insinuating a thing. But, think about it. Every time a long time resident dies, they rent out his unit to a new resident at a higher rent and with a higher entry fee. If that resident who dies has also put this place in their will, then Vista de Alameda gets a triple whammy. Bigger upfront fee and higher rents going forward, and a bequest from the deceased."

Max looked as though he was about to laugh, but shook his head instead. "Maybe we should go somewhere else to eat. Someplace safer."

CHAPTER 18

Susan stood twenty yards from Karl Quintana's grave. She felt cold, despite the warmth of the late afternoon sun. The prospect of seeing Quintana's casket lifted from the ground chilled her. She gazed around the cemetery, which took up several square blocks. A long line of limousines and other vehicles trailed a hearse two lanes over from where she stood, on their way to an open grave next to a green tarpaulin-covered dirt pile.

"Another corpse on the way to its eternal rest," she whispered. She noticed there were at least a dozen brightly-colored lowriders in the caravan and wondered if some gangbanger had met an untimely end.

When Susan heard someone approach her from behind, she turned and recognized Dr. Hugo Blake, the Bernalillo County Coroner and Medical Examiner. He was accompanied by another man.

"Detective," Blake said. "This is David Caruso, Funeral Director from ABQ Funerals."

"Good afternoon, Dr. Blake, Mr. Caruso. I appreciate your attention in this matter."

Blake wore a sour expression. "You know, we've got more than enough new cases to deal with as it is, without digging up bodies."

Before Susan could respond, Blake turned around, walked a few steps, and pointed at the front-end loader that had just lifted

Karl Quintana's casket from the grave and gently placed it on the ground. Four cemetery employees lifted the casket into the back of a Coroner & Medical Examiner van. He said, "If you're correct about the man in that casket over there, we're about to be part of a three-ring circus."

Susan nodded. Then her cell rang. She looked at the screen and saw Barbara's number. "Hey, Barb," she answered.

"We're done here. The coroner's van just took off with Emily Watrous's casket. How are things there?"

"Locked and loaded, so to speak," Susan said. "We on for dinner?"

"Well, sort of. Henry called to tell me that he and Roger will pick us up at 6:15. We're going to the Balloon Fiesta. Boots and jeans, girl."

"Oh, hell. Do they have any idea about the traffic and the crowds? We'll have to walk a mile from the parking lot. You didn't agree, did you?"

"It's a test, Suze. They want to see if we're real down-to-earth women."

"Henry said that?"

"No, of course he didn't. I was just kidding."

Susan looked at the time on her phone. "It's 4:30. I want to go home, shower, and change. Hanging around dead bodies always makes me feel dirty."

After ending the call from Barbara, Susan apologized to Blake and Caruso for the interruption. "That was my partner. Your guys are en route with the other body."

"Yes, I know," Blake said. "They already called me."

"What happens next?" Susan asked.

Caruso said, "There has to be a licensed funeral director at a disinterment. That's why I'm here. I'll sign over the body to Dr. Blake, so the chain of custody is intact."

"Then we'll transport the body to our facility on the UNM campus," Blake added.

"Are you bringing in Dr. Beringer?"

"Absolutely. He'll observe the autopsy."

"How long will it take?" Susan asked.

Blake let out a loud breath. "Now, now, Detective, let's try to be patient. I assume you want a thorough job done."

"Of course, I just—" The look on Blake's face stopped her. She smiled. "I look forward to receiving your timely and thoroughly detailed report."

Blake gave her a fatherly pat on the arm, then walked over to the M.E. van. Caruso took off in a black sedan.

On the way home, Susan called Barbara and asked, "You think we should let the staff at Vista de Alameda know that we're investigating the deaths there?"

"I thought we agreed to keep it under wraps, rather than show our cards."

"Yeah, I know, but what if another person dies . . . is murdered? By keeping quiet, the killer might feel safe to continue murdering residents."

Barbara didn't immediately respond. Finally, she said, "Why don't we wait until the Medical Examiner finishes with Quintana and Watrous? If he finds evidence that either of them, or both, for that matter, were murdered, we'll go in there with guns a-blazing, so to speak."

"What if they find nothing?"

"We interrogate the staff about Mr. Matthews's death. You're right. We can't hide this from the staff and the residents any longer. Too great a risk."

Stuart Armstead carried two glasses of iced tea to a table in the Vista de Alameda dining hall, placed them on the table, and moved one across to Violet Hawkins, an eighty-five-year-old long-time resident. He took packets of sugar and artificial sweetener from his suit jacket pocket and dropped them in front of Mrs. Hawkins. The old lady was so stooped from arthritis that she could barely lift her gaze above the tabletop. From the side, she looked like a question mark.

"I want to thank you for your consideration regarding a bequest to Vista de Alameda."

"Well, Mr. Armstead, it's the least I can do," Hawkins said, her dry voice still full of the Alabama accent she'd brought with her decades earlier when she and her husband moved to New Mexico. "You all have taken such good care of me for going on fifteen years now, ever since Harold passed away. Besides, I have nobody to leave my money to." She labored with one of the sugar packets, trying to rip the top off with arthritic fingers.

Armstead's hand jerked as his instinct was to assist the woman. But he quickly pulled his hands under the table and let Mrs. Hawkins work at the packet. He knew how independent she was and didn't want to insult her by offering assistance that probably wouldn't be appreciated.

Hawkins finally tore a corner off the sugar packet, tipped it over her glass and poured the contents into her tea. She tilted her head as she lifted a long-handled spoon from the table, placed it in her glass, and slowly stirred the tea. Then she carefully removed the spoon and put it down beside the place mat. After sipping from the glass—a laborious process that required her to hold the glass in both hands, barely lifting it, and tipping it to her lips—she genteelly patted her lips with a cloth napkin, folded it, and returned it to her lap.

When Hawkins looked at him, Armstead asked, "Were you able to discuss a bequest with your attorney?"

"I already talked with her. I signed a codicil to my will to cover a gift to Vista de Alameda. Everything has been arranged. All you have to do is agree to my terms and sign the documents." The old lady paused and smiled. "Would you like to know how much the bequest will be?"

Armstead waved a hand as though to indicate that any amount would be appreciated.

Mrs. Hawkins smiled again and made a cackling sound that he knew was the old woman's way of giggling. "Don't be disingenuous, my dear. I can tell from the flush on your face and the way you're holding your breath that you're dying to know."

Armstead let out his breath. "I can never fool you, Mrs. Hawkins."

She cackled again, took another sip of her drink, and then went through the agonizingly-slow process of patting her lips, folding the napkin, and replacing it on her lap.

Armstead thought: *How in God's name does this woman dress herself with those hands and her posture?*

"Before I tell you how much my gift will be, there will be three requirements before the gift can be made."

Armstead had a sinking feeling. *What now?*

"The first requirement is, of course, that I have to die." She cackled as though she'd told the greatest joke of all time.

"Let's hope that's a long time off."

Hawkins cleared her throat. "The second condition is that only the income off the bequest can be used to help cover operating costs here at Vista de Alameda. The principal amount cannot be touched."

"Understood," Armstead said. "And the third requirement?"

"You must dedicate the community room to my late husband. I want it named the Harold Hawkins Community Room."

"Well, of course, that would depend on the size of the bequest, Mrs. Hawkins. I don't think we can just dedicate rooms here for any amount—"

"I don't think two million dollars is just *any amount*, dear."

His sinking feeling turned into a heart-thumping, pulse-pounding sensation. He barely stopped himself from exclaiming, "Wow!"

"No, ma'am. That is not *any amount*. I will talk with our attorney. I'm sure we can quickly approve the dedication of the room to Mr. Hawkins's memory." He took a couple of seconds to reflect, then continued, "Wouldn't you rather have the room named after both you *and* your husband?"

She waved a hand. "Oh, no, that isn't what I want. I want Harold recognized."

"Whatever you wish, Mrs. Hawkins."

"Thank you, dear."

Armstead watched Mrs. Hawkins struggle to stand. He hovered beside her in case she lost her balance, then stepped back when she was stable behind her walker.

"Thank you, again, Mrs. Hawkins. Your bequest will make a big difference."

She smiled, then began her slow, obviously painful trek toward the elevators.

Armstead returned to his office. *Two million dollars*, he thought as he dropped onto his desk chair. *That'll help immensely. It'll also give me time to carry out my long-term plans. But Old Lady Hawkins, despite her health issues, could live another five years or more.* He tapped his desk blotter with a chrome-plated letter opener that looked more like a dagger, and dialed Lisa French's extension.

"Lisa, you got a minute?"

"Sure."

"Come to my office. I just got good news."

As soon as French arrived, before she'd even taken a seat, he began to tell her about his meeting with Violet Hawkins.

"Is this a joke?"

Stuart Armstead laughed. "No joke, Lisa. She's going to gift two million dollars."

"That's wonderful. When will the gift take effect?"

"Upon her demise and after we dedicate the community room to her husband's memory. I want you to begin the process of naming the room after Harold Hawkins. We'll need signage and an agreement signed by our board members and Mrs. Hawkins."

"Are there any restrictions on the use of the funds?" Lisa French asked.

"They will go into our endowment fund. The income from the account will go toward subsidizing our operating costs. I'm sure I don't have to tell you that the extra one hundred thousand or so dollars in income will help keep our entry fees and monthly rents affordable."

French thought: *Or you could use the income from the endowment to pay for salary increases and benefits to the senior staff.* "Sounds good, Stu."

"Let's get the paperwork completed as soon as possible."

"Yeah," she said. "God forbid something happens to Mrs. Hawkins before the deal is closed."

Armstead frowned. He opened his mouth as though to say something, but French interrupted, "I'm just being practical, Stu. She's a very elderly woman who's not in the best of health. I'm just thinking about you and the facility."

"Fortunately, she's already arranged things with her lawyer and signed the papers. The only thing we need to do is sign that we agree to the terms of the deal.

"Please call our attorney and put him in contact with Mrs. Hawkins's counsel." He let out a sigh. "I've got to go home and check on Kathy."

"I hope the new treatments will work."

"From your lips to God's ears," Armstead said. "The concern I have is that the treatments will aggravate her heart arrhythmia. That's apparently a possible side effect."

French showed him a sympathetic look. "I'll pray for her, Stu."

"Thanks, Lisa."

"I'll call our attorney right now," she said.

"I appreciate it. I know you'll take care of everything." He gave her a huge smile, stood, and came around to her chair as she stood. He placed a hand on her shoulder. "I don't know what I would do without your help."

French's eyes widened and her face flushed. She placed a hand on his. "I'm always happy to help in any way. You know that, Stu."

He met her gaze for a long beat, smiled, and said, "Of course I know that." He withdrew his hand and waited for her to leave his office, all the while watching her long, shapely legs and tight ass. After she closed the door behind her, he chuckled, returned to his desk, and thought, *What a needy bitch. She'll take care of the details and then want me to pat her on the back and tell her what a good girl she's been. She's so damned easy to manipulate.* Then he blew out an exasperated breath as he thought about what awaited him at home.

It had taken Violet Hawkins twenty minutes to negotiate the hallway to the elevator, ride the car to the fourth floor, and then shuffle to her room. She was utterly spent by the time she backed into the easy chair in her living room. She'd put her head against the back of the chair, closed her eyes, and drifted off. An hour had passed by the time she awoke from her nap. She reached for the television remote on the small glass table next to the chair, but fumbled it to the floor. "Oh my," she said as she took in a deep breath and exhaled, then edged forward on the chair and bent over to reach for the remote.

The device was a few inches from her deformed fingers. She scooted forward a couple more inches and walked her fingers toward the remote. She took in another breath, expelled it, leaned forward a bit more, wrapped her fingers around the remote, and gasped as she tried to right herself. A wave of dizziness overwhelmed her. It wasn't an uncommon phenomenon. She often had dizzy spells when she got out of bed or stood after sitting in a chair. But, this time, the dizziness was worse than usual. She experienced a falling sensation. The last things she was aware of, were the sound of a knock on her apartment door and air rushing from the hallway into her unit.

CHAPTER 19

"You guys are full of surprises," Susan said.

Roger looked across at Susan, seated next to Barbara in the bench seat at the back of the limousine, and smiled. "Nothing's too good for you ladies."

Henry, in a captain's chair that faced backward, was separated by a mini-fridge from Roger in his own captain's chair. "This was Roger's idea," he said.

Susan favored Roger with a glowing smile.

Henry pulled a bottle of vintage *Gilbert Gruet Grand Reserve* from the fridge. "I've been saving this for an occasion."

"Since this is my first time in a limo, I have to admit this *is* an occasion," Barbara said.

Henry poured two glasses and handed them to Susan and Roger. Knowing that Barbara no longer drank alcohol, he reached into the fridge for a can of ginger ale, which he opened and poured some of the contents into a champagne flute. He handed the flute to Barbara, then poured a glass of wine for himself. After placing the bottle in an ice bucket between his feet, he raised his glass and toasted, "To good friends."

The sun was low in the sky as the limo crawled in heavy traffic to the Albuquerque Balloon Park on the north side of the city. Susan glanced toward the Sandia Mountains to the east. "We could have a beautiful sunset tonight," she said. "The Sandias are already tinged with pink."

The others looked toward the mountains.

"The evening just gets better and better," Barbara said. "The paper said the balloon glow was scheduled to go off around 8:00. The winds are supposed to be very light."

"That's good," Henry said. "All it takes is an eight-mile-an-hour wind and they'll cancel the thing."

"I've never been out here before," Roger said. "I'm looking forward to it."

Susan shot Roger an incredulous look. "I can't believe you've never been to a balloon fiesta. You've lived here for over ten years."

"I lived in Philadelphia for ten years, too, and I never went to Betsy Ross's house or the Liberty Bell. That's tourist stuff."

"Oh, you poor thing. I have so much to teach you."

Roger gave her a lascivious smile. "You've already taught me so much."

The limo driver announced over the intercom, "We're almost there, Mr. Smith. What time do you want to be picked up?"

Roger looked at Susan and Barbara. "Will three hours be enough?"

"Sounds good to me," Barbara answered.

Susan nodded.

The four of them exited the limo after the driver pulled over near a line of six white pavilions. The first one in line was sponsored by New Mexico Mutual Insurance. The next one had a Wells Fargo Bank sign on it.

"That's the way to watch the balloons," Susan said. "Seated at a pavilion, overlooking the field."

"Funny you should mention that," Roger said as he pulled tickets from his jacket pocket. He led the way to the entrance to the insurance company's pavilion, handed the tickets to a young woman, and stepped aside as the others entered. Tables and chairs covered an area about the size of a basketball court. At the back of the area were a bar and an alcove into a section with a large buffet setup.

Susan hooked her arm in Barbara's and whispered, "I think Roger and Henry are keepers."

Barbara squeezed Susan's arm. "You just figure that out?"

The sun was fifteen minutes from going below the horizon, the mountains now resplendent with a reddish-pink hue, when Henry took Barbara's hand. "I want to show you something," he said.

"What?"

"Just come with me. You'll see."

He led her out of the pavilion and down a small slope to the field, where dozens and dozens of spectacular, multi-colored hot air balloons bobbed in the slight breeze. Their crews finalized preparations for the glow, when all of the balloon crews would simultaneously fire up their propane burners, making their balloons shine like gigantic lanterns. On the south end of the field, just below the insurance company's pavilion, was a fully-inflated red, blue, and yellow balloon overlaid with a rearing white stallion. Henry held Barbara's hand all the way to the balloon. A woman stood next to the basket below the envelope and greeted them.

"Hey, Henry." She shook his hand, then said, "And this must be Barbara." She extended her hand to Barbara, who shook it and asked, "What's going on?"

"You ready, Henry?" the woman asked, ignoring Barbara's question.

"Actually, I'm a little nervous," he said.

The woman patted him on the back. "Nothing to it. Just climb on in."

Barbara pulled back a step. "I hope you're not planning on us getting into that thing."

Henry reached for Barbara's hand but she pulled it away.

"I can't stand airplanes, and they have engines." She pointed up at the balloon. "These things go wherever the wind takes them. Into power lines, in rivers, on highways. Don't even think—"

Henry stepped forward and took hold of both of her hands. "We're just going up thirty feet or so. The balloon will be tethered to the ground the whole time."

Barbara pulled her hands free and looked around at the thick ropes that secured the balloon. She was still about to object, when she saw the disappointed look on Henry's face, sucked in a breath, and said, "Okay, Henry."

The woman who had stood aside during the exchange between Henry and Barbara now opened a gate in the basket. Henry again took Barbara's hand and led her into the basket. The woman followed, closed the gate, and announced, "Hold on, folks." She turned up the burner, which shot a huge blue flame into the already inflated envelope. The balloon jerked upward, then rose steadily until it reached the limits of its tethers.

"All set," the woman told Henry.

Barbara looked at Henry and frowned. "What are you up to?" she said.

Henry took a small black box from a jacket pocket, dropped to one knee, and held the box up toward Barbara. He opened it and said, "Barbara Lassiter, I've loved you from the moment we met. You make my heart soar and my knees tremble. I want us to spend the rest of our lives together. Barbara, will you marry me?"

Barbara was stunned, at a loss for words. Sure, she'd wondered where their relationship would ultimately go, and had wondered if marriage was in their future. But she hadn't expected a proposal today, and surely not in a hot air balloon surrounded by over a hundred other balloons and at least ten thousand people. Her mind reeled with sudden thoughts of her first husband who'd died from cancer. Then her eyes met Henry's and an overwhelming feeling of warmth flooded through her. She said, "Henry Simpson, you bet I'll marry you, but only if you stand up and kiss me."

Henry blew out a loud breath, stood, slipped the ring from the box onto Barbara's finger, and put his arms around her. As they kissed, Barbara heard the female pilot dial a cell phone and say, "She said yes."

As they broke off their kiss, the balloon fiesta announcer shouted over the sound system, "Let's hear a round of applause for Henry Simpson and Barbara Lassiter. They just got engaged in the White Stallion balloon."

Barbara poked Henry. "Jeez, Henry, I can't wait to see what you plan for our wedding."

Susan and Roger stood next to one another and watched the tethered white stallion balloon descend to the field.

"Did you know what Henry had planned?"

"Of course. Pretty romantic, huh?"

Susan chuckled. "Yeah, except for the fact that the one thing Barbara hates more than dead bodies is heights."

Roger twisted toward Susan. "You're serious?" he said.

"As a heart attack."

"I'm glad she accepted his proposal."

"Me too," Susan said. "Henry's a great guy."

"By the way," Roger said, "speaking of heart attacks, what's going on with your case?"

Susan huffed. "I'm on pins and needles. We're waiting to hear from the coroner about the two bodies that were exhumed. We'll look like idiots if there was no foul play."

Roger hugged her. "Susan, you've got the best instincts of anyone I know. I'll bet you a dollar that one or both of the bodies have traces of poison in them."

"Gee, Roger, one whole dollar. That's quite a show of confidence."

"Okay, let's raise the stakes. If I'm right, you have to sleep with me. If I'm wrong, I have to sleep with you."

Susan giggled and kissed his cheek. "Sounds like a no-lose situation for both of us."

Roger pointed out Henry and Barbara as they exited the balloon basket. Then an enormous chorus of *oohs* and *aahs*, mixed with the roars from the propane burners, swept the field as the balloon glow kicked off. The crowd's response, mixed with the blasts from the balloon burners, prevented Susan from hearing the ring of her cell phone. But she felt the phone's vibrations through her purse. She quickly pulled out the cell, looked at the screen, and pressed it against her ear. She shouted, "Hi, Uncle Alberto. Is everything all right?"

She could barely hear her uncle's voice and shouted, "Say that again, Uncle Alberto. I couldn't make out what you said."

"There's been another incident here, *mija*. Lady named Violet Hawkins."

Susan felt her stomach clench. "Hold on a minute," she yelled, as she ran toward the back of the pavilion, away from the crowd and the balloons. From a corner at the back, she said, "Okay, tell me what happened."

Her uncle's voice was clearer now. "A woman named Violet Hawkins just had some kind of attack. The paramedics took her to Presbyterian Hospital. They think she had a heart attack."

"Okay, Uncle Alberto. We'll check into it." She thought: *Every heart attack at a retirement home isn't necessarily foul play.* "Thanks—"

"One other thing, *mija*," Alberto said. "Max was down in the dining room when Mrs. Hawkins met with Stuart Armstead, the owner of this place. Armstead brought over a glass of iced tea to Mrs. Hawkins. She apparently suffered the attack shortly after their meeting ended."

By the time Susan rejoined Roger, Barbara and Henry had returned.

"What's up?" Barbara asked.

"Another Vista de Alameda resident may have had a heart attack. She was transported to Pres downtown."

"And?" Barbara said.

"The woman met with the owner of the center just before the attack."

"You think he slipped her something?"

"I don't know, Barb. But we already know that liquid nicotine would have to be injected in some way."

"Coulda slipped her something to make her drowsy and then injected the nicotine later."

"Maybe. I'm going to the hospital to check it out. I want to make certain that, if she passes away, they don't declare her dead from natural causes until an autopsy is performed. In the meantime, I'll try to get them to do a tox screen."

"How will you get to the hospital?" Roger asked.

"There are sheriff's deputies and city police all around here. I'm sure I can get a ride. You guys stay here and have a good time."

Susan noticed that Barbara wore a hangdog expression. She guessed Henry must have noticed it as well when he said, "Oh, you go ahead and join Susan. You'll be miserable wondering what's going on down at the hospital."

Barbara brightened. "You sure you don't mind?"

"For better or for worse, babe," Henry said. "I took your job into account when I proposed."

Barbara embraced Henry and kissed him enthusiastically. She whispered in his ear, "I'll come by your place when I'm done."

Barbara and Susan hitched a ride with a deputy named Watkins in a BCSO SUV. Barbara sat shotgun, while Susan took a seat in the back. The deputy turned on the vehicle's roof rack lights and deployed the siren, which helped them to get through balloon fiesta traffic fairly quickly. Once they reached Interstate 25, traffic thinned and they made good time. They were a half-mile from the Central Avenue exit when Susan's phone rang again.

"Martinez," she answered.

"Detective, it's Dr. Blake."

She pressed the speaker icon on her phone and mouthed to Barbara who was looking over her shoulder at her, "It's Blake."

"Yes, Dr. Blake," she said.

"We just finished the autopsy on Karl Quintana."

Susan closed her eyes and tightened her lips.

"We found nothing that indicated he'd been poisoned. There was no trace of nicotine or *continine* in his liver. Because of decomposition, there was no way of discovering an injection site. Cause of death was exactly as the emergency room physician determined. Myocardial infarction."

A wave of disappointment hit Susan. She looked at Barbara and saw that she looked as ill as Susan felt.

"No question?" Susan asked.

"None. But I want you to remember something. It's been almost three months since Mr. Quintana died. The only way we would have been able to discover traces of *continine* would have been through analysis of his hair. The fact that there was no trace of poison in his liver, we didn't bother testing his hair."

A shiver went through her. "You didn't test his hair?"

"No. It's a very expensive test. Considering the absence of *continine* in the liver, I didn't want to waste—"

"Did Dr. Beringer agree?"

Blake didn't immediately respond. Susan waited.

"I'm the coroner, Detective. It's my decision to make."

Susan sucked in a breath and let it out slowly. "Dr. Beringer wanted to test his hair, didn't he?"

"That's neither here nor there, Detective. I decided—"

"Please, Dr. Blake. If there's a chance that an analysis of Mr. Quintana's hair will show that he was poisoned, you've got to order the test. We're talking about possible murder here."

Susan waited. Finally, he said, "All right, Detective. But if the test comes back negative, I'm sending you the bill."

"Thanks, Dr. Blake." She was about to sign off, when a thought struck her. "Did you notify the D.A.?"

"Not yet. That's my next call." He sighed and added, "Now I'll wait until the hair analysis is complete."

"Anything on Emily Watrous?"

"Jeez, Martinez, how about giving me a break?" Then Blake cut off the call.

Susan stared out her window and muttered, "Bureaucrats."

CHAPTER 20

Susan stopped a nurse in the Presbyterian Hospital emergency room and asked, "Where has Violet Hawkins been taken?"

The nurse asked, "Who are you?"

Susan felt her face warm. It took a great deal of self-control to not raise her voice. She glanced at the nurse's nametag, flashed her I.D., and said, "Look, Ms. Panagopoulos, your cooperation would be much appreciated. Where is Mrs. Hawkins?"

The nurse looked from Susan to Barbara, and back to Susan. Then she shrugged and pointed at a corner of the area. "She's behind that curtain. The physician just confirmed that she was deceased."

"Did you take blood specimens when she came through here?" Barbara asked.

"Sure, just like we always do."

"Have those specimens gone to the lab?"

"I was just about to do that."

Barbara said, "Have the lab check for the presence of liquid nicotine."

"You serious?" the nurse asked.

"Do I look like I'm playing games?" Barbara said.

The woman nodded.

Barbara and Susan exited the hospital emergency room and returned to the SUV.

"Where to now?" Deputy Watkins asked.

"Take us to headquarters," Susan said. "We'll get a vehicle from the motor pool."

"I can drive you around," the deputy said. "This is more interesting than hanging out at the balloon fiesta arresting drunks and pickpockets."

"Thanks, Watkins. But I suspect we're going to be tied up way beyond the end of your shift."

It was a few minutes past 9:30 p.m. when Barbara and Susan parked their department sedan outside Vista de Alameda and entered the front lobby. A woman behind the reception desk greeted them.

"Would you mind calling Alberto Martinez?" Susan said. "Please tell him his niece is here."

"No need to call," the woman said. "Alberto and Max are in the reading room. Alberto told me he might have visitors tonight." She pointed to the left, at a cross corridor. "It's the second door on the right side of that hall." Then she added, "Please sign the visitors' log."

Susan was about to object, but overcame her impatience and signed in both her and Barbara. When she finished, she said to the woman, "I wonder if Mr. Armstead is here."

"Oh, no. Mr. Armstead is never here this late."

"Do you have a home telephone number for him?"

"Of course."

"How about calling him and asking him to come here?"

The woman's face paled. "I hate to bother him at home," she said. "What with the time and his wife's illness."

Susan handed the woman her card. "This is important, ma'am. Call Mr. Armstead and have him call my number." Then she followed Barbara to the reading room.

As soon as they entered the room, Alberto dropped the playing cards he held, slowly stood, and walked over.

"I'm sure glad to see you two," he said. "Any news about Violet?"

Barbara shook her head. "She didn't make it."

Max had come over and now stood next to Susan. He whispered, "Was she poisoned?"

"We haven't heard anything about that," Susan answered. "Why

128

don't we sit down and you can tell us what you know."

They moved to a four-top table in a corner. Max had barely begun to tell them what he'd seen earlier that day about Violet Hawkins and Stuart Armstead meeting in the dining room, when Susan's cell rang again. She picked it off the tabletop, stood, quick-walked to the other side of the room, and answered the call.

"Detective, it's Stuart Armstead."

"Thanks for calling me, Mr. Armstead. I'm a detective with the Bernalillo County Sheriff's Office."

"Is something wrong?"

"Are you aware that one of your residents was transported to the hospital earlier this evening?"

"Of course. Violet Hawkins. I believe she suffered a heart attack."

"That's why we're here."

Armstead didn't immediately respond. When he did, he sounded out of sorts. "I don't understand," he said. "Why would the police be involved?"

"Perhaps we could meet to discuss the matter."

"Now?"

"If that's convenient."

"I couldn't possibly meet tonight. My wife is ill and I have no one here to stay with her."

"Perhaps my partner and I could meet you at your home."

Armstead paused again. "What's the urgency?"

Susan detected anger in his voice. "A resident in your facility died today. I would think you'd want to know what happened."

"What are you implying? That Mrs. Hawkins didn't have a heart attack?"

Susan said, "I think it would be good if you talked with us tonight."

Armstead's voice was now louder and more strident. "What department are you with?" he demanded.

"I'm a homicide detective, sir."

"My God. Maybe I'd better call my attorney."

"Only if you feel you need one, Mr. Armstead."

CHAPTER 21

Stuart Armstead and his attorney were scheduled to meet with the detectives at 10:30 p.m. at Vista de Alameda. Normally, he would have refused to meet at this late hour, but Kathy had a treatment scheduled in the morning and, besides, he wanted to know what the hell was going on with the cops. He called the visiting nursing agency to get someone to be with his wife but there was no one available until early the next morning. Then he called Lisa French. She sounded groggy when she answered.

"Did I wake you?"

"Oh, no, it's all right."

"Would it be possible for you to come over and stay with Kathy for a couple hours? I called the visiting nursing service and they can't get anyone over here for at least eight hours."

"What's going on, Stuart?" French asked.

"I'm not quite sure, but a detective is at the center. She seems to have suspicions about Violet Hawkins's heart attack." His voice broke as he said, "What in the world is going on? Since when do the police follow up on heart attacks?"

French didn't respond. For a moment, Armstead thought he'd lost her.

"Lisa, are you there?"

"Oh, I'm sorry, Stuart. Of course I'll come over. Don't you worry about a thing."

"I have to leave here in ten minutes. I'll leave the front door key under the mat."

French dressed quickly and rushed out to her car in her garage. But she suddenly stopped, placed both her hands on the car door, and breathed deeply. *Slow down,* she thought. *Think.* After ten seconds, she reversed direction, re-entered her home, and thought about what she wanted to do. She paced from kitchen to den, contemplating steps she would take. When she hit a snag in her plan, she backtracked and began all over again, until she was satisfied. Then she moved to the garage, unscrewed a vent cover in the wall next to a freezer, and took out a zippered pouch. After checking inside the pouch, she closed the zipper, and slipped the pouch inside her purse. She took a hammer and screwdriver from a tool rack; went into her kitchen, where she collected a pair of rubber gloves; and went back out to her car.

She anticipated that the drive to the Armstead house in North Albuquerque Acres would take fifteen minutes. About halfway there, as she crossed Spain on Eubank, she called Calderon Towing, one of her brother Frank's companies.

"Calderon Towing," a man answered.

"I need my car towed."

"Lady, it's going to be at least three hours. We're swamped tonight. Unless it's an emergency, it'll have to wait—"

"Listen, asshole, this is Frank's sister, Lisa. You think I'd call at this hour if it wasn't an emergency?"

The guy didn't immediately respond. Finally, he said, "I can take care of it right away. Give me the location and the make and model of the vehicle."

"Silver Mercedes E 400. How soon can you get here?"

"About thirty minutes."

"Is that thirty minutes, New Mexico time, or thirty minutes, real time?"

She could tell from the guy's tone that he was aggravated, when he answered, "I'll be there in *thirty minutes.*"

"Good. I'll leave the keys on the top of the right rear tire. I want you to take the car to the following address." She gave him her home address. "I have a medical emergency I have to take care of."

She didn't like making the call out of sequence, but the last thing she wanted was to have her car sitting on a city street at midnight, ready prey for some thief. If some bastard broke into the vehicle, or stole it, he could ruin everything.

She looked at her watch: 10:45. *This is going to be tight.*

Stuart had told her he would leave a key under the front mat and would not set the alarm. French found the house key, unlocked the door, and entered. She knew that the Armstead's master suite was on the second floor, but Stuart had told her he'd set up his wife in a spare bedroom on the first floor to avoid having to go up and down stairs.

She found Kathy Armstead asleep in a bedroom at the end of a long hallway. A clear tube snaked from a plastic bag on a tall, metal, wheeled rack on the right side of the bed into a shunt in the woman's hand. A bedside lamp on the opposite side of the bed bathed the woman's pale face in anemic light. *She looks twenty years older than Stuart,* French thought. *He's wasting his life on this old hag.*

She placed her purse on a corner of the bottom of the bed, removed the rubber gloves, and slipped them on. Then she took out the pouch, unzipped it, and removed a glass vial and a syringe. She loaded the syringe with the contents of the vial, replaced the vial in the pouch, and set it down on the bed by her purse. She walked around to the far side of the bed, to the metal rack, and inserted the needle into the port of a connector on the intravenous line. About to depress the plunger on the syringe, she was startled by a willowy, muted voice.

"Stu . . . is that you?"

French looked at Kathy Armstead and quietly said, "Stu had to go out, Kathy. He asked me to come over until he came back."

The woman's eyes looked bleary as she looked at French. "I'm sorry, Lisa. I hate to be a bother."

"No bother, Kathy. I'm happy to help out."

Kathy Armstead now wore a smile. "Did Stu tell you about the"—she stopped and took a slow, deep breath, then exhaled raggedly—"about the experimental treatment?"

"Uh huh."

"He wants so badly for the treatments to work." She groaned as she shifted her position. "I hope, for his sake, that it's successful." She sighed. "But I'm so tired of . . . being sick. If it wasn't for the effect on Stu, I would have refused the treatments."

"You should go back to sleep, Kathy. You need your rest."

She said, "That's all I do anymore. Sleep." She groaned again and closed her eyes. Only a half-minute passed before her breathing had slowed to a regular pattern.

French stared at the woman for a full fifteen seconds, then depressed the syringe's plunger.

After putting the syringe and vial back in the pouch and the pouch back in her purse, she left the bedroom, went out the front door, locked it, and replaced the house key under the mat. She returned to her car, drove half the distance to her home, did a U-turn on Eubank Boulevard just south of Academy Boulevard, and parked against the curb on the east side of Eubank, ten feet away from a sewer opening. She removed the pouch from her purse, picked up the hammer and screwdriver from the front seat, and left the car. After dropping the pouch into the sewer opening, she moved to the right front wheel, bent over, inserted the sharp blade of the screwdriver between two of the tire treads, and whacked the head of the screwdriver with the hammer. The blade slipped downward and stabbed the side of her ankle.

"Dammit," she cursed. She dropped the hammer and swiped at the cut on her ankle with her hand. Then she lifted the hammer from the street, put the end of the screwdriver against the side of the tire, gripped it with all her strength, and hit the tool's handle with the hammer. This time, the screwdriver punctured the hard rubber. As she pulled the blade from the tire, sour, hot air blasted her face. She quickly stood, moved to the sewer opening, stripped off the rubber gloves and tossed them, along with the hammer and screwdriver, into the sewer. She then used the Uber app on her cell phone to call for a driver. Then she grabbed her pocketbook off the front seat of the Mercedes, took the car keys from her jacket pocket, and placed them on the top of the right rear tire.

At 11:10, the Uber driver arrived.

"Damned tire," French exclaimed. She gave the driver the Armstead address. "I was supposed to go to that address to sit with a very ill woman. I should have been there twenty minutes ago." She again said, "Damned tire."

The driver dropped her at the Armstead residence. She re-entered the house as she had before, went to Kathy Armstead's bedroom, and checked her pulse. No heartbeat. She checked again to make certain. Still no pulse. Then she sat in a rocking chair in a corner of the room, removed her cell phone from her purse, and called 9-1-1.

Stuart Armstead tried to remain open-minded and patient with the two female detectives, although he thought their questions were inane. But when one of them asked about his meeting with Violet Hawkins in the dining hall, and mentioned her heart attack a short time after that meeting ended, he lost his cool. He shot to his feet and jabbed a finger at the one named Martinez. "Are you nuts?" he shouted. "What do you do, sit around making this stuff up?" When his attorney reached for his arm, he shook off the man's hand and was about to continue his tirade, when his cell phone interrupted him. He took the call and listened to Lisa French cry, "She's dead, Stu. Kathy's dead."

By the time he'd ended the call, Armstead had collapsed back into his chair.

"Mr. Armstead, what's wrong?" Detective Lassiter asked.

He glared at her, then at her partner. In a broken voice, he ranted, "I should have been with her, not here with you two. I should never have left her."

The lawyer asked, "What's happened?"

Armstead turned and looked at the man. "It's Kathy," he said. "That was Lisa. She told me that Kathy died."

"Oh my God," the lawyer said. "I'm so sorry. I thought she was getting better."

Armstead stood again, ignored the two detectives, told his attorney, "I've got to go home," and rushed from the conference room.

CHAPTER 22

After her call to Stuart Armstead, Lisa French watched the street through the living room window at the front of the Armstead home. The headlights and colored flashing emergency lights of the ambulance that responded to her 9-1-1 call reminded French of New Orleans during Mardi Gras. She smiled at the memory of that visit when she and her first husband went there on their honeymoon. Like then, this was also a cause for celebration.

She watched the paramedics scramble. One of them moved quickly toward the front door while the other one lugged a case from the back of the vehicle. Since she'd worked at Vista de Alameda, she'd seen many people die, so she told herself to be careful and not overdo her emotional reaction to Kathy Armstead's death. She put on a sad expression, opened the front door, and pointed the paramedics toward the first floor bedroom hallway. While they went to work on Kathy, she returned her attention to the street and waited.

The sounds of the paramedics carried to the living room as French looked out through the front window. She heard the squeal of tires before she saw headlights. Then Stuart's car pulled to the curb in front. French wondered for a moment whether she should meet him outside or wait where she was. She opted for the latter. By the time she heard the *thunk* of Stuart's car door, she'd manufactured tears. When he opened the door and rushed inside, she was in full-blown crying jag mode. He glanced at her as he moved past her to the hallway and toward the bedroom.

She listened to the conversation in the bedroom. Stuart momentarily full of hope. One of the paramedic's expression of sadness for Stuart's loss. Then his mournful grief that echoed through the house as though the sound was seeping out of the walls.

Do I put my arms around him to console him when he comes out? she wondered. *The sooner he learns to depend on me, to come to me for comfort, the better.*

She held a wadded tissue in her hands and waited. When Stuart finally left the bedroom, following the paramedics as they wheeled his wife outside on a gurney, she released a soft sob and dabbed at her eyes. But he hadn't seemed to notice.

Ten minutes later, after the ambulance departed, Stuart came back inside, walked to the bar in the den, and poured three inches of an amber-colored liquid into an Old Fashion glass. He downed a third of the drink, moved to the chair across from the couch where she sat, and stared at her. When she looked up and their eyes met, she was startled by the coldness in his.

"What happened?" he demanded.

French sniffled. "I found her . . . she was gone when I arrived. I'm so sorry, Stuart. I know what Kathy meant to you. I—"

"The paramedics told me what time you made the 9-1-1 call. That was almost forty minutes after you told me you would come here."

She shook her head and gave him a sorrowful look. She began, "I left to come here ten minutes after you called, but I got a . . . ." She gulped, then continued: "I got a flat tire on Eubank. I had to call Uber to get a ride."

He exhaled a moan that sounded as though it had escaped his throat of its own volition. More to himself than to her, he said, "I should never have left her." He gave her an apologetic look. "I'm sorry for my tone before. It wasn't your fault; it was mine. She was my responsibility."

Tears flowed down his cheeks and onto his shirt. His shoulders shuddered. In a hoarse voice, he said, "I really thought she was going to make it. The experimental treatment, and all. But it was apparently her heart that finally gave out."

"What can I do, Stu?"

He stood, placed his glass on the coffee table, and moved toward the front door. "You need to go home and get some rest. I'll have to depend on you to run things at the center until I can get things settled here."

She stood and hung her purse on a shoulder. "You can count on me."

He patted her back as she moved to the door. "I know that, Lisa." He swallowed hard and added, "I'm sorry I put you in this situation. It must have been awful."

She shook her head, but didn't say anything. Then she turned to face him, put her arms around his chest, and hugged him. She exhaled a sigh when she felt him hug her back. "I'm so sorry," she said, then backed up, turned, and went outside. But before Armstead closed the door, he said, "Wait a minute. You don't have your car."

She tapped the side of her head with a finger. "What a ditz I am. I can't believe I forgot that. I'll just call Uber."

"No, you won't," he said. "I'll drive you. It's the least I can do."

Despite the fact that they didn't speak more than a couple dozen words to one another during the drive to her house, she felt a warm sensation flow through her body just being with him during his time of need. As he pulled up in front of her place, she was happy to see that the tow company had delivered her car as they'd promised. They'd even replaced the flat with the spare. *I'll have to put in a good word about the driver with my brother*, she thought.

"Thanks for the ride, Stu," she said as she opened her door.

"You going to be okay handling things at the center while I'm out?"

She looked back at him and thought, *Shit, I already do everything there.* "Sure, Stu. But I can call you if anything comes up that I can't handle."

He nodded.

She got out, closed the door, and waved at him as he drove away. Then she quickly went to her car, found the keys on the top of the right rear tire—where she'd told the tow truck driver to leave them, hummed a tune, and pulled the car into the garage.

TUESDAY
OCTOBER 7

CHAPTER 23

Barbara and Susan arrived at the Homicide Division offices at 7:00 a.m. Barbara found on her blotter a telephone message slip left by the night duty detective: *Call Dr. Beringer.* The pathologist had called at 6:35 a.m. She waved the slip at Susan. "Beringer called."

"Any message?" Susan asked.

"Just his number," she said as she dialed Beringer, pressed the speaker icon, and placed her cell on her desk. As soon as he answered, she said, "Dr. Beringer, it's Barbara Lassiter and Susan Martinez." She held her breath as she waited for him to speak.

"Thanks for calling back so quickly. You sitting down?"

"No. Do we need to?"

"Yes, I think you do. We found traces of *continine* in Mr. Quintana's hair." After a short pause, he added, "There's no question in my mind. Dr. Blake and I both agree that he was poisoned with nicotine."

Susan whooped.

"I'll be damned," Barbara said.

"There's more," Beringer said. "Mrs. Watrous was also poisoned."

"Holy Mother of God," Susan said. "How soon can we get your reports?"

"I'll email them to you by the end of the day. But I may have more for you."

"More poisoned residents of Vista de Alameda?" Barbara asked.

"No, not yet, anyway. I had a thought about the poisoning agent and had the lab break down the components of the liquid nicotine we found in all three bodies. The chemical makeup of what we discovered in Mr. Matthews's and Mrs. Watrous's bodies were identical. Unfortunately, there wasn't enough trace evidence in Mr. Quintana to determine the chemical DNA of the *continine* in his body."

"How does that help us?" Barbara said.

"Good question. I checked with the FBI. They can identify the manufacturer of over two hundred different types of liquid nicotine. If what we found matches one of those nicotine types, then we can identify the manufacturer, and—"

"We might be able to find out who bought the stuff from the manufacturer," Susan said, finishing Beringer's comment.

"You got it, Detective. I'll send off samples to the FBI lab today."

After thanking Beringer, Barbara said, "Partner, I think we should take that nicotine vial we found in Scott Matthews's house and have Dr. Beringer test it to see if it's the same stuff that was in Mr. Matthews and Mrs. Watrous."

Lisa French came to work at 8:00 a.m. and immediately went to the reception desk. She took the sign-in log off the desk and checked the log sheets for the day before. She spotted the names of the detectives—Barbara Lassiter and Susan Martinez—who had met with Stuart Armstead and his attorney. The same two who had questioned her the other day.

She went to her office, closed the door, and sat in her desk chair. After she rummaged around in her center desk drawer, she found the calling cards for the two detectives. She placed them side-by-side on her blotter and stared at them for a long while. *What do I do about these two?* she thought.

"They could ruin everything," she muttered to herself.

Stuart Armstead, seated in a recliner in his living room, propped a framed photograph of his wife on his thighs and looked down at it. His throat felt tight and his mouth was dry. She'd been the love of his life, from the time they'd met in college, through over two decades of marriage. But the last two years had changed things. Cancer had debilitated her, aging her, causing her body to bend to the ravages of the disease. He'd been ashamed of his reaction to her illness, of how he couldn't look at her without feeling disgusted. Of how he had come to resent the time he'd committed to playing nursemaid. *How many times did I ask myself, what happened to the woman I married,* he thought.

Kathy had had no siblings and her parents were long since gone. Many of the friends she'd made in Albuquerque had drifted away as her disease progressed. The three women who had been closest to her had just left after paying a visit to him. Now he had to get through the next few days. After the funeral, he'd be able to focus on the rest of his life. He still felt vibrant and, now that the finances of Vista de Alameda had improved, he was optimistic about the future.

His cell phone rang. Before answering the call, he checked the caller ID and saw it was Lisa. He breathed out a sigh and cleared his throat. He knew he should talk with her, but the last thing he really wanted to do was listen to her platitudes about his loss and what a wonderful woman Kathy had been. He cleared his throat again, sipped from a glass of wine, and waited for the ringing to stop. He breathed a sigh of relief, took another drink of wine, and was about to turn on the stereo when his phone rang again: Lisa French. "Shit," he blurted. He answered the call.

"Everything all right?"

"I should be asking you that question. Everything's fine here. I just wanted to check in with you to see if there's anything I can do."

"Thank you. I appreciate your concern. But I'm fine. I just need some time alone."

"Of course. But please don't hesitate to call me if you need something. Anything."

"Okay. Will do. I'll call you in a couple days to check in. Thanks again."

"Oh, Stu, one other thing. The employees and some of the residents asked about the funeral services. They want to be able to attend."

Armstead sucked air in over his teeth. He thought, *I guess I'll have to play the game.* "The funeral will be on Saturday. I'll let you know time and place when it's all set."

"Okay. Thanks. Don't forget. Call me if—"

"I'll be in touch, Lisa. Thanks again. I appreciate everything you're doing."

He terminated the call and stared at the phone screen. "I gotta figure out how to get rid of that cloying bitch," he whispered. "What a useful idiot she's been." *But her usefulness is about over,* he thought.

His cell phone rang again, interrupting his thoughts: Dr. Isaac Bain.

"Hello," he answered.

"Stu, it's Isaac. I heard about Kathy. I'm so sorry."

Armstead put on a fake aggrieved tone. "It's a shock. I was so optimistic that the experimental treatment you put her on was going to work." He groaned. "After all she'd been through because of cancer, a heart attack takes her."

Bain said, "You just never know. I'm really sorry."

"Thanks, Isaac."

"Listen, I need to know where Kathy's . . . body was transported to. I have to arrange for the autopsy."

"What are you talking about? What autopsy?"

"The contract with the drug company that provided the experimental cancer treatment requires that any patient who dies during the treatment protocol must be autopsied. It's part of the deal. They want to make certain that the treatment wasn't the cause of a patient's death."

"Horse shit!" Armstead blurted. "I'm not putting Kathy through an autopsy after all she went through over the past couple of years. Besides, the mortuary might have already cremated her remains."

Bain took a few seconds to respond. "You'd better hope they haven't. Apparently, you didn't read the fine print in the contract with the drug company. If you violate any of the terms of the contract, you're liable for the costs of the experimental treatment regimen. The whole regimen, regardless of where Kathy was in the process. You'd owe the pharmaceutical company over half-a-million dollars."

"Are you friggin' kiddin' me?"

Bain didn't respond.

Armstead's stomach felt as though it was full of snakes. He licked his lips. "She was taken to Albuquerque Funeral Home."

"Okay. Thanks. You'd better call them right now and hope they haven't started the cremation. Tell them to do nothing until further notice. I'll arrange for transport to the coroner. I'm sorry about this, but we don't have a choice."

Armstead called the mortuary and talked with the representative assigned to him. "Have you started processing my wife's body?" he shouted, knowing his voice was too loud, but not able to speak calmly.

"No, Mr. Armstead. We plan to start cremation this—"

"Don't do anything. Her body has to be sent to the Office of the Medical Investigator. Dr. Isaac Bain will call you to explain things."

"All right, sir," the man said.

Armstead hung up, refilled his glass from the wine bottle on the table beside him, and drank half the contents. Then he thought about what had happened last night. He didn't know why the idea came to him, but it did and he shuddered. *I wonder if Lisa had anything to do with Kathy dying. Couldn't be,* he thought. *She wasn't even at the house when it happened.* At first, the idea that Lisa could have done something to Kathy made no sense. *She's not a murderer. Sure, she's clingy and has been nauseatingly obvious about her feelings for me, but MURDER?* He shook his head as though to rid it of unwanted thoughts. But then the thought returned and he wondered, *by calling her and asking her to stay with Kathy, did I, in effect, provide her the opportunity to act?* His hands shook as though he'd been struck with palsy. His heart beat as though he'd just finished a marathon. As much as he tried to deny to himself that he was culpable in any way for his wife's death, he couldn't erase the thought. He'd known for quite a while that Lisa French was more than infatuated with him and that she would do anything for him. He shuddered as he considered that he could have set up Lisa's opportunity to murder his wife.

He closed his eyes and reflected on the time, several months ago, when he'd entered her office looking for her, and saw her open purse on the floor beside the left leg of her desk. He'd barely paid any attention to it and turned to leave the office. But suddenly stopped and turned back around. Something had registered in his mind's eye. He walked over to the purse and looked down at a syringe. He leaned over and stared at the needle, and then saw a tiny glass bottle next to it. He read the label on the bottle: CTX CHEMICAL PRODUCTS, LLC. Below the name of the manufacturer were the words: Savory Scent Liquid Nicotine.

As he returned to his own office that day, he'd considered what he'd discovered. He'd never known Lisa to smoke anything, and he wasn't aware of her needing injections for anything. He couldn't make heads or tails of the bottle or the syringe, but he put any thought of them out of his mind.

Later that day, however, shortly after lunch, he'd been conversing with one of the maintenance staff in the room across from the elevator lobby. He'd seen Lisa, purse hanging from her shoulder, take the elevator. He'd watched the lights over the elevator register the floor numbers 1 through 4. Her taking the elevator to one of the resident floors didn't surprise him. There were plenty of reasons for her to visit with residents. What surprised him was that she'd brought her purse along. It seemed odd.

Ninety minutes later, the emergency alarm went off in the administrative offices. Someone had pulled the alarm cord in one of the resident's suites. He'd run into the large room that housed a secretary, the security desk, and the reception counter, and noted the light blinking for suite 416. Susan Vincent's apartment.

Armstead and the security guard had run to the elevator lobby. By the time the car door opened, Lisa French had joined them, having come from the direction of her office.

"It's apartment 416," the guard said.

"That's Mrs. Vincent's suite," Lisa had said.

Armstead remembered Lisa's surprised expression.

When they'd arrived at Mrs. Vincent's apartment, the woman stood in the hall outside her door.

"What's wrong?" Armstead had asked.

"We were supposed to play bridge in my apartment, but Karl didn't show. When I knocked on his door, he didn't answer." The woman shrugged. "That's why I pulled the emergency cord in my apartment."

The guard knocked on Karl Quintana's door. After a long wait, and no answer, he used a passkey to enter the apartment. Quintana was on his back in bed. Dead. It was later determined that he'd suffered a heart attack.

On the way back to his office, after paramedics had transported Quintana's body, Armstead recalled the glass bottle and syringe he'd seen in Lisa's purse. Once in his office, he closed his office door, booted up his desktop computer, and Googled "Liquid Nicotine."

Later, when Lisa had met with him about re-leasing Quintana's apartment, he'd experienced a chill that pervaded his entire body. Her reaction to Quintana's death and what he'd learned on the Internet about liquid nicotine had scared him to death.

"We can bring in another tenant at a higher up-front fee and a higher rent," she'd said. "And we can put rent escalators in the lease."

As he recalled what had happened those several months ago, he also remembered how shocked he'd been at her reaction. Quintana had just died and all she focused on were the financial benefits that could accrue from his death. In fact, he recalled that had been her reaction in the instance of each of the resident deaths over the past year or so.

A thought now percolated in his brain and sent fingers of fear through his nervous system: *If Lisa French murdered Karl Quintana, could she also have murdered other residents? Could she have murdered Kathy? It's too hideous to contemplate,* he thought, and took another sip of wine.

It was a few minutes after 5:00 p.m. when Barbara called Frederick Beringer and asked if anything new had come in from the FBI.

"No. I'm afraid that might take a while."

"Any way to speed up the process?"

"I already put in a call to a colleague there. She said she'd do her best to expedite things."

Barbara visualized Beringer shrugging.

After Barbara hung up, she asked Susan, "Did you ever call the D.A. about releasing Scott Matthews?"

"No. I thought we should go visit him once more before making the call. Once he's out, I suspect he'll never want to talk with us again."

"You want to visit him now?"

"Yeah." Susan looked at her watch. "I arranged with the ADA and Matthews's lawyer to meet us at the detention facility in thirty minutes."

"For what purpose? I thought we both agreed that we don't think he's guilty."

"I keep going back and forth on that," Susan said. "Let's see how he reacts to the latest news."

Scott Matthews looked as though he'd aged ten years. Dark circles etched his eyes and his complexion had changed from pale-white to pale-gray. His hair was mussed and a metal splint was affixed to his nose with surgical tape. A scab etched his upper lip.

Barbara grimaced at Susan as they took chairs against the wall, behind ADA Elinore Freed, who sat across from Matthews and his attorney.

The attorney jabbed a finger at Freed and growled, "You see what happened to my client? He was attacked by some psychopath. This is on you." Then he switched his accusing finger toward Barbara and Susan. "You two, as well."

Freed gave the attorney a cold, hard stare. "Nice speech," she said. "Now, are you calm enough to have an intelligent conversation?"

The lawyer just glared back at her while Matthews looked down at his folded hands.

Freed turned her glance on Matthews, who continued to look down. "Mr. Matthews, this may be your last chance to make a deal."

"What the hell are you talking about?" the lawyer said. His expression was venomous.

Freed said, "Liquid nicotine was found in your client's bathroom. It was also found in his father's body, and in two other Vista de Alameda residents who passed away." She paused for effect, then added, "All of the nicotine found in the bodies matched the contents of the vial in Mr. Matthews's home." Another pause. "The FBI lab is doing tests on the contents of the vial found in your client's home to determine where the nicotine was manufactured. It will be easy to determine if Mr. Matthews was a customer of that manufacturer."

The attorney's expression went from anger to shock when he glanced at his client. He turned back to Freed. "I need to talk to my client in private."

CHAPTER 24

Barbara drove Susan home from downtown. Neither of the women seemed inclined to talk, both deep in thought about the meeting with Scott Matthews. When Barbara pulled into Susan's driveway at 6:15, she said, "What do you think about Matthews now?"

"He's a sad case."

"But did he murder his father?"

"We arrested him, didn't we?"

"Yeah, we did. Because he had means, motive, and opportunity. But there's something niggling at the edges of my brain telling me he really cared about his old man. And he doesn't impress me as a violent type."

"Don't forget about him assaulting his former wife."

"You didn't find his story about the wife and her boyfriend setting him up to be credible?"

Susan shrugged.

They sat in silence for half-a-minute, then Barbara said, "Let's commit to not being narrow-minded about Matthews. Maybe he had the means, motive, and opportunity in his father's death, but what would his motive have been to murder Karl Quintana or Emily Watrous?"

"We're never narrow-minded, partner. That's why we're such good detectives."

"And sexy, too."

149

"And honest and fair, friendly and helpful, considerate and caring, courageous and—"

Barbara laughed. "You never told me you were a Girl Scout."

"I was a Gold Award scout. That got me a college scholarship. Best thing that ever happened to me. Anyway, when are you and Henry going to make it official?"

"We're talking about it. You'll be the first to know when we set a date. Can't have my maid of honor in the dark."

"I wondered when you were going to ask me to stand up with you."

"I had considered another friend until you told me you were a Gold Star scout. I mean, I couldn't very well miss the opportunity to have you wear your scout uniform at my wedding."

Susan chuckled. "Be careful, girlfriend. I might just do that."

"You don't have the nerve." Before Susan could respond, Barbara said, "Scratch that. Forget I mentioned anything about wearing a Girl Scout uniform at my wedding." She looked at Susan's expression and grimaced. "Please, Susan, you wouldn't embarrass me like that, would you?"

Susan opened the passenger door and stepped out onto her driveway. She waggled one hand, looked back at Barbara, and said, "Depends."

"On what?" Barbara shouted.

"On how you treat me between now and then."

The OMI contract with Essex Pharma & Health, Inc. specified that patients who were on their onco-infusion experimental treatment regimen and who died during or within six months after the end of treatment had to be autopsied. The autopsy had to focus on four basic areas: body fluids, liver, lymphatic system, and brain. DR. Francis Nixon, an OMI staff pathologist, had already sent specimens of various body fluids to the lab for screening.

Kathy Armstead's body was laid out on a stainless steel autopsy table at OMI. Nixon voice-recorded pertinent information about Armstead into the recording system, then glanced at the wall clock: 6:30 p.m. *Another long day,* he thought. He guessed it would be at least 9:30 before he finished with Armstead, cleaned up, and began his drive home. Nixon made his initial incision into the body.

Susan had arranged to have dinner with her uncle Alberto at 7:00. After Barbara dropped her off, she'd quickly changed into jeans, a white blouse and cross-trainers, and drove her Corvette to Vista de Alameda. She paced the lobby as she waited for her uncle to come downstairs. On her third circuit of the area, someone behind her asked, "Are you waiting for someone, ma'am?"

She turned around and recognized Lisa French.

"Oh," French said. "It's you."

Susan found the woman's response a little off, but she smiled and said, "I'm here to pick up Alberto Martinez for dinner."

"How nice." Then French asked, "Anything new with your investigation?"

Susan thought about what she and Barbara had told the woman when they'd met with her before. Something told her to play her cards close to the chest. "Oh, it turned out to be a false lead."

French shot her a look that appeared to Susan to be one of part relief and part disbelief.

"Well, that's good news. I mean, it would have been bad for our reputation here if Mr. Matthews had died of something other than natural causes."

Susan nodded. "I can imagine." She considered for an instant bringing up the subject of Violet Hawkins's death, but thought better of it. Besides, her uncle walked up at that moment.

Susan and Alberto hugged.

"Have a nice time," French said to them as they passed her on their way out.

Susan helped her uncle drop down into the passenger seat of the Corvette. The old man groaned as he fastened his seat belt and complained about the vehicle.

"Why don't you buy something practical? This damned thing is like a coffin on wheels."

"This car's a classic, I'll have you know."

Alberto grunted as she closed the door.

Susan got behind the wheel and asked, "Where do you feel like eating?"

"How about Trombino's?"

"Italian sounds good to me."

She pulled out of the parking lot and turned left onto 2nd Street. At Alameda Boulevard, she took another left and accelerated up the incline toward Interstate 25.

"Can't this thing go any faster?" her uncle said.

"I thought you didn't like my car."

"I hate getting in and out of it. It makes me feel decrepit. But I love it when you speed."

"You like to live dangerously, don't you?" she said.

He laughed. "Sure, as long as I don't have to pay the speeding tickets."

Susan smiled. This was part of their usual banter.

"How's Max?"

Alberto scowled. "He has a date tonight. By my count, he's dated at least thirteen women at the retirement center."

"Don't the ladies get jealous?"

"Nah. A couple of dates with Max is about all a woman can stand. They're happy to see him move on."

"I think Max is cute."

"Hah. That's because you've never spent more than a couple hours with him at any one time." Alberto took a quick breath and added, "Anything new on Violet Hawkins?"

"We're still waiting for word from the medical examiner."

"I gotta tell you, *mija*, I'm really worried."

"I understand, Uncle Alberto. Our problem is that other than Mr. Matthews's son, Scott, we don't have any suspects. And Scott Matthews was in jail when Violet Hawkins died. If the coroner finds liquid nicotine in her body, we have a real problem. Matthews couldn't have killed her and may not have murdered any of the others."

"I thought you found liquid nicotine in his home."

"We did, and it was determined to have come from the same batch that was injected into Mr. Quintana and Mrs. Watrous."

"Maybe he had someone else kill Mrs. Hawkins."

"For what purpose. What's his motive?"

Alberto scratched his forehead and muttered, "Dunno." Then

he said, "Maybe to deflect attention from himself."

"That's possible," Susan said. "But why would he kill Quintana and Watrous?"

"Same answer. To try to make it appear like there's a mass murderer running around Vista de Alameda who just happened to murder his father along with other residents."

Susan shook her head. "It just seems like too much of a stretch. Too diabolical. Barbara and I have already started second-guessing the decision to arrest Matthews."

"What about the nicotine in his house?"

"It could have been planted there."

"Talk about a stretch."

"I know. I know. But Matthews doesn't smoke, and he claims he has no idea how the bottle of liquid nicotine got in his place."

"What would you expect him to say?"

Susan laughed. "You're as cynical as I am." She turned onto Academy Boulevard and stopped at the first red light. While she waited for the light to turn green, she said, "But if Matthews is not the killer, then it has to be someone with ready access to the retirement home. That would increase our suspect list to hundreds of people."

"*Madre de Dios*," Alberto exclaimed.

Susan pulled into the Trombino's parking lot, found an open slot on the south side, and killed the engine. She stared ahead and watched the traffic on Academy.

"*Que paso*, Susan?" Alberto asked.

"I'm missing something."

"You know what my beautiful Carmela used to say, God rest her soul?"

"As I recall, my Aunt Carmela always had a lot to say."

Alberto chuckled. "Yes, Carmela did have an opinion about everything." He chuckled again. "Whenever I had a problem and couldn't come up with a solution, she would say, '*Mi corazon*, you need to drink some wine, eat a good meal, and get a good night's sleep. It will come to you in the morning.'"

Susan slapped the steering wheel. "That's pretty good advice, Uncle Alberto. Let's eat."

CHAPTER 25

Barbara and Henry sat together on the couch in her den and held hands while they watched an episode of *Outlander*.

"That love scene was pretty steamy," Henry said.

Barbara poked him with her elbow. "What's your point?"

"I was just making an observation."

"I detect an ulterior motive in that observation."

"Jeez, girl, can't a guy say something without you thinking he's got something else on his mind?"

She poked him again. "So, are you saying that you don't have something else on your mind?"

He kissed her cheek. "I didn't say that."

Barbara laughed, picked up the remote control, and paused the program. "Come on, big boy, let's find out what's really on your mind." She stood, pulled him by the hand, and led the way to her bedroom. Halfway there, her cell phone rang.

"Don't do this to me, Barb. Don't you dare."

"I'll just see who it is," she said.

She rushed to the kitchen where her phone was charging and checked the screen. When she saw Frederick Beringer's name, she answered the call.

"Detective, we've got another death by liquid nicotine."

"Violet Hawkins?"

"That's right. Someone injected her with a dose that would

have stopped the heart of a race horse. It took us a while to find the injection site. Mrs. Hawkins's hands and arms were covered with dark purple bruises, probably from bumping herself. Not uncommon for a woman her age. She'd had blood drawn recently, which left a nasty bruise on the inside of her left elbow. Someone injected her in the same spot where blood had been drawn. Between the needle mark and the large bruise, we had difficulty finding the site."

"I'll be damned," Barbara said.

"I don't mean to tell you how to do your job, but you'd better get on top of whatever's going on at that retirement home."

Barbara didn't feel a need to respond to Beringer's comment. It wasn't as though she hadn't already figured out that they were dealing with a huge problem that just got bigger. "Anything else, Doctor?"

"Oh yes. I heard back from my friend at the FBI. They were able to identify the manufacturer of the liquid nicotine: CTX Chemical Products, LLC. in Phoenix. The product DNA was a perfect match to CTX's Savory Scent product."

"Did they identify their New Mexico buyers?"

"CTX has thirty-eight hundred customers in New Mexico— three thousand in Albuquerque alone. Eight hundred Albuquerque customers have purchased their Savory Scent product. The FBI knew we had three deaths dating back six months, so they asked CTX for a list of customers who'd bought Savory Scent prior to April."

"Please tell me that lowered the number of customers to three or four."

"Sorry, Detective. They had over three hundred buyers of Savory Scent dating back six months or more."

"That's still a lot of people, but knowing their names, we could run the list against the names of the employees and residents of Vista de Alameda. Maybe we'd get a hit."

"There's a problem with that. CTX won't release the names. Not without a court order."

"Dammit."

After Barbara hung up, she looked around for Henry. She

finally found him in her bedroom, fully clothed, fast asleep. "Oh, Henry," she whispered. "You sweet, sweet man. How do you put up with me?"

She went back out to the den and called Susan. "Can you talk?" she asked when Susan answered.

"Sure. I just dropped off my uncle at Vista de Alameda."

"I heard from Beringer. Violet Hawkins died of cardiac arrest caused by an injection of liquid nicotine."

"Holy Mary," Susan said.

"Also, the FBI traced the liquid nicotine to a company in Arizona. The specific product is branded under the name Savory Scent, and at least three hundred customers in Albuquerque have done business with them for at least six months."

"That's a nice round number," Susan said.

"Yeah. But the company won't release the names of their clients without a court order."

"So, we now know that four residents of Vista de Alameda died from liquid nicotine injections, that the poison used on at least three of them came from the same company in Arizona, and that our suspect list could include over three hundred people."

"Hate to burst your enthusiasm bubble," Barbara said, "but the suspect list could be a lot bigger than that. Who's to say that the killer lives in Albuquerque?" She blew out a long breath through her mouth and added, "And what if the killer didn't buy the nicotine? What if he stole the liquid from a friend or relative?"

"Or she."

"What?"

"You said 'What if *he* stole the liquid.' "

"Right. But most serial killers are men."

"Yeah, but most killers who use poison are women."

"Are you suggesting we just concentrate on women?"

"No, I was just making the point that we can't assume anything."

Barbara said, "Unfortunately, that's about all we have at this point. Assumptions."

Dr. Francis Nixon finished the autopsy on Kathy Armstead; took slices of brain, liver, lung, and kidney tissue to the laboratory, and then collected a copy of the recording of his remarks. He locked it in his desk, planning to send it over to Essex Pharma & Health, Inc. as soon as the toxicology screen was complete. He looked at his watch: 9:50.

WEDNESDAY
OCTOBER 8

CHAPTER 26

"You know, you really don't have to be here today," Lisa French said. "My God, Stu, you just lost your wife. You need to take time for yourself."

Stuart Armstead's mind wandered as Lisa French droned on with platitudes and what, to him, seemed like insincere sympathy.

"Did you hear what I said?" she asked.

"Of course," he answered. He quickly changed the subject. "Tell me where we are with Violet Hawkins's bequest."

French briefed him about her conversation with Hawkins's attorney and about how all the documents were prepared and ready to be executed by Vista de Alameda.

Armstead slowly shook his head. "I was just thinking about how much pain Mrs. Hawkins must have been in. Her arthritis was horrible."

"The old woman's death was apparently from natural causes," French said.

"What else could it have been?" he asked.

He noticed French look down and to her left.

"Is there some reason to suspect that she didn't die of natural causes?"

"No, no. Of course not."

"So, Vista de Alameda winds up getting two million dollars without having to wait." He rolled his shoulders and stretched his back. "I gotta tell you, I was surprised we lost Mrs. Hawkins right after she and I met."

"She was quite old and in poor health. I'm just glad she decided to make a gift before she died." She smiled at him. "Her gift will make a big difference."

He tried to focus his gaze on Lisa, but her fawning, sycophantic tone and wet doe-like eyes made him want to wretch.

Be careful, he warned himself. *I need to ensure I keep her on my side until I no longer need her.*

As French continued to drone on about operational matters, Armstead remembered how charged with optimism he'd felt that morning after going over the business's financial statements for the year to date through September. He thought: *Between the future interest and dividend income off Hawkins's gift, and the turnover at higher entry fees and higher rents of so many units in the past year, Vista de Alameda is now profitable and should be even more so in the new year.* He'd completed an Excel spreadsheet that showed, with average annual unit turnover of five percent over the next five years, the property would be highly marketable. *Based on projected cash flow, the business now justifies a sale price of between twelve million and thirteen-and-a-half million dollars. The national retirement home chain owner/operator I contacted a couple years ago will now surely be interested in acquiring us.* He mentally tallied what he thought he'd be able to walk away with: *minimum four million in equity in the facility, four hundred thousand equity in his home, five hundred thousand from Kathy's life insurance policy, and three million from her trust fund.* He had a momentary pang of guilt. That trust fund had covered the operating losses at Vista de Alameda for the last four years. Kathy had never complained about using the money she'd inherited from a grandmother to help him keep the retirement home afloat. *Seven point nine million dollars total walking-away money. I'll be able to leave this one-horse town and put fucking Lisa French in my rearview mirror.*

"What was that, Stu?" French asked.

Armstead came out of his reverie and met her gaze. Suddenly flustered, he said, "What?"

"You said something."

160

He wagged his head and assumed a self-deprecating expression. "I don't know. I guess you're right. I shouldn't be here. It's too soon after . . . Kathy."

French stood, came around the desk, and took Armstead's hand. "Come on, Stu; I'll walk with you to the lobby."

He allowed her to lead him through his office to the hallway outside. He pulled his hand from hers, thanked her for her concern and friendship, and said, "I'm okay, Lisa." He gave her a soulful look. "I can't tell you how much I appreciate you."

She placed a hand on his arm and whispered, "Anything, Stu. All you have to do is ask."

"I know that, Lisa. I know I can depend on you." He paused and met her gaze. "It's been a tough few years. I appreciate you hanging in there."

"Things will get better. You'll see."

"I thought that everything was going in the right direction. Kathy getting on the experimental treatment; the business improving." He swallowed and looked away. When he looked back at her, he closed his eyes for a couple seconds. When he opened them again, he said, "What the hell is going on with those two female detectives. I mean, what was with them investigating Mr. Matthews's heart attack?"

"I don't have a clue. But I heard that Mr. Matthews's son, Scott, was arrested in connection with his father's death."

"How's that possible? That man was completely dedicated to his father. He was here several times a week to visit him."

French shrugged.

"God, I hope I don't have to worry about the police now."

She stepped closer and placed her hands on his arms. "I'm sure it's nothing. You'll see."

He half-hugged her quickly, turned, left the building, and went to his car. He started the Cadillac and pulled out of the parking lot. After he turned onto the Coors Bypass, he punched in the number for the owner of Congregate Care Retirement Solutions.

"Hey, Stuart; long time no talk," Clifford Grant answered.

"Cliff, you guys still interested in expanding to New Mexico?"

"Absolutely. But you know what kind of bottom line we're interested in."

"I understand. We've made big changes around here. When we roll a unit, we collect a higher upfront fee and we now have rent escalators in the new leases. Also, one of our former tenants just gifted two million dollars to our operating fund."

"How'd you turn things around so quickly?"

"It was a freakish two-year period. We usually have around ten units turn over due to deaths or severe health issues. We had forty-one units turn over in the past twenty-four months."

"Wow. That's twice the normal rate for the industry."

Armstead felt his heartbeat accelerate. *Will Cliff Grant think there's something wrong here?*

He swallowed hard, cleared his throat, and said, "It was a shock to all of us here. We lost people we really cared about. But you'll probably recall that the average age of our residents is five years older than the industry average. I suspect that's why we lost so many of them. The good news is, from a business standpoint, the New Mexico market is underserved. Our residents don't just come from Albuquerque. They come from all over the state."

"I remember," Grant said. "Maybe I should send my acquisitions people down there to do another assessment. What's the rest of your week look like?"

"It's pretty clear."

"Okay. We'll call you back this afternoon to set a date. In the meantime, email me the financials for the last two years and the proformas for the next five."

"Sounds good."

"By the way, how's your wife doing? Last I heard, she was pretty sick."

"She passed away, Cliff."

"Oh, I'm so sorry, Stu."

"At least she's not suffering any longer."

After he hung up, Armstead wondered if he should have mentioned that Kathy had died less than twenty-four hours ago and that her burial was planned for this coming Saturday. *He'd think I was a cold-hearted bastard for calling him less than a day after my wife died.*

After Armstead left the building, Lisa French returned to her office. She felt faint as her heart beat a frenetic riff. She'd tried to calm Stuart by downplaying the detectives coming to the complex. But she knew it was *not* nothing. Despite what Detective Martinez had told her when she picked up her uncle the previous evening, French had a very bad feeling. The police wouldn't have visited Vista de Alameda if they didn't have strong suspicions about something. She mentally backtracked to the first time she'd administered liquid nicotine—eighteen months ago. The Slovinski woman had been eighty-seven years old, had survived one heart attack, and was going downhill fast. The woman had been in pain and would probably not have survived another year. She'd rationalized at the time that she was on a mission of mercy. There had been six more residents that she'd *helped* over the following few months. Like Mrs. Slovinski, they were all on their last legs, so to speak. But, since then, her "mercy missions" became something else altogether. Seth Franks had been healthy.

She'd picked Franks because of opportunity. He was the chairman of the residents' advisory committee and had asked to meet with her. They'd met in her office. As they were close to wrapping up the meeting, she'd refilled his iced tea and dosed it with four sleeping pills she'd crushed earlier. As he began to yawn and get dreamy-eyed, she terminated the meeting and suggested he return to his unit. He'd gladly agreed. Five minutes later, she'd taken the fire stairs to the third floor, used her master key to enter his unit, found him asleep in a recliner, and injected the nicotine behind his right ear. Franks had been a robust eighty-year-old. Probably had at least another decade in him. It was his death that, French knew, changed her from an angel of mercy to a killer.

She shuddered at the memory but stiffened her spine and sucked in a big breath as she thought, *there's nothing I won't do for Stuart.*

French mentally scrolled through the deaths she had caused (not including Kathy Armstead) and realized it was John Matthews's death that had changed things. She hadn't known at the time that he'd donated his body to the medical school. She clenched her hands into fists and slammed them on the top of her desk. "That nosey bastard, Alberto Martinez. He and his damn niece."

I should take care of old man Martinez, she thought. But she knew that would be stupid now that the sheriff's office was investigating Matthews's death.

She stood, paced, and tried to think of all the angles. Her heart rate had slowed a bit, but she found it difficult to think clearly.

"Calm down," she whispered. "Think."

She returned to her desk and took a legal pad from a desk drawer. After she jotted down the names of the residents she'd injected, she thought about each one.

I met with all the victims in their apartments at widely disparate times, from early in the morning to late at night. There was never anyone in the hallway when I entered or left an apartment. There are no cameras in the hallways to the residential units.

"No witnesses," she said.

She then thought about ways the police could track down the cause of the deaths. She suspected that forensic analysis could identify the chemical signature of the nicotine and then trace that signature to the manufacturer, but there could be tens of thousands of people who had bought from the same lot.

"I'm in the clear," she muttered.

But then her heart rate accelerated again as she thought about the reputational damage that would be done to the facility if it came out that residents had been murdered. She forced herself to breathe steadily, slowly. She thought about the research she'd done on nicotine poisoning. How the substance could be detected in a body for several months after death and that it broke down quickly thereafter. So, at most, maybe four deaths could be attributed to poisoning. *News about four murders would be bad enough; twenty-one would be a P.R. disaster. I need to get control.*

She thought about every person she'd injected and felt good about her conclusions when it came to each one, until she stopped at Kathy Armstead. "That's the only one where the police can place me at the scene," she muttered. She moaned. *What the hell can I do?*

After a long minute of musing, she announced, "Frankie'll fix this for me."

Frank Calderon had always worried about his sister. Lisa had made a series of bad decisions since she was a teenager. Two failed marriages, a bankruptcy caused by her compulsive shopping and a gambling addiction, and an affair with a married man that led to her being fired from a job at a local insurance company. She'd been cursed with good looks and bad judgment and thought she could skate her way through life. He sipped from his beer and wondered what the hell she wanted from him now.

He stared out the front window of Emilio's Café and watched his sister slip from her Mercedes. *Another extravagance she couldn't afford if it wasn't for the money I give her every month*, he thought.

When she entered Emilio's and walked to his back corner table, Calderon stood and hugged her. "*Quieres cerveza?*" he asked.

As usual, she frowned and answered him in English. "No thanks. I have to go back to work."

Calderon compressed his lips and shook his head. His sister wanted nothing to do with her Hispanic heritage. She refused to speak Spanish; didn't even like to drink Mexican beer.

"What's going on?"

"That thing you did for me before . . . ." She made a little sound that was like a whimper, then continued, "You know, when you had that . . . thing placed in that guy's house."

Calderon nodded. "What about it?"

"I need you to have someone do it again."

He scrunched up his face as though he'd sucked a lemon. "What the hell's going on, Lisa?"

He saw her expression change. Her eyes flashed anger. "I need your help, Frankie. It's better if I don't explain."

"That's not gonna work this time. I gotta know what's up."

Tears leaked from her eyes. "Can't you do one little thing for me without getting an explanation?"

Calderon leaned in and whispered, "Listen to me, Lisa. This ain't like helping you pay off credit cards or threatening to kick your ex's ass when he gets behind on his alimony. I already had a guy do a B&E for you. Now, you want me to arrange another one. I wanna know what's going on."

She looked around and caught the stare of a woman two tables over. She turned back to her brother. "Not here. Let's go out to your car."

CHAPTER 27

"What the hell were you thinking?"

Lisa French, seated at the opposite end of the bench seat in the back of her brother's car, tried to speak but all that came out was a hoarse croak.

Frank Calderon looked out through the windshield of his Lincoln Navigator and watched his driver wander around the parking lot, cigarette in one hand, cell phone in the other. He thought about all the excuses their parents had made for Lisa from the time she started to walk. She was their father's favorite, their mother's *princesa*. He shuddered as he thought of all the times he'd bailed her out of trouble. *But murder is a whole other thing.*

French finally got her voice. "I wanted to help Stuart. He's such a good man. The place was going under."

"The last I heard, your boss was married. Have you been sleeping with him?"

Her eyes went hard as they bored into Frank's. "Of course not. I was just trying to help a good man. And, for your information, Stuart's wife just died."

Calderon's jaw dropped. "When?"

She shrugged as though the woman's date of death was inconsequential. "What difference does that make?"

He was about to ask her if she'd been responsible for Stuart Armstead's wife's death, but decided he didn't want to know. "What do you want from me?"

"I got the nicotine from the locker of a former employee at the retirement home. The guy left it when he was fired. We can put the police on his trail. Frame him for the murders."

"You want an innocent man to go to jail for murder?"

"The guy's a low life. I mean, he can't even hold down a maintenance job. We can put the blame on him as a disgruntled former employee who kept a set of keys when he was terminated, who smoked e-cigarettes, and who bought liquid nicotine that he used to poison Vista de Alameda residents."

Her tears now gone, her anger rising, Frank recognized the metamorphosis taking place in his sister. He'd seen this performance several times before. First came the "little girl" pleading, then tears, then anger, then the rationalization that what she was doing was righteous, then the dumping of guilt onto him. *If you really love me, you'll do whatever is necessary to help me.*

Her eyes narrowed and her lips formed a cruel slash. "If you love me, you'll—"

Calderon reached out and grabbed his sister's arm, squeezing until she squealed. "Don't you fuckin' go there. You've played that game on me too many times."

She snatched her arm away and pressed back against the corner of the seat. Then tears flowed again as sobs wracked her body.

"Aw-w-w," Calderon moaned. "What a mess! Give me the guy's name. You still have some of the nicotine he left in his locker?"

Before he'd even finished the question, she'd opened her purse and taken out a plastic bag. Inside it, Calderon noticed a glass vial, several syringes, and a slip of paper. *She knew I'd help her*, he thought. Out of nowhere, a word came into his mind: *Psychopath.* Then a thought: *My sister's a fucking psycho.*

Barbara and Susan were working two other cases in addition to the John Matthews murder. They knew they'd given short shrift to those cases since getting involved with the Matthews's murder. They'd basically ignored them once they'd discovered that Vista de Alameda was a killing ground. They'd discussed talking to Lt. Salas about reassigning them, but knew their fellow detectives were already overwhelmed.

"Let's spend a few hours working the Carruthers murder," Barbara suggested.

"Good idea," Susan said. "Before Salas starts ripping us for ignoring it." After a quick breath, Susan added, "Besides, we know who killed Samantha Carruthers."

"We do?"

"Sure. It was the butler, with the knife, in the master bedroom."

"Does the fact that the Carruthers didn't have a butler and that Mrs. Carruthers was murdered by a blow to the head change your thinking?"

Susan rolled her head around as though her neck was stiff. "Well, she was killed in the master bedroom. One out of three ain't bad."

"All kidding aside," Barbara said, "I think we should interview the husband again. He seemed evasive when we talked to him at the scene."

Susan frowned. "You know it's not always the spouse. Besides, Carruthers had just found his wife's body. He was bound to be distraught."

"I said he was evasive, not distraught."

"Yeah, I got that." Susan wandered around the homicide division's bullpen area, doing a circuit of the desks.

Barbara watched the effect she had on the two male detectives seated at their stations. The men followed her with their eyes as she wandered the room. The *clack-clack-clack* of her heels only seemed to make them focus more on her. By the time Susan returned to her desk, one of the detectives had wiped his forehead with a tissue and the other appeared to have hung up on a call in mid-sentence.

"Besides getting the boys all hot and bothered, did your little saunter through the department do any good?" Barbara asked.

"I just remembered something. When we responded to the 9-1-1 call and went to the Carruthers's residence, I went through the woman's purse. You know, looking for an address book, cell phone, business cards. Anything that might give us names of people she knew."

"If I recall correctly, you didn't find any of those things. Also, there was no wallet."

"Don't you find that strange?" Susan said.

"Yeah, now that you mention it. I don't have a problem with you not finding an address book or business cards, but no cell phone or wallet is very strange. Who doesn't have a cell phone and wallet?"

"No one," Susan said. "And with a cell phone, you don't need an address book and you don't need to keep business cards. You just upload that stuff into your phone."

"Right."

"There was something else in her purse that I didn't really think about at the time. Condoms."

"Huh," Barbara said. "Why does a fifty-year-old married woman need condoms? She's not about to get pregnant."

"Disease prevention," Susan offered.

"You think Spence Carruthers has an STD?"

"No. If he did, the condoms would probably be at home in a bedside table."

"Ah, the plot thickens," Susan said. "The deceased was playing hanky-panky."

"It's a possibility."

Barbara said, "It could also be a motive for murder. Spence Carruthers discovers his wife is cheating on him and . . . . You know he could have tossed out the phone and wallet to make it look like someone killed his wife and then took her stuff."

"Let's go talk with him."

Barbara looked at the wall clock. "If we get that done, we can stop by Vista de Alameda and talk to Stuart Armstead. Our conversation was curtailed when he got the call about his wife's death."

No one other than Frank Calderon knew Churro's real name. But the savvier of Calderon's men knew how the man had gotten his nickname. There was a Spanish Matador named Francisco Romero Lopez, known as Churro Romero, who was so successful that he was invariably awarded the ears of the bull at the end of his fights. Calderon's Churro always took the ears of his victims. He was Calderon's "go-to" guy. He assigned him jobs that involved risk and required someone who was tight-lipped. Churro always performed and never questioned anything that Calderon told him to do. Including hits. But as Churro drove past Oscar Vigil's place in Albuquerque's South Valley, he couldn't help but wonder about this assignment.

Oscar Vigil's place was a dump. The little porch on the front of the dilapidated shack slanted to the right and half the windows on either side of the front door were cracked or missing. The missing panes had been replaced with pieces of cardboard. A twenty-year-old pickup truck with one wheel missing was propped up on a jack on the left side of the shack in a pot-holed, dirt driveway. Thorny, orange berry-laden pyracantha bushes grew between the driveway and an adobe house on the north, as well as on the south side of the property, separating Vigil's place from his neighbor. *Good,* Churro thought. *The bushes will provide cover.*

He pulled into a Mexican bodega lot half-a-block away on Bridge Street, parked, walked back to Vigil's shack, moved swiftly down the driveway, and peeked in windows. The rooms on the north side were surprisingly neat, but unoccupied. He skirted the back end of the property and saw no one in the kitchen there. On the south side of the house, he spotted a man lying spread-eagle face-down on a bed.

Piece of cake, Churro thought.

Satisfied that there was only one person home, he jimmied the back door lock, padded through the kitchen, down the hallway to the first bedroom, and looked into the space. The man on the bed snored like a bull moose in rut. Churro took a syringe from his coat pocket, removed the protective cover and placed it in the same pocket, and cleared the syringe of air. He walked into the bedroom, pressed the man's head into the pillow, and injected *Trazodone* into the side of his neck, knocking him out and wiping out any memory of what had happened. After replacing the protective cover on the needle and putting it into his pocket, he removed from another pocket a Ziploc bag that Calderon had given him. The bag held a six ounce bottle of liquid nicotine and three unused syringes. He took the items from the bag, pressed Vigil's fingers against each of them, returned them to the bag, and resealed it. Then he walked to the bathroom and placed the plastic bag in a back corner of the cabinet under the sink. He retraced his steps, not worrying about noise as he exited through the back door, and calmly strolled back to the bodega parking lot. He had stripped off the rubber gloves he'd worn and discarded them in a dumpster, along with the syringe he'd used to inject Vigil. As he drove back to Calderon's office to report in, he felt a spasm of regret. He'd been amazed at the size of Oscar Vigil's ears. They would have been wonderful additions to his collection.

CHAPTER 28

The Carruthers residence was on a one-acre lot in North Albuquerque Acres, an upscale neighborhood bordered on the south by Tanoan Country Club and on the north by the Sandia Pueblo. Paseo del Norte, a speedway for east- and west-bound traffic bisected the area. Barbara took Paseo del Norte east to Eubank Boulevard, turned south, then turned left just past the Mormon Temple. She drove past large homes on one-acre lots until she came to the Carruthers address.

Susan pointed at the house. "Looks like Spence Carruthers is taking advantage of the unseasonably warm weather."

Barbara looked left and spied Carruthers watering a tree that looked as though it had just been planted. The man apparently spotted them. He dropped the hose, walked over to a wall faucet and shut off the water, and then came out to the front gate. He just stared at them as they got out of the unmarked and moved toward him.

"Would you mind talking with us for a few minutes?" Barbara asked.

Carruthers shrugged, opened the gate, did a one-eighty, and walked toward the front door.

Barbara gave Susan a wide-eyed look, spread her arms, and whispered, "After you."

Inside the house, Carruthers pointed at a couch, told them to sit down, then dropped into a chair across from them.

"Everything all right, Mr. Carruthers?" Barbara asked.

His forehead wrinkled and his eyes narrowed. "What do you think?" he said.

"Sorry. This must be awfully difficult for you."

He gave her a disdainful look. "Have you ever lost a spouse, Detective?" He asked the question as though he didn't think that someone as young as Barbara could have suffered loss.

"Actually, Mr. Carruthers, both my partner and I have. My husband died from cancer several years ago."

The look on the man's face suddenly changed. His eyes closed and he breathed out a large breath. "I'm sorry," he said.

Barbara waited for him to open his eyes. When he did, she said, "We have a few questions to ask you. Are you up to it?"

He waved a hand as though to dismiss the notion that he couldn't answer their questions. "Of course," he said. "Ask away."

"When we were here the day you found your wife's body, we looked around your home for evidence of who might have attacked her. We found neither a wallet nor a cell phone. We assume your wife had both."

He looked confused for a moment, then said, "That's strange. She always had her wallet and phone with her." He expelled a short, little laugh that sounded more like a cough and added, "She must have spent ten hours a day on that damned phone."

"You have any idea where her wallet and phone might be?"

He frowned and licked his lips. After a few seconds, he said, "Other than the killer stealing them, the only other thing I can think of is that she might have switched purses and hadn't finished transferring everything to the new purse when the killer came into the house."

Barbara said, "Could we look at her other purses? It would be good to eliminate other reasons for those things going missing."

"Absolutely," he said as he stood. "Why don't you come with me?"

Carruthers led them up the stairs to the second-floor bedroom where his wife had been murdered. Barbara noticed he walked along the wall to avoid the blood-stained spot where he'd discovered his wife's body. "I assume it's okay to get the carpet replaced," he said.

"No reason not to," Susan said.

Inside a walk-in closet that had obviously been his wife's alone, they passed ten yards of a seven-layered shoe rack on the left and two levels of clothes on the right. Carruthers pointed at a four-shelved back wall crammed with boxes. Hidden lights illuminated each shelf. The designer names on the boxes included Hermes, Dior, Louis Vuitton, among others.

"Those are her handbags," Carruthers said.

Susan exhaled a breath that came out like a half-whistle. She quickly apologized.

Carruthers smiled at her. "That's okay, Detective. When I found out what those damned things cost, I whistled too." After a few seconds, during which he glanced around, he said, "I don't think my theory holds water. There are no bags sitting out. Before she put a bag in a box, she emptied it entirely." He spread his arms. "You're welcome to look through the boxes, of course."

Barbara looked at Susan, who shook her head.

"I don't think that will be necessary, Mr. Carruthers."

"Okay," he said. He walked out of the closet and moved back to the staircase. About to take a step down, he suddenly turned and said, "I'd better call the banks and cancel the credit cards."

Susan nodded. "That would be a good idea."

"The phone, too," he said.

"Maybe you could hold off doing that for a couple days, sir."

"Why?"

"Because we might be able to track the signal. It would be helpful if you called the phone company and gave them permission to share data with us."

He nodded. "I'll do that."

Back downstairs, he asked, "Did you have any other questions?"

"Just a couple," Barbara said. "What was your relationship like with Mrs. Carruthers?"

He visibly swallowed and his face reddened. "Complicated," he said.

"How so?"

He gulped and sat down on the couch. "Samantha was my second wife. We met on a cruise a few years after my first wife died.

She was vivacious, funny, and beautiful." A sad, dark expression briefly crossed his face as though a cloud had passed in front of him. When he continued, he seemed to have aged ten years. "I never fooled myself that it was true love. At least it wasn't on her part. But I was knocked senseless the first time I saw her. She was fifteen years younger than me. But I didn't care. The thought of having someone like her in my life outweighed the negatives."

"Negatives?" Susan asked.

He breathed loudly. "She spent my money like there was no tomorrow, and she had an eye for younger men. Much younger men."

"How did that make you feel?" Barbara asked.

Carruthers looked at her as though he couldn't believe she'd asked such a thing. Finally, he said, "Sad. It made me feel sad."

"That must have been awful," Susan said.

"Yes, Detective, it *was* awful. But not awful enough to murder her."

CHAPTER 29

"The human condition can suck," Susan said.

"You talking about Samantha Carruthers's cheating?"

"That, too. Infidelity is bad enough, but getting killed because of it is even worse."

"We don't know that's what got Mrs. Carruthers killed," Barbara said.

"No, we don't. But I'm placing two to one odds on that possibility."

Barbara said, "Carruthers had a weekly Thursday golf game at the Tanoan Country Club. He thinks his wife was sleeping with her Pilates instructor when he was out on the golf course. His wife scheduled her exercise classes on the same day."

"Why don't you call Severino Torres, the Pilates guy, and see if he can meet with us now?"

"Thought we were going to Vista de Alameda?"

Susan took a moment to respond. "Find out where Torres is located. Maybe he's on the way to the retirement home."

Severino Torres had a Pilates/Yoga studio in a storefront on Osuna Boulevard, three blocks west of Interstate 25. The receptionist there told Susan that he was in a class, but would be available to speak with her at 1:00 p.m. Barbara took Eubank south to Academy, west to San Mateo, and then turned back north to Osuna. She stopped at Wecks Restaurant where they ordered salads and Diet Cokes. At ten minutes to one, they returned to the Crown Vic and drove west on Osuna to the studio.

Inside the storefront, Susan badged the receptionist. "We're here to see Mr. Torres."

The young woman looked off to her left at an open door and said, "They're just about finished."

Susan, followed by Barbara, walked to the doorway and looked into a wood-floored studio where fifteen or so sweat-glistened women in yoga outfits lay on mats, their eyes closed, deep breathing, apparently decompressing from their workout. A soundtrack played what sounded like whale noises. Susan nudged Barbara with her elbow and pointed to the far side of the room at a fortyish-looking man with jet-black hair tied into a twelve-inch ponytail. The guy was tan and ripped and lay on his back on a mat. Susan shook a hand to indicate that the guy was "hot."

"Try to control yourself," Barbara whispered.

A minute passed before the man stood and the students followed suit. They quietly rolled up their mats and had whispered conversations with the male instructor, who moved among them handing out words of praise and encouragement, along with light touches on arms, shoulders, and backs.

Barbara closely watched the man as he meandered through the women, reminding her of a serpent casually slithering through a jungle hunting for prey. As the students dispersed and moved toward the door where Barbara and Susan waited, one of them hung back, then attached herself to the man, one hand resting on his bulging bicep, her hip touching the side of his thigh. The woman was small, almost tiny, and had a card or piece of paper in her free hand. She appeared to be about to press it into the man's hand when she glanced at Barbara. Her face reddened and she quickly disengaged from the man. In too loud a voice, she said, "Thanks. It was a great class." Then she quickly moved to a mat, rolled it up, and slipped sideways past Barbara and Susan.

"Severino Torres?" Barbara said as she entered the workout room.

The man wore a skin-tight muscle shirt and a pair of yoga pants that left nothing to the imagination. His tan looked as though it was machine-generated. *If he has five percent body fat, I'd be shocked,* Barbara thought.

He slowly eyed Barbara, then Susan, doing a full-body scan of each of them. He smiled as though he liked what he saw. "Interested in signing up for classes?" he asked.

Susan, who still had her cred pack in hand, flashed her ID. "We're here to ask you some questions."

Torres's smile disappeared and his posture stiffened. "What about?"

"You had a student named Samantha Carruthers," Susan said.

"That's right." He showed a momentary grimace, but it was quickly replaced with a belligerent frown. "It was terrible what happened to her."

Barbara had dealt with innumerable macho men before and had long ago learned that there were two ways to handle them. One, you could play the shrinking violet and appeal to their inner machismo; or, two, you could come on strong and antagonize them. She opted for window number two.

"We want you to come down to our offices and make a formal statement."

The guy looked confused. "I don't understand. A statement about what?"

"About your affair with Mrs. Carruthers." Barbara waited, then added, "About how your relationship with Samantha Carruthers might have led to her murder."

The guy babbled for a couple seconds. Before he could respond coherently, Susan said, "We'd like you to take a lie detector test."

It took him a while to regain his composure. When he did, he said, "I think I'd better call my lawyer."

"Probably a wise thing to do if you have something to hide," Susan said. "But if you do that, I would be surprised if the news media doesn't pick up on you being questioned." She shook her head as though to say, 'What a shame.' "The next thing you know your customers will be reading about you being involved with Mrs. Carruthers's death. We won't be able to control what people will think."

Torres's face paled, despite his deep tan. He slumped a bit, then said, "Let's go to my office."

"You change your mind about calling your attorney?" Susan asked.

"Yeah. For now, anyway."

When they were all seated in Torres's office—the man behind a small desk; Barbara and Susan in armless, metal chairs across from him—he asked, "Are you going to read me my rights?"

"You're not under arrest, Mr. Torres," Barbara said. "Are you telling us you want us to recite your rights?"

He waved his arms around. "No . . . no, I was just wondering."

"How about you tell us about your relationship with Samantha Carruthers?" Susan said.

After breathing out a loud sigh, he said, "You gotta understand about women. They—" He made eye contact with Barbara, then Susan, and appeared to realize he was about to go down the wrong path. "I mean, there are a lot of lonely women out there." He swallowed and didn't seem to know what to say next.

"So, you help some of those women be a little less lonely," Barbara offered.

He spread his hands and nodded. "Yeah, something like that."

"Was Samantha Carruthers one of those *lonely* women?" Susan asked.

A lascivious smile quickly came and went. "She was lonelier than most."

"Lonely or horny?" Susan said.

Torres narrowed his eyes as he looked at Susan and nodded. "Okay, she was more horny than lonely."

"When was the last time you saw her?" Barbara asked.

He paled again. He looked down at his desktop. "The day she died. She came to my place that morning. It was a Thursday. That's when we always met. About nine o'clock. We always got together on Thursdays. Her husband has a regular golf game and my first class doesn't start until eleven." He did the hand waving thing again and, in a louder voice, said, "She left my house at half-past ten. We each drove to my studio for the eleven o'clock class."

"You keep a record of who attends your classes?" Susan asked.

"Of course. Jannie, my receptionist, checks in each person. That's how we know who owes what." He suddenly brightened. "Sam always paid with a credit card. I'm sure we have a record of her paying that day."

Barbara knew that Samantha Carruthers was murdered at 2:15 p.m. A small decorative clock had been broken in the struggle between the victim and her attacker. That's the time the clock showed. The coroner had determined time of death at around that same time. And she remembered that Mr. Carruthers had found his wife's body when he returned home at three o'clock from the golf course.

"Where did you go after your eleven o'clock class ended?" Barbara asked.

"I stayed right here," Torres said. "I have back-to-back classes on Thursdays from eleven through four. I have an hour break until 5:00, then I have two hour-long classes." He shuffled some papers on his desk and picked up a printed schedule. He passed the sheet of paper over to Barbara, who studied it.

"It's the same every week?" she said.

"Pretty much."

Barbara noticed notations on the schedule on Monday and Wednesday from 8:00 a.m. to 9:00 a.m.: CM on Monday and VA on Wednesday. More out of curiosity than searching for clues, she asked, "What do the initials mean on Monday and Wednesday? CM and VA?"

Torres showed an anemic smile. "I'm paid to give weekly classes at two retirement facilities in town. CM is Colonial Manor and VA—"

"Vista de Alameda," Barbara interrupted.

"Right. How'd you know?"

Barbara waggled a hand in answer and stood.

"Jannie can confirm this schedule?" Susan asked.

"Absolutely."

Barbara sidestepped to the office door, opened it, and said, "Don't make plans to leave Albuquerque, Mr. Torres."

The man visibly swallowed and nodded.

Susan followed Barbara to the doorway but stopped, turned,

and glared at Torres. Relief at their departure seemed to etch every part of his face. "Your relationship with Mrs. Carruthers was purely physical," she said.

He dropped his gaze to his hands which were clenched on his desk top. After a second, he looked back at Susan. "I told you she was a lonely woman. I filled a void in her life. That's all."

"You're a real humanitarian, Torres."

The guy's eyes blazed with indignation, but he had the sense to keep his mouth shut.

Then Susan asked, "What did you do with Mrs. Carruthers's wallet and phone?"

Torres's jaw dropped. "How'd you know?"

"Answer my fuckin' question."

He made a frustrated sound, somewhere between a groan and a loud hum. "Her purse must have fallen off the side of my bed when we were . . . . I found it later that evening by the side of the bed. Her wallet and phone were in it. By that time I'd heard she'd been killed. I threw away the purse in a dumpster." He breathed in deeply, his muscular chest threatening to split his shirt. "I didn't want her things found in my place."

Susan glared hard at the man. "Like I said, Torres, you're a real humanitarian."

CHAPTER 30

After confirming with Jannie the receptionist what Torres had told them about his schedule, Barbara and Susan went back to the unmarked sedan and drove west.

"I could use a shower," Susan said. "That guy made me feel grimy."

"Real sleaze bag," Barbara agreed. "I wonder how many other of his students he's helping to *fill a void.*"

"Nice coincidence that Torres gives classes at Vista de Alameda."

"I know you don't believe in coincidences, so what do you really think?"

Susan made a *tsk-tsk-tsk* noise as she took a moment to think. Then she said, "I got a shiver down my back when you read 'VA' from his class schedule. I knew in my gut he was going to say Vista de Alameda. What are the odds?"

Barbara shot a glance at Susan. "It has to be coincidence. What else could it be?"

"I'm getting a headache, partner."

"How did you know about the wallet and phone?"

Susan shook her head. "I didn't. It was just a guess."

"Nice guess," Barbara said. Then she chuckled. "Some dumpster diver is probably walking around Albuquerque with a two thousand dollar designer bag."

On the drive from Torres's studio to Vista de Alameda, Susan called and asked to speak to Stuart Armstead. The receptionist informed her that Armstead wasn't in and that Lisa French was taking his calls. She was put through to French.

"We're on our way to your location, Ms. French. We'd like to ask you a few questions."

"Of course," French said. "I'll be here all afternoon."

"We should be there in twenty minutes," Susan told her.

After she hung up, Susan grunted a "huh."

"What?" Barbara asked.

"She actually seemed happy to hear from me."

"It's your winning personality."

Barbara parked the Crown Vic in a visitor's slot near the front entrance. On the way to the lobby, she suggested to Susan, "Since you're Lisa French's new best friend, I think you should take the lead."

Susan showed her a thumbs-up sign and moved to the reception desk. Before she could give the woman their names, Lisa French came out of her office and greeted them.

"Good afternoon, Detectives. It's good to see you again." She pointed toward the interior hallway. "Why don't we meet in the dining room. The lunch hour is over and it should be quiet." She smiled and added, "We can get something to drink there." French then turned to Agnes at the front desk and said, "We can dispense with signing in the detectives."

The elderly woman's expression changed from welcoming to almost fearful. "But that's against the rules."

French ignored her and led the way to the dining hall. On the way, Susan scrunched up her face and crossed her eyes at Barbara, as though to send the message: what's with the sweetness and light routine?

Barbara shrugged.

French pointed at a table near the center of the spacious room. "Please sit down. I'll get us iced teas."

Seated in the dining room, Susan and Barbara watched French fill three glasses from a tea dispenser, place the glasses on a tray, and return to the table. She put the tray on the table. "Help yourselves," she said. When neither Susan nor Barbara took a glass, French passed glasses to each of them, took one for herself, moved the tray to a nearby unoccupied table, and sat down.

"You have questions you want to ask me?" French said.

"That's right, Ms. French," Susan said.

"Oh, please call me Lisa."

The tendons in Susan's cheeks twitched. She paused a beat, then smiled. "Thank you, Lisa. We won't take much of your time. We were wondering if you have any thoughts about how John Matthews could have ingested liquid nicotine."

"Liquid nicotine? I didn't know there was such a thing." French's brows knit and her eyes narrowed. Then she said, "Is that somehow relevant to his death?"

"You've never heard of liquid nicotine?"

"That's right."

"Then you don't know that liquid nicotine is used in e-cigarettes."

She shrugged. "I don't smoke and Vista de Alameda is a smoke-free facility."

"I see," Susan said. "Can I conclude that you're not aware of anyone here—resident or employee—who smokes e-cigarettes?"

French rapidly shook her head. "No, I can't think of . . . ." Then she stopped. Her mouth made a large "O." She looked from Susan to Barbara, then back at Susan. "There was a man who used to work here who I recall smoking e-cigarettes." She spread her arms and frowned. "But what does any of this have to do with Mr. Matthews's death? I thought he went into cardiac arrest."

Susan glanced at Barbara and received a nod in response.

"Mr. Matthews did have a heart attack. But we now know that it was caused by his being injected with liquid nicotine. Someone drugged him with a sleep-inducing medicine and then injected him."

"But why would anyone do such a thing?" French asked.

"*That* is the question, isn't it, Lisa. You were about to say something about a former employee."

She slowly shook her head as though she was incredulous. "Yes, there was a maintenance man here named Oscar Vigil. We terminated him about two years ago for poor performance and absenteeism."

"Two years ago?" Barbara said.

"That's right. He made an awful scene. Made all sorts of threats." She closed her eyes and made a small humming sound, as though she was recalling events from the past. "He told me that I would be very sorry for firing him."

"And he was an e-cigarette user?"

"That's what I remember."

"But if he left here two years ago, it's unlikely he could have murdered Mr. Matthews," Susan said.

"Well, that's true," French said. Then her eyes went wide and she said, "You know, Mr. Vigil never returned his keys when he was fired. He had keys to every room in the building."

Susan looked at Barbara and arched her eyebrows.

"Do you have an address for Mr. Vigil?" Barbara asked French.

"Of course."

"What else can you tell us about Oscar Vigil?" Barbara asked.

French raised a finger as though she'd just recalled something else. "When I called him about returning the keys, he cursed me in the vilest language you can imagine and hung up on me."

"So, you never got the keys?" Susan said.

"Nope."

"I assume you changed the locks."

French's eyes widened. "To every door in the complex? That would have cost a fortune."

"So Vigil still has keys to every room in the building, including all the residents' apartments?"

"That's correct." Her complexion turned rosy and her mouth made an "O" again. Then she said, "Oh, my God, he could have snuck in here and . . . ."

CHAPTER 31

"Hello, Stu. It's Cliff."

"Oh, hey, Cliff. Did you get the financial information I sent you?"

"I got it. Thanks. Your projections look really good. Depending on the condition of the property, I think we ought to be able to put an offer together."

Armstead let out a silent breath of relief. "That's good to hear, Cliff. When would you like to do an on-site inspection?"

"I'm thinking this Saturday. Will that work for you?"

Armstead thought about Kathy's funeral service and burial on Saturday. Then the open house at his place afterward. "It will have to be in the late afternoon, if that's okay."

"Perfect," Clifford Grant said. "Our flight won't arrive until 2:00 p.m. Can you pick us up at the airport?"

It's going to be tight, Armstead thought. *I'll have to leave while the open house is still going on. I'll just have Lisa handle things.* "Sure, Cliff. Send me your flight information. I'll meet you in baggage claim."

Barbara dialed Elinore Freed's office number, hoping the Assistant D.A. was still in her office. When Freed answered, Barbara said, "Thank goodness you're still there."

"Where else would I be?" Freed said.

"Sounds like you need to get a life, Elinore."

"There's the understatement of the year. What can I do for you?"

"It's about the poisonings at Vista de Alameda. We have a lead on a possible suspect. I want to be armed with a search warrant when we confront him."

"How good a suspect is *this* guy?" She went silent for a couple seconds, then said, "We've already been through this with Scott Matthews."

"I know, Elinore. Matthews looked good for the murder of his father."

"He still does. But now you're telling me there might be another perp?"

"Yeah. A former employee of the retirement center, fired for cause, threatened the owner and his staff, and was an e-cigarette user."

"That's it?"

Barbara chuckled. "Not quite. He walked off with a set of keys to every door in the complex. He had access to the complex and to every residential unit."

"Sonofa—"

"Yeah."

"It's late. I'll have to call a judge at home. Give me a couple hours."

Oscar Vigil's mouth was so dry that his tongue stuck to the roof of his mouth. He felt groggy, disoriented, and listless. He turned his head to the left and tried to focus on the clock on the bedside table. He blinked several times before he could make out the clock face. His heart leaped when he realized it was already past 8:00 p.m. *I set the alarm to go off at 7:00. What the hell happened?*

"Sonofabitch," he barked. "I'm late for work."

He felt panicked. He couldn't afford to lose his job with the janitorial company. After stripping off his underwear, he washed his face, ran a brush through his thinning gray-streaked black hair, and put on clean clothes. All the while, he tried to recall something that picked at the edges of his brain. But it wouldn't come.

House keys, wallet, cell phone, loose change and bills, and an e-cigarette in a fanny pack, his JCJ Janitorial cap in place, he rushed to the front door just as someone knocked.

"What the fuck," he muttered, as he opened the door.

"Oscar Vigil?" asked a woman who pointed a badge at him.

Vigil was stunned for a moment. "Ye-yeah," he answered as he stared wide-eyed at the group of four people outside his door. Two women in suits; two uniformed deputies. A cruiser with flashing lights was parked out front. Another vehicle sat behind the cruiser. He turned his gaze back to the woman. "What do you want?"

"My name is Susan Martinez. This is my partner, Barbara Lassiter. We're detectives with the Bernalillo County Sheriff's Office. We have a warrant to search the premises."

"Search for what?" he asked.

"We'll let you know when we find it," the woman said as she pushed past him.

"I'm already late for work. I've got to call my boss."

One of the uniformed deputies took his arm and guided him to a chair in the small living room. "Sit down and don't move," the deputy said.

Vigil watched the other deputy and the two women disperse through his house while the second deputy hovered over him like a storm cloud.

What in God's name is going on? he wondered.

Then he heard the other cop shout, "Detectives, you better come in here."

"Long day," Barbara told Susan.

"The job of a peace officer is never done," Susan said.

"How do you feel about the bust tonight?"

Elbows on her desk, head in her hands, Susan ran her fingers through her hair and compressed her lips. When she lifted her head and looked at Barbara seated across from her, she tried to guess where her partner was coming from. But Barbara's expression didn't give her any clues.

"Why do you ask?"

"It was pretty easy, wasn't it?"

"Yeah. Sometimes we get lucky."

"You think that's what it was?"

Susan said, "What do you think?"

"I asked you first."

Susan rolled her neck from side to side, then stood and paced the detective bureau. When she'd completed a circuit of the room, she stopped in front of Barbara's desk. "Okay, it was easy. Maybe too easy. We got a lead about Vigil, we searched his house, and we found a bottle of liquid nicotine along with syringes."

"What else?" Barbara asked.

"The date stamp on the bottle was from over two years ago and the product name was identical to the product the FBI lab said killed John Matthews, Violet Hawkins, and Emily Watrous: Savory Scent."

"Sounds like we've got the guy dead to rights."

Susan nodded. "Except for one thing. Vigil had three bottles of liquid nicotine sitting on his kitchen counter. Those bottles were from the same manufacturer as was the bottle we found under the sink. Same product, too. But those bottles had production dates of three months ago. So, why would he hide a bottle with a production date of over two years ago under his sink, but leave three more recently purchased bottles out in the open?"

"That's exactly what I was wondering," Barbara said. "Also, there was no sleep medication anywhere in Vigil's house. Remember that Matthews had been doped up before he was injected with nicotine."

"What's your female detective instincts tell you about Vigil?" Susan asked.

"He was as surprised about us finding the bag in the cabinet under his sink as we were excited about finding it. He's either the greatest actor of all time or he's an innocent man."

"Uh huh," Susan said. "You know, I was just thinking about Scott Matthews. We found liquid nicotine in his house, too. Made by the same manufacturer; same product. But Violet Hawkins died when he was in jail. What if we've got the same problem with Oscar Vigil?"

"You worried about our reputations as super sleuths?" Barbara asked.

Susan's knee-jerk reaction was to answer no. But, after a beat, she said, "Maybe a little of that. But what I'm really concerned about is that if Vigil isn't our guy and Matthews isn't our guy, then we're no further along in this case than we were on the day we learned about the nicotine poisoning." After a beat, she added, "And what happens if there's another death?"

Barbara bit her upper lip for a second. "That could clear Vigil. With him in jail, that would mean someone else is the murderer."

"That makes me feel so warm and fuzzy."

Barbara spread her arms in a helpless gesture. "What's the one common denominator?"

Susan scrunched up her face. "You mean, besides Vista de Alameda?"

"Dig deeper."

Susan rested her chin in the cup of her hand, then pushed back in her chair. "What are you thinking?"

"Who gave us Vigil's name?"

"Lisa French."

"Right. And who gave us Scott Matthews's name?"

"Matthews's name was on the visitors' log. French just made us a copy of the log. It's not like she gave us a doctored log."

Barbara sat back in her chair, stared at Susan, and said, "I didn't say she did. I'm just saying that she was the source of information on both Matthews and Vigil."

THURSDAY
OCTOBER 9

CHAPTER 32

OMI Staff Pathologist Dr. Francis Nixon placed the Flying Star coffee cup on the edge of his desk, shed his down coat, and hung it on a hook on the inside of his office door. As he turned back to his desk, he noticed the file folder in the center of his blotter. He walked around his desk, sat down, and picked up the file. A label on the tab read: Armstead, Katherine, 00198123.

He reached for his coffee cup, took a sip and exhaled an "*aah*." Then he flipped over the front cover of the file and turned to the toxicology results. He didn't expect anything out of the ordinary. He'd performed a dozen autopsies for Essex on people who had participated in the trials the company was conducting in New Mexico. None of those individuals had died because of Essex's drug. It had always been something else that killed the patients. Cardiac arrest, kidney failure, stroke.

After he took another sip of coffee, he read the first couple of lines that showed the results of tests performed on Katherine Armstead's body fluids. He coughed, spraying coffee onto the file and on his shirt and tie. Using his handkerchief, he blotted the spots on the papers in the file and then tried to clean his splattered clothes. He gave up when he realized the coffee had already been absorbed into the fabric. The coffee cup set to the side, Nixon continued down the tox screen, and then moved to the lab results of the tissue samples he'd submitted. His heart rate accelerated as he finished reviewing the results.

Nixon called Dr. Frederick Beringer and asked to see him.

"You sound worried."

"I don't know whether I'm worried or surprised. I need to show you something."

Nixon walked to Beringer's office, dropped the Armstead file on his desk, opened it to the toxicology results section, and stabbed the top sheet with a finger. "Look at these," he said.

Beringer studied the first page of the tox screen, then moved to the next page. When he'd finished, he looked up at Nixon. "I don't suppose Katherine Armstead was a smoker." Before Nixon could respond, Beringer said, "Hell, even if she had been a smoker, there's no way she could have had that much nicotine in her body fluids and tissues."

"Strange, isn't it? I mean, it couldn't have been Essex's drug that caused this?"

Beringer rubbed his face with his hands. When he finally looked back at Nixon, he said in a hoarse voice, "No, this has nothing to do with Essex. This is an entirely other matter."

"What's that?" Nixon asked.

Beringer pointed at the chair behind Nixon and told him to sit. Then he picked up his desk phone receiver and called Dr. Hugo Blake, the County Coroner.

"You have a few minutes to meet with me and one of my associates?"

"Not really," Blake said. "I have a meeting in thirty minutes. Can it wait?"

"No, I don't think so. We've had another nicotine poisoning."

Blake's voice rose a couple octaves when he asked, "Another resident at that retirement home?"

Beringer quickly turned to the front of the Armstead file and looked at the subject's personal information. Then he told Blake, "Doesn't look like it. The woman lived in a home in the Northeast Heights."

When Blake didn't respond, Beringer asked, "Did you hear what I said?"

"Yes, Fred, I heard you. I was trying to calculate the odds of a nicotine poisoning unrelated to those at the retirement home."

"What do think?"

Blake cleared his throat. "I think you should call those detectives who are working the other poisonings."

Henry Simpson spent the night at Barbara's house. In the morning, they jogged the three point two miles around the Albuquerque Academy property, showered, changed, and had breakfast together. Over breakfast they'd discussed a date and venue for their wedding and had finally agreed that June would be good. Barbara wanted a small affair in Albuquerque. A small wedding was fine with Henry but he preferred a location that he termed "exotic."

"I want to take you to Greece," he'd said. "A wedding on the island of Samos would be special."

More practical with money, Barbara pushed back on his suggestion. "Besides," she'd said, "some of my friends wouldn't be able to afford the trip."

The upshot was that they'd agreed to have a small ceremony in the chapel on the UNM campus. Susan would be her maid of honor and Roger would be his best man. Then they would honeymoon in Greece. When Barbara objected to an expensive honeymoon, Henry had told her that he'd made up his mind and there was nothing else to say on the subject.

"It's what I want to do for you," he'd said.

Now 9:00 a.m., Henry having left for the university, Barbara was on the road to meet Susan at Vista de Alameda. They'd arranged to meet Stuart Armstead there to gather background on Oscar Vigil. They also wanted to question other employees about Vigil. About to turn off the interstate onto Alameda Boulevard, Barbara's cell phone rang. She saw Lt. Salas's name on the screen.

"Hey, Lieutenant," she answered.

"You keeping bankers' hours? You missed roll call this morning."

Barbara cringed at Salas's high-pitched voice. She waited a couple seconds before telling him that she'd left a message on his voicemail about their meeting at the retirement home.

"Oh, I guess I need to check my messages."

Barbara waited. She knew her boss wouldn't have called just

because she'd missed roll call.

"I received a call from the FBI SAC this morning. I don't know what they did but I suspect it might have had something to do with threatening the company with an IRS audit."

Barbara's fingers nervously tapped the steering wheel as she forced herself to be patient. It usually took Salas at least a minute to get to the point.

"Where was I?" he said.

"The FBI threatened some company."

"Oh, yeah. Anyway, the FBI got CTX Chemical Products in Phoenix to turn over the list of their New Mexico clients on the condition that we would only compare the list against the Vista de Alameda tenant and employee lists. I have an email here with the CTX customer list attached."

"That's great, Lieutenant. Susan and I should be in the office in a couple hours. Thanks for letting us know."

As Barbara drove the department sedan into the Vista de Alameda lot, she spotted Susan parked in her Corvette. She appeared to be in an animated phone conversation. As she pulled into a slot a couple cars away, her partner leaped from her car and hustled over to her.

Barbara stepped from the Crown Vic and said, "I've got good—"

Susan cut her off with the same words. They laughed and Barbara told Susan to go ahead.

"That was Dr. Beringer on the phone. They have another death by nicotine poisoning."

"Oh, shit," Barbara said. "We should have warned everyone here about this." She frowned. "I thought you said you had good news."

"Well, maybe I overstated the situation. We do have another death, but it wasn't anyone at the retirement home."

"What?"

"Yeah. If I wasn't afraid that you'd draw down on me, I'd give you ten guesses as to who our victim is." She smiled for a second, then said, "It's Katherine Armstead. Stuart Armstead's wife."

Barbara crossed her arms and blew out a loud breath. "I thought she had cancer."

"She did. If it hadn't been for the cancer and the fact that she'd

196

been on an experimental drug regimen, we might never have discovered the nicotine. The drug company that administered the drug trial requires that any patient in the program who passes away must be subjected to an autopsy. That's how Beringer found the nicotine."

"Did OMI find an injection site?"

"Nope. But that's probably because Mrs. Armstead was on an IV. He said it would have been easy for someone to inject the poison into one of the IV ports."

Barbara turned and looked at the entrance to the retirement home. "Are you thinking what I'm thinking?"

"If what you're thinking is that we have an appointment with the possible murderer of several residents at Vista de Alameda, as well as of his wife, then I'm thinking what you're thinking." Susan nudged a pebble with the toe of her right shoe. "How do you want to handle this?"

Barbara uncrossed her arms and arched her back. "Let's dance around the subject for a while. I want to see his reaction to a few things."

Susan nodded. As they moved toward the building entrance, she said, "You were about to tell me good news."

"Salas called. The company in Arizona that made the liquid nicotine found in the bodies of Mr. Matthews, Mrs. Watrous, and Mrs. Hawkins has agreed to share their New Mexico customer list with us."

"Damn. It's a red letter day."

CHAPTER 33

Stuart Armstead's expression told Barbara everything she needed to know about the tone of the interview she and Susan were about to conduct. The man was red-faced and, other than a brief glare, wouldn't look them in the eyes.

"I've got thirty minutes for you, Detectives. Then I need to go to the funeral home to finalize arrangements for my wife's service and burial." He whipped a look over a shoulder at them as they trailed him into his office. "I assume you can understand where my priorities are."

"Of course, Mr. Armstead," Barbara said. "We apologize for having to bother you during this troubling time. Our condolences over your wife's death."

They took chairs across the desk from Armstead and waited for him to silence his cell phone.

"What's so important that you needed to meet with me now?"

"We wanted to talk with you about Oscar Vigil. I assume you heard that he was arrested as a possible suspect in the poisoning deaths here at Vista de Alameda?"

Armstead's complexion went from red to scarlet. "Poisoning deaths? What are you talking about? And, no, I had not heard about Mr. Vigil's arrest. The last I knew, Scott Matthews had been arrested for murdering his father. Something about insurance proceeds." He paused a couple moments, then said, "Are you inferring that a former employee of ours has been murdering residents?"

Barbara glanced at Susan, then back at Armstead. She shot him an innocent smile. "Oh, no, Mr. Armstead, I wasn't *inferring* any such thing. We're way past the inference stage. We know for a fact that at least four of your residents were poisoned with liquid nicotine." She gave him the names of the four. Barbara had never before seen anyone go from scarlet-faced to pale in a matter of a second.

Armstead groaned and opened and closed his mouth like a beached fish for several seconds. Then he said, "You can prove this?"

"Absolutely. Toxicology tests were performed on all four individuals. The FBI lab also identified the source of the nicotine in three of the cases. In the case of Mr. Quintana, the poison had degraded to the point that the lab couldn't identify the substance's DNA, so to speak, other than to confirm that he had liquid nicotine in his body. We've been in contact with the manufacturer, who provided us with a list of customers who purchased the particular product used to murder the three residents."

"The FBI?" Armstead said in a whiny, tremulous voice.

"Yeah, the FBI," Barbara said sarcastically. "They tend to help out in mass murder cases."

Armstead stared wide-eyed at Susan and then back at Barbara. "Oh my God. This is a disaster. You can't release any of this information. It would ruin me. I would never be able to se—"

Barbara and Susan waited for him to finish his sentence, but he didn't continue.

"What can you tell us about Oscar Vigil?" Susan asked.

The change of subject seemed to disorient Armstead. He blinked several times, poured himself a glass of water from a pitcher on a credenza to the left of his desk, drank half the contents, and then pushed back into his chair.

"I understand you talked with Ms. French about Mr. Vigil."

"We did," Barbara said. "We were hoping you might have something more to add."

"I don't deal with the employees on a day-to-day basis. I mean, Lisa handles employee issues. At the time she terminated him, she told me she'd cleaned out his locker and called him to come pick up his things." He paused a beat, then added, "If I recall correctly, she told him that he could have his personal things if he returned the set of keys he hadn't turned in."

"What personal items did he leave behind?" Susan asked.

Armstead shook his head. "I have no idea. I'm sure they've been disposed of by now."

Barbara said, "Perhaps there are other employees who were here when Mr. Vigil worked here. We'd like to talk to them, if possible."

Armstead looked peeved, but finally nodded. "I'll have Lisa arrange that." He picked up his desk telephone and pressed an intercom button. Lisa French's voice answered.

"Can you come here, Lisa? Detectives..."

Barbara prompted him: "Lassiter and Martinez."

"Detectives Lassiter and Martinez would like to interview employees who worked here with Oscar Vigil."

"Be right there," French said.

While they waited for French, Barbara said, "Again, I'm sorry about your wife."

Armstead waved a hand as though to dismiss the sentiment. "Cancer probably contributed to her death." He wagged his head as though confused. "Go figure. She suffered from cancer for a couple years, but ultimately died of cardiac arrest." He seemed defeated for a moment, but then suddenly became red-faced again. He looked angry when he said, "The goddamn pharmaceutical company required that an autopsy be performed. Probably worried about liability in case it was their drug that killed Kathy."

Susan said, "So you haven't received the autopsy results?"

He sagged and slumped in his chair. "Not yet. Why?"

Before Susan could respond, a knock on the door sounded and Lisa French entered. "Are you ready to meet with the employees?" French asked.

Barbara nodded as she and Susan stood and stepped away from their chairs.

Before they turned to leave, Armstead said, "You asked about my wife's autopsy. Have you heard something?"

Susan said, "Actually, we—"

But French cut her off and, in a shrill voice, said, "An autopsy was done on Kathy?"

Armstead looked shocked at French's interruption but quickly recovered. "Can you believe the drug company demanded it?" He turned to Susan. "What were you about to say?"

Barbara cut in, "We haven't heard anything yet. The M.E. wouldn't have any reason to call us."

Armstead looked from Barbara to Susan. "Of course," he said.

Barbara and Susan spent the next two hours interviewing Vista de Alameda employees about Oscar Vigil. The only thing they learned was that Vigil had been a "good ole boy" who liked time off more than time on. There had apparently been plenty of reasons for Lisa French to fire him. As French escorted them to the building entrance, Susan asked her, "Do you still have the personal effects that you removed from Vigil's locker?"

"No. When he didn't return our keys, I dumped the whole kit and caboodle into the trash. There was nothing there but some clothes and toiletry items."

"Okay," Susan said. "Thanks for your help."

"No problem."

About to go through the front door, Barbara suddenly stopped and turned. "I suppose Mr. Armstead will inform you about this, so I might as well bring you up to date. Autopsies done on Messrs. Matthews and Quintana and on Misses Watrous and Hawkins proved that all of them were poisoned."

French's features sagged and her eyes looked like a deer in headlights. "Autopsies?" she said.

"Yes," Susan said.

French looked ill as she asked, "Do you think Oscar Vigil poisoned them?"

"That's the operative theory at the moment."

French seemed to recover a bit. Her expression turned almost hopeful.

CHAPTER 34

In the parking lot of the retirement home, Susan asked, "Why didn't you tell Armstead what we learned about his wife's death? About the nicotine in her body?"

Barbara bit her lower lip and stared at Susan. She finally said, "I don't know. It was just an instinct not to say anything more. Having learned about the nicotine in his wife's system before we went in there, I was leaning toward Armstead being the killer. But, after seeing his reactions during our interview, I wasn't so sure. Then, when French reacted the way she did when she learned that an autopsy had been done on Armstead's wife, I decided to hold onto that information for a while."

"Maybe we should call Beringer and ask him to put off disclosing the autopsy results to anyone else for now."

"That's a good idea. Why don't you call him on the way back downtown?"

"Okay." Susan pulled out her phone and, as she dialed, said, "I think I'm going to stop at the detention center and talk with Vigil. I'll see you in the office."

"Why?" Barbara asked.

"Something's bothering me. I'll let you know when I organize my thoughts."

On the drive to the Bernalillo County Metropolitan Detention

Center, Susan received a call from Barbara.

"You there yet?" Barbara asked.

"Almost. What's up?"

"I went over the list of New Mexicans who bought the Savory Scent product from CTX Chemicals and compared it against the list of Vista de Alameda tenants and employees. Guess whose name was the only one on both lists."

"Oscar Vigil," Susan said.

"You got it right the first time. Maybe you should hold off talking with him. We don't want to jeopardize this investigation. Let's get the D.A. in on questioning him."

Susan considered what Barbara had just told her, then said, "I understand. I won't say anything about the CTX list. But there's something else I want to ask him."

"Are you sure?"

"No. But I'm kinda sure."

After hanging up with Barbara, Susan second-guessed meeting with Vigil. The more she thought about driving all the way to Albuquerque's southwest side to meet with the man, the more she felt that she was wasting her time.

"Aw, hell, I'm almost there. Might as well do it."

She pulled into the facility's parking lot, went through security, relinquished her weapon, and was directed to a room to wait for Vigil.

When a deputy brought in a shackled Vigil, she was shocked by his appearance.

"What happened to you?" she asked.

"What do you care?"

"I asked you a question."

Vigil tried to stare her down, but conceded defeat after a few seconds. "I'm not a gang member. So a couple guys decided they wanted to be my new best friends." He pointed at a sutured cut on his left cheek and his blackened left eye. "I wasn't in the mood for a jailhouse romance."

Susan looked at the deputy who hovered by the inside of the room door. She said, "Is that right?"

The deputy shrugged.

She turned back to Vigil. "I've got a couple questions for you. You want an attorney present?"

"Fuck an attorney," he answered. "I ain't done nothin'."

Susan nodded. "When you worked at Vista de Alameda, did you have a locker?"

"Sure. All employees had one. You know, to keep a change of clothes there. Like that."

"Is that what you kept in your locker?"

"Among other things."

"Like what other things?"

He just glared at her.

Susan shifted forward in her chair. "Listen, Oscar, I'm a homicide detective, not vice. I could care less if you had drugs in your locker. Just tell me what was there when you got fired. Did you clear it out?"

"Nah, I didn't get the chance. They bum-rushed my ass off the premises before I could get my stuff."

She arched her eyebrows at him and waited.

He finally huffed a loud sigh. "I had a change of clothes and some . . . personal things."

"Come on, Oscar, what personal things?"

He huffed again. "You know, a bit of weed and a few vials of nicotine for my e-cigarette."

A shiver went down Susan's spine. "You recall where the nicotine came from?"

"Sure. I buy it on the Internet from a company in Arizona. I like their Savory Scent stuff."

"And you never got your things back?"

"That's right. They wanted me to return the keys I took with me in return for giving me my stuff back." He chuckled. "I figured if I kept the keys, they'd have to change all the locks, which would have cost them a bunch of money. I could always buy more nicotine and shaving gear."

"And weed?"

He smiled for a moment and nodded.

"What happened to the keys?" Susan asked.

He laughed out loud. "I buried them in the backyard a week after they fired me."

"You think you can find them?"

"Sure. I dug a little hole right under my barbecue grill." He squinted at her and asked, "What do you care about a bunch of old keys?"

"More than you know, Mr. Vigil."

She thanked him and stood. Then she followed the deputy and Vigil from the room. Back in the reception area, she asked to talk with the chief administrator. After a fifteen minute wait, she was ushered into his office by another deputy.

"What can I do for you, Detective?" Chief Reed asked.

"You have detainees named Oscar Vigil and Scott Matthews."

Reed tapped on his computer keyboard, looked at his terminal, and then turned back to Susan. "Yes, that's correct. What about them?"

"It appears that they've both been targeted by other inmates and have suffered injuries."

"Detective Martinez, we can't very well watch over every inmate in the center twenty-four hours a day."

"Yeah, I got that. But I need a favor."

The guy just stared back at her.

"Warden Reed, I screwed up. I was so certain Scott Matthews had murdered his father. Now, I'm convinced he's innocent." She lowered her head and slowly shook it. "I think I screwed up with Oscar Vigil, as well. I really need your help. I don't want to see them hurt anymore because I made mistakes. I'm going to correct my error as soon as I get back to my office."

After a meeting at the funeral home, Stuart Armstead returned to Vista de Alameda. He'd barely sat in his desk chair when Lisa French entered his office without knocking.

"How did it go with the detective and the employees?" Armstead asked.

French threw up her hands. "Total waste of time." She shook her head as she seemed to be trying to get her brain in gear. "What was that about an autopsy?"

"You seem upset."

"Why would an autopsy be done on Kathy?"

"It was required by the drug company that provided the cancer medication. Nothing I could do about it. I didn't like the whole idea. Autopsies are so . . . so . . . I don't know . . . violent, I guess. Kathy had already been through so much."

French bounced her head like a bobble-head doll.

"What's the matter?" Armstead asked. "Why are you so upset?"

French moved around Armstead's office like a tigress in a cage. "It's all a mess," she whined. She stopped pacing and stared at him. "It was all for you, Stu. All for you. I saw what was happening with this place and how your wife's illness was dragging you down. I did it *all* for you."

Armstead now wore a confused expression, but he had a sinking feeling that he knew what she was referring to. Sure, he'd had doubts about whether the woman had done something to his wife, but French's demeanor had now erased any lingering doubts. But his gut clenched as her words rolled over him: 'I did it all for you.' The emphasis on the word *all* was the clincher. *I need to handle this very, very carefully*, he thought.

"We need to leave. It will be the only chance for us to spend our lives together."

The confused expression still in place, he said, "What are you talking about, Lisa?"

He swiveled his chair toward her as she came around his desk. She went down on her knees, took one of his hands in hers, and cried, "I know you feel about me the way I feel about you. I love you, Stu. I killed them all for you."

Armstead yanked his hand from her grasp as he leaped to his feet and backed away, pushing his chair back against the wall. "What have you done, Lisa?"

Susan called Barbara as she drove from the detention facility toward Oscar Vigil's house. She told Barbara what she'd discovered.

"You believe him?" Barbara asked.

"Yeah, I do. But I'm on my way to Vigil's place to see if I can find the keys he took from Vista de Alameda. The search warrant we got before is still in force. I already called the dispatcher to have a uniform meet me there. I want a witness."

"Good idea."

"Barb, why don't you give the lieutenant a heads-up? I think we all ought to meet to discuss where this goes from here."

Susan parked in front of Vigil's ramshackle home. The uniformed deputy, Tom Cantwell, was already there.

"You wouldn't happen to have a shovel in your vehicle?" she asked Cantwell.

"No, ma'am."

"Okay, let's see if we can find something in the backyard."

Cantwell came up with a trowel he found inside a cracked, empty flowerpot and brought it over to Susan. She led the way to the back of the dirt yard, which apparently hadn't seen grass or flowers or bushes in years. A small barbecue grill with two wheels sat at the back, two feet in from the three-foot-high cinder block wall that enclosed the yard.

"Stand beside the grill," Susan instructed the deputy. Then she took a video of the man and the grill with her cell phone.

"Now, pull the grill away from the wall a couple feet."

Cantwell again obeyed her order as she continued to record the scene.

Susan gave her phone to Cantwell and told him to continue the video until she told him to stop. She squatted in front of the spot where the grill had been and dug a half-a-trowel's worth of dirt at a time. After she'd dug a hole a foot deep, she spotted something which she carefully lifted from the hole with the trowel.

"Get a shot of this," she told the deputy.

The deputy leaned in and took several shots. When he'd finished, he said, "Looks like a key ring with dozens of keys on it. Must have been in there a while. They look corroded."

Susan stood, told the deputy to stop filming, took her phone from him, and put it in her left jacket pocket. She handed him a plastic bag she pulled from her right jacket pocket and waited for him to open it. Then she dumped the keys from the trowel into the bag.

She thanked Cantwell, then fast-walked to her Corvette.

CHAPTER 35

Lisa French had given Stuart Armstead plenty of reason to know she was infatuated with him, but he'd never really taken it seriously. After all, he was married and he'd never considered himself a particularly good catch. He knew he was well past his prime. But hearing her proclaim her love for him had been almost as unsettling as was her confession of murdering people. He got her to move to a chair in front of his desk, and then returned to his own chair. His mind reeled as he tried to fathom the implications of what she'd just told him. What she'd just confessed to could be the end of Vista de Alameda. *How in God's name can I ever sell this place now? I need to get this situation under control so I can decide how to handle things*, he thought.

"I'm flattered, Lisa," he finally said, knowing it sounded lame. But he couldn't think of anything else to say. "I thought you and that Pilates guy were seeing one another. I had no idea you felt this way about me."

French blurted a sound that was more cackle than laugh. "Severino Torres and me? You thought we were serious?"

He waggled a hand. "Well, I saw you two together when he gave classes here. I thought you were dating."

French leaned forward, which caused Armstead to push back in his chair. "Okay, okay, so we dated a couple times. It was nothing serious. Especially when I discovered he was sleeping with other women." A bitter twist came to her mouth and her eyes went dark—like shark's eyes. "When I found out he was sleeping with that old hag, Samantha Carruthers, I called it quits with him." She smiled. "He was really never anything more than a boy toy."

Armstead had already been jolted to his core by Lisa's revelations, but her mention of Samantha Carruthers made him feel electrified.

"Samantha Carruthers? That's the woman who was murdered in her home." He forced himself to remain calm and asked in a quiet voice, "Did you . . .?"

French showed him a toothy smile that sent chills through his body.

"We don't need to talk about her, Stu. She was nothing but scum."

Armstead now knew that the chills he felt had less to do with shock than with fear. He couldn't maintain eye contact with the woman. When his cell phone rang, he jerked as though he'd been hit with a cattle prod. He looked at the phone screen: Cliff Grant, Congregate Care Retirement Solutions. He didn't want to answer the call with Lisa in his office, but he didn't want to take the chance of missing the call, either. He raised a finger to tell French to hold on for a minute.

"Hey, Cliff, what's up?"

"Just calling to confirm my flight on Saturday. We still on?"

"Absolutely. Give me the flight number and time of arrival."

Grant recited the information and Armstead wrote it down. As he did so, he noticed French peer at what he'd written.

"I'll pick you up," he told Grant, then signed off the call.

"Was that Clifford Grant with that company in Washington?"

Armstead swallowed hard. It took him a couple seconds to get his voice and finally said, "Yeah."

"He's coming here?"

Armstead nodded.

French's face went through a series of expressions ranging from disappointment to anger. She leaped to her feet and stabbed a finger at him. "You're selling the place, aren't you?"

"Nothing's been agreed to, Lisa. Calm down."

"Why didn't you tell me you'd talked to Grant? I've worked my ass off here for years. You should have kept me in the loop."

As she sagged back into her chair, he said, "It was premature to tell anyone, Lisa."

She jumped out of her chair again and shouted shrilly, "I'm not just *anyone*. I've been like a partner to you for all these years. What were you going to do? Sell out, then take the money and run? You owe me, Stu. You *owe* me."

Armstead had experienced a multitude of emotions over the last few minutes, but now anger supplanted surprise, shock, fear, shame he'd felt a moment earlier.

"You crazy bitch," he growled. "I paid you good money to work here. As an assistant manager, not as a partner. I didn't ask you to kill anyone. You did that on your own. My God, four of our residents and Mrs. Carruthers. You're going down big time." The woman's crazed expression told him he should have remained in control.

Still on her feet, she made the cackling sound again. Then she made a stabbing motion with her finger as she screamed, "You think I only killed four residents? What a fool you are. Twenty-one people. That's how many I killed so we could replace them with new people paying higher rents and entry fees. All for you." She laughed. "Twenty-one, not including Samantha Carruthers. Twenty-one, not including your fucking wife."

Then French showed him a sick smile that erased Armstead's anger and took him back to feeling abiding, unadulterated fear.

She moved forward, her thighs against the front of the desk, snatched a letter opener from the blotter, and jabbed it repeatedly into the edge of the desk as she screeched, "I freed you from that wife of yours. All for us. Us, you see."

"Sit down, Lisa," Armstead croaked, his voice barely audible, his words almost indiscernible. "Let's talk this through."

Maybe it was the fear, or maybe the contempt that she saw in his expression, that caused her to suddenly leap at him. He tried to push his chair back, but his feet slipped on the glass mat under his chair. She was on him before he could retreat.

Armstead felt an enormous punch to his chest. Then French's body hit his and toppled his chair over backward. Despite the pain he felt, his vision was clear. He watched her roll off him, stand up, and look down at him with venom in her eyes and cruelty in the set of her mouth. He attempted to get up, but couldn't seem to gather the strength to do so. Something seemed to have short-circuited his ability to move. He looked down at his chest and couldn't rationalize what he saw protruding there. Then he suddenly couldn't breathe. He closed his eyes and heard the hoarse sounds of his labored breathing.

French adjusted her suit jacket and skirt, ran her fingers through her hair, and took a deep breath. She opened Armstead's office door, exited into the hallway, and glared at the frightened faces of three employees gathered there.

"What are you doing out here?" she barked. "Get back to work."

CHAPTER 36

Assistant D.A. Elinore Freed looked up from her notes and glanced, in turn, at Rudy Salas, Barbara Lassiter, and Susan Martinez. Then she asked Susan, "You're absolutely certain that Lisa French said she personally opened Oscar Vigil's locker?"

"Absolutely," Susan said.

"I was there at the time," Barbara said. "That's what French told us. She also told us about the keys and suggested that Vigil might have used them to re-enter the facility after he was fired."

"That's right," Susan said.

Barbara said, "And it was French who called 9-1-1 to the Armstead residence when she supposedly found Katharine Armstead in cardiac arrest. We now know Mrs. Armstead was poisoned with the same substance that killed the four residents at the retirement home."

"Four that we know of," Salas interjected.

"God," Freed exclaimed. Then she said, "I thought she arrived at the Armstead place after the woman had already died."

"We haven't put that together yet. We think she set the whole thing up to look as though that's what happened."

"Elinore," Salas said, "we need to have Matthews and Vigil released A-S-A-P. And we need to go pick up Lisa French."

"Lieutenant, I'll issue an arrest warrant for French and arrange for Matthews's and Vigil's release. Why don't you have Detectives

Lassiter and Martinez immediately go to the retirement home? I'll email the warrant to Detective Lassiter's cell phone."

Alberto Martinez adjusted his black Trilby hat and zipped his black leather coat all the way to his neck. Despite the sun and the blue sky, the wind coming out of the east was bitterly cold. He looked back into the Vista de Alameda lobby. No sign of Max. He checked his watch and saw that the van was due to pull up in two minutes. "Damn Max," he mumbled. "Always late." He was looking forward to seeing the new Clint Eastwood movie and decided he would board the van, whether Max showed or not.

Lisa French was drenched in perspiration. Her body shook as though she had a fever. She had rushed to the employee parking area behind the retirement home and now sped around toward the front of the complex in her Mercedes, toward Alameda Boulevard. She was about to skirt the front of the building when she spied Alberto Martinez in the alcove outside the entrance and thought about Martinez's detective niece and her partner. "Those bitches," she shouted.

An idea came to her that gave her a warm feeling. She stopped shaking as she pulled into the circle in front of the entrance, stopped by Martinez, and lowered the passenger side window. She said, "Did you hear about your niece?"

Martinez stepped up to the car and bent over. "What about her?"

The panicked expression on the old man's face made French feel like a kid at Christmas.

"Oh, I assumed you'd heard. There was a shooting. Two officers were taken to UNM Hospital. The news mentioned your niece."

"Oh, my Lord."

"I don't know what happened, Mr. Martinez." She paused for a second. "I have an appointment downtown. If you'd like, I can drop you off at the hospital and bring you back here after my meeting's over."

"Are you sure?"

"Hop in."

Max Katz exited the retirement home just as the van pulled up. He looked around for Alberto and was surprised he wasn't there. *Alberto is always on time, if not early*, he thought.

He climbed into the van and asked the driver if he'd seen Alberto.

"Yeah. I just saw him drive off with Ms. French. He looked worried."

The driver had just closed the van door when Max stood and shouted, "Let me out." He stepped down and entered the building. He couldn't reconcile Alberto driving off with Lisa French and not calling him. He vacillated between returning to his apartment or going to the administrative offices to see if someone there knew something. When he heard voices coming from the hall outside the offices, he opted to go there.

A couple of the female staff were in the hall outside Stuart Armstead's office. One of the women, a leggy redhead of about fifty named Joan who Max liked a lot, glanced his way, turned away, took the other woman's arm, and tugged her toward their work area.

"Hey, Joan, what's up?" Max called out.

Still holding onto the other woman's arm, Joan waved at Max over a shoulder, and said, "Nothing."

The other woman jerked her arm free of Joan's grasp, stopped, turned toward Max, and beckoned him with a finger wag.

When Max reached the women, he asked, "What's wrong? You two look upset."

Joan said, "It's probably nothing. We heard Mr. Armstead and Ms. French shouting something awful, then Ms. French stormed out of the office, yelled at us, and then left the building."

Max said, "Have you seen Mr. Armstead since then?"

"No," the second woman said. "We talked about knocking on his door but we—"

"Didn't want to get into trouble," Joan said, finishing the thought.

Max smiled at the two women. "Well, hell, ladies, what's he going to do to me? Kick me out of the building?"

He turned and went back to Armstead's door, knocked once, and waited a few seconds. When there was no response, he knocked again, with the same result. Max then opened the door and peeked into the office. One of the chairs in front of the desk was on its side. There didn't appear to be a chair behind the desk. He walked into the office and noticed that the blotter and desk phone were askew and the nameplate that usually rested on the front of the desk wasn't there. He went around one side of the desk, and stopped in his tracks. "Holy shit," he exclaimed. He looked back at the two women who now stood in the doorway and shouted, "Call 9-1-1. Tell them we need an ambulance and the police."

Max pressed three fingers against the side of Armstead's neck, trying to find a pulse, although he knew the man was already dead. A letter opener stuck out of the man's chest and blood saturated his shirt. He'd seen enough dead bodies while serving as a medic in Korea during the war. Then he had a sinking feeling and went out to the hall and found Joan.

"Is he dead?" she asked.

"As a doornail," Max answered. Then he asked, "Were you in the hall when Lisa French left?"

"Yes. Maggie and I were there, along with another employee."

"Did you see anyone else go into the office after she left?"

"No. We were out in the hall the whole time from when Ms. French left until you showed up."

"Sonofabitch," Max barked.

Joan touched his hand. "You were very brave doing what you did, Max. Going in there."

"Oh, give me a break," he growled. He jerked his cell phone from a coat pocket and called Susan Martinez.

Shortly after they'd left Vista de Alameda, Alberto Martinez realized he'd left his cell phone in his apartment. When he asked Lisa French if he could use her phone, she told him it was in her briefcase in the trunk of the car.

"Can't you dial using Bluetooth?"

"I've tried it before. It won't work when the phone's in the trunk. I'm sorry. I'm always forgetting to take it out of my briefcase."

Traffic on Coors Boulevard in the early afternoon flowed well and they made good time to Interstate 40. But instead of driving east to Interstate 25, French took the Rio Grande Avenue exit and drove south.

"This isn't the way to the hospital," Alberto said.

As she turned right on Central Avenue, French said, "I have to drop something off first. It won't take but a minute." She pulled into a lot that fronted a strip center with six storefronts.

Alberto didn't like it that the woman was putting something ahead of Susan, but he figured they were only about five minutes or so from UNM Hospital.

Barbara and Susan were still on the interstate going north when the call came in that a 187 had occurred at the Vista de Alameda Retirement Center. They responded that they were on their way to that location. A second after that call came in, Susan's cell phone rang. She saw Max Katz's name on her screen.

"Max, if you're calling about a . . . incident at Vista de Alameda, we're already on our way there."

"That's not why I'm calling. It looks like Lisa French stabbed Stu Armstead to death, then took off. The van driver here saw Alberto get in French's car before she drove away."

Susan's breath caught in her chest. "Did anyone see where they were headed?"

"No."

"Okay, Max. Thanks. Can you do me a favor?"

"You bet."

"See if you can get me Lisa French's cell phone number, then call me back."

"Okay. You gotta find him, Susan. She's crazy."

"Just get me that number, Max."

After Susan ended the call, Barbara said, "I heard what Max said. Call the dispatcher and have him send another unit to the retirement home. We're going to find French and your uncle."

After Susan called the dispatcher, she tried her uncle's cell phone. No answer. Then Max called her back with French's number. She tried that phone, with the same result.

"I thought you said your phone was in the trunk," Alberto said as he watched French take her cell from a jacket pocket, glance at the screen, tap the screen, and put away the phone.

"I guess I was mistaken."

"What's going on?" he said.

"Nothing. Relax."

French got out of her car, told Alberto that she would be back in a minute or two, then went through a grocery store to a door in the back and knocked, which brought a beefy guy armed with a pistol in a shoulder holster.

"¿Qué quieres?" he demanded.

French pushed past the guy. "I want to see my brother Frank."

She marched through a large room where men lounged around, ate, smoked, played cards, talked on cell phones, and—in the instance of one guy—napped. The place smelled like cheap cigar smoke and sweat infused with the odors of chilies and tortillas.

The men in the room went quiet and watched her storm toward the offices in the back.

She opened the door to Frank Calderon's office and announced to the two other men in the room with her brother, "*Salte. Quiero hablar con mi hermano.*"

The men looked at Frank, who, after a couple seconds, nodded. After the men left and closed the door, Frank Calderon squinted at his sister. "Nice to know you can still speak Spanish," he said. "What is it this time?"

"I'm in terrible trouble, Frankie. I need to get out of New Mexico. Maybe out of the country."

Calderon just stared and waited.

Tears filled her eyes and her chin trembled. "It's bad, Frankie. They'll start digging up bodies. When they do, they'll discover that I poisoned a bunch of people."

"Humor me, Lisa. How can they pin that on you?"

"Maybe they can't. But I just stabbed my boss and I poisoned his wife. Those two deaths they can put on me. You have to help me get out of here."

Calderon's stomach seemed to do a flip-flop. "What the fuck is wrong with you? You want me to cover your ass for . . . what, how many murders?"

She shrugged.

"How many, Lisa?"

"Twenty-three."

Calderon's mouth dropped open. He couldn't seem to muster the strength to speak.

"So what's the difference between one or two dozen? You're my brother. You've got to help me."

He finally caught his breath and closed his mouth. He thought about the implications of helping his sister flee the country and the risks he would be taking. *She is my little sister*, he thought. *What else can I do*?

Then the manic, vicious little girl he remembered from his youth crawled to the surface. Her pleading tone gone, she skewered him with a look that reminded him of a viper on the hunt. In a voice that sounded as though it emanated from the depths of hell, she said, "You either help me or I'll ruin you."

He thought, *you'd do that, Lisa, after all I've done for you*. He knew without a doubt that she was referring to telling the police about his businesses.

"And there's another thing you need to do," she said, after a pause. "There's an old man in my car that I want dumped somewhere."

"And what has this old man done to deserve such treatment?"

"His niece is a cop who's made my life miserable."

"I see."

"You going to help me with this?"

Calderon sucked in a huge breath and let it out slowly. He got up from behind his desk, opened the door, and shouted, "Someone tell Churro I need him."

Calderon shut the door and pointed at his sister. "Does the old man in your car know why you came here? Does he know this is my office?"

"No, of course not. You think I'm stupid?"

Calderon was about to tell Lisa that killing twenty-three people wasn't the smartest thing in the world to do but stifled the urge and, instead, said, "Follow me."

He walked out of his office, pointed at two men in the lounge, and barked, "You and you, come with me." At the entrance to the store, Calderon ordered Lisa to get the old man out of her car. "Take him over to that red pickup on the right side of the parking lot, then come back to my office." While Lisa moved to her car, Calderon told one of his men, "Go to the pickup truck and take the old man wherever he wants to go. You don't say a word to the guy except, 'Where do you want to go?' You got it?"

"Yeah, boss."

"Then get to it."

To the other man, he said, "Tomas, I want you to call the tow company and have them send a driver over here to pick up that Mercedes and take it to the body shop. Have Enrique chop it up."

Tomas's eyes went wide. "That's a beautiful car, boss."

"A beautiful car that the cops will soon be looking for."

"What a shame," Tomas said.

He pointed at Lisa who was beside the pickup truck, saying something to the old man. "Get the Mercedes keys from that woman. Let me know as soon as the job's done."

"Right, boss," Tomas said.

Calderon whipped around and hurried back toward his office. As he passed the lounge, he waved at a man. "Churro, come with me," he ordered. When they were both in Calderon's office, Frank explained what he wanted done.

Churro's only response was a frown.

When Lisa re-entered the office, she visibly shuddered when she looked at the man with her brother. The guy had features that looked as though his face had been chiseled from granite. His right eye was white, with a slight blue tint. A jagged scar wound from his forehead, across his right eyelid, to his right ear.

"Churro, this is my sister. She needs to get out of Albuquerque; needs to disappear before the police find her. Take good care of her."

Lisa smiled at her brother, thanked him, and followed Churro out of the office. As she reached the doorway, Frank told her, "This is the last time we'll ever see one another. Is there anything you want me to tell Mama?"

She smirked and shook her head.

Calderon trembled as he watched his sister depart. Then he

hit the switch under his desk to stop the recording function on the equipment in his bottom right desk drawer. He opened the drawer and backed up the disk to the point where Lisa had first entered his office; he then played the conversation up to but not including the part where he'd called Churro into his office. He erased everything after that. Then he turned the machine back to recording mode, said a few words, got up and opened and then slammed shut his office door. He shut off the machine and closed the desk drawer.

Churro led Lisa to a black vintage El Camino. He opened the passenger door for her, then walked around to the driver's side. After he drove away from the lot, Lisa asked, "What's the plan?"

"Frank told me to take you to Juarez." He shot a glance at her. "You don't got no bags?"

She laughed. "I can get whatever I want once I cross the border. But I have to make a stop first."

"Frank didn't say nothin' about a stop."

"It'll be quick. I need cash. So, stop at the bank at the corner of Lomas and Third Street. I have a safety deposit box there."

Churro wasn't used to making independent decisions, but he didn't want this woman going off on him. He'd heard her screeches through the walls of the boss's office. He drove to the bank—not even a five-minute-trip—and parked in the lot.

"I'll only be a few minutes," she told him.

In a cubbyhole with her safety deposit box, Lisa French lifted the box lid and stared at the entirety of her net worth: eighty-seven thousand dollars in cash, about five thousand dollars worth of gold coins, seven hundred dollars of U.S. Savings Bonds left to her by an uncle, and a .38 caliber revolver. *I should have saved more and spent less,* she reflected. She was glad that she'd leased the Mercedes and was renting the house. *No big financial loss there.* But she knew that as long as she had her looks and her brains, she could always find a sugar daddy. She shuddered and clenched her fists when she thought of the years she'd spent with Stuart Armstead. She'd always assumed she'd be able to lure him away from his wife. *What a waste,* she thought. As she stuffed the contents of the box into her purse, she considered what she'd do once the gorilla in the El Camino dropped her off in Juarez. She'd try to find a way to acquire Mexican documentation and then, maybe, travel to Costa Rica. A former boyfriend had taken her to that country for a vacation. She'd liked the place and the people.

Alberto Martinez had long since figured out that something screwy was up with Lisa French. He'd been just about to bail out of her Mercedes and walk to a gas station he spied a block away, to hopefully use their phone, when a tough-looking man with a large bald head came to the Mercedes and beckoned him with a finger waggle.

Alberto opened the door and asked, "Who are you?"

"Where was Ms. French going to take you?"

"UNM Hospital."

"I'm supposed to take you there. She's tied up."

Alberto made eye contact with the man and decided to trust him. For whatever reason, he felt more comfortable with this stranger than he had with French.

The ride to the hospital lasted eight minutes, during which neither man spoke a word. When Alberto exited the pickup, he thanked the man, who only grunted in return.

At the reception counter, Alberto asked a woman who looked ten years older than he was for Susan Martinez's room number.

After checking a computer, the woman said, "I'm sorry, sir, but no one by that name has been admitted to the hospital. How long ago was she supposed to have been admitted?"

"My niece is a policewoman. I was told she was in a shooting." He swallowed to try to loosen his throat muscles. "She might have been hurt—"

"Are you sure?" the woman asked. "We get notified immediately of any such incident. I haven't heard anything about a shooting."

Alberto was about to contradict the woman when the thought struck him that it was Lisa French who'd told him about a shooting. He stared down at the floor for a long beat and then looked back at the woman and asked, "Would it be all right to use your phone to call my niece's partner? Maybe she was taken somewhere else."

The woman said, "I'm not allowed to let anyone use the hospital—" She suddenly stopped what she was about to say, reached under the counter, took a purse from the floor, and placed it on her lap. She removed a cell phone from the purse and handed it to Alberto.

He dialed Barbara's number from memory and when she answered, "Lassiter," he said, "Are you okay? Where's Susan? I heard—"

"Susan's right here with me. Where are you? What's going on?"

"*Iheardtherewasashootingand Susanwas—*"

"Whoa, Mr. Martinez, slow down. There's been no shooting and Susan's fine. Where are you?"

"Oh, thank God. I'm at UNM Hospital. Lisa French told me—"

"Is Lisa French there with you?"

"No."

"Do you know where she is?"

"She drove to a building on Central a couple blocks west of Rio Grande. It has a grocery store in it. That's the last I saw of her. What's going on?"

"I'll explain later. I'm going to have a deputy come by the hospital and pick you up and bring you to our office. Wait in the main lobby for him. While I call in on the radio, here's Susan."

"Uncle Alberto, are you okay?"

Susan's voice caused Alberto to choke up again. He cleared his throat. "I'm fine, honey," He said." He coughed, then added, "I was so worried about you."

"I'm fine. We were really worried about you when we heard that French took you somewhere. Max called us in a panic."

"Did French do something?"

"Oh, yeah, Uncle Alberto."

CHAPTER 37

After leaving the safety deposit vault, French exited the bank lobby and stopped at the glass entrance doors that led to the parking lot. She looked left and right, in case there were any cops around. Satisfied that it was safe to exit the building, she quickly went to the El Camino, slid onto the seat, and announced, "Let's get the fuck out of here."

Churro pulled away and turned right to Lomas Boulevard. Then he drove east to Interstate 25 and took the southbound ramp. They hadn't even cleared the Albuquerque city limits before French complained about the temperature in the car and her bucket seat. Churro adjusted the heater and apologized for the seat. By the time they reached Los Lunas, she whined about being hungry.

"I don't think it's a good idea to stop and eat too close to Albuquerque," he said.

"Are you retarded?" she said. "If they're looking for me, it will be the Mercedes they'll be watching for. Not this piece of shit *cholo*-mobile."

Churro clenched his jaws and breathed out a calming breath. He stifled the urge to pull off the interstate at the next exit and put a bullet in the head of this silly broad. *Cholo-mobile, my ass*, he thought.

"I think it would be best if we wait 'til we get to Socorro. I know a good restaurant there that serves the best enchiladas in New Mexico."

"Wonderful," she groused. "Peasant food."

She didn't speak again until they approached the northern-most Belen exit. He'd caught her staring at the scar on his face. "¿*Qué?*" he barked.

"How'd you get that scar," she asked.

He shrugged.

"How long have you worked for my brother?"

"Long time."

"What do you do for him?"

"Odd jobs."

"Jeez," she said. "You don't say much, do you?"

He didn't have an answer for that, so he just shrugged again.

Barbara and Susan interviewed Alberto Martinez in a room at BCSO headquarters. Unfortunately, Alberto wasn't able to shed light on where Lisa French had gone after leaving the location on Central Avenue. He hadn't seen an address and could only tell them that it was somewhere near a grocery store in the first three blocks west of Rio Grande Boulevard. He was able to describe the man who'd driven him from there to UNM Hospital, but didn't have a name. After arranging for a deputy to take her uncle home, Susan checked to see if there had been any responses to the APB they'd issued on Lisa French's Mercedes.

An APB on a vehicle associated with a murder suspect got significant attention from every law enforcement officer in Bernalillo County. But an APB issued for a serial killer driving a silver Mercedes jacked up the adrenaline level of every law enforcement type within a one hundred mile radius of Albuquerque, including FBI personnel. Despite the excitement the APB generated, Susan had reached a level of frustration she'd never known before because not a single viable sighting of the vehicle had come in.

The only information about Lisa French that they'd come up with in that time was generated from social media. French had a Facebook page that featured "selfie" screen shots of her in bathing suits, yoga outfits, and dresses that showed plenty of leg and cleavage. Susan had looked at the woman's Facebook friends and found the name Walter French among them. From Walter French's Facebook page, she'd discovered that he was an administrator at the University of New Mexico. She called Walter French at his office and learned he was out that day. Then she called Roger Smith's cell.

"Hey, beautiful," Roger answered.

"Sorry, but this needs to be quick," Susan said. "Do you know a guy at UNM named Walter French?"

"Absolutely," Roger said. "He's been here for a couple decades, at least. Good guy. Why do you ask?"

"We're trying to locate someone named Lisa French and thought he might know her."

"Know her? That shrew nearly ruined his life."

Susan waved at Barbara to come over, then put her phone on speaker. "You said Lisa French nearly ruined Walter French's life. How so?"

"They were married until, maybe, eight years ago. She treated him like a prince until their wedding day, then she drained his bank and retirement accounts. I heard she was sleeping around with every man who caught her fancy. Poor Walter had a nervous breakdown and barely avoided bankruptcy." Roger took a breath and said, "What's she done now?"

"You remember me telling you about that little wake we had in that bar for my uncle's friend, John Matthews?"

"Sure."

"You recall how my uncle couldn't believe that Mr. Matthews had died because he was in such good health?"

"I remember. Hey, wait a minute. Didn't you tell us that Matthews was murdered?"

"Yes. And Lisa French works at the same facility where Matthews lived."

"And where your uncle lives."

"Correct."

"Are you telling me that Lisa French had something to do with Matthews's death?"

"I shouldn't say anything else. But I suspect if you watch the news, you'll learn a lot about why I have to cancel our dinner date tonight. I'll tell you all about it when I can. In the meantime, do you have a home phone number for French?"

"Hold on. I'll get my university personnel directory."

Her desk phone on speaker, Susan asked, "Mr. French?"

"Yes. Who's calling?"

"Sir, my name is Susan Martinez. I'm a detective with the Bernalillo County Sheriff's Office. Would you mind answering a few questions?"

"What's this about, Detective?"

"Were you married to Lisa French?"

A good five seconds passed before French answered, "Yes. A long time ago."

"We're trying to locate Ms. French. Would you know where she might be?"

"Detective, I haven't heard from my ex-wife in at least seven years."

"I noticed that you are Facebook friends."

French made a dismissive hand gesture. "Pure maudlin curiosity," he said.

Susan wasn't sure that she believed the man, but she went on to ask, "Would you be able to refer me to someone who she might be close to?"

"What's going on?" French said.

"Please answer my question, sir."

Another long pause, then French said, "Not until you tell me what's happening."

It was Susan's turn to pause. After she thought about what she wanted to tell French, she said, "Your ex-wife is wanted for questioning about the death of her boss."

"You think she killed him?"

"I can't really answer that question."

"I understand," he said. "I figured she'd kill someone sooner or later."

"Why do you say that?"

"She's a predator, Detective. A predator without conscience. All she needed were the right circumstances and enough motivation."

226

"Does she have any close contacts?"

"There's only one person in this world who Lisa is close to. The one person she would always go to for help in getting her out of a jam. Her brother Frank."

"What's his last name, and do you have a contact number for him?"

"I don't know his number. I do know he owns a towing company, among a lot of other businesses."

"His last name?"

"Oh, sorry. Calderon. Frank Calderon."

Susan gasped. While she made eye contact with Barbara, she asked, "*The* Frank Calderon?"

French said, "If you mean, is her brother the Frank Calderon who's frequently mentioned in the press regarding certain nefarious activities, the answer is they are one and the same person."

While Susan finished up with French, Barbara called Detective Joe Manzanares in Vice and asked him if he had contact information for Calderon.

"Ah, my favorite sleaze ball," the detective said. The man chuckled. "What do you want with that bastard?"

"You see that APB we put out on Lisa French?"

"Yep. A female mass murderer. That's a new one. What about it?"

"That woman is Frank Calderon's sister."

"Jeez. What a family. Give me a minute. I'll pull up Calderon's address."

Barbara stalked the floor of the Homicide Division as she waited for Manzanares to return to his phone. When he did, he gave her an address on Central Avenue.

"Thanks," she said.

"You want some backup?"

"You know, Joe, that's a good idea. How about we meet you at the address on Central in fifteen minutes?"

Barbara felt energized as she drove onto the lot of the building address Detective Joe Manzanares had given her. She parked the car and pointed at the grocery store in the center of the strip mall that occupied the property.

"Susan, didn't your uncle mention a food store?"

"Yeah, he did. And notice that we're three blocks from Rio Grande."

"I'll be damned. Maybe Lisa French did exactly what her former husband suggested she would do. Run to her brother."

Barbara looked around to see if Manzanares had arrived yet. When she didn't see him, she said, "While we wait for Joe, let's walk around the lot and see if we can spot French's Mercedes."

Susan opened her door and stepped out. She buttoned her coat and looked over the car roof at Barbara as her partner exited the vehicle. "It's getting colder every day. I hate winter."

Barbara laughed. "Fall's not even half over and you're already complaining about winter."

They strolled the perimeter of the parking lot and then looked behind the building, but had no luck finding the Mercedes. "Probably on the road by now," Susan said.

"Yeah, probably."

They returned to their vehicle just as Manzanares drove up.

"How do you want to do this, Barb?" Manzanares asked.

"What's your relationship with Calderon?"

"We're on speaking terms. I get the impression he likes pulling my chain. I know he's dealing, among other things, and he knows that I know, but I think he loves playing cat and mouse with me. I really wish I could pin something on the bastard."

Barbara considered what Manzanares had said and then suggested, "How about you take the lead? We'll observe. After you warm him up a bit, Susan and I can jump in."

Manzanares nodded. "Okay by me."

They walked through the store to a locked door in the back. Manzanares knocked and told the man who opened the door that they were there to see Frank Calderon.

"You got an appointment, Detective?" the man said with a scowl.

Manzanares scowled back. "Tomas, since when do I need an appointment?"

The man laughed. "Come on in. The boss is always happy to see you." He led the three of them through a lounge area occupied by several hard-looking men to an office and announced, "Detective Manzanares to see you, boss."

Frank Calderon was a tall, good-looking man with jet-black hair streaked with gray, strong features, and intelligent mahogany-colored eyes. Barbara's first impression was that he was no thug, but rather an executive dressed in a custom-made suit with a one hundred dollar haircut.

"Hey, Frank. ¿Qué pasa?" Manzanares said.

"*Nada más,* Joe. Just trying to make a living."

Manzanares sneered. "Yeah, business is a bitch. Must be tough being a legitimate businessman."

Calderon blurted a laugh. "What can I do for you?" He took a long moment to eyeball Barbara and Susan and added, "You're keeping better company than usual, Joe. Don't tell me these ladies are with the sheriff's office."

Manzanares turned slightly and introduced Barbara and Susan.

"My, my," Calderon said. He pointed at chairs in front of his desk and invited them to sit.

As soon as he was seated, Manzanares said, "Any idea where we might find your sister?"

Calderon put on a surprised expression that Susan considered immediately as dissembling.

"Which sister are you referring to, Joe?"

"How many do you have, Frank?"

"Three."

"And how many live in New Mexico?"

Calderon smiled. "Only one of them."

"Okay, well then let's concentrate on the one who lives here."

"Oh, you mean Lisa. Why are you asking about her?"

"Let's stay on point here, Frank. Answer my question. Where might we find Lisa?"

"I really have no idea. She dropped by here earlier in the day, and then took off to parts unknown."

"Why'd she drop by?"

He shrugged. "Just to say hello." He put on a patronizing smile and added, "I'm her big brother. She comes to me for advice."

"What kind of advice was she looking for today?"

He shook his head. "No advice, really. Like I said, she just stopped to say hello."

Susan said, "You having fun, Frank?"

The question seemed to confuse Calderon, who settled back into his chair, steepled his fingers, and tipped his head to one side. "What do you mean?"

"You're sitting here in a three thousand dollar suit pretending to be a member of the chamber of commerce, while you're surrounded by *matónes*."

Calderon waved a hand in the direction of the lounge. "Those men are loyal employees. They're not thugs."

Susan laughed as she caught a glimpse of the change in Manzanares's surprised expression. "We know you're an asshole; we know you're knee-deep in shit; and we know you're normally pretty damned smart. But I want to leave you with a thought. Being knee-deep in shit is bad. But once it rises above your chin, all the fancy suits and clever banter won't be able to cover up the fact that you're drowning in it." She stood as though she was about to leave, but said, "I have a feeling that you won't do well at the state pen. That's where you'll be after we nail you for being an accessory to murder."

She moved to the door, wiggled her fingers at Calderon, and said, "Ta, ta."

Barbara and Manzanares followed Susan out, but before they'd all cleared the hall to the lounge, Calderon called out, "Joe, come back here."

Barbara and Susan turned to follow Manzanares back to the office, but he gestured at them with a hand, telling them to wait in the hall. He went to the office and shut the door behind him.

"What?" Manzanares said, his voice full of impatience.

"What the hell's going on?"

"You tell me, Frank. You told us your sister was here. So that's not even in question. We know she didn't stop by to just say hello, having just murdered her boss. We suspect she also murdered a bunch of other people. You expect us to believe a woman on the run took time out to visit her brother, who's been pulling her ass out of hot water for years? Your little lie was witnessed by three detectives. When we find Lisa, we'll question her about everything, including her stopping here for your help. You think she's going to cover for you? You're going down, Frank."

Manzanares wheeled out of the office, joined Barbara and Susan, and followed them back out to the parking lot. Next to their cars, he said to Susan, "Do you always go off like that or was what happened in there a one-time thing?"

"Actually, I thought what Susan said was pretty damned effective," Barbara said.

Manzanares chuckled. "In truth, I did too. I just wanted to know if that was unusual behavior."

Susan looked away as Barbara said, "No, that's pretty much normal."

CHAPTER 38

The fall sun was almost down as Churro took the first Socorro exit, cruised North California Street, went west on Bullock, and skirted the New Mexico Tech Golf Course. He reached Blue Canyon, west of the golf course, before his passenger woke up.

"Where the hell are we?" she demanded.

"I think I took a wrong turn," Churro said.

"Gee, you think? We're out in the middle of nowhere."

He drove forward one hundred yards to the edge of an eighty-foot drop-off into a narrow canyon that looked more like a fissure in the earth. The distance to the ledge on the other side of the canyon was no more than ten feet. Churro got out from behind the wheel and walked forward. He peered into the chasm and thought, *perfect*.

French lowered her window and shrank back as a steady blast of cold air struck her face, wildly swirling her hair. She shouted, "What the fuck are you doing?"

He walked back toward her side of the car and said, "I think we ran out of road."

"No shit, Sherlock. Get back in here and get us the hell out of this godforsaken place." She lifted her purse from the floor and placed it on her lap. She took out a compact and told Churro, "I thought you said you had a favorite restaurant around here. I'm hungry."

"*Jesus, Maria, y Jose*," he intoned. "You are one pain in the ass.

232

No wonder your brother wants you dead."

As he threw open the passenger door, Churro derived great satisfaction from the surprised expression on the woman's face. "Get out," he growled.

It took French a few seconds to process what she'd just heard. "What are you talking about?" she shouted as she dropped the compact.

"Get out," the man ordered in a low, threatening voice as he grabbed her right arm.

French tried to jerk her arm free, but the man was too strong, his grip painful. She screamed for help but knew it was useless, considering where they were. As he pulled, her upper body now parallel with the rocky ground, her purse tipped off her lap and dropped onto the rocky ground. The envelopes of cash and gold coins scattered beside the car. Then she saw the glint from the chrome-plated barrel of the .38 caliber revolver. Only her feet were still in the car as the man pulled her. In desperation, she swept her left hand toward the spot where she'd seen the shiny pistol barrel. She grasped the top of the pistol and tried to adjust it in her hand, to get her fingers around the grip. But she dropped it as Churro heaved on her arm and dumped her on the ground.

"Don't, don't," she cried out.

The man slammed the passenger door shut, pulled out a knife that reflected the moonlight, and pointed it at her. "Your ears are going to make a nice addition to my collection."

French scuttled sideways a foot or two, all the while sweeping the ground with her hand. She gasped for breath as her fingers scraped over small, jagged rocks and sand. She couldn't take her eyes off the man's face, which seemed ghastly in the dying light.

"I'm going to enjoy this, *puta*," he said.

When she scooted back another foot, her hand found the pistol. She righted it in her hand and turned it upward toward the man just as he straddled her. The noise of the hammer striking the empty chamber sounded unnaturally loud. Her lungs seemed to deflate. The man stopped for a second, as though he couldn't reconcile the noise he'd heard. Then he smiled and growled, "*Estupida, olvidaste poner balas en tu arma.*"

French pulled the trigger again, shocked by the noise as the weapon fired. The man made an *oomph* sound and staggered backward. She continued to pull the trigger until it dawned on her that she was out of bullets. Back on her feet, she half-stumbled as she approached the man. His scarred face was contorted in pain and his breathing was labored.

"Who's the stupid one now?" she said as she dropped the pistol.

"*Hija de puta,*" he groaned.

French spotted the man's knife lying next to him. She squatted, picked it up, and placed the blade under his left ear.

After French finished with Churro, she tried to calm down, to think about what to do next. After gathering up the knife and pistol and wrapping them in a handkerchief she found in one of the man's pockets, she placed them behind the El Camino's front seat. Then she went to retrieve her purse and things. When she discovered that the wind had scattered her cash into and beyond the ravine, she howled like a wounded animal. She thought she could see the bills being chased by the wind along the bottom and on the far side of the depression. The only things she was able to recover were her purse, the gold coins, her wallet, her cell phone, and her compact.

After scanning the ground to make certain she hadn't left anything behind—besides Churro and his ears—she got into the car and drove away.

Frank Calderon looked at his watch: 7:15 p.m., and wondered why he hadn't heard from Churro. His man should have taken care of business by now. He also wondered why he had not even a minute sense of regret about ordering his man to kill his sister. He'd always known that all the things he'd done for his sister, all the times that he'd rescued her from trouble, had been grounded in responsibility, not in love. As the eldest son, he'd been indoctrinated by his parents from an early age to take responsibility for his siblings. That indoctrination had only bred contempt bordering on hatred for his sisters and brothers. That had especially been the case with Lisa, who was perpetually inciting trouble and getting into scrapes from the time she was five or six. Those episodes steadily escalated to more and more serious matters the older she got, the more beautiful she became. *Now, she's a fuckin' mass murderer*, he thought.

He dragged his cell phone over to the middle of his table at Zinc and dialed Churro's number.

The coyote that had gobbled up one of the pieces of meat on the body had just dropped his snout to the second morsel and grabbed it with its front teeth when something inside the corpse made a loud noise. The animal tucked its tail between its legs and dashed off.

"Come on, Churro, answer your phone," Calderon whispered. When it went to voicemail, he hung up.

Lisa French stopped for gas at a station on the south end of Socorro. She could only afford twenty dollars worth. That left her ninety dollars in cash to get to Mexico and get settled there. *Who am I kidding?* she thought. *That's not enough.* The memory of her eighty-seven thousand dollars scattered in the wind caused her chest to ache. Thank God for the gold coins. But, then she thought, *I'll need a lot more than the cash I get from selling them.* "Who can I call for help?" she mumbled. But she came up with no names. *I can't even trust my brother. The bastard was going to have me killed.* She considered calling Walter French. *He's always been obsessed with me, even when I screwed around on him.* But she erased that thought from her mind, figuring that the cops would probably have already contacted him about her whereabouts. She knew that regardless of Walter's obsession with her, he was too much of a wimp to defy the police.

Then the idea came to her that she held one trump card that could save her. She'd threatened to expose her brother to the police. That had gotten his attention. *That threat was why he told that scar-faced monster to kill me. That's still the ace up my sleeve.*

She pulled her cell phone from her purse and dialed her brother's number.

Calderon recognized the number on his cell phone screen. He

jumped out of his chair and rushed outside to the front of the restaurant. He quickly moved around the corner and answered the call.

"Hello," he said.

"Well, well, if it isn't my loving brother."

"Where are you?"

"Oh, I'm sure you would love to know that."

"Where's Churro?"

"Probably being eaten by vultures by now." Her tone went from mischievous to violently angry. "You sonofabitch, I'm going to make you pay for what you tried to do."

"Hold on, Lisa. Let's think about this. I know you're upset, but we can work this out."

"You're damned right we can work it out."

"What do you want?"

"In return for me not going to the cops and telling them what I know about your operation, I want two million dollars."

A tidal wave of fear washed over Calderon. Despite the cold and wind, he felt wet with perspiration.

Lisa laughed. "Brother, remember that I know a lot about your operation. I kept your books for your businesses while I was in college. I know about your businesses, your drug distribution network, your money-laundering scheme, and your overseas bank accounts."

Calderon expelled a slow, steady breath. "How do you want to do this?"

"I think that will be pretty easy. You just have to wire money from one of your Mexican banks to my account in Mexico. You get that done by noon tomorrow and I'll be gone."

She'll never be gone, he thought. "What are the account and bank routing numbers?"

"I'll call you in the morning with that information." She paused a couple seconds, and then said, "Sleep tight."

FRIDAY
OCTOBER 10

CHAPTER 39

Barbara was startled awake by knocking on her front door. She shrugged into a robe, went to the door, and looked in the peephole: Henry.

She opened the door and stepped into him, hugging him and nearly causing him to drop a cardboard tray of coffees and a bag of something that smelled very good. She stepped back, grabbed the tray from his hand and ushered him inside. After placing the tray on the table by the door, she turned and kissed him. When she finally let him go, he said, "You have anything on under that robe?"

She asked, "What time is it?"

"Eight."

"Oh, damn, I've got to meet Susan and Salas in an hour."

"You didn't answer my question about what you have on under your robe."

Barbara flashed him, showing Henry that she had nothing on other than the robe. She said, "Eat your heart out, Big Boy," turned to the table, snatched up one of the coffees, and escaped toward her bedroom. As she retreated, she heard him mutter, "No good deed goes unpunished."

After she promised Henry that she would meet him for dinner at Scalo's in Nob Hill, Barbara ran to the Crown Vic and drove to Susan's. They then rode together to headquarters for a meeting with Lt. Salas.

They briefed Salas on where the Lisa French case was as of yesterday at 9:00 p.m., when they'd finally called it a day.

"Still nothing from that APB on the Mercedes?" Salas asked.

"Nothing, Lou," Susan said. "It's as though the car flew off into space."

Salas nodded. "I'll give you ten-to-one odds that it's been parked in a garage, put on a semi headed for Mexico, or chopped for parts."

"No bet," Barbara said.

Susan said, "Dammit. If I recall correctly, Frank Calderon owns a body shop. Let's go down there and see if we can find something."

Salas said, "Don't waste your time. Calderon's too smart to have any evidence lying around."

"It's worth a try," Susan said.

"You've got better things to do," Salas said. "Send a deputy over to the body shop and have him look around."

"They'll never let him in without a warrant," Barbara said.

"Probably right," Salas said. "But, as Susan said, it's worth a try. In the meantime, I want you two to spend the day at the retirement home. And get hold of that ADA, Elinore Freed, and have her start the process of disinterring every person who died of a heart attack at Vista de Alameda at any time during the past twenty-four months. We need to build a case for trial."

"If we ever find Lisa French," Barbara said.

Salas shrugged. "What choice do we have?"

"None," Barbara said.

Lisa French had driven straight through from Socorro to Mexico, arriving in Juarez at midnight. She'd taken a room in a one-star motel near the dog track and tried to sleep on a lumpy, sway-backed mattress. After a fitful night and a breakfast of coffee as thick as mud and two pieces of toast with the consistency of cardboard slathered with orange marmalade that was more rind than jam, she cashed in the gold coins and used the cash to open an account at a *Banco Mexico* branch. She then called her brother, gave him the account and routing numbers, and signed off with, "Remember, Frank, no later than noon, or I'll have to make a call to the cops."

She disconnected the call before Frank could respond.

Frank Calderon knew that his sister would always be a threat to him. The money he would send her would only appease her until she ran out of it. He saw no alternative to wiring the money to her, but he wasn't about to sit back and assume she'd go away forever. He'd guessed that Lisa had made it to Mexico by now. There was no way she would remain in the States. The fact that she'd opened a bank account in a Mexican bank told him that, more than likely, she'd done so in Mexico. He knew a few Mexican banks had branches in some U.S. cities, but those U.S. branches would have to comply with Federal Reserve and U.S. Treasury rules about reporting deposits in excess of ten thousand dollars.

Calderon had another thought: Churro's El Camino. *Lisa must have taken off in the vehicle after she somehow killed Churro.* Every time he thought about her eliminating his best man, he was amazed. He'd underestimated his sister. After he'd wired the cash to Lisa's account, he used a burner phone to call Estevan "*Toro*" Sandoval.

"Hola, amigo, ¿qué está pasando?"

"Toro, I need your assistance."

"So, you're not calling about the next shipment?"

"No, my friend. I need to locate someone in Juarez."

"And if I can locate this person, what should I do with him?"

"Her, my friend. It is a woman I want to find."

Sandoval said, "Huh. That's what every man wants."

Calderon vented a curt laugh. "I want this woman to disappear."

"Oh."

After a few seconds, Calderon said, "She has two million dollars in an account in a Mexican bank. If I give you the routing number, can you come up with the bank's location?"

"Of course. But if the bank isn't here in Juarez, it will be difficult to find this woman."

"I'm assuming she's in Juarez." He chuckled. "I presume, with your powers of persuasion, you will be able to encourage her to transfer that money to you."

"This is a very important favor you want from me."

Calderon laughed again. "I think that two million dollars takes this request from being a favor to being a very lucrative business deal."

It was Sandoval's turn to chuckle. "I think you are correct, *mi amigo.*"

Calderon gave Sandoval Lisa's name, the description of the El Camino, and the bank's routing number.

"Who is this woman?" Sandoval asked.

"Is that important, Toro?"

"No, my friend. *No es importante.*"

CHAPTER 40

Barbara and Susan found Vista de Alameda in a state of turmoil. Television news had carried the story of Armstead's murder and the manhunt in progress to find Lisa French. Although the media was not privy to the extent of French's crimes, even one murder at a retirement home was more than enough to become "our top story," as the news programs put it.

After inspecting Armstead's office, Barbara and Susan met with Susan's Uncle Alberto and Max Katz in Alberto's apartment.

"You seem to have your ear to the ground around here," Susan told Max. "What's the scuttlebutt?"

Max chuckled. "It's like the end of the world. The old gals around here are in a panic. I've had to console so many of them, I feel like a friggin' rabbi."

"Max," Alberto said, warning his friend to watch his language.

Max waved off the warning. "It was like a goddamn Miss America Contest around here last night. Women running around the halls in curlers and nightgowns." He chuckled again. "What's a man to do?"

Susan leaned forward in her chair. "That's not quite what I had in mind when I asked my question. Tell us about the rumors. Any word on Lisa French? Anyone say anything about where she might have gone?"

Alberto said, "I talked with some of the staff. They are as

shocked about what happened as the residents. I learned that none of them was close to French. Several thought she and Armstead were having an affair. No one knows where French might have gone." He paused and then added, "I have my suspicions."

Barbara said, "And they are?"

"I think she's in Mexico by now."

Barbara nodded. That was Susan's and her presumption, as well.

"Who's in charge around here now that Armstead and French are gone?" Susan asked.

Max said, "Probably the board of directors. They're meeting in the conference room now."

"What are you going to do now?" Alberto asked.

"Interview the employees who heard Armstead and French arguing," Susan said. Then she looked at Barbara. "We should try to get the name of every person who passed away here since Lisa French started working at Vista de Alameda."

Max's eyes widened and his mouth gaped. "You think . . . ?"

Susan shrugged.

Toro Sandoval had earned his nickname when he was only ten years old. Already stocky like a bull, he would charge a schoolyard opponent like a rampaging animal, his head down, his fists extended like horns. He was five feet, eight inches tall in eighth grade—his last year of formal education. Over the next four years, he added fifty pounds to his bovine-like frame. He hadn't been paid to do a hit since he was twenty-eight. That was twenty years ago. But that hit on a police captain had been the foundation of his reputation and his criminal career. Now, head of the Juarez Cartel, he was rich beyond his dreams and most people's imaginations. But, despite his wealth and position, the thought of killing someone still caused his juices to flow. Besides, for two million dollars he'd whack his own mother. He'd put out the word all over Juarez that he would pay ten thousand dollars to anyone who provided information that led to him finding a woman driving a renovated, black El Camino with New Mexico plates. The owner of a food truck called in at 9:25 a.m. He'd seen the woman get into the El Camino in front of a *Banco Mexico* branch. The man now followed the black vehicle.

"*Primo*," Toro said, "where is she headed?"

"*Jefe*, it looks like she's going toward the dog track."

"Stay with her, my friend."

"*Si, Jefe*, you can count on me."

Toro wondered as he looked around at the opulence of his den, *how many tortillas would the peon have to sell to make ten thousand dollars?* While he waited for the food truck driver to update him, he put his cell phone on mute and shouted at one of his men, "Call Rodrigo and have him go toward the dog track."

"What do you want him to do with the woman?" the man asked.

"Have him bring her to the warehouse. And tell him to scare her, but if he hurts her so she can't talk, I'll feed his *cajones* to the pigs."

Lisa French was finally feeling good about her prospects. She'd confirmed that the money from her brother had been wired to her account. She'd withdrawn ten thousand dollars for additional walking around money. Now she needed to get new documents and make arrangements to travel to Costa Rica. *Almost home free,* she thought.

She glanced in the rearview mirror and muttered, "What the hell." There was a large yellow truck with garlands of plastic flowers bracketing the windshield and the word BURRITOS scrolled across the hood. The vehicle was no more than six feet off her rear bumper.

French lowered her window and waved her arm at the truck's driver, trying to get him to pull back from the rear of the El Camino. But the guy didn't seem to get the message. Finally, after a minute of waving and cursing, she pulled off the cracked asphalt road onto the dirt shoulder. She took her purse off the passenger seat, draped it over her right shoulder, and stuck her hand inside it as she exited the Chevy. She moved toward the truck, pulled her empty pistol from her purse, and aimed it at the driver, who shouted something incoherent, dived off his seat, and disappeared from view.

"Serves you right, *pendejo*," she screeched. "Get off my ass."

French turned back toward the El Camino, thinking about finding a place to buy ammunition for her .38, when a white Ford sedan with heavily-tinted windows skidded to a stop beside her. As she jumped back a foot, three men armed with pistols pointed at her leaped from the car, bum-rushed her, shouting like crazed creatures from hell. She threw up her hands, dropped the pistol, and screamed, "Stop! Stop!"

The men threw her to the ground, knocking the wind out of her. They stripped her purse from her arm, secured her hands and feet with plastic ties, and stuffed a rag that tasted like oil in her mouth. Gasping to catch her breath, she saw one man toss her purse into the front of the sedan. She was thrown into the back seat and pushed to the floor. One of the men shouted in Spanish, "Go!" and the car drove off.

After he received a call from Rodrigo, Toro Sandoval dialed Frank Calderon's number. "Your problem has been solved," he said.

"You work quickly, my friend."

"What are friends for, *mi amigo*?"

CHAPTER 41

"We're screwed," Susan said. "This will be the case that keeps on giving. It'll never end."

Barbara slowly shook her head, her eyes giving away her frustration. "Yeah, you're right. Forty-one residential units turned over in the past two years. Twenty-seven involved residents' deaths. I assume that some of those deaths were from natural causes, but we're going to have to disinter every one of them to make sure they weren't murdered." She took a deep breath and then said, "What the hell might we find when we go all the way back to when Lisa French started working here?"

Susan gave her partner a sympathetic look. She knew how much Barbara hated looking at corpses. "Well, we'd better call Elinore Freed and give her a heads-up."

"We could be working this case until we retire," Barbara said.

"Nah, that's an exaggeration. Probably only five years or so."

Barbara groaned. "We might as well return to headquarters. We've done all we can here."

"Too bad none of the employees heard what Armstead and French were arguing about."

As they left the building and walked toward their unmarked, Susan asked, "What should we do about Frank Calderon? That S-O-B must have helped his sister get out of town."

"I'd sure like to take him down," Barbara said.

Almost to their car, Barbara's cell phone rang. She saw Joe Manzanares's name on the screen.

"Yeah, Joe. What's up?"

"I just received a call from Frank Calderon. He wants to meet as soon as possible."

"We were just talking about him. Why are you calling us?"

"He wants you and Susan in on the meeting."

"You're kidding."

"Nope. That's what he said."

"When and where?"

"His office as soon as you can get there."

"Thirty minutes, Joe."

"I'll meet you."

Barbara cut off the call and looked at Susan. "Frank Calderon just called Manzanares. He wants to meet with us."

Susan grinned. "I guess he liked the way I talked to him." She gave Barbara a lascivious look. "You know, some men like aggressive women."

"Yeah, yeah, yeah."

Frank Calderon replayed the disk he'd recorded to make certain there was nothing incriminating on it. Now that Lisa was out of the picture, there was no one who could contradict his story. And helping the cops now might earn him a pass in the future. He smiled and thought about how much easier his life was going to be now that his psycho sister was gone.

He looked at his watch and saw he had about ten minutes before Manzanares and the two female detectives were due to arrive. He took a drink from his iced tea when one of his men knocked on the door. Calderon waved him in.

The man opened the door partway and stuck his head inside. "Boss, a call just came in from that Asian cop you got on the payroll. Someone found Churro's body down in Socorro." The man grimaced. "Critters had been feeding on him."

Calderon felt his stomach do a little somersault. *Churro will be missed and will be difficult to replace.* "Anything else?"

"Yeah. They found his cell phone on him. Your number was in

his recent calls list."

Calderon's stomach rolled over again as his man closed the door and walked away. He thought about the last conversation he'd had with Churro. Unless the man had recorded that conversation, there was nothing incriminating about his number being on Churro's cell phone call list. He might have to answer some questions about why one of his employees was murdered, but that would be no big deal.

The detectives arrived and were shown into his office. Calderon greeted them as though they were long-lost friends, offered them something to drink—which they all declined—and then invited them to sit.

"Thanks for making time out of your busy schedules to meet with me," he said.

"What's on your mind, Frank?" Manzanares said.

Calderon looked disappointed at the detective's abrupt response. He took a deep breath, let it out, and smiled. "I have something I want you to listen to."

Without further preamble, he opened a desk drawer, leaned over, and flipped a switch. Lisa French's voice suddenly came from speakers mounted in the two corners of the wall behind Calderon.

"I'm in terrible trouble, Frankie. I need to get out of New Mexico. Maybe out of the country."

French's voice continued after a short pause. "It's bad, Frankie. They'll start digging up bodies. When they do, they'll discover that I poisoned a bunch of people."

Calderon's voice then came from the speakers: "Humor me, Lisa. How can they pin that on you?"

"Maybe they can't. But I just stabbed my boss and I poisoned his wife. Those two deaths they can pin on me. You have to help me get out of the country."

Then Calderon again: "What the fuck is wrong with you? You want me to cover your ass for . . . what, how many murders?"

There was dead space for a couple seconds, then Calderon's voice again: "How many, Lisa?"

"Twenty-three."

Calderon looked at the detectives in turn, gratified that they each sat seemingly mesmerized.

French continued: *"So what's the difference between one or two dozen? You're my brother. You've got to help me."*

Then French's tone changed as she said: *"You either help me or I'll ruin you."*

After a small break, French added: *"And there's another thing you need to do. There's an old man in my car that I want dumped somewhere."*

"And what has this old man done to deserve such treatment?"

"His niece is a cop who's made my life miserable."

"I see."

"You going to help me?"

Calderon's voice replaced French's: *"You're out of your friggin' mind. Get out of here and never come back."*

Then the sound of a door opening, followed by a *slam*.

The speakers went quiet. After about ten seconds, Calderon reached over and clicked off the machine. When he looked back at the detectives, he said, "I hope that was helpful."

Manzanares looked left at Barbara and then right at Susan. "Any questions?" he asked.

"I assume you'll give us a copy of that recording," Barbara said.

"Of course. I anticipated that." He pulled open his center desk drawer, withdrew a disk in a plastic case, and tossed it onto his desk within Barbara's reach.

As Barbara picked up the disk, she looked across Manzanares at Susan and raised her eyebrows. Susan smiled back and said, "I do have one question." She turned to look at Calderon. "What did your sister mean when she mentioned ruining you?"

Calderon shot Susan a smug look and spread his hands. "I have absolutely no idea what she was referring to. I'm a legitimate businessman and have nothing to hide. I pay my taxes and am a good citizen."

"Yeah, you're a saint," Susan muttered.

Calderon sat up straighter; his upper body appeared to stiffen. "There's no cause for sarcasm or disrespect, Detective." He glared at Susan. "If my sister knew anything about me or my businesses that would have put me in jeopardy, do you think I would have refused to help her?"

"Sure," Susan said. "If you knew she was going to be dead and couldn't testify against you."

Calderon's voice rose in pitch as he jabbed a finger at Susan. "I resent the insinuation, Detective. I loved my sister. I would never do anything to harm her."

"*Loved?*" Barbara asked.

"What?" Calderon said.

"You said, 'loved,' not 'love.' Why did you refer to your sister in the past tense? Do you have some reason to believe she's dead?"

Calderon shook his head. "I used the past tense because as far as I'm concerned my sister is out of my life. I want nothing more to do with her."

"Do you have any idea where your sister might be?" Barbara asked.

"I know nothing about my sister, her whereabouts, or her plans. As I said, she's out of my life." After a beat, he asked, "Are we done here?"

"One other question," Manzanares said. "Earlier today, we got a call from the Socorro County Sheriff that a body was found out past the New Mexico Tech golf course. ID on the body was for a man named Ernesto Leon. Our records show that he went by the street name Churro."

"Oh my God," Calderon said. "Churro was one of my employees. What happened to him?"

"He was shot multiple times." Manzanares paused, then added, "His ears had been cut off, although they weren't at the scene."

Calderon hoped the expression he now wore sufficiently showed grief. "He was a good man," he said.

"So, you have no idea why one of your employees was down in Socorro or why someone would have wanted to do him harm?"

Calderon forced an innocent look. "None. Churro didn't have an enemy in the world."

"That's not quite correct, Frank. He must have had at least one." Manzanares stood, thanked Calderon for the disk, and led Barbara and Susan out of the office.

Susan halted in the doorway and smiled at Calderon. "You

wouldn't happen to have any other disks you'd like to share with us?"

He smiled back. "That was the only one."

"Uh huh," she said, and then followed Barbara and Manzanares.

Calderon waited until the cops were gone, then stood and closed his office door. When he returned to his chair, he thought about what Manzanares had told him about Churro's ears and shuddered. He whispered, "Lisa, you sick bitch." Then he felt a warm surge flow through him as he wondered how the cartel leader, Toro Sandoval, had dealt with his demented sibling.

CHAPTER 42

Barbara and Henry sat on one side of a six-top table across from Susan and Roger in a semi-private alcove on the east side of Bravo Cucina. Alberto Martinez and Max Katz had taken chairs at the opposite ends of the table. They hoisted wine glasses, except Barbara, who lifted her water glass, while Susan said, "Barbara and I want to thank Uncle Alberto and Max for your help with the '*Geezer Killer Case*'"—as a reporter on an Albuquerque radio station had dubbed the murders committed by Lisa French. Then she turned to Roger, kissed his cheek, and smiled at Henry. "And we also want to thank the two greatest guys in the world for your patience with us."

The men all responded in some way, either pooh-poohing Susan's comments or thanking her.

Alberto sipped his wine, placed his glass on the table, and asked, "How can you close the case without arresting the murderer?"

"The case isn't officially closed," Barbara said, "but there's little likelihood that French will turn up. The DEA sent us a message today that Ernesto "*Churro*" Leon's El Camino was found abandoned near the Juarez Race Track. Our assumption is that Lisa French killed Leon, drove his car across the border, and dumped it there." Barbara frowned. "That woman could be anywhere by now."

"And she'd be nuts to ever return to the States," Max said.

Henry chuckled. "Well, we already know she's nuts."

Max grinned. "Okay, okay, you're right. I'll change that to stupid.

She'd have to be stupid to come back here."

"You still think you're going to be tied up with the case?" Henry asked Barbara. "Even though the killer has probably left the country."

"Oh, yeah," Barbara said, her expression now morose. "The D.A. will try French in absentia. To do that, she'll want OMI to examine every one of the bodies of the people French more than likely murdered."

"I sure hope Vista de Alameda has a large liability policy," Susan said. "The relatives of the men and women French killed will be suing that place big time."

Max laughed. "There was a midget lawyer with a pompadour and three inch platform shoes wandering around the place today looking for information. I heard he paid the receptionist three hundred dollars for the names of every resident who passed away over the past couple of years. He also left flyers in the lobby asking people with PTSD to call him."

"PTSD?" Roger said.

"Yeah," Max said. "Supposedly we're all suffering from trauma from living in a place where residents were murdered."

"What happened at the board meeting?" Barbara asked.

"The board's going to try to sell the place to some big out-of-state operator," Alberto said. He shrugged and added, "I suspect any buyer will want to pay a hugely discounted price."

Two waiters arrived bearing serving trays laden with food and placed plates in front of each of them.

"This sure beats Vista de Alameda food," Max said.

Alberto scowled. "I sure hope the insurance policy is a good one, otherwise, we'll be eating beans and franks for the rest of our lives."

The others laughed until Alberto added, "I wasn't kidding."

"What do you want us to do with her, *Jefe*?"

Toro Sandoval tipped his head and squinted at the woman suspended from a steel girder by a rope around her wrists. Her eyes were puffy and closed and her face had already begun to "purple." The only clothes on her were a bra and bikini panties. He walked around her, as though inspecting a side of beef. Finally, he said, "She's not half-bad looking." He slapped her ass and laughed. "She obviously takes good care of herself."

His man, Rodrigo, said, "She looked a lot better before we worked her over."

"No disrespect, *Jefe*," another man said, "but isn't she a little old for you? I mean, you usually like them much younger."

Sandoval laughed again. "Sometimes you have to season your life with experienced women. This one looks like she's had a lot of experience."

Sandoval walked another circuit around the woman and stepped in close as he came around in front of her. He reached out and pried open one of her eyelids and was surprised when the woman kicked at him, barely missing his groin. He sidestepped the kick and moved back a half-step. He peered at her face with added interest.

"You're a fighter, aren't you?"

The woman groaned, muttered something that sounded like, "*Pendejo*," and spat at him.

Sandoval wondered who this woman was and why it was so important to Frank Calderon that she disappear. He turned to Rodrigo. "Clean her up, feed her, and then bring her to the hacienda."

SATURDAY
OCTOBER 11

CHAPTER 43

Toro Sandoval stared at the woman seated in the straight-backed chair in front of his desk. He was impressed. Despite being handled roughly by his men and now confronted by a stranger in unfamiliar surroundings, she showed no fear. In fact, she glared back at him as though he were something she'd scraped off her shoe.

"What's your name?" he asked.

She continued to glare back. The only change in her expression was a small grin.

"I got two men waiting outside that door over there who can't wait for me to hand you over to them. If you don't change your attitude and don't give me immediate answers to my questions, I'll let my guys do whatever they want with you. Then, when they're finished playing their games, they'll sell you to a brothel in town." He gave her a cruel smile. "You won't last long."

"What the fuck do you care what my name is?"

Sandoval shook his head and barked, "Arturo."

The office door opened and a man stepped inside. He asked, "*Si, Jefe?*"

"She's all yours," Sandoval said.

"Whoa, wait a minute. I'll—"

The woman shouted and begged as Arturo dragged her toward the door. Sandoval watched her kick and scream and thought, *good riddance*, until she shouted, "I have information about Frank

256

Calderon's operation."

Sandoval raised a hand, stopping Arturo. "Bring her back here." The man jerked the woman to her feet and pulled her by one arm to the chair. He pushed her into it and backed away. Sandoval waved him out of the room.

"You've got thirty seconds," Sandoval told the woman.

"My name's Lisa French. I used to handle the books and cash for Frank Calderon. I know the names of every one of his distributors, how much product they move, how much money they make for him."

"And why would I be interested in that information?"

The woman swallowed and licked her lips. "Because Calderon's three-state distribution network throws off over thirty million dollars a year. If you had the names of the distributors in all three states, what would you need Calderon for? He's the middle man. That's thirty million more in your pocket."

Sandoval rested his chin on one hand and scratched the side of his nose with a finger. He looked into the woman's eyes and knew instinctively that she wasn't bullshitting him. For years, he'd thought about how eliminating his primary clients in eight states would increase his profit margins. But the buyers in those states protected the identities of their distributors like the DEA protected the identities of their informants. He also knew that if he tried to set up his own distributors, he would start an all-out war, which wouldn't help anyone. But, with the names of the distributors, he could easily eliminate men like Frank Calderon. The men who bought drugs from Calderon wouldn't care one bit if he was out of the picture, as long as someone else quickly took his place.

Sandoval shifted against the back of his chair and squinted at the woman. "So, Miss Lisa French, why should I believe you?"

She stared back at him with an arrogant smile. "How difficult would it be to verify what I tell you? I give you the name and location of one distributor, you send a couple tough guys to talk with him, he answers their questions." She dusted her hands together, then spread them apart and shrugged.

"How did you come by this information?"

"I worked for Calderon part-time while I was in college." She smirked. "I set up the system for moving cash from the States to Mexico, and then on to banks in the Caribbean. He's still using the same process."

Sandoval squinted and shook his head. "You expect me to believe that Calderon let you walk away with all this information in your head?"

The woman's eyes narrowed and went hard; her lips formed a slash. "He didn't want me too close to the action anymore. He was afraid that, if he was ever arrested, I would wind up in prison, too."

"And why would he care one way or the other?"

"French is my married name. I was born Lisabeta Calderon. I'm Frank's sister."

Sandoval's breath caught in his chest for a moment. When he let it out, he coughed, then blurted a laugh.

The woman's expression evolved over the next few seconds. Her face softened and her eyes now gleamed with apparent glee.

Sandoval now wore a toothy smile. "You'd do this to your own brother?"

"He ordered one of his men to kill me. Then he obviously called you when his man failed to get the job done."

Sandoval was beginning to enjoy the conversation. "What happened to the man who was supposed to kill you?"

"I shot him and cut off his ears."

Sandoval had a momentary shiver run up his spine. Then he smiled again. "I guess, if we're going to work together, I'll have to keep my eyes on you."

The woman just smiled back.

Barbara stood under a leafless cottonwood tree on the edge of a cemetery that had been in Albuquerque's South Valley for well over one hundred years. She watched a backhoe loader operator jam his shovel into the pebbly earth that covered Peter Giacomo's grave. She knew someone needed to be present to ensure that chain of custody rules were adhered to, but had tried, without success, to get Salas to assign someone else to the duty. To take her mind off the gravesite activity, she called Susan who was serving a similar purpose at a cemetery in the town of Bernalillo, about fifteen miles north of the Albuquerque city limits.

"How are things there?" Barbara asked.

"I thought we'd have difficulty with the disinterment orders," Susan said. "I figured families would be up in arms about loved ones being dug up and picked at. Man, was I wrong."

Barbara chuckled. "Nothing like a prospective lawsuit and a big payday to make people put aside their sensitivities."

"My uncle told me that Vista de Alameda has a large liability policy that covers up to five million dollars per incident and twenty-five million overall."

Barbara said, "They're going to burn through that coverage pretty damned fast. The board of directors of that place will be living with a mess for quite a while."

"That's an understatement," Susan said.

"Where are you going next?"

"Sunset Memorial Park."

"You okay, Barb?"

"I'm okay. Thanks for asking." Barbara swallowed hard, glanced over at the backhoe loader. "You think we'll ever find out what happened to Lisa French?"she asked.

"Nah," Susan said. "That woman might be psycho, but she's not stupid. She knows what's waiting for her here. Lisa French is in the wind."

TEN WEEKS LATER
WEDNESDAY
DECEMBER 24

CHAPTER 44

"What do you think Salas wants with us?" Barbara asked Susan on the ride to BCSO headquarters.

Susan shrugged. "Can't be good," she said. "We were supposed to be off today."

Barbara pulled the Crown Vic into the underground parking lot and, as she circulated to find a space, said, "I can't wait for this year to be over. All we've done for the past two-and-a-half months is watch bodies get dug up and go to autopsies."

"Yeah. Ain't law enforcement glamorous and exciting?"

Barbara parked and shut down the car. Then she shifted in her seat to look at Susan. "I have a bad feeling, partner."

"About what?"

"About the lawsuits brought by Scott Matthews and Oscar Vigil."

"Nonsense. The only thing we could be criticized for is getting the search warrant of Matthews's home after I'd already found the liquid nicotine in his medicine cabinet. Everything else was by the book." She huffed a breath and added, "I screwed up. I should never have looked in that cabinet without a warrant."

"More nonsense," Barbara said. "You had probable cause. Matthews was on the visitors' log at Vista de Alameda on the day his father was murdered. He had a rap sheet. He had means, motive, and opportunity."

Susan put on a whimsical smile, which quickly metamorphosed

into a sour, tight-lipped expression. "We'll see. Let's go see Salas."

Salas was seated behind his desk. Instead of the normal setup of two chairs in front of his desk, there were three there today. One of the three, occupied by a fifty-something dirty-blonde who had a cherubic face and a *Cruella De Vil* body, was turned slightly toward the other two chairs.

"Who's that?" Susan asked as they moved toward Salas's open door.

"No idea," Barbara said.

As they approached their boss's door, he waved them in. His complexion looked wan; he didn't make eye contact with either of them.

Uh oh, Barbara thought.

"Sit down," Salas said, as he stood, went around to the door, and closed it.

Susan took the middle chair; Barbara sat on her right.

After Salas returned to his chair, he pointed at the other woman. "This is Candace Saunders, the new Sheriff's Office H.R. Director."

Barbara looked over at Saunders, who wore as neutral an expression as Barbara had ever seen. She had the *uh oh* feeling again. She glanced at Susan to see her reaction but her partner's expression was no less neutral than was Saunders's.

"Thanks for coming in today," Salas said, his usually squeaky voice now almost shrill.

Barbara didn't trust her voice, so she just nodded. Another glance at Susan told her nothing about what was going on inside her partner's head.

Salas swiveled his chair toward Saunders. "Why don't you tell Detectives Lassiter and Martinez about the . . . settlement."

Barbara and Susan shifted slightly to look at the H.R. Director.

"The county manager just signed off on a settlement agreement with Scott Matthews over his wrongful arrest lawsuit. The county agreed to settle out of court. I—"

"How much?" Susan asked, her neutral expression now gone, replaced with white-hot anger that showed on her cheeks. Barbara couldn't see Susan's eyes, but she suspected they were like burning coals.

Saunders said, "Four million dollars."

"Bullshit," Susan blurted.

Saunders face reddened. "No, Detective; not bullshit. The county attorney figured a jury trial would have led to a judgment of at least twice that amount."

"A gelded horse has bigger balls than the county attorney," Susan said. "But what does he care. It's just taxpayer money."

Saunders was obviously getting hotter by the second. She opened her mouth as though about to say something, but Salas cut her off. "Susan, Barbara, why don't you let Ms. Saunders finish."

They all looked back at Saunders and waited.

"Thank you, Lieutenant," Saunders said. She shot Susan a cold look, but quickly brought her emotions under control, licked her lips, and said, "The same attorney who represented Mr. Matthews also represented Oscar Vigil. The county has agreed to pay Mr. Vigil three million dollars for unlawful arrest and for the injuries he suffered while in custody."

While Susan steamed, muttering something in Spanish, Barbara looked from Saunders to Salas, and back to Saunders. She had a visceral feeling that what the woman had told them was merely prelude to the real reason they'd been called in. She took a deep breath, slowly let it out, and cleared her throat. Saunders began to speak again, but Barbara held out her arm like a running back fending off a tackler and quietly said, "Lieutenant."

It took Salas a couple seconds to meet her gaze.

"What's the bottom line here?"

Salas released a blast of air that came across like a moan. He closed his eyes for a moment, then looked back at Barbara. "The plaintiffs' attorney wants you two terminated. That's part of the settlement. The county attorney has agreed."

"And if we choose to fight it?" Barbara said.

"Toward what end?" Salas said. "Both cases will go to court. You'll spend the next two years in legal proceedings, juries will probably award the plaintiffs twice as much as the amounts in the settlement agreements, and your names will be dragged through the muck by the media." He swallowed and looked from one of them to the other. "You'll be transferred out of Homicide, you'll never be promoted, and you'll be assigned every shit case that comes along or put on permanent clerical duty. I already talked with the union rep. His take on your situation is about the same as mine."

Barbara nodded her understanding. Susan continued to mutter something.

"It's a shitty deal," Salas said. "I'm sorry."

He stood and said, "Ms. Saunders will explain how your exit from the department will work." Then he walked around his desk and out of the office.

Saunders stood, moved her chair so that she could face Barbara and Susan head-on, and took a file from a briefcase beside her chair. She took two stapled sets of papers from the file and handed one to each of them.

"Your severance information is on those papers. You'll receive your regular pay through the end of this year. You also have unused vacation time, which you'll be paid for. Also, the county manager has agreed to put you on consulting contracts for a six-month period, during which you'll receive full pay, but no benefits. There will be nothing derogatory put in your personnel files. In return, you will agree to not fight termination." After a beat, she asked, "Any questions?"

Susan leaned toward the woman. "You're really enjoying this, aren't you?"

Saunders seemed to take a calming breath, then said, "Women have fought for years to get the opportunities you two had. It's too bad you didn't recognize what you had. You blew it."

Barbara was surprised at how calm her partner's voice was when she said, "You have no idea how hard we've worked to get where we are . . . were. You sit behind your desk and breathe air untainted by the filth and blood and violence that we experience. And, instead of fighting for two women who fully understand our opportunities, you take them away without even thinking about standing up for us."

Saunders sneered. "Good riddance to you and Salas. You're all dinosaurs."

Susan was about to respond, but Barbara touched her arm,

stopping her. "What did you mean when you said good riddance to Salas?" she asked the woman.

Saunders sniffed, then showed a victorious smile. "When the sheriff wouldn't stand up for you two, Salas resigned. He took early retirement." She sniffed again. "What an idiot!"

Susan jumped to her feet, her fists clenched, and growled, "You silly bitch. I ought to—"

Barbara grabbed Susan's arm and pulled her away from Saunders. She said, "Susan, she just wouldn't understand." Then Barbara looked at Saunders and asked, "How long before we have to sign these papers?"

"Monday by five p.m."

CHAPTER 45

Toro Sandoval looked at the clock beside his bed and noted the time: 9:12 p.m. *Should be any time now*, he thought. He shook his head in wonderment as he got out of bed and stared at the woman who slept as though she didn't have a care in the world. *Even if I hated my brother, there's no way I could sleep knowing he was about to be destroyed.*

He admired the curves of her body under the silk sheet and marveled at how she'd changed his mind about his relationship with women. He no longer craved young women. Lisa French had showed him what a "real woman" was all about. She twisted his insides as no woman had ever done before. And, though he knew she was using him for her own purposes, he didn't care.

Sandoval put on a robe and slippers and padded out to his office. He poured himself a shot of Laphroaig Islay Single Malt Scotch Whisky, inhaled the liquor's nose, then sipped it. Seated in a plush armchair, he thought about the events that would take place before midnight tonight. Lisa French had devised the scheme over the past two-and-a-half months. He felt a slight tremor of fear go through him at the thought that the woman in his bed had been able to manipulate him so easily. Initially, he'd been motivated by greed, but, somewhere along the line, things had changed. For an instant, he'd thought he'd fallen in love, but he quickly discarded the thought. He realized he was incapable of loving anyone. He finally settled on obsession as his true motivation. Just as he was obsessed with money and power, he'd become obsessed with Lisa French.

He checked the time on the clock on the credenza across the room: 9:30.

Mondo Garcia and his brother Rico had lived in Chimayo, in Rio Arriba County, New Mexico, their entire lives. Their county of forty thousand people had, for years, led the nation in the rate of heroin overdoses with an overdose death rate of ten times the national average. The Garcia family that spawned Mondo and Rico also produced four other sons. Two of those boys had died from heroin overdoses. The two others were serving time in the New Mexico State Penitentiary for heroin distribution.

Mondo and Rico, the two youngest of the six boys, both in their late twenties, had learned their lesson from watching their older brothers flush their lives down the toilet. So, instead of using and dealing drugs, the two young men decided to follow a safer line of work. They became enforcers and, ultimately, hit men for whomever would pay the price. They traveled all over the United States on assignments. Rarely were they given targets in their home state.

"Nice to be home for Christmas, bro," Mondo told Rico as they waited in a stolen late model white Honda Odyssey van.

"Mama and Pop will be asleep by the time we get home," Rico said.

"Don't matter, *cuate*. As long as they leave some *posole* and tortillas for us. I can taste Mama's *posole* like I'm eating it now."

"Stop that shit, Mondo. You're driving me crazy talking about it." He laughed. "How the fuck am I gonna concentrate on the targets if I'm thinking about Mama's *posole*, *esse*?

Mondo stared across the parking lot at the Sandia Casino building, a good one hundred yards to the north. "They been in there three hours already. Maybe they're playing some blackjack."

"Gringo assholes," Rico said. "You see how hot those gals were. I wouldn't be spending my time gambling. Hell, I'd rent a room and take care of my needs right there in the hotel. Wouldn't even wait to drive home."

"Shh," Mondo hissed. "I think that's them."

"Shoulda valet-parked the car, Henry," Barbara said. "These heels are killing me."

"We would have been in the valet line for an hour," Henry said. "There were at least thirty cars ahead of us. Christmas Eve is a big night at the casino."

Barbara snuggled against Henry, her arm in his. "I know, sweetie. I'm just not used to wearing high heels."

He looked down at her legs and whispered, "I think you look very sexy in them."

Barbara pinched his arm. "You're drunk."

He giggled. "That's an astute observation, Detective." Then he groaned and said, "Oh, I'm sorry. I shouldn't have said that."

She snuggled closer to him. "It's okay. Technically, I'm still a detective. I'll be on the payroll for another week. You can call me Detective Lassiter until then."

"Those bastards," Henry said. "I can't believe—"

"Let's not talk about it tonight, Henry. It's Christmas Eve. We've got better things to talk about."

"What are you guys talking about?" Susan asked as she and Roger came around a car in the lot and intercepted Barbara and Henry.

"My sexy heels," Barbara said.

"Ooh, girl, those are some hot heels," Susan said, giggling as she bumped up against Barbara. "I'm surprised all the men in the restaurant weren't hanging all over you."

Barbara laughed. "Ha-ha. As the designated driver, you all better shape up or I'll leave you here in this parking lot."

"I didn't say a thing," Roger said.

"Yeah, but you were about to," Barbara said.

Just a few steps from Henry's Infiniti SUV, which was backed into a space that fronted the circulation lane between rows, Barbara heard a car door open somewhere beyond the row where they were parked. Always on alert, she looked in the direction of where the sound had come from but didn't see any courtesy lights come on. She found that odd, but didn't want to read too much into it. After all, this was New Mexico. A lot of people drove older vehicles that they couldn't afford to maintain. *Stop thinking like a paranoid cop,* she told herself. *It's Christmas Eve. Enjoy yourself. Relax.*

Henry used the key fob to remotely unlock the Infiniti's doors, then handed Barbara the key fob. He followed her around to the driver side door while Roger and Susan piled into the back seat. He held the door open for Barbara, made a production of helping her into the driver's seat, and then kissed her on the cheek.

The sound of a golf cart suddenly came from somewhere behind them. *Maybe parking valets coming for a vehicle,* Barbara thought as she placed her purse on the console between the two front seats. As Henry closed the car door, she slipped off her heels and kicked them back toward the front of her seat. "Ah-h-h," she moaned as she rotated her ankles.

As Henry turned to his left toward the front of the vehicle, she put a foot on the brake pedal and pushed the ignition button. The headlights came on automatically as the big engine roared to life. Barbara stared through the windshield and smiled at Henry as he made his way across the front of the SUV. He stopped by the right front headlight, placed a hand on the hood, and blew her a kiss with his other hand. She laughed and whispered, "You silly, sweet man."

Then her stomach lurched as she spotted two men quickly striding toward them, one on either side of a car across from them, beyond the circulation lane. She did a momentary double-take when she thought she saw pistols in their hands.

Barbara shouted, "Guns," as she reached for her purse and pressed the clasp. Her heart seemed to stop as her fingers felt like wooden stumps. She fumbled with the clasp, trying to depress it, all the while staring at the approaching men. She heard Susan yell, "Roger, get down," and then heard the back door on the other side of the vehicle swing open and felt the rush of cold air. Barbara finally popped the clasp, gripped her .9 mm pistol, and jerked it from her purse.

The windshield was like a television screen. It framed the two men and Henry, all lit by the surreal brightness of the Infiniti's headlights. Barbara flicked the light bar on the SUV's column, turning on the hi-lights, which seemed to surprise the two men. She saw shock and confusion on Henry's face. His mouth seemed to form the word, "What?" He apparently had not noticed the two men. He spread his arms as though to ask, "What are you doing?" when the men opened fired. Barbara barely heard the *pfft, pfft, pfft* sounds of silenced rounds being fired as she grabbed the door handle, just as a bullet pierced the windshield. Her left shoulder felt as though she'd been smacked with a sledge hammer. Her entire body felt as though she'd been struck with a huge electrical charge. She tried to open the door with her left hand but her arm seemed paralyzed. She placed her pistol in her lap, reached across her body with her right hand, and pulled on the door handle as she banged her left shoulder into the door. She screamed from the pain but slid down from the seat, crouched behind the open door as bullets impacted the vehicle.

The noise of Susan's .9 mm was deafening as she fired off rounds at the men. Barbara didn't know where Susan was exactly, but it sounded as though she was on the right side of the Infiniti. Maybe behind her own open door.

Peering through the space between the door frame and the car body frame, Barbara spied one of the men moving at an angle away from the headlight beams. She placed her weapon on the "V" between the door and the car's frame, took aim at the man, and fired three times. She saw him jerk backward for an instant. Meanwhile, more rounds thudded into the Infiniti as Susan shouted, "I'm out." Then a flash of light from the left hit the man and a voice shouted, "Drop your weapon."

Barbara saw the front end of a golf cart about twenty yards off to her left. A uniformed security guard crouched behind the cart, a pistol in his extended hand. Then someone yelled something in Spanish that sounded like 'Vamos.'

"Susan," Barbara shouted.

"I'm okay. You?"

"I've been hit. You see them?"

As Barbara moved slowly around the edge of her door, she heard a vehicle engine start and then tires screech on the pavement. The driver did not turn on his lights. Near the front left side of the Infiniti, Barbara's body shook as though she was suffering convulsions. As the adrenaline high of the gun battle began to subside, she focused her mind on Henry. She called out his name as she rounded the front of the vehicle. Then her emotional and spiritual world seemed to collapse when she saw him lying on the pavement, his eyes closed, his body spasming, a spreading pool of blood haloing his head.

Somewhere off in the distance, seemingly a long way away, she heard Roger talking to someone, demanding an ambulance and police officers. Then Susan was beside her, using her pashmina to try to stop the blood flowing from Henry's head. As Susan worked on Henry, she asked Barbara, "Where are you hit?"

"Shoulder." She tried to say something else but nothing would come. She heard Susan scream for Roger's help, but then she heard nothing at all.

CHAPTER 46

As he used one hand and his teeth to knot a handkerchief around his wounded forearm, Rico Garcia told his brother, "We gotta dump this van."

"And do what then? Walk? *Pendejo*, nobody saw this van. We'll finish the job, then dump it."

"What the fuck was that?" Rico asked. "Sandoval say anything to you about those women carrying?"

"He didn't say shit. Everything looked easy until they started shooting." He groused, "I mean, who the hell goes out to dinner on Christmas Eve carrying?"

"Where the hell did that security cop come from? Fuckin' rent-a-cop?" Rico said.

"You hit any of them?"

"Yeah. One of the guys. How about you?"

"Maybe I got one of the women."

"What a disaster!"

It was 11:00 p.m. and Toro Sandoval was worried because he hadn't heard from the Garcia brothers. He hadn't been happy about putting out a hit on the two cops, but Lisa had been adamant that it had to be done. 'Those bitches ruined everything,' she'd shrieked. It was easier to put out a hit than to deal with the woman's hysterics.

About to pour another scotch, he was startled when his phone rang. "*Si*," he answered.

"We just heard on the radio that the women you sent us after are cops."

"What do you mean, 'are cops'? They're still alive?"

"Yeah. You should have told us they might be armed."

"What difference would that have made? You're supposed to be professionals. Did you take care of business, or not?"

"One of them is wounded."

"So, you failed," Sandoval said. He looked at the clock on the credenza. Almost midnight. His voice full of scorn, he said, "I assume you'll be able to take care of the other assignment."

Mondo Garcia didn't immediately respond. When he did, his voice vibrated with anger. "I don't like surprises. You shoulda told us about the policewomen."

"Watch your tone, Garcia." Sandoval waited a second, then said, "Like I told you before, Calderon will be at his parents' home until midnight, exactly as he always is on Christmas Eve. He'll be accompanied by a bodyguard who is also his driver. One guy. That's all. I hope you and your brother can manage to at least do this right."

"Yeah, we'll take care of business."

Sandoval bit his tongue. As angry as he was at Garcia's surly tone, he didn't see any point in alienating the man. "Can you finish the job?" he said.

"Count on it. We'll take care of the cops later."

"Forget the cops. Just take care of Calderon."

After terminating the call, Sandoval set his scotch glass on the side table and pressed his fingertips into his temples. It suddenly struck him that he'd experienced more frequent headaches during the past two months . . . during the period of time that Lisa French had come into his life. He'd just about come to the conclusion that she was more trouble than she was worth, when she walked into the room. Dressed in a filmy negligee that left nothing in doubt, she approached him and asked, "News?"

He shook his head. "They wounded one of the women."

"What do you mean, 'wounded'? I thought the men you hired were professionals." She took a large breath, then shouted, "Tell them to finish the job." Her voice rose in pitch as she screamed, "I want those bitches dead."

"I told them to forget about the women. Going after them is stupid. It could just bring heat down on us, and there's no benefit to killing them. You need to think rationally."

"No benefit? No benefit? I told you I want them gone."

"Keep your voice down," Sandoval growled.

"Screw you," she roared. "What the fuck good are you?"

The look in the woman's eyes made Sandoval cringe for a moment. He'd never seen that look before. It reminded him of the rattlesnakes that were all over the desert around Juarez. Before he could say something, she screeched, "You damn Mexicans are all the same; a bunch of worthless *maricons*."

Sandoval, about to explode in anger, pointed a finger at French. He took a calming breath.

"What? You gonna shoot me with your finger?" She laughed. "Typical."

He dropped his hand and stared at her. It was as though he looked into the face of pure evil. Her eyes were bright with malice, while her mouth curled with contempt.

"*Que lastima!*" he said in a voice slightly louder than a whisper, as he moved to his desk, opened a drawer, and removed a massive chrome-plated pistol.

He pointed the weapon as he came around from behind the desk, approached French, who backed up, her palms out toward him.

"Wait, wait," she whimpered. "I was just kidding." She gasped, then said, "I love you, Toro. We're going to be great together. I—"

The .357's report careened off the walls. Within thirty seconds, two of Sandoval's men stormed into the room, each man carrying an AR-15. They stopped and lowered their weapons when they saw that their boss was safe.

Sandoval pointed his pistol at French, who was on her knees, crying. He looked at the huge hole in the wall behind her and the fine powdery plaster debris that hung in the air.

"What do you want us to do, *Jefe*?" one of the men asked.

Sandoval looked at French again, then said, "Take her to *Casa de Julia*. Tell Julia that this *puta* is my gift to her, to do with as she wishes."

Sandoval watched his men lift the cursing French from the floor and drag her from the room. Then he moved to his desk chair and sat. His mind raced through a series of thoughts that left him disquieted. The disrespectful way Mondo Garcia had spoken to him was worrisome. Garcia's failure to rub out the cops was, in the end, okay, but it made him wonder if the brothers could eliminate Frank Calderon. Then an idea came to him that gave him a warm feeling all over. *Maybe I can get everything I want without killing Calderon,* he thought. *I already know the names and locations of his distributors, the names of his key employees, and his money laundering system. Lisa shared all of that with me. All I need to do is get Calderon out of the picture, and there are ways of doing that other than killing him.*

He snatched up his cell phone, glanced at the clock, and saw that it was three minutes shy of midnight. He rapidly dialed Frank Calderon's number and paced back and forth around the room as he waited for his call to be answered. Finally, someone answered with a shouted, "What?"

"Frank?" Sandoval asked.

"Yeah. Who's this?"

"It's Toro."

"Jeez, Toro. I didn't recognize the number."

"It's a burner phone. Listen, where are you?"

Calderon hesitated. "Why do you want to know that?"

"I just heard the Guadalajara Cartel put out a hit on you."

"Are you kidding? Since when would they target one of your partners?"

"All I can guess is they want to disrupt my distribution network. Maybe put their own people in your territory. With you gone, their chances of taking over the southwest region would be a simple matter."

"You know anything about the hit men?"

"Yeah. I heard they're out of some place called Chimayo. The Garcia brothers."

"I'll be damned. I've used those guys. What—"

Sandoval cut off Calderon. "Listen, Frank, from what I heard, they might come after you tonight. The word is they'll hit you as you leave your parents' house."

Calderon hesitated again, then said, "How do you know I'm at my parents' place?"

"I don't. I'm just telling you what I heard."

After another short hesitation, Calderon said, "Okay. Thanks, Toro."

Sandoval set down his phone and clenched his jaw. He knew he'd made a mistake when he mentioned Calderon's parents' house. He hoped his explanation had been believed. He also knew that the only risk he was taking in warning Calderon was if the man captured one or both of the Garcias. That would be the smart thing to do. But Calderon had a reputation for shooting first and asking questions later. Besides, the Garcias were savvy enough to know that the worst thing that could happen to them would be to be captured. That would lead to very bad deaths.

As he walked back to his bedroom, Sandoval realized that his head no longer hurt. The headache was gone.

THURSDAY
DECEMBER 25

CHAPTER 47

Frank Calderon made a call from the bedroom he'd slept in while growing up in this house. As he waited for the call to go through, he looked around the room at the posters and trophies, the old baseball glove, the photos of him as a kid, the Dallas Cowboys bedspread. Nothing had changed since he'd moved out. He wondered if Lisa's old room was still intact. He thought, *it probably has candles burning in it, now that she's dead.* Then he thought again about how the Garcias could know he was at his parents' home. That was information only his family members and his driver knew. He always spent Christmas Eve with his parents because they wanted their children with them to welcome in Jesus' birthday. Now that Lisa was dead and his other siblings lived out of state, he was the only Calderon child left in New Mexico to spend the eve of the birth of Christ with their parents.

"Hello," a man answered. He sounded groggy.

"Tomas, it's Frank. I need you to do something for me. Fast." He explained what he needed, then hung up and waited.

Mondo Garcia liked the setup. The Calderon house was at the end of a dirt lane that went east off Edith Boulevard. There were no side streets that branched off from the dirt lane. Calderon was trapped.

"What the hell is keeping him?" Rico complained. "It's already half-past twelve."

278

"Stop whining," Mondo said. "Maybe it's taking him a while to say his goodbyes."

"My arm's killing me."

"We'll get Mama to fix you up as soon as we take care of business here."

"Hey," Rico said. "Someone just came out of the house."

Mondo looked at the front door of the old adobe home and saw a man step through the door and up the path to a low metal gate. As the man opened the gate, Mondo said, "That's Calderon. Let's do it."

They left the van and watched the target move toward a dark-colored Lincoln Navigator that was parked nose-out, facing away from the Calderon house. They fast-walked in the direction of the Lincoln, quickly eating up half the distance—about forty yards—from the stolen Honda and the big SUV. Pistols in hand, they bracketed the vehicle. Rico approached from the street side, in case the bodyguard exited the vehicle, while Mondo walked up with the weed-congested lane's shoulder on his left, toward the SUV's passenger side, toward Calderon.

Not wanting their target to enter the Navigator, Mondo shouted, "Hey, Frank." The man whipped around and faced him. Just as Mondo raised his pistol, all hell broke loose. Two cars abreast raced down the lane, their lights pinioning the Garcias in their glare. Mondo, then Rico turned to face the cars, trained their weapons on the vehicles, and fired round after round after round. One of the vehicles slid to a stop on the left side of the lane coming even with Mondo, who was still ten yards from Frank Calderon. The second car, its motor screaming, sped toward Rico, rammed him, and catapulted him into the air over the car roof. While Rico's body did two full gainers in the center of the lane, then landed on its head, three men scrambled from the other vehicle and opened fire. They turned Mondo into a jiggling, spinning marionette who danced a spastic jig on the shoulder, then collapsed on his back.

Susan frenetically paced the length of the hall outside the surgery suite at UNM Hospital. A nurse had tried to get her to go to the visitors' waiting room, but one glare from Susan had been enough to get her to go away without another word. The emergency room doctor had told her hours earlier that Barbara's wound wasn't too bad. The danger, he'd said, was that she'd lost a lot of blood. As she walked up and down the hall, she murmured prayers over and over, demanding that God, Jesus, the Virgin Mary, and every saint whose name she could remember heal her partner. She was on yet another circuit of the hall when her cell phone rang. It was Roger. He'd gone to Presbyterian where Henry had been taken.

"Hey, babe," Roger said. "Any news?"

"Nothing yet. How about over there?"

Roger made a little sound that made Susan's stomach tighten.

"Oh, Roger, don't tell me." Her voice broke. "What happened?"

"Hold on, Suze. He's in surgery. But, based on what the surgeon told me, it's not good. He lost an incredible amount of blood and had stopped breathing for a good five or six minutes." He cleared his throat. "That could have caused brain damage. Also, the bullet went into the left hemisphere of his brain and specifically contacted the temporal lobe."

"What's that mean, Roger?"

Roger coughed, as though trying to keep his voice strong. But his voice shook as he said, "The temporal lobe is where language understanding, memory, hearing, and information sequencing and organization are controlled. If he survives—and that's highly questionable, Henry could be a . . . completely different person."

Roger finally left Presbyterian Hospital at 10:15 p.m., Christmas Day. He called Uber for a ride to his home in Nob Hill, showered and changed into fresh clothes, and drove over to UNMH. He met Susan in the Intensive Care Waiting Room and got an update from her about Barbara. Her wound had been cleaned and closed; she had been given three units of blood and a massive dose of antibiotics, and was drugged up almost to the point of being comatose.

"Let's go home, honey," Roger said. "We'll come back here in the morning."

Susan just nodded; too fatigued to form words. When Roger told her that the surgeon had no idea at that time what the prognosis was for Henry, she slumped as though her bones had turned to sand. Roger put his arm around her and supported her on the long walk to his car.

FRIDAY
DECEMBER 26

CHAPTER 48

Toro Sandoval called one of his men by radio. "Is the shipment ready?"

"Just about, *Jefe*. We're loading it now."

After he shut down the radio, Sandoval thought about how it would work. He smiled and thought, *muy elegante*. Then he had one of his men call Frank Calderon to confirm with him that the next shipment of heroin would be delivered on Saturday, December 27th.

Twelve million dollars was wired from a Cayman Islands bank account owned by Frank Calderon to a Monaco account owned by Toro Sandoval. The deposit was authenticated at 10:13 a.m. Within sixty seconds of authentication, one of Sandoval's accountants notified Calderon that the money had been received and that "the merchandise will be delivered by noon tomorrow."

Sandoval rubbed his hands together, not even trying to hide the glee he felt. He told one of his men, "Go to the warehouse and make sure everything is set."

The man turned and left Sandoval's office.

Frank Calderon immediately made the manager of his produce distribution business aware of the impending shipment and made certain that the man would have a large enough crew on hand. After all, the shipment would arrive on a Saturday, just a couple days after Christmas. Another load of sweet onions that would be distributed to grocery stores, including some of the largest chains serving cities like Albuquerque, Denver, Phoenix, and Tucson. Calderon laughed at the genius of the operation. He was amazed at the craftsmanship and ingenuity of the Mexicans. Hundreds of kilos of narcotics—handcrafted ceramic onion shells around black tar heroin—placed in the center of a load of two thousand mesh bags of real onions. Between the ceramic coatings on the fake onions and the smell of the real onions, even the noses of the drug-sniffing dogs couldn't detect the contraband.

By noon on Friday, Susan had already spent four hours at UNMH with a deathly-pale, semi-coherent Barbara. It wasn't until noon that Barbara understood where she was and exactly what had happened. The first words Barbara spoke were, "How's Henry?"

"He's at Pres. He had surgery yesterday. Roger called an hour ago and told me he's still in a medically-induced coma."

Barbara's eyes widened. "Coma?"

Susan wanted to sugarcoat what she had to say, but had never lied to her partner and wasn't about to start now. "His brain was injured. Swelling occurred. They put him in a coma because it's safer."

Barbara waved her hand as though to say, "What else?"

Susan shook her head. "It's not good, Barb." She swallowed. "They have no idea whether he'll recover."

A long, low moan came from Barbara, sounding as though it had originated in her soul. Then tears flowed from her closed eyes. Susan watched Barbara sleep for the next few hours, then decided to get something to eat. She squeezed Barbara's hand, whispered, "I'll be back in a little while," not certain that her partner had heard her, and went to the elevator bank. She rode down to the cafeteria level, bought a sandwich and a bottle of orange juice, and sat at a table. She'd just picked up her sandwich, when a man came over to her and said, "That's you, isn't it?"

Sandwich suspended in front of her mouth in both hands, she said, "What? What are you talking about?"

The man pointed at the television on a wall bracket in the corner of the cafeteria. "That's you, isn't it?" He asked again.

She looked at the television and saw file photos of Barbara and her on the screen. The screen then flashed to the Sandia Casino parking lot where police car and ambulance lights strobed through the darkness, making the scene seem other-worldly.

An announcer spoke over the video of the shooting scene about what had happened at the casino two nights before. To Susan, the episode seemed to have happened well in the past, not just less than thirty-six hours ago. Then the screen segued to another location where, again, there were police vehicles and ambulances with multi-colored flashing lights making the night sky appear to be on fire. This time, there were two bodies in body bags being rolled to the backs of two ambulances. The announcer said that two men had been killed at the scene and that an unidentified source had called the television station and speculated that the men were the same ones who had attacked two BCSO detectives in the Sandia Casino parking lot. That speculation was based upon the fact that the two detectives had been investigating Frank Calderon in connection with a murder case, that the two bodies were found on Bear Paw Lane in the North Valley, just a few feet from the home of Frank Calderon's parents, and that a security guard at the casino had identified one of the dead men from mug shots as Ricardo "Rico" Garcia.

The man looked down at Susan and smiled. He said, "That's been all over the news for the last twenty-four hours." His smile faded when he asked, "How's your partner? I heard she was shot."

Susan put down her sandwich. "I think she's going to recover nicely," she said.

"Oh, that's good to hear." He then said, "I'm sorry to have disturbed you."

"That's okay. Thanks."

He turned away, but turned back and asked, "Did I hear correctly that the sheriff's office fired you and your partner for some bullshit reason?"

Susan just shrugged.

The man smiled again. "I saw on Facebook and Twitter that thousands of people have called into the sheriff's office ripping him a new one. Social media is all over the guy. He won't be able to run for dog catcher." The guy laughed, waved, and walked away.

Susan returned to Barbara's room and saw Rudy Salas standing at the window, looking out at the Sandia Mountains. When she moved into the room, she was startled to find Candace Saunders, the H.R. officer, seated in a chair. Seated next to Saunders was a man who Susan recognized as the county's communications director.

Salas turned as Susan moved to the far side of Barbara's bed. He tipped his head at Susan but didn't say anything.

"To what do we owe the pleasure of this visit?" Susan asked, all the while glaring at Saunders.

The communications director, Wayne Cummings, replied, "I'm glad to see Barbara's doing so well."

Susan looked at Barbara and met her gaze. Barbara's eyelids fluttered and she made a shushing movement with her lips.

Okay, Barb, she thought. *I'll hold my tongue as long as I can.*

Susan looked at Cummings and waited.

"You ladies are the big story in the news." He chuckled, but it sounded forced to Susan.

Cummings went silent for a beat, seemingly waiting for Susan or Barbara to say something. When neither did, he continued, "The sheriff called this morning and told me he'd thought about you all leaving the department and suggested I talk with you about reconsidering."

Susan and Barbara looked at one another again. Barbara wore a tiny smile.

When they again stayed silent, Cummings added, "The sheriff feels it would be a loss to the department if you two were to leave."

This time, Susan looked at Salas. The muscles in his cheeks bounced around as though they were convulsing. His eyes were as black as coals and as hard as diamonds.

When she looked back at Cummings, he spread his arms. "What do you say?"

A glance from Barbara told Susan that she was okay with her speaking for both of them.

"So, let me get this straight, Mr. Cummings. Now that my

partner and I are all over the news and the word is out that *Little Miss Candy Ass* there next to you and the *No Cajones* Sheriff fired us, you've decided that the politically expedient thing to do is to revoke our terminations, is that about right?"

Cummings hemmed and hawed for a moment. Before he could say a coherent word, Susan added, "And, by the way, we didn't decide to *leave the department*. We were fired because of a couple specious lawsuits that none of you had the guts to fight."

"Well, I'm sure there are differences of opinion about how things occurred. But the upshot is that we would like you to return to duty." He then quickly added that there would be no derogatory comments in either of their files.

Barbara tried to say something but all that came out was a raspy sound. Salas passed her a plastic cup with a straw. She took a couple short sips, handed the cup back to Salas, in a hoarse voice, said, "A couple conditions. I go back only if Lieutenant Salas goes back."

Cummings looked desperately at Salas and asked, "Is that acceptable?"

Salas's expression was indecipherable. "Let's see what Detective-Sergeant Lassiter's other conditions are," he said.

Barbara held up two fingers. "My next condition is that Ms. Saunders writes a letter to my partner and me apologizing for her attitude and for what she said to us."

Saunders leaped from her chair, looked at Cummings, and shouted, "That's bullshit. There's no way I'm going to write—"

"Sit down and shut up," Cummings said.

Barbara continued: "Ms. Saunders's behavior was unprofessional and unbecoming a manager in the sheriff's office. I want those words put in the letter. I also want her to write an apology to Lieutenant Salas for the things she said about him."

Salas looked at Barbara and then at Susan. "She said something about me?"

"Oh yeah," Susan said. "Something about you being a Neanderthal."

Salas looked at Saunders. "You're an H.R. expert, Saunders. Would that sort of comment qualify as a form of age discrimination?"

Saunders groaned and slumped in her chair.

"What else?" Cummings asked Barbara.

"I guess that's it," Barbara said.

"I'll see that it's all done," Cummings said. "I wish you a rapid recovery, Detective Lassiter, and look forward to you being back on duty soon."

"Thank you, Mr. Cummings."

An awkward silence fell over the room. No one seemed to know what to do or say next. But then a doctor and a nurse came into the room, shooed everyone out, and closed the door. Susan turned down the hall to call Roger. As she walked away, she looked over her shoulder and saw Salas buttonhole Cummings and Saunders and say, "I've got a couple conditions of my own." Then Saunders groaned again, but apparently had the sense to keep her mouth shut.

Susan smiled.

Salas said, "You paying attention?"

"Go ahead," Cummings said.

"I want medals of valor awarded to Lassiter and Martinez. And I want them presented in a public ceremony with the press present."

Cummings looked at Saunders and said, "I'm sure the sheriff will see the wisdom of doing that."

Salas's voice hardened when he added, "It's got nothing to do with wisdom. It's got everything to do with doing the right thing. They earned those medals."

Cummings nodded.

Salas continued: "And I want them put on the promotion list for advancement to the rank of lieutenant. They're the best detectives in the department and they've earned the promotions."

"I can't guarantee when openings will come up," Cummings said.

"I understand. As long as they're on the promotion list."

"Done."

SATURDAY
DECEMBER 27

CHAPTER 49

The open-topped semi-trailer had a canvas tarpaulin affixed by carabiners through eyelets in the tarpaulin to twelve eyehooks welded into the top of the trailer. Sandoval's men shut the double doors at the back of the trailer, locked them, and then waved at the driver. The truck pulled out of the warehouse and headed north toward the border crossing. After a two-hour wait at the border, including a perfunctory inspection of the vehicle, the truck driver crossed into *Los Estados Unidos* at 3:00 p.m. and began the five-hour trip to Albuquerque.

Since Barbara had sworn off booze, she'd also avoided using pain relievers of any kind. She wouldn't even take a couple Advil for a headache out of fear that she'd become dependent on them. But when the pain in her shoulder rose to an "8," she abandoned her abstinence and pressed her call button to get a nurse's attention. She'd just chased down an 800 mg Ibuprofen tablet with a swallow of water when Susan walked into her room and stood at the foot of the bed.

"How's things, Barb?" Susan asked.

"Just peachy."

Susan smiled. "They tell you when you can get out of here?"

"Maybe tomorrow, assuming there's no indication of infection."

"I'll pick you up and take you home. I've already moved some of my stuff into your spare room."

"What are you talking about?"

"Someone's got to take care of you. I appointed myself."

Barbara was about to argue the point but decided Susan was correct. With her shoulder mummified, she couldn't even dress herself. She sighed and whispered, "Thanks."

"I stopped to see Henry this morning. There's been no change."

Barbara's eyes filled with tears. Her chest felt too small for her heart. Susan came around to the side of the bed and took Barbara's left hand. "Oh-h, Susan," she said, sounding mournful, defeated. Then she devolved into soul-wrenching sobs.

Susan released Barbara's hand, took a tissue from a box beside the bed, and handed it to Barbara. After a couple minutes, her emotions more under control, Barbara dabbed at her eyes and said, "You have any ideas about why those men came at us?"

Susan paced, her hands bouncing around as though she was juggling invisible balls. "I've racked my brain trying to figure it out. We know there was some tie between those men, Frank Calderon, and us. Somehow we're all connected. But, for the life of me, I haven't been able to figure it out.

"The only connections we had with Calderon were our two meetings with him about his sister. I never heard of the Garcia brothers before. They came after us, then apparently went after Calderon. We don't know this, but the presumption is that Calderon was at his parents' house on Christmas Eve."

Barbara said, "Kinda interesting that when deputies showed up at the scene, all they found were the two Garcia brothers' bodies and a few exercised neighbors. No Calderon."

Susan continued pacing but didn't respond.

Barbara said, "Let's take it one connection at a time. You already said it. The only connection between Calderon and us is Lisa French."

"Yeah, but she's long gone. Got to be in Mexico or some other place by now."

"I agree." Barbara paused a beat, and then added, "When I was coming out of the anesthesia after surgery, I had a weird dream. It was about French and that body the Socorro Police found. The dead guy was one of Frank Calderon's men. I've been thinking about that dream for the past two days. My theory is that Calderon had his man take French on a road trip with the intent of killing her and dumping her body out in the middle of nowhere. Somehow, French turned the tables on the man, killed him, stole his car, and headed for Mexico."

Susan picked up on Barbara's thought process. "So, French realizes that her own brother ordered her murder and wants payback."

"Exactly. And we're the unreasonable detectives who investigated murders at French's place of employment and disrupted her plans."

"How awful of us," Susan said.

Barbara shifted and grimaced as pain shot through her shoulder. She tried to get into a more comfortable position, then said, "I can't prove it, but I believe that the connection between us, Calderon, and the Garcias is Lisa French. I'll bet you she hired the Garcias to get rid of the people she now hates the most: her brother, you, and me."

"How would she know the Garcias?"

"That's a mystery in and of itself. But anyone who's as obsessed about avenging wrongs done to her is probably not going to stop until she's completely satisfied."

Susan stopped pacing, stood at the bottom of the bed, and said, "Maybe I'd better go talk with Calderon."

Two of Sandoval's men dragged a bound and gagged Lisa French through the back entrance of *Casa de Julia* where they were met by a beefy, ham-fisted, dark-skinned woman of fifty.

"This is the gift you called me about?" Julia Cardenas said.

"*Si, senora,*" one of the men said. "*El Jefe* Sandoval wanted us to make sure you understand that this woman is yours to do with as you please." Now emphasizing his words with a jab of his finger, he added, "Our boss will be extremely displeased should this woman ever leave this place." He chuckled. "Of course, if she dies, that will be fine."

Cardenas said, "So this gift has strings attached to it."

"*Si, senora.* But she is a good looking woman who should bring you profits."

Cardenas ripped the gag from French's mouth, gripped her chin, and stared at her. "She's a little older than most of my girls, but she'll do. Please thank *Senor* Sandoval. Tell him I will keep a close eye on his gift."

As the two men left the building, Julia Cardenas pressed a hand against French's chest and shoved her hard against a wall. She leaned into her arm and ordered, "Don't move." Then she shouted, "Gordo, come here."

Fifteen seconds passed, as Cardenas continued to hold French against the wall, all the while staring into her eyes with an appraising look. "You must have screwed up in a big way," she said in Spanish. When French didn't reply, Cardenas said, "You don't understand Spanish?"

"Yeah, I understood you."

"Good." She laughed. "My clients like it when they can communicate with my women."

"I don't—"

Cardenas punched French in the stomach, knocking her to her knees. As French wretched, Cardenas rapped a fist on the top of her head and said, "You don't speak unless I tell you to."

French looked up at the woman just as an enormous man wearing a pair of faded, discount store jeans and a soiled tee shirt that only reached to a point three inches above his navel entered the corridor.

"*Si, Ma . . . ma. Que qui . . . eres?*"

The man's speech was guttural, slow, unnatural, as though he had a cleft palette. French glanced at his face and shuddered. Drool glistened on his crooked mouth. One eye drifted in its socket as though afloat.

"Take her to room thirty-nine. Make sure you lock the door."

"*Si Ma . . . ma.*"

The man grabbed French's arm and lifted her off the floor as though she weighed nothing. He pulled her to a staircase, climbed two flights while half-lifting, half-pulling her, and dragged her to a room at the back of the third floor. He pushed her into the room, turned her around, untied the ropes that secured her hands behind her back, and pointed at a sheetless bed with a filthy sway-backed mattress in a corner.

"*Tú du . . . er . . . mes allí.*"

Her nausea from Cardenas's punch had passed, but her abdominal muscles felt as though knives had been stabbed into them. She stared incredulously at the bed and shuddered. "I'm not lying on that thing."

The man tilted his head as though to see her better. "*Er . . . es muy her . . . mo . . . sa,*" he said agonizingly slowly.

"Oh wonderful," she muttered in English, her tone full of contempt, but tinged with fear. "Quasimodo thinks I'm beautiful."

The man tilted his enormous head, his face full of confusion.

Susan parked in the grocery store lot on Central Avenue, walked through the store to the back, and rapped on the door. When a man answered, she asked to see Frank Calderon.

"You got an appointment?" the man asked.

"Yeah. Tell him it's the health department looking for bugs."

"What are you, some kinda smartass?"

Susan pulled her cred pack from a coat pocket, showed it to the guy for no more than a second, put it back in her pocket, and waited. Frank Calderon opened the door a few seconds later and welcomed her as though she was a visiting potentate.

"What a pleasure, Detective," he said. "I can't imagine having a more delightful visitor."

"Cut the horse shit, Calderon. I don't want to spend any more time here than is absolutely necessary."

Calderon led the way to his office, dropped into his chair, and asked, "What can I do for you?" He didn't invite Susan to sit, but she did anyway.

"Bad scene outside your family's home on Christmas Eve," she said.

"Awful. Just awful. What's the world coming to? My poor father and mother are still shook up." He exhaled a breath that whistled. "And how about what happened to you and your partner?"

"Must have been tough on you, too."

"Well, I feel bad for my parents."

Susan smiled. "A lot of lead flying around. You could have been hurt."

Calderon showed her a supercilious smile. "I don't know where you get your information, Detective. I was nowhere near my parents' place that night. Hell, by midnight, I was already in bed dreaming about what Santa Claus was going to bring me."

"Okay, Calderon, let's stop playing games. We both know that it wasn't a coincidence that the Garcias attacked my partner and me before coming for you. It was probably easy for them to find Barbara and me. After all, our lives are kind of an open book. But you're a different story. You've got personal security and you have a vested interest in keeping a low profile. Have you stopped to wonder how the shooters discovered you were at your parents' house?"

"I already told you that I wasn't there."

"Okay, asshole, let's pretend you were there. How would anyone know that?"

Calderon shrugged.

"Who would know you would be there at that time of night on Christmas Eve? Humor me. Let's make a list."

Calderon grinned. "Okay," he said, "I'll play along. My parents, of course."

"Sure. But they wouldn't tell anyone. They know what business you're in and would have the sense to keep their mouths shut."

He nodded. "My brothers and sisters would know."

"You told us that all but one of your siblings live outside New Mexico. We checked on them. They're good citizens who don't even have parking tickets. Only your sister, Lisa, has gone off the rails."

Calderon nodded.

"You stop to think that maybe she hired the Garcias?"

"First of all, there's no way Lisa would have even been aware of the Garcias. Second, she couldn't have had anything to do with hiring them."

"Why are you so certain of that?"

He put on a triumphant smile. "Because she was killed in Mexico almost three months ago."

Calderon's statement was about the last thing Susan had expected to hear. "You're kidding."

"Nope. A guy down in Juarez called me recently. Told me she

was dead."

"Is that a fact?"

"Yep. Kinda shoots the shit out of your theory, doesn't it?"

"Yeah, it does. But my question still hasn't been answered. Who knew about you being at your folk's house?"

"Hypothetically?"

"Yeah, hypothetically."

"Other than my driver, no one."

"Maybe you ought to talk to your driver. He might have loose lips."

"I could do that. Anything else?"

"Yeah. Let's say somebody mentioned you planning on being at your parents' house. That *somebody* is part of the puzzle. But who would have had knowledge of the Garcias and would have wanted you killed? We could be talking about two different people. And when you're thinking about all of this, ask yourself who would also have wanted my partner and me dead." She paused a couple seconds. "I've beat this thing up one side and down the other and there's only one name that keeps popping up in my brain."

"Who's that?" Calderon asked.

"Lisa French."

"But she's dead."

Susan shrugged. "Maybe you should check with your friend down in Mexico again."

CHAPTER 50

Toro Sandoval used a burner phone to call the DEA offices in Albuquerque. He asked to talk with the Agent in Charge and was told by a guy who sounded fifteen that Agent Fratanelli wasn't in.

"You got a duty officer?"

"Yes, sir. That would be me."

"And what might your name be?"

"What's this about, sir?"

"It's about a heroin shipment that's headed for Albuquerque. You want the information I have?"

"What's your name, sir?"

"None of your business, Boy Wonder. You got a pencil and paper?"

"I do."

"Well, get ready to start writing."

"Go ahead," the agent said.

Sandoval gave the agent Calderon's warehouse address. "A truck will arrive there at 8:00 p.m. tonight. You'll find two hundred kilos of heroin disguised as onions under a load of real onions. You show up there at a couple minutes after eight and you'll hit the mother lode."

Sandoval cut off the call and destroyed the burner phone. Then he made a series of calls to men he'd sent to the cities where Frank Calderon maintained key distribution centers. He confirmed that each man and his team, who had snatched Calderon's top people in each location, were ready to take action. He told each of them, "The minute Calderon goes down, you explain the facts of life to Calderon's people. They either agree to work with us or they get eliminated."

The onion truck driver had bypassed a Customs checkpoint on Interstate 25, south of Elephant Butte Lake. He was cruising along at seventy miles per hour, in the process of passing a bus that looked as though it had come off an assembly line in the 1960s and had the words Evangel Mission on its side, when the bus drifted into the left lane. The truck driver tried to dodge the bus, steering onto the left shoulder, but the bus just kept coming. The truck driver madly cursed the man behind the wheel of the other vehicle. He had an instant in which to make a decision: steer into the deep, "V"-shaped dirt strip that served as a median and risk rolling his truck and cargo, or hit the gas and steer back into the bus, possibly driving the vehicle and its twenty or so passengers into the hereafter. In a split second, he opted for the latter course of action. He stomped on the accelerator, turned back onto the highway, and gritted his teeth as he anticipated the collision with the bus.

But, the bus driver apparently realizing what was about to happen, steered to the right, and hit his brakes. The bus stuttered as it decelerated, and then slid into a screeching stop on the right shoulder. The truck driver had over-corrected expecting to crash into the side of the bus. But the bus was no longer beside him as he drove the big semi across both lanes and into a ravine on the right side of the highway. The trailer rolled onto its side, dragging the truck with it, and came to a stop fifty yards down a ten degree slope. It hung precariously on the rock and dirt slope as two thousand bags of onions, and hundreds of kilos of black tar heroin disguised as onions, tore the canvas tarp loose and shot down onto a dry riverbed like yellow cannon balls.

The truck driver muttered a string of curses in Spanish as he tried to extricate himself from the cab. He knew he was royally screwed. There would be no excuses that would placate Toro Sandoval or Frank Calderon.

The passengers on the church bus poured out of the vehicle. Some cried, some screamed, and a few went to the truck cab and pulled out the driver, who was shook up but uninjured.

A teenage girl from the bus looked down at the onion field that spread out below the highway and shouted, "Holy shit. Look at all those friggin' onions," which earned her an admonishment from one of the adults.

Another of the adults happened to look for the truck driver, who he spied hoofing it across the interstate to the southbound lane.

By the time the local news media picked up on the accident on I-25, Frank Calderon was getting dressed after an afternoon with his latest girlfriend, Vickie Long, a red-head with freckles the size of shirt buttons and breasts the size of cantaloupes. While he shrugged into his jacket, Vickie watched television. She had a show on that featured a bunch of screeching housewives who were richer than Croesus and more immature than a bunch of thirteen year olds.

"Why do you watch that shit?" Calderon asked.

"It makes me feel superior."

He laughed. "You don't need that dumbass show to make you superior, Vickie. You're about the most superior person I've ever known." He leaned over the side of the bed and planted a kiss on her mouth. "I'll see you next week."

Vickie giggled. "That's the nicest thing you've ever said to me." She picked up the TV remote and switched the channel.

As Calderon walked toward the apartment door, she shouted, "Look at that shit."

He chose to ignore her. He had a large shipment coming in. His hand was on the doorknob when she blurted a laugh. "Frank, you gotta see this. I never saw so many onions in my entire life."

Calderon was miserable as his driver, Johnny, left Vickie's apartment complex and headed to his warehouse. He was out twelve million dollars, which he'd paid Toro Sandoval for the heroin, and he had no way to recoup the money. But it was the sixty million in street value that he would never earn that really had him upset.

Johnny took Wyoming to Interstate 40, went west to Interstate

25, then drove south to the Central Avenue exit. From there, he went west on Central to Broadway and then south toward Calderon's warehouse. With six blocks to go, he caught the red light at Lead Avenue and waited in line for the light to change.

Calderon had just about accepted the loss of the truck load of heroin when a caravan of black SUVs and sedans, their bubble and grill lights flashing and their sirens blaring, turned at high speed off Lead and raced down Broadway.

"Bunch of cowboys," he muttered.

When the light turned green and Johnny followed the cars in front of them toward the street on which the warehouse was located, Calderon's heart rate leaped when he realized that the caravan of black vehicles had turned onto that street. His warehouse was the only building there. He shouted, "Johnny, don't turn in. Keep going down Broadway." Then he called his attorney.

"Find out what's going on," he told Greg Switzer. "Then call me."

By the time Switzer arrived at the warehouse, three of Calderon's men were handcuffed and seated on the building's concrete floor. DEA agents armed with automatic weapons stood guard over them.

"Who's in charge here?" the attorney demanded.

A young agent wearing a nylon windbreaker with "DEA" screen-printed on the front and back, stepped forward and said, "Who are you?"

"I'm Greg Switzer, the attorney for the owner of this property. What in God's name are you people doing here?"

"This is drug bust, Mr. Switzer. What's the name of your client?"

"Drugs?" Switzer said. He did a slow turn, his arm extended, pointing at one wall, then the next, until he'd turned three hundred and sixty degrees. "What drugs?"

The agent waved an envelope at Switzer. "We have a search warrant here and—"

Switzer gaped at the agent. He looked dumbfounded when he said, "Show me the drugs."

"They're not here yet."

The attorney snickered. "So, you got a search warrant for these premises based on contraband that isn't on these premises. Is that about right?"

The agent's face went crimson. His voice squeaked a bit as he said, "I was told that the drugs would arrive in an onion shipment at eight this evening."

Switzer looked at his watch. "I've got ten after eight. How long do you plan to wait for this fictitious shipment of onions to show up?"

The agent couldn't seem to concoct an answer.

"Have you heard the news?" Switzer asked.

The agent looked confused. "What news?"

"A load of onions spilled on I-25 earlier today. Do you have something that tells you that those onions were bound for this warehouse and that my client was even aware that there might be contraband hidden in that shipment?"

"Well, I got a call and—"

"Oh, you got a call. I suppose it was from an anonymous caller."

"Yeah, but—"

Switzer stepped forward, took the agent's arm, and gently guided him away from the rest of his men. He said, "Listen, Agent"—he looked at the man's nametag—"Lockhart. I think it would be a really good idea if you and your men vacated the premises as quickly as possible. I suggest you call your supervisor and advise him or her of how badly you screwed up here today." Switzer sighed and added, "I'll try to convince my client and his men here to not file charges against you and the DEA for illegal trespass, false arrest, and emotional distress." He spread his arms and added, "But you know how litigious our society has become."

At 9:25 p.m., attorney Greg Switzer called Frank Calderon and briefed him on events at Calderon's warehouse.

"Did you learn who put the DEA on my warehouse?"

"No, Frank. They were there based on an anonymous call. The senior agent in charge was out of town. Some kid who got the shit detail of being duty officer on Christmas weekend took it upon himself to raid your place." Switzer chuckled. "Probably had dreams of becoming a decorated agent." Switzer paused a couple seconds, then said, "Frank, I hope that truckload of onions that overturned on I-25 this afternoon wasn't headed for your warehouse. I just heard that narcotics were found secreted in the truck."

"What truckload of onions?"

"Good answer, Frank."

Calderon's spine seemed to vibrate with anger-generated energy. As Johnny drove him to his North Valley home, he recycled events of the past couple of days through his memory banks. By the time they pulled into his driveway, he'd come to the conclusion that recent events represented nothing less than a coup against his operation. He sat in the front passenger seat of the Lincoln Navigator and mentally chewed on who would have the guts, the resources, and the motive to execute a coup against him. The only name he could come up with was Toro Sandoval. Then he remembered what that female detective, Susan Martinez, had said to him: '*Maybe you should check with your friend down in Mexico again.*'

He opened his car door, stepped out, and told Johnny to pick him up at eight the next morning. Then he closed the door and turned toward his front door. He rested his palms on the door and took a long moment to catch his breath. "Sonofabitch," he whispered. "This has the smell of Lisa all over it."

SUNDAY
DECEMBER 28

CHAPTER 51

Her arm in a sling, Barbara was rolled in a wheelchair outside of UNMH by a nurse. She spotted Susan standing next to a Crown Victoria twenty yards from the front entrance and tried to get out of the chair, but the nurse gently pressed down on her right shoulder, said, "You're getting the royal treatment, Detective," and rolled her to the sedan.

Susan took Barbara's right hand and helped her out of the chair, then stood like a mother hen beside her as she maneuvered into the front passenger seat.

"I imagine you'll be glad to get home," Susan said, once she got behind the wheel.

"You bet. But after I go see Henry."

"You sure you're up to it?" Susan asked.

Barbara shot Susan a determined look.

"Okay, okay. We'll go see Henry."

Susan parked the Crown Vic just a few yards away from the entrance to Presbyterian Hospital and placed a placard that read: "BCSO-Official Business" on the dashboard. By the time she scooted around to the passenger side of the vehicle, Barbara had already gotten out.

"Might be a good idea to let people help you until you're healed," Susan said.

"I'll think about it," Barbara said.

"Stubborn as a mule," Susan muttered.

Barbara touched Susan's arm. "I apologize for being grouchy," she said. "I really appreciate your help."

Susan smiled. "I know, partner." She exhaled a sharp breath. "I know you're worried about Henry."

Barbara nodded.

Other than for the beeping of monitors, the Intensive Care Unit was library-quiet. A couple nurses sat behind a counter. One was on a telephone; the other jotted something in a file. Barbara moved to the counter and said, "I'm Barbara Lassiter, Henry Simpson's fiancée."

The nurse with the file jerked a look at Barbara. "Oh, you're the one." She seemed embarrassed. Her face went red and her eyes rounded. "I mean, we heard what happened to you." The woman pointed at Barbara's arm. "How are you doing?"

"Better. Thanks. Would it be possible to see Mr. Simpson?"

The nurse stood and came around the counter. "I'm Betty Winslow. Of course. Come with me."

Barbara and Susan followed the nurse across the unit to a glass-fronted room. The door to the room was open. The lights were muted but not so dim that Barbara couldn't make out Henry lying in a bed, or see his head swaddled in bandages, or see the tubes and breathing device that he was hooked up to. She moaned and her eyes flooded with tears. The only other sounds in the room were the suction noise made by the respiratory device and the beeping of electronic monitors.

"Oh, my God," she murmured. "Oh, Henry."

She felt Susan touch her good shoulder and reached up with her hand and squeezed it.

The nurse said, "You should talk with the doctor. He can explain . . . everything."

"When will he be here?" Barbara asked.

"He just finished making rounds. Probably not for another four or five hours."

Susan turned to face the nurse. "I need to get Ms. Lassiter home. She was just released from the hospital. What can you tell her?"

The nurse looked a bit uncomfortable. "I really shouldn't—"

Then she seemed to change her mind and said, "Mr. Simpson is in a medically-induced coma. There's been some brain swelling and accumulation of fluid, but nothing out of the ordinary with his kind of injury. In fact, the doctor is pleased with his progress." She smiled briefly. "It's encouraging that there has been no sign of infection."

"When will the coma . . . be reversed?" Barbara asked. "Is that the correct terminology?"

"Close enough," the nurse said. "If there is no swelling, we might be able to administer drugs to reverse the coma in the next couple of days."

"Then what?" Barbara asked.

The nurse's expression was almost mournful. "I wish I could tell you something definitive. Unfortunately, we have no idea. Although the injury to Mr. Simpson's brain was not as severe as others I've seen, it did impact a part of the brain that controls a lot of important functions, including memory, information processing, understanding of language, and the like." She shrugged. "We'll just have to wait and see."

Barbara stepped toward the bed as she heard Susan and the nurse back out of the room. She took Henry's hand in hers, bent over, and kissed it. "You listen to me, Henry Simpson," she whispered, her throat constricted, her voice hoarse. "You promised to marry me in June and take me to Greece for our honeymoon. I'm holding you to those promises. You hear me, Henry?" A short-lived wail escaped from her throat. "Goddammit, Henry, you promised me." Then she broke down and cried as though she would never be able to stop.

Lisa French was moved to another room on Sunday morning. Julia Cardenas assigned two women the task of supervising her bathing and dressing. The women kept up a continuous banter while they watched her, joking about what awaited her downstairs. Despite the heat of the water and the warmth of the central heating system, Lisa shivered as though she were in an icy pond. She could guess what was in store for her. After all, she'd slept with many men. But those men had been of her own choosing. The prospect of what she was about to experience was frightening.

After she'd dressed and the two women had watched her comb

her hair, one of them pointed at makeup on a counter in the bathroom and told her to "fix your face." Her hand shook as she tried to apply lipstick. The two women giggled for a while, then shoved her into a chair and applied makeup to her eyes, cheeks, and lips.

"It's okay," one of them said. "You'll see. Julia will give you something to calm your nerves."

"What?" French asked, her voice quavering.

"Cocaine, heroin," the woman told her. "You will think the men are all movie stars with enough of that stuff in you." Then they both laughed.

The women had just finished applying makeup when Julia Cardenas came into the room. She told French to stand and then walked around her, as though inspecting a horse at a livestock auction.

"Ah, *chica*, you are going to make my clients very happy. They like it when a new woman is available." She laughed. "They get tired of being with the same women all the time."

The shaking began again and French dropped back into the chair.

Cardenas snapped her fingers and told one of the other women to bring "*el jugo feliz*—the happy juice."

"No, I don't want—" She stopped in mid-sentence when Cardenas's face turned stormy.

"Don't be a fool," the madam said.

When the woman returned with a small pouch, Cardenas removed a syringe and nodded at the two women. One of them pressed down on French's shoulders, pinning her to the chair. The other grabbed French's left arm in her two hands and stretched the arm out to the side. Cardenas stuck the needle into the inside of French's elbow and injected the drug. Almost instantaneously, French was overwhelmed with an infusion of heat that ran from her arm to every part of her body. She felt sleepy and suddenly calm, and then her brain seemed to go fuzzy. The upshot was that she couldn't remember ever feeling so at peace in her life.

She was only partially aware of being moved to a staircase and then being helped down a flight of steps to a room where a dozen or so other women sat, stood, or lounged. They all gabbed away like teenage girls at a pajama party. Not too long after being brought to the room, men entered and disappeared with some of the women. Then, as she became a bit more aware of her surroundings, a man who smelled like a mixture of horse, hay, sweat, and manure took her hand. She cringed at the feel of his skin, which seemed to be rough as sandpaper. He said something to her in Spanish. When she didn't respond, he yanked her up, wrapped an arm around her waist, and dragged her to a room.

FRIDAY
JANUARY 2

CHAPTER 52

When Barbara and Susan arrived at the Presbyterian Hospital ICU, five days after Barbara had been released from UNMH, they ran into Dr. Simone Carteret as she was about to leave the unit.

"Hey, Barbara," Carteret said. "I was hoping I'd run into you."

"How's Henry?" Barbara asked.

The doctor tipped her head to the side and spread her arms. "We'll see. But he's a whole lot better than he was the last time you saw him. We administered the drugs to reverse the coma last night, which is good news in and of itself. The swelling in his brain had subsided and we'd been able to drain the fluid in his skull, so I thought it was time to bring him out of it. He's breathing on his own, but he's not responding to stimuli yet. That can take several days." She touched Barbara's arm and said, "Think good thoughts."

After the doctor left, Barbara went into Henry's room and felt a surge of optimism. Seeing him without a breathing device now that he was off a respirator made a major difference. *He looks . . . more human*, she thought. She stood next to him and held his hand as she talked about everything and nothing. She brought him up to date on the Vista de Alameda case, on the crash of the onion truck, on her plans to shop for a wedding dress, and on her and Susan's reinstatement with the BCSO. She talked about what she'd had for breakfast that morning and where she and Susan planned to eat lunch. Finally, she prayed aloud that he would get better soon.

And during the thirty minutes that she talked, her heart ached and her eyes burned because there was zero indication that Henry had heard a word she'd said.

In the Crown Vic, Barbara said, "Susan, there's something I've been thinking about since all this happened. What if Henry doesn't get better? I mean, what if he has to be institutionalized? Or, what if he dies?"

Susan pulled the car into the lot of a Vietnamese restaurant on Menaul Boulevard and parked it. She left the car running and turned in her seat. "You're getting way ahead of yourself."

"Maybe," Barbara said.

"Spill, girl. What's going on in your head?"

Barbara showed Susan a small smile. Her eyes were moist, vulnerable. Then, as though a dam had burst, she cried inconsolably. Her shoulders and chest heaved. After a couple minutes, she looked at Susan and wailed, "What have I done to bring this on myself? It's like I'm being punished for something. I've only loved two men in my life. One's dead and the other one could be any day now."

Susan touched Barbara's hand. "You're the best person I know. This isn't about punishment. It's about life. There's good and bad. Sometimes the good is spectacular and sometimes the bad is horrible. You just need to pray for Henry's recovery."

"God, I feel awful. So impotent. I wish there was something I could do to help him."

Susan pulled a pack of tissues from her purse and handed it to Barbara. She said, "Other than praying, I don't see that there's much for you to do. Why don't you wait and see how things turn out?"

Barbara nodded.

Susan drove out of the lot and turned west on Menaul. They drove in heavy silence to BCSO headquarters.

Lisa French's drug hangover had diminished. She was lucid enough to understand that the longer she stayed in *Casa de Julia*, the fewer her options. The only outcome she could foresee was bad: disease, drug addiction, injury, suicide. She had come to the conclusion that the drugs alone would ultimately render her incapable of making any sort of self-preservation decision. The last five days had been hell on earth.

She listlessly rolled out of bed and, with an arm, shielded her eyes from the glare of the sunlight that sliced through the little window up near the ceiling. *Like a window in a cell,* she thought. A *tap-tap-tap* on her door startled her. *It can't be a client,* she thought. *It's too early.* Then she remembered that Julia Cardenas's son, Gordo, came by her room every morning. She cracked the door and looked out at his misshapen head.

"O . . . la, Sen . . . or . . . ita . . . Lisa," he said. "*Ten . . . go el desay . . . uno para ti.*"

She thanked him for bringing her breakfast and invited him into the room.

"Please put the tray on the table there," she told him. She followed him to the table and patted his back as he set down the tray. She felt him press back slightly against her hand. "That looks very good, Gordo."

He asked her if she wanted anything else.

"I would love a cigarette, Gordo."

He told her that he would get a pack for her.

"I don't want a pack of regular cigarettes. I prefer e-cigarettes. Do you know what they are?"

"*Si.*"

"Maybe you could get me an e-cigarette and a few vials of liquid nicotine."

"*Si, yo pue . . . do ha . . . cer eso.*"

"I'm sure you can, Gordo." She put her arms around him and kissed his cheek.

The young man stammered for a few seconds, making him even more difficult to understand. Then he told her he would return *inme . . . dia . . . ta . . . mente* as he backed out of the room and closed the door.

French then took out money she'd hidden under a loose floorboard: tips some of her clients—mostly young men from Ft. Bliss—had given her. One hundred and twenty-eight dollars. *It's now or never,* she thought.

BCSO Communications Director Wayne Cummings, and A.D.A. Elinore Freed sat on one side of the conference room table in the BCSO Homicide Division, across from Barbara and Susan. Dr. Frederick Beringer sat at the head of the table. This was the first weekly meeting arranged to discuss progress in the *Geezer Killer Case.*

"Fifteen of seventeen bodies that we want to disinter have been delivered to OMI," Freed said. "The remaining two are proving problematic because they were buried out of state. Different laws and regulations."

"Have you talked to the family members of those two?" Beringer asked.

"Yes," Freed said. "They're very supportive and have intervened with the authorities." She frowned. "The families obviously want to be part of the class action suit brought against the retirement home and its insurance carrier."

Beringer passed out sheets of paper on which the names of the Vista de Alameda residents who had died in the past two years were typed. "We've completed eleven autopsies." He pointed at the paper in front of him. "As you can see," he said, "the results in every case were positive for liquid nicotine and/or *continine.*"

"Any word about Lisa French?" Cummings asked.

Susan answered, "I talked with French's brother, Frank Calderon. He swears his sister died down in Juarez."

"You believe him?" Freed asked.

Susan bit her lower lip for a second. "I believe that he *thought* she was dead, but I detected a degree of uncertainty after our conversation. If you asked me if *I* thought she had died, I would tell you that I have reservations."

"I would love to put that woman on trial," Freed said.

"I wouldn't hold my breath," Barbara said. "She's too smart to ever come back to the States."

"Is that your belief as well, Detective Martinez?" Cummings asked.

Susan shrugged. "She'd be crazy to ever come back here."

"That's not what I asked," Cummings said.

"Yeah, I know," Susan said. She paused a beat and then said,

"There's no question that Lisa French is crazy."

Gordo returned to French's room at around three in the afternoon. He wore a huge, crooked smile, like a little boy who had run an errand for a parent he wanted badly to please. He handed French a brown paper bag and stuttered, "*Es . . . lo que quer . . . ías.*"

She turned the bag upside down on her bed, smiled up at him, kissed his cheek, and said, "Yes, it's exactly what I wanted."

He beamed.

"You are my best friend, Gordo."

This time, his smile was accompanied by a grunt that French had come to understand was his grotesque way of showing happiness. His mouth lolled open, giving her a full shot of his crooked teeth and protruding tongue.

"I think we should go for a walk one of these days, Gordo, so all the people in Juarez can see that you are my boyfriend."

He made the grunting sound again, smiled briefly, but then his expression changed to one of abject panic. In his halting Spanish, he said, "Oh, no, I could never go outside. The people make fun of me. And Mama would be very angry."

It took French a few seconds to decipher what Gordo had said. When she had, she quickly took one of his hands in hers and said, "No one would dare make fun of you when we are together. They would envy you."

"¿Crees eso?"

"That's exactly what I think, Gordo." She smiled at him and whispered, "We should take a short walk tonight after your mother closes up. I'll show you how jealous of you all the men will be."

Gordo did a little dance while he swept his hands in the air.

After Gordo left her room, French had to force down the wave of nausea that suddenly washed over her. Another night on her back servicing all manner of men made her retch. According to the other women, Friday nights were the worst, when the clients had a week's wages in their pockets to buy booze. The place would be packed. And tonight she would have to perform without the benefit of drugs. She had to remain alert. There was too much she had to do that required a clear head.

CHAPTER 53

Frank Calderon had worked out in his mind what he would have done if he were Toro Sandoval and wanted to take over a drug distribution network in the States. It hadn't been very difficult to guess at what the Juarez Cartel leader would do once Calderon was out of the picture. He'd co-opt all of the leaders of his network, promise them that he'd supply them with product, and maybe even lower the price of his drugs. Sandoval would be able to afford to pay the men a bigger share once Calderon was no longer acting as middleman. He wasn't certain that's what Sandoval did until he made calls to his network heads in Tucson, Phoenix, and Denver and couldn't get through to any of them. *They're either dead, being held prisoner, or cooperating with Sandoval,* he thought.

He and his bodyguard/driver, Johnny Turturro, chartered a plane to Tucson, rented a car, and drove to the home of one of the low-level men who worked for Emilio Benavidez, Calderon's head man there. The low-level guy had never met Calderon. So, when two strangers showed up at his house, the man was understandably confused and frightened. But when Calderon told him the name of his crew boss and who that guy reported to, the man became a believer.

"Let's go find your crew boss," Calderon told the man. By the time the sun had gone down, Calderon and Turturro had gone up the food chain and connected with every leader of his Tucson organization, except the top man.

Calderon promoted the second in command to the top position, having told him that his boss was either dead or cooperating with the head of the Juarez Cartel. "If he's dead, so be it." Calderon told the man. "If he's not, then you've got permission to take him out the first time he pops up."

"What are you going to do about Sandoval?" his new Tucson network leader asked.

"Don't you worry about him," Calderon responded.

It was after 10:00 p.m. when Calderon and Turturro boarded the chartered aircraft and flew to Phoenix. He hoped that things would go as smoothly in the other cities as they had in Tucson. While the plane headed for Phoenix, he called Jaime Suarez, the leader of the Guadalajara Cartel.

"I hear you have problems," Suarez told him.

"Problems are nothing but opportunities in disguise, Don Jaime. I'm calling you with an opportunity."

"And will this opportunity involve a . . . reshuffling of loyalties and commitments here in Mexico?"

"Without a doubt," Calderon said. "But thirty million dollars a year in additional product sales should more than compensate for a reshuffling, as you put it."

Suarez went silent for several seconds. Calderon waited.

"Perhaps we should arrange to meet," Suarez finally said. "Perhaps my beach house in Puerto Vallarta."

Calderon had figured that it would take him three more days to re-establish his chain of command in his other cities. "Will four days from today be convenient?"

"Perfect," Suarez said.

At 8:00 p.m., Julia Cardenas had made the rounds of her girls' rooms, passing out drugs to "anesthetize" them for their night's work. When she stopped at French's room, she handed her a syringe, smiled, and said, "Enjoy yourself."

French had convinced the madam of her dependency on the drug so that Cardenas no longer injected her. She relied on French to inject herself and then discard the syringe. After Cardenas left,

French removed the safety cap from the needle, disposed of the syringe's contents into the toilet bowl, uploaded one hundred milligrams—nearly twice the lethal dose to kill an adult—of liquid nicotine into the syringe, and replaced the safety cap. She placed the syringe under her bed and waited.

By 11:00 p.m., Lisa French had already serviced three of Julia Cardenas's clients. The fourth client was so rough that she was tempted to scream for help, which would bring Julia Cardenas running to the room, armed with a machete. But the last thing French wanted was for Cardenas to possibly see that she hadn't taken the heroin she'd given her. So, instead, French suffered the abhorrent man, hoping that his rough behavior wouldn't turn into true violence.

SATURDAY
JANUARY 4

CHAPTER 54

The last client left *Casa de Julia* at a few minutes after 3:00 a.m. Someone rang a bell that reminded French of the chimes that the ice cream vendor used to ring when he drove onto the street where she and her siblings grew up in Albuquerque. That bell told the girls that their work was done for the night. French washed herself at the sink in her room and then changed into the jeans, peasant blouse, and sandals that Julia Cardenas had so "graciously" provided the women in her whorehouse. She pried up the board in the floor and removed the cash there. She put the cash in a jeans pocket, then retrieved the syringe from under her bed.

She knew that Cardenas's bouncers would have congregated in the bar for a last drink before they went home. The whores would be locked in their rooms, essentially dead to the world. Julia Cardenas would be nearly comatose from the Kentucky bourbon that she loved and sipped most of the night. She whispered over and over again, "Come on Gordo, you freaking idiot." She hoped he would come through as he had with the e-cigarette and liquid nicotine. Would he unlock her door and take the little walk with her that she'd suggested and that he'd seemed so enthused about?

Nearly an hour passed before she heard footsteps in the hall outside her door. She hoped again that it was Gordo, but was prepared for anything. She removed the safety cap from the needle and held the syringe in her other hand, moved to the door, and waited for someone to open it. There was a light *tap-tap-tap*, then the sound of a key in the lock. She stepped out from behind the door when she heard Gordo say, "*Sen . . . or . . . ita?*"

She put the cap back on the needle and slid the syringe into a jeans pocket. Then she squeezed the man's left arm with her other hand and said, "Let's go for our walk, Gordo. Everyone will know that I am your girlfriend."

He made the grunting sound, said, "*Bue . . . no,*" and stepped through the doorway to the hall. He turned to the right, toward the staircase down to the bar, but French stopped him.

He looked at her, confused.

She whispered, "Let's take the back stairs, in case your mother is in the bar. I wouldn't want her to get mad at you and spoil our walk."

He made a sound in his throat that sounded both humorous and lascivious, gave her a wet kiss on her forehead, and turned toward the back of the building.

Frank Calderon used the same M.O. in Phoenix as he had in Tucson. The low-level man he confronted in his home at 3:10 a.m. answered the knock on his door armed with a cannon-of-a-pistol. Johnny Turturro knocked the piece out of the man's hand, threw him to the floor inside his front door, and ordered him to keep quiet or he'd slit his throat. They hefted the guy off the floor, tossed him on a couch, told him what they wanted, and quickly got his cooperation.

Barbara was in the nether world of a bad dream, when her ringing cell phone woke her. She looked at the clock on the table beside her bed and groaned: 4:05 a.m. Then her heart rate accelerated when she thought that Henry had taken a turn for the worse.

"Hello," she said, fully alert and on edge.

"Miss Lassiter?" a woman asked.

Barbara saw the Presbyterian Hospital caller ID name on her phone screen and exhaled a small whimper. "Yes. What is it?"

"Dr. Carteret asked me to call. Mr. Simpson just asked for something to drink."

"He what?"

"He just asked for something to drink."

"I'll be right there," Barbara said. "Thank you."

Then Barbara shouted, "Susan, wake up."

After Gordo Cardenas unlocked the back door to *Casa de Julia*, he took French's hand and walked down the alley to the street as though he was a king. He stood up straighter than French had ever seen him stand. He made a sound like he was humming, but she couldn't be certain.

The main street that ran along the front of Cardenas's place was still brightly lit and crowded with men and a few street walkers. The vendors were all gone, however, and vehicular traffic was about one tenth of what it was during peak hours. French steered Gordo to the left out of the alley, avoiding the front of *Casa de Julia*. Then she led the way up the street to a row of bars where she remembered Americans tended to hang out. She remembered the places from her college days, when she and friends would drive down to Juarez to buy cheap booze and stay up for twenty-four hours.

At the entrance to one of the bars, she told Gordo, "Let's go in here."

He seemed enthusiastic about entering the bar.

Inside the place, there were still a couple dozen or so patrons that looked like Americans. French surveyed the crowd and immediately spied a group of what appeared to be six twenty-somethings—three men and three women. Two of the women were blondes. French told Gordo to wait for her by the bar, then made her way toward the table. She slowed as she passed by. She'd anticipated that the kids would stop their conversations and stare at Gordo, who, under any circumstance, was a sight to behold. In the glare of the bar lights, he appeared surreal.

One of the men pointed and blurted, "Holy shit," which caused the others to gawk. While their attention was on Gordo, French quickly stooped and snatched the long strap of a leather pocketbook lying on the floor next to a chair, stuffed the pocketbook under one arm, and exited the bar. She moved briskly up the sidewalk and scooted into the next alley and waited. Gordo followed her into the alley, which smelled like piss and was as black as ink. He stopped a couple feet into the alley, backlit by the gaudy lights of the street.

"Gordo, I'm in here," French said.

"Are you playing a game?" he asked in his stunted Spanish.

"Yes, it's a game. Come find me."

He snorted a laugh and came forward. When he was a few feet away, French came forward, put her arms around his neck, and pulled his great head toward her. "Give me a kiss, Gordo," she said.

He made a lip smacking sound and bent forward as she brought her mouth to his cheek, said, "*Lo siento,* Gordo," and injected the full syringe into the side of his neck.

Gordo cried out, stepped back, and slapped at his neck. Then he stretched his arms out and moved toward French. She took mincing steps further down the alley while the big man lumbered forward. She turned to run, but slammed into the side of a trash dumpster and bounced onto the ground. She shouted, "No," when Gordo's hand clamped onto one of her ankles.

"*Eres ma . . . la,*" he groaned. Then his hand fell away and he cried out, "*Du . . . ele. Me du . . . ele el bra . . . zo.*"

She scrambled to her feet, shifted the stolen purse higher on her shoulder, and looked down at Gordo. "Your arm won't hurt for long." Then she stepped around him, walked out to the main drag, and walked six blocks to the Bridge of the Americas. The crossing at that early hour only took thirty minutes. As she approached the personnel entry gate, she brushed her hair in front of her cheeks, obscuring all but her eyes, nose, and mouth. She told the U.S. Customs & Border Protection Officer who interviewed her that the reason for her visit to Mexico was to party with friends, from whom she'd become separated. He cursorily checked her stolen driver's license photo and then stared at her face.

"I looked a lot younger when I crossed over. Too much drinking and too little sleep will do that to you."

The officer chuckled. "I hope you have a way home, ma'am," he said.

"Thanks, Officer," she said. "I'll grab a cab."

She walked to a line of taxis on the El Paso side of the border, told the driver, "Take me to the bus terminal," then scrunched down in the back seat and closed her eyes. As tired as she was, her mind raced with thoughts about her brother.

He's going to pay for what he did, she thought.

"What was that, lady?" the cabbie asked.

She hadn't realized she'd spoken her thought. "Nothing. Just talking to myself."

Susan dropped Barbara off at the Presbyterian Hospital entrance, then drove around the driveway to the closest parking lot. Barbara made her way to the ICU floor and stared across at Henry's room. She saw two people bracketing Henry's bed. As she moved closer to the doorway, she recognized his doctor and one of the nurses.

As Barbara walked to the foot of the bed, she looked at Henry who was propped up on a couple pillows. Other than seeming slimmer and the blood- and antiseptic-soaked bandage on his head, he looked like the old Henry.

"Look who's here," the nurse said, as she moved away from the bed to allow Barbara to stand next to Henry.

Barbara moved, took Henry's hand in hers, bent over, and kissed his forehead. "Hey, honey," she said.

Henry's voice was thick. *Probably from the breathing tube that had been in his throat and from medication,* Barbara thought. "I like it when . . . beautiful women . . . call me honey," he said. "But . . . maybe you should . . . tell me your name."

Barbara laughed, thinking Henry was joking. But then she noticed his confused expression. Her breathing stuttered and her throat went dry. She forced a smile and tried to speak, but nothing came out.

Dr. Carteret said, "Mr. Simpson, don't you recognize Barbara?"

Henry now wore an apologetic expression. He looked from Carteret to Barbara. "I'm sorry," he said. "Do we know each other?"

Barbara squeezed his hand, then released it, said, "It's nice to see you doing better, Henry," then, before she lost control of her emotions, left the room. Susan intercepted her outside the ICU.

"What's going on?" Susan asked.

Barbara's voice broke as she said, "He's better. He can actually talk. But—"

"That's wonderful," Susan said. She stepped forward and put

her arms around Barbara.

Barbara gently pushed Susan away. "He doesn't know who I am," she said. Tears flowed as she added, "Oh, Susan, Henry didn't recognize me."

Before Susan could respond, Dr. Simone Carteret exited the ICU and put a hand on Barbara's shoulder. "What happened in there," she said, "is not uncommon. I encourage you to focus on the good news. Mr. Simpson's speech appears to be unimpaired. His thought processes seem to be solid. His responses to questions are organized." She took a sharp breath and let it out slowly. "It's his memory that isn't functioning correctly."

"What does that mean?" Barbara asked. "Can he remember how he was injured?"

"No, he has no recollection of the incident. Interestingly enough, he does remember his own name, date of birth, where he was born and raised, where he went to school, everything prior to the past couple years. But he still thinks the previous UNM president is in office. Preliminarily, it appears that Mr. Simpson has lost all memory since two years ago."

"About the time that he and I met," Barbara said.

Carteret's lips compressed and her eyes closed. When she opened her eyes again, she said, "I'm going to keep Mr. Simpson here for at least two more days. Then I'll transfer him to our Physical & Occupational Therapy unit. We'll have a better idea of what's going on by this time next week. In the meantime, I suggest you visit every day. But don't push him to remember things. Have conversations about his formative years, about his family and friends, about his schooling. Concentrate on the stuff that's easy for him to remember."

"Thanks, Doctor," Barbara said. "One other thing. How should I respond if he asks me about how we know one another?"

"Answer it honestly, but don't pressure him to try to remember what you had together." She touched Barbara again and said, "I'm sorry."

Barbara said, "He's alive. That's a major miracle."

"Yes, it is," Carteret said.

Barbara walked back into the ICU to sneak a peek at Henry,

leaving Susan and Carteret standing in the hallway.

"Would you answer a question for me?" Susan said.

"If I can," the doctor said.

"How often does someone who's lost short-term memory recover fully?"

"I assume you're asking me if Henry will remember Barbara." Susan nodded.

"You want the long answer or the short one?"

"Short will do."

"I'm surprised Mr. Simpson's doing as well as he is. But after a severe injury like the one he suffered, the patient almost never recovers his short-term memory, Detective. Almost never."

CHAPTER 55

Lisa French hung out at the El Paso bus terminal for a couple hours. The first bus destined for Albuquerque was scheduled to leave at 8:00 a.m. The clock on the terminal wall told her she had a couple hours to wait. Then she had a thought and asked the ticket agent if there was a big box store in the neighborhood. He gave her directions to a Walmart a couple miles away. She thanked the man, hailed a cab, and rode to the Walmart. With a credit card from the purse she'd stolen, she bought a floppy-brimmed cowboy hat, a jean jacket, a light-blue work shirt, a towel, sunglasses, black hair dye, lipstick, and mascara. She took her purchases into the store bathroom, dyed her hair, applied the makeup, and changed into her new shirt and jacket. She dumped the towel in the trash can. Before leaving the bathroom, she counted the money she had left: Three hundred eighty-three dollars and some change, most of which had come from the wallet in the purse.

I need to figure out a way to get some more money, she thought as she left the store.

She took another cab back to the terminal, boarded the bus for Albuquerque thirty minutes later, took a seat in the back, and tried to nap. But images of her brother, of Toro Sandoval, and of the two female detectives kept scrolling through her mind's eye. The people who she blamed for everything that had happened to her tormented her and destroyed her chance at sleep.

The view out her window was stark and overcast. Storm clouds made the eastern sky appear purple-black. Flashes of lightning from the bottoms of the clouds speared in almost straight lines toward the ground and, even through the shuttered bus, she heard the massive rumbles of thunder. There was something soothing about the weather change. The darkness and intermittent lightning strikes seemed to match her mood.

She smiled at her reflection in the bus window and thought, *what's another four dead bodies?*

THE END

ACKNOWLEDGEMENTS

To my readers, thank you for your loyal support. You virtually keep alive my passion for writing. Your kind feedback and suggestions are invaluable, and your reviews make a difference.

I have been fortunate to receive reviews and blurbs for my novels written by many successful and prolific authors, including Mark Adduci, Tom Avitabile, Parris Afton Bonds, Steve Brewer, Catherine Coulter, Philip Donlay, Steve Havill, Anne Hillerman, Tony Hillerman, Paul Kemprecos, Robert Kresge, Jon Land, Mark Leggatt, Michael McGarrity, David Morrell, Michael Palmer, Andrew Peterson, Mark Rubinstein, Meryl Sawyer, and Sheldon Siegel. I know how busy these men and women are and it always humbles me when they graciously take time to read and praise my work.

Special thanks to John Badal for information that helped out some of my characters.

My sincere thanks go to Tom Antram, French's Mortuary Services; Amy Rosenbaum, Director of The University of New Mexico Medical School's Anatomical Donation Program; and Nancy Joste, Director of Anatomic Pathology, Department of Pathology, University of New Mexico Health Sciences Center for their advice regarding legal, medical, and other technical aspects of this story.

Finally, my heartfelt thanks and appreciation go to John and Shannon Raab and all their staff at *Suspense Publishing* for their professionalism, support, advice, and friendship. You have all made the publishing side of writing a pleasure.

ABOUT THE AUTHOR

Joseph Badal grew up in a family where story-telling had been passed down from generation to generation.

Prior to a long business career, including a 16-year stint as a senior executive and board member of a NYSE-listed company, Joe served for six years as a commissioned officer in the U.S. Army in critical, highly classified positions in the U.S. and overseas, including tours of duty in Greece and Vietnam, and earned numerous military decorations.

He holds undergraduate and graduate degrees in business and graduated from the Defense Language Institute, West Coast and from Stanford University Law School's Director College.

Joe is an Amazon #1 Best-Selling Author, with 14 published suspense novels, including six books in the *Danforth Saga* series, two books in the *Curtis Chronicles* series, three books in the *Lassiter/Martinez Case Files* series, and three stand-alones. He has been recognized as "One of The 50 Best Writers You Should Be Reading." His books have received two Tony Hillerman Awards for Best Fiction Book of the Year, been top prize winners on multiple occasions in the Mystery/Thriller category in the New Mexico/ Arizona Book Awards competition, received gold medals from the Military Writers Society of America, and Finalist honors in the International Book Awards.

His latest novel, "Natural Causes," the third in the *Lassiter/ Martinez Case Files* series, will be released by Suspense Publishing on April 9, 2019.

Joe has written short stories which were published in the "Uncommon Assassins," "Someone Wicked," and "Insidious Assassins" anthologies. He has also written dozens of articles that have been published in various business and trade journals and is a frequent speaker at business, civic, and writers' events.

To learn more, visit his website at www.JosephBadalBooks.com.

"EVIL DEEDS"
DANFORTH SAGA (#1)

"Evil Deeds" is the first book in the *Bob Danforth* series, which includes "Terror Cell" and "The Nostradamus Secret." In this three book series, the reader can follow the lives of Bob & Liz Danforth, and of their son, Michael, from 1971 through 2011. "Evil Deeds" begins on a sunny spring day in 1971 in a quiet Athenian suburb. Bob & Liz Danforth's morning begins just like every other morning: Breakfast together, Bob roughhousing with Michael. Then Bob leaves for his U.S. Army unit and the nightmare begins, two-year-old Michael is kidnapped.

So begins a decades-long journey that takes the Danforth family from Michael's kidnapping and Bob and Liz's efforts to rescue him, to Bob's forced separation from the Army because of his unauthorized entry into Bulgaria, to his recruitment by the CIA, to Michael's commissioning in the Army, to Michael's capture by a Serb SPETSNAZ team in Macedonia, and to Michael's eventual marriage to the daughter of the man who kidnapped him as a child. It is the stops along the journey that weave an intricate series of heart-stopping events built around complex, often diabolical characters. The reader experiences CIA espionage during the Balkans War, attempted assassinations in the United States, and the grisly exploits of a psychopathic killer.

"Evil Deeds" is an adrenaline-boosting story about revenge, love, and the triumph of good over evil.

https://amzn.com/B00LXG9QIC

"TERROR CELL"
DANFORTH SAGA (#2)

"Terror Cell" pits Bob Danforth, a CIA Special Ops Officer, against Greek Spring, a vicious terrorist group that has operated in Athens, Greece for three decades. Danforth's mission in the summer of 2004 is to identify one or more of the members of the terrorists in order to bring them to justice for the assassination of the CIA's Station Chief in Athens. What Danforth does not know is that Greek Spring plans a catastrophic attack against the 2004 Summer Olympic Games.

Danforth and his CIA team are hampered by years of Congressionally mandated rules that have weakened U.S. Intelligence gathering capabilities, and by indifference and obstructionism on the part of Greek authorities. His mission becomes even more difficult when he is targeted for assassination after an informant in the Greek government tells the terrorists of Danforth's presence in Greece.

In "Terror Cell," Badal weaves a tale of international intrigue, involving players from the CIA, the Greek government, and terrorists in Greece, Libya, and Iran—all within a historical context. Anyone who keeps up with current events about terrorist activities and security issues at the Athens Olympic Games will find the premise of this book gripping, terrifying, and, most of all, plausible.

"Joe Badal takes us into a tangled puzzle of intrigue and terrorism, giving readers a tense well-told tale and a page-turning mystery."
—Tony Hillerman, *New York Times* bestselling author

https://amzn.com/B00LXG9QNC

"THE NOSTRADAMUS SECRET"
DANFORTH SAGA (#3)

This latest historical thriller in the *Bob Danforth* series builds on Nostradamus's "lost" 58 quatrains and segues to present day. These lost quatrains have surfaced in the hands of a wealthy Iranian megalomaniac who believes his rise to world power was prophesied by Nostradamus. But he sees the United States as the principal obstacle to the achievement of his goals. So, the first step he takes is to attempt to destabilize the United States through a vicious series of terrorist attacks and assassinations.

Joseph Badal offers up another action-packed story loaded with intrigue, fascinating characters and geopolitical machinations that put the reader on the front line of present-day international conflict. You will be transported from a 16th century French monastery to the CIA, to crime scenes, to the Situation Room at the White House, to Middle Eastern battlefields.

"The Nostradamus Secret" presents non-stop action in a contemporary context that will make you wonder whether the story is fact or fiction, history or prophesy.

" 'The Nostradamus Secret' is a gripping, fact-paced story filled with truly fanatical, frightening villains bent on the destruction of the USA and the modern world. Badal's characters and the situations they find themselves in are hair-raising and believable. I couldn't put the book down. Bring on the sequel!"
—Catherine Coulter, *New York Times* bestselling author of "Double Take"

https://amzn.com/B00R3GTLVI

"THE LONE WOLF AGENDA"
DANFORTH SAGA (#4)

With "The Lone Wolf Agenda," Joseph Badal returns to the world of international espionage and military action thrillers and crafts a story that is as close to the real world of spies and soldiers as a reader can find. This fourth book in the *Danforth Saga* brings Bob Danforth out of retirement to hunt down lone wolf terrorists hell bent on destroying America's oil infrastructure. Badal weaves just enough technology into his story to wow even the most a-technical reader.

"The Lone Wolf Agenda" pairs Danforth with his son Michael, a senior DELTA Force officer, as they combat an OPEC-supported terrorist group allied with a Mexican drug cartel. This story is an epic adventure that will chill readers as they discover that nothing, no matter how diabolical, is impossible.

"A real page-turner in every good sense of the term. 'The Lone Wolf Agenda' came alive for me. It is utterly believable, and as tense as any spy thriller I've read in a long time."
—Michael Palmer, *New York Times* bestselling author of
"Political Suicide"

https://amzn.com/B00LXG9QMI

"DEATH SHIP"
DANFORTH SAGA (#5)

"Death Ship" is another suspense-filled thriller in the 45-year-long journey of the Danforth family. This fifth book in the *Danforth Saga*, which includes "Evil Deeds," "Terror Cell," "The Nostradamus Secret," and "The Lone Wolf Agenda," introduces Robbie Danforth, the 15-year-old son of Michael and Miriana Danforth, and the grandson of Bob and Liz Danforth.

A leisurely cruise in the Ionian Sea turns into a nightmare event when terrorists hijack a yacht with Bob, Liz, Miriana, and Robbie aboard. Although the boat's crew, with Bob and Robbie's help, eliminate the hijackers, there is evidence that something more significant may be in the works.

The CIA and the U.S. military must identify what that might be and who is behind the threat, and must operate within a politically-corrupt environment in Washington, D.C. At the same time, they must disrupt the terrorist's financing mechanism, which involves trading in securities that are highly sensitive to terrorist events.

Michael Danforth and a team of DELTA operatives are deployed from Afghanistan to Greece to assist in identifying and thwarting the threat.

"Death Ship" is another roller coaster ride of action and suspense, where good and evil battle for supremacy and everyday heroes combat evil antagonists.

"Terror doesn't take a vacation in 'Death Ship'; instead Joseph Badal masterfully takes us on a cruise to an all too frightening, yet all too real destination. Once you step on board, you are hooked."
—Tom Avitabile, #1 Bestselling Author of "The Eighth Day" and "The Devil's Quota"

https://amzn.com/B016APTJAU

"SINS OF THE FATHERS"
DANFORTH SAGA (#6)

The Danforth family returns in this sixth edition of the Danforth Saga. "Sins of the Fathers" takes the reader on a tension-filled journey from a kidnapping of Michael and Robbie Danforth in Colorado, to America's worst terrorist-sponsored attacks, to Special Ops operations in Mexico, Greece, Turkey, and Syria. This epic tale includes political intrigue, CIA and military operations, terrorist sleeper cells, drug cartels, and action scenes that will keep you pinned to the edge of your seat.

Joseph Badal's twelfth novel is complex, stimulating, and un-put-down-able. You will love his heroes and hate his villains, and you will root for the triumph of good over evil.

This is fiction as close to reality as you will ever find.

"Outstanding! Joseph Badal combines insider knowledge with taut writing and a propulsive plot to create a stellar thriller in a terrific series. Well-written, intense, timely and, at times, terrifying. Highly recommended."
—Sheldon Siegel, *New York Times* Bestselling Author of the Mike Daley/Rosie Fernandez Novels

http://a.co/eZTFJlO

"BORDERLINE"
THE LASSITER/MARTINEZ CASE FILES (#1)

In "Borderline," Joseph Badal delivers his first mystery novel with the same punch and non-stop action found in his acclaimed thrillers.

Barbara Lassiter and Susan Martinez, two New Mexico homicide detectives, are assigned to investigate the murder of a wealthy Albuquerque socialite. They soon discover that the victim, a narcissistic borderline personality, played a lifetime game of destroying people's lives. As a result, the list of suspects in her murder is extensive.

The detectives find themselves enmeshed in a helix of possible perpetrators with opportunity, means, and motive—and soon question giving their best efforts to solve the case the more they learn about the victim's hideous past.

Their job gets tougher when the victim's psychiatrist is murdered and DVDs turn up that show the doctor had serial sexual relationships with a large number of his female patients, including the murder victim.

"Borderline" presents a fascinating cast of characters, including two heroic female detective-protagonists and a diabolical villain; a rollercoaster ride of suspense; and an ending that will surprise and shock the reader.

"Think Cagney and Lacey. Think Thelma and Louise. Think murder and mayhem—and you are in the death grip of a mystery that won't let you go until it has choked the last breath of suspense from you."
—Parris Afton Bonds, author of "Tamed the Wildest Heart" and co-founder of Romance Writers of America and cofounder of Southwest Writers Workshop

https://amzn.com/B00YZSAHI8
Now Available at Audible.com: http://adbl.co/1Y4WC5H

"DARK ANGEL"
THE LASSITER/MARTINEZ
CASE FILES (#2)

In "Dark Angel," the second in the Lassiter/Martinez Case Files series, Detectives Barbara Lassiter and Susan Martinez pick up where they left off in "Borderline." Assigned to a murder case, they discover that their suspect is much more than a one-off killer. In fact, the murderer appears to be a vigilante hell-bent on taking revenge against career criminals who the criminal justice system has failed to punish.

But Lassiter and Martinez are soon caught up in the middle of an FBI investigation of a monstrous home invasion gang that has murdered dozens of innocent victims across the United States. When they discover a link between their vigilante killer and the home invasion crew, they come into conflict with powerful men in the FBI who are motivated more by career self-preservation than by bringing justice to innocent victims.

Award-Winning and best-selling author Joseph Badal presents another intricate, tension-filled mystery that puts readers on the edge of their seats from the first page to the last, and will have them demanding more Lassiter/Martinez stories.

"Badal delivers a nice tight mystery and two wonderful female detectives you'll be cheering for."
—Catherine Coulter, *New York Times* bestselling author of "Nemesis"

http://a.co/5fFx9vs

"THE MOTIVE"
THE CURTIS CHRONICLES
(#1)

In "The Motive," Joseph Badal presents the first book in his new series, *The Curtis Chronicles*. This latest addition to Badal's offering of acclaimed, best-selling thrillers delivers the same sort of action and suspense that readers have come to expect and enjoy from his previous nine novels.

Confronted with suspicious information relating to his sister Susan's supposed suicide in Honolulu, Albuquerque surgeon Matt Curtis questions whether his sister really killed herself. With the help of his sister's best friend, Renee Drummond, and his former Special Forces comrade, Esteban Maldonado, Matt investigates Susan's death. But Lonnie Jackson, the head of organized crime in Hawaii, afraid that Matt has gotten too close to the truth, sends killers after him.

This is an artfully written book that will appeal to readers who like thrillers with fully-developed characters, a big plot, and plenty of action, seasoned with friendship and romance.

"The Motive" puts the reader on a roller coaster ride of non-stop thrills and chills, propelled by realistic dialogue and a colorful cast of characters. It is another entertaining story from a master story-teller where good and evil struggle for supremacy and everyday heroes battle malevolent antagonists.

" 'The Motive' is a nail biter I couldn't put down. Joseph Badal knows how to make his legion of readers sweat to the very last paragraph. He has mastered the art of writing—and suspense. Bravo!"
—Parris Afton Bonds, Award-Winning Author of "Dream Time"

https://amzn.to/2VCFwPL

"OBSESSED"
THE CURTIS CHRONICLES
(#2)

A world-class thriller with non-stop, heart-pounding tension and action, "Obsessed" brings back Matt Curtis and Renee Drummond and their villainous nemesis, Lonnie Jackson. This second installment in Joseph Badal's *The Curtis Chronicles* takes the reader from Rio de Janeiro to the mountains of New Mexico to the Mexico/United States border, following a crazed Jackson on his single-minded quest for revenge against the two people he blames for the deaths of his mother and brother and for the destruction of his criminal empire in Hawaii.

"Obsessed" is another master stroke of fiction from this Amazon #1 Best-Selling Author, two-time winner of the Tony Hillerman Award for Best Fiction Book of the Year, and three-time Military Writers Society of America Gold Medal Winner.

If you like fast-paced stories that put you on a breathless, adrenaline-filled journey, with realistic good guys and believable bad guys, "Obsessed" will have you begging for more.

"Joseph Badal's characters play on a world stage—and that world is a dark and dangerous place, seen through the pen of a master story teller."
—Steven F. Havill, Award-Winning Author of "Easy Errors"

https://amzn.to/2VCFwPL

"THE PYTHAGOREAN SOLUTION"
STAND-ALONE THRILLER

The attempt to decipher a map leads to violence and death, and a decades-long sunken treasure.

When American John Hammond arrives on the Aegean island of Samos he is unaware of events that happened six decades earlier that will embroil him in death and violence and will change his life forever.

Late one night Hammond finds Petros Vangelos lying mortally wounded in an alley. Vangelos hands off a coded map, making Hammond the link to a Turkish tramp steamer that carried a fortune in gold and jewels and sank in a storm in 1945.

On board this ship, in a waterproof safe, are documents that implicate a German SS Officer in the theft of valuables from Holocaust victims and the laundering of those valuables by the Nazi's Swiss banker partner.

"Badal is a powerful writer who quickly reels you in and doesn't let go."
—Pat Frovarp & Gary Shulze, Once Upon A Crime Mystery Bookstore

https://amzn.com/B00W4JVIYC

"ULTIMATE BETRAYAL"
STAND-ALONE THRILLER

Inspired by actual events, "Ultimate Betrayal" is a thriller that takes the reader on an action-packed, adrenaline-boosting ride, from the streets of South Philadelphia, through the Afghanistan War, to Mafia drug smuggling, to the halls of power at the CIA and the White House.

David Hood comes from the streets of South Philadelphia, is a decorated Afghanistan War hero, builds a highly successful business, marries the woman of his dreams, and has two children he adores. But there are two ghosts in David's past. One is the guilt he carries over the death of his brother. The other is a specter that will do anything to murder him.

David has long lost the belief that good will triumph over evil. The deaths of his wife and children only reinforce that cynicism. And leave him with nothing but a bone-chilling, all-consuming need for revenge.

" 'Ultimate Betrayal' provides the ultimate in riveting reading entertainment that's as well thought out as it is thought provoking. Both a stand-out thriller and modern day morality tale. Mined from the familial territory of Harlan Coben, with the seasoned action plotting of James Rollins or Steve Berry, this is fiction of the highest order. Poignant and unrelentingly powerful."
—Jon Land, bestselling and award-winning author of "The Tenth Circle"

https://amzn.com/B00LXG9QGY

"SHELL GAME"
STAND-ALONE THRILLER

"Shell Game" is a financial thriller using the economic environment created by the capital markets meltdown that began in 2007 as the backdrop for a timely, dramatic, and hair-raising tale. Badal weaves an intricate and realistic story about how a family and its business are put into jeopardy through heavy-handed, arbitrary rules set down by federal banking regulators, and by the actions of a sociopath in league with a corrupt bank regulator.

Like all of Badal's novels, "Shell Game" takes the reader on a roller coaster ride of action and intrigue carried on the shoulders of believable, often diabolical characters. Although a work of fiction, "Shell Game," through its protagonist Edward Winter, provides an understandable explanation of one of the main reasons the U.S. economy continues to languish. It is a commentary on what federal regulators are doing to the United States banking community today and, as a result, the damage they are inflicting on perfectly sound businesses and private investors across the country and on the overall U.S. economy.

"Shell Game" is inspired by actual events that have taken place as a result of poor governmental leadership and oversight, greed, corruption, stupidity, and badly conceived regulatory actions. You may be inclined to find it hard to believe what happens in this novel to both banks and bank borrowers. I encourage you to keep an open mind. "Shell Game" is a work of fiction that supports the old adage: You don't need to make this stuff up.

"Take a roller coaster ride through the maze of modern banking regulations with one of modern fiction's most terrifying sociopaths in the driver's seat. Along with its compelling, fast-paced story of a family's struggle against corruption, 'Shell Game' raises important questions about America's financial system based on well-researched facts."

—Anne Hillerman & Jean Schaumberg, WORDHARVEST
https://amzn.com/B00LXG9QFA